The
Truth

Prelude

There is a fine line between a lie and a truth. Between siding with what you know is right, even when it is something unknown. I always knew I was different from the rest of my family. They have warm, clear eyes like a sunny day and golden-tan skin. Compared to my eyes that are black and ice cold and my skin being as white as snow. My hair is black as the night while everyone else is blonde as the sun. On holiday they like to go out in the sun and play on the beach, I like to stay in my room or go to caves when I am forced to go out. Friends used to joke and say I must have been adopted and we would laugh. But then everything changed, and I stopped laughing with them. I found out the truth and everything I thought I knew, turned out to be a lie. A lie that changed my life for ever.

Chapter 1

I heard my mum banging on my door, waking me up from my deep sleep.

"Go away I am sleeping" I shouted back at her.

I heard my mum going downstairs singing 'wake me up before you go go; out of tune of course like she does every morning. The like clockwork my 13-year-old pain in the neck brother Ben shouted outside my door,

"Time to get up we are going to be late for school again."

I heard him run downstairs for breakfast making as much noise as he could. It was like Groundhog Day in this house, nothing ever changes. I don't think anything will ever make it changed.

I hate getting up in the morning, I like to sleep in but then, and so do most of my friends. But one thing I know which is different between me and my friends is that they don't sneak out in the middle of the night and walk around the village of Hillstrength. I hate staying in bed at night, it feels wrong, for me, I could never sleep. The village was a small one, it had a park with some woods nearby, but they wasn't anything else for kids to do. There was only a high school in the village and the nearest hospital is a bus ride away. Apart from that, there was nothing in the village apart from walking around it.

When parents go to bed, I open my window and climb down the big old oak tree, which has been there since as long as I could remember, and I just walk around the village on my own. I love everything about the night and everything connecting with it. The cold fresh air on my face and skin, no noise from cars or any people bumping into you in a rush, getting in your way when you are trying to get to places. At night they are empty and mine, my own little world. I feel like I belong more in the dark then I do in the day. The darkness is who I am.

When I finally manage to drag myself downstairs for breakfast my dad had already left for work. This was not unusual as I don't see him much because he works 6 days a week and, on his day, off, he sleeps for most of it. Every so often he has few days off where we see him all the time and spend time together. He just had a few weeks off as he has just got a new assignment and is now back working. Him and mum both seem happy about the new job even though I still don't know what he does for a living. When I ask him about it in the past, he just replies it is a job that involved helping people, but he won't go into any details about it.

I got to the kitchen where I found my mum was standing in her normal place by the sink.

"You are not wearing that to school Ingrid Jones. You're a young lady and you are only 15, those clothes are not acceptable for school." Stated my mum when I walked in. I looked down at the clothes my mum was talking about. I was wearing knee length black boots and a black flowing skirt that was knee length. The top I was wearing was a red and black stripe top with a skull on it. It was no uniform day, so I didn't need to wear the usual boring clothes. But I didn't think it was that bad of things to wear, but then again, any clothes I wear my mum has a problem with it due to them being dark in colour.

"Why what is wrong with it?" I asked not bothering with the answer and rolling my eyes at the same time. I knew what was going to happen as it happens all the time its non- uniform day. She says it's not good for a young lady to wear black and dark clothes all the time like I do. I would reply that I'm wearing red, purple or whatever as well and that I'm 16 in a few months and I am not a kid anymore. She would say stop being cheeky, I would reply that I was not etc. Even when I did wear my uniform, she would find something wrong with it. This would normally go on for about an ½ hour, but this morning I could not be bothered with any of that and go through the same routine. So instead I grabbed some toast, grabbed my bags, one for school and one with clothes for a party that I was going to later and headed out of the house. I went towards my boyfriend Luke's house where I go every morning, so we can walk to school together. We always spend a while at his house before we head to school, so we only just make it to school with minutes to spare, but we have always managed to be on time.

As I was walking to Luke's, I kept thinking about how I wish I was adopted, that they were people who didn't shout at me for my clothes or sleeping in late. That they don't like going outside and playing on the beach like me but go to caves and dark places to explore. That I had a sister, someone I could talk to and swap things with and I had a better connection to then Ben. I was walking and in my own world when I noticed that Miss Smith's house finally had people moving into it since they sold it a few weeks back.

Nobody liked Miss Smith or her daughter Chloe that use to live in the house with her. At Halloween they didn't give kids sweets or anything like that, they just chuck water at them and the same at Christmas, if you sang at their house. Everyone was glad when they said they were moving away. Everyone wanted them to move quickly as no one had anything nice to say about them. I wonder who is moving into the house now, I hope they are nice since Luke lives next door to them, I felt sorry for him having to live next to the Smith's for so long and needing to deal with them all the time. I knocked on the door and Luke's mum opened it with a smile. I wish my mum was a lot more like Luke's. She always has bright clothes on, which I don't mind on other people just not on me. Luke's mum always has something orange on her as it was her late husband's favourite colour; today is was her top that was orange. It always went great with her dark chestnut hair and blue eyes. She was funny, nice and loves to walk in the dark like me. When she catches me out at two in morning, she doesn't tell my mum or dad about me being out and agrees with me about it being better than the day. The best thing about her is that she doesn't go on about my clothes like my mum, she loves them and even buys me new ones without my parents knowing.

"Hi Ingrid, you're early today, Luke is only just getting up. Why don't you come in?" I smiled at her and entered the house with her following me into the living room. "I like your top it suits you really well, you should wear it more often."

I love how Luke's mum is always happy no matter what. Luke's 6-year-old twin's brothers were running round the living chasing each other. Life at Luke's is never boring with them in the house. Luke brothers were identical, they had the same blue eyes and short browns hair that the same colour as their mum. They always play tricks on everyone as no one can tell them apart and running around the house laughing. How Luke can cope with 2 younger brothers when I have trouble with 1, I don't know.

"So do you known who is moving in next door to you, have you met them yet?" I asked wanting to know what they were like and who would move to a boring place like Hillstrength.

"Well I haven't..." 'Bang, bang; I jumped. Tim and Jim were now playing cowboys and they had just found Luke's BB guns and were shooting each other now. Luke's mum grabbed the guns off them and put them on top of a cupboard out of reach of them. I couldn't help but laugh at them and how they are failing to look innocent about the guns.

Just when I was about to ask about next door again Luke walked into the room. Every time I see him my breath gets caught in my throat. He was wearing black trainers with skinny black jeans and no top on, showing off his 6 pack. Every girl wants to be with him, with his perfect smile that melts anyone hearts and his eyes blue and clear as crystal. His hair the same colour as his mum and brothers, but his was longer on the top then his brothers.

My mum hates me being with Luke because he 2 years older than me, but I don't care, and she hasn't tried that hard to stop us from seeing each other. We're in most classes together at the moment due to classes being merge together due to sickness of Luke's teachers and the teachers not being replaces yet. It means that most classes are doubled up which means Luke and I get to spend more time together inside class.

"Hi you're early, your mum nagging you about your clothes again?" He chuckled. I could listen to him laughing all day. It was something he said most morning when he saw me at his house.

"Yeah, it was the same old speech, so I decided to leave. Couldn't be bothered with all the nagging this morning."

"Can I talk to you in the den please?" He asked, his tone suddenly serious.

"Sure." Not understanding the sudden change of ton but I didn't mind going into Luke's den. I love everything about it and hanging out in it. The walls were covered with wooden panels and the window has a balcony on it, which is used for bonfire night, where we can just stand there in each other arms watching the fireworks lighting up the sky. There is a wall full of books about people and ever place in the world with a 50-inch flat screen TV and wall speakers which fills the whole of one wall and is perfect for watching films together. Because Luke's uncle travels a lot around the country, nearly every surface is covered in souvenirs from all the places he been too. Photos, masks, paintings anything and everything you could think off. I sat on one the chair in front of the TV while Luke stood in front of me.

"Have you seen who's moving in next door yet?" I asked Luke. "I asked your mum but then Tim and Jim got a bit loud."

"I haven't seen them yet. I know it's a girl called Elizabeth and she lives with her grandparents. That all I know by asking around."

"That sounds nice. I meant to ask when we go to Rose's party tonight will we be leaving from? My mum wants to know where to pick us up from here or my house?" I spotted some hesitation in Luke face. "We are still going, aren't we? We got to go, I promised Rose."

"Erm Ingrid..." Luke Started to say when Tim and Jim suddenly burst through the door.

"Can we come in, mums going next door to say hello and we're board." Shouted the twins together in their normal loud way jumping around the room.

"Will you two just beat it; I am trying to talk to Ingrid! Why don't you two just watch some stupid TV and leave us alone for 10 minutes?!" yelled Luke at them.

I jumped; I have never heard or seen Luke shout at the twins before, I never heard him shout before full stop. They took one shock look at me and then ran down the stairs, closing the door behind them with a bang.

"You didn't need to shout at them, they're only 6 years old. They not done anything wrong, they were just playing with us." I half shouted back at him defending them. "What is wrong with you?"

"Look Ingrid it about Emma."

"Emma?" I echo back. Emma has been my friends for years. Our mums grew up together, so we were more like sisters then friends as she sleeps over almost every week. She knows that I sneak out at night, she never comes with me, but she never tells on me either. We always work together with my other friends Rose on all our group project. "What about Emma, is she OK? She must be OK, or I would've heard something." I started to panic. What could have happened to her?

"Ingrid. You asked if I was going to Rose party. I am but..."

"But?" I asked, suddenly not liking where this conversation is going.

"But not with you. I'm going with Emma; we been dating for a while now."

"NO! Emma would never do that to me. She just wouldn't!" I shouted at him, why was he saying this. Why was he doing this to me?

"I'm sorry Ingrid but, what he is saying is true." Said a familiar voice from behind me. I turned and saw Emma coming in from another door, the spare room I stay in. It was set up so you could get to the room without needing to go through the main house and without anyone even knowing you were there.

"Why would you do this to me Luke? And you, Emma I thought we were friends?" I asked as Emma stood next to Luke near the door.

"Because Ingrid," Emma said cruelly, not the quite voice she normal has. "You're simply weird. A freak. Sneaking away at night, never going out during the day unless forced. You are just sad and lonely. He never really liked you, he just using you. He never loved you."

"It's this true Luke?" I asked shocked on how normal my voice sounded with what I was seeing in front of me.

"Sorry Ingrid." Said Luke putting his arm round Emma and kissing the top of her head. "But every world is true. I was just using you to see Emma, or are you so stupid that you couldn't see that?" Luke voiced now had an evil tone to it now.

I thought back over the last 2 years of us being together and the few months of me crushing on him before he knew how I felt about him. When we play hide and seek with Tim and Jim, they were also found together. They would sometime go off with one another when a group would meet up. I was the same with my friends though, so I didn't think much about it. At school when I was working with Emma, I would talk about Luke and she would listen to every word I said. I could see she was thinking of someone, was it Luke she was thinking about all that time? Thinking back when I would call for them, they always seem to be not in at the same time. I never thought for one moment that they were together. I suddenly felt sick to the stomach with all the information going through my mind. I looked at them both, Luke's arm round Emma shoulder, Emma looking smug as she snuggled closer to Luke. I couldn't stand it anymore, I stood up and ran; I had to get away from them, I needed to get far away. I ran back though house and out the front door. I didn't notice Luke's mum coming through the front door and neatly knocked her over.

"Ingrid are you OK?" She asked in surprise getting her balance back.

I was at the end of the path when I turned round to answer her, that was when I saw Luke's new neighbour for the first time. She was standing by an upstairs window in the house, slightly obscured by a set of black curtains but I could see some part of her. My breath got caught in my throat making it impossible to breath. It wasn't that her clothes looked something a mystery movie stair would wear or that her skin was as white as clouds or her hair was as black as coal. It was her eyes. Her eyes were exactly like mine in every single way.

Chapter 2

"I can't believe it." I whined. It was lunch time and I had somehow managed to get to school and sit through 3 lessons, I was on my own as Luke and Emma luckily didn't show up to any of the classes.

"Just forget about it, he's no good for you anyway. He was just using you and Emma is clearly a back stabber. "Replied Rose. I looked at her when she replied. She has got no problems getting boys. Every boy in the school wanted to be with her, even those with girlfriends already. She has long blond hair that goes halfway down her back which at the moment she had in 2 plaits. Her eyes were like melted chocolate and her skin was a golden tan colour, no matter what the weather is like.

"That easy for you to say." I sighed. "You can have your pick of any boy in this school, you can click your finger and they would come running."

"Look why don't you come early to my house and we can talk about it. Get it of your chest so you can have a fun time at the party."

"I don't know if I'm coming to the party, not if Luke and Emma going to be there. Kissing and dancing, people looking at them then at me. They are going to be asking me stuff and then I am going be leaving crying."

"Look don't worry, no one knows about him and Emma. They haven't been seen by anyone, they have not been in any of yours lesson or mine. I don't think they are even in school. So you can still come and have a fun time. If people ask where he is, say he is ill or something. Lock him in his house to stop him coming or something, get his mum to stop him if you have too."

Rose pleaded, trying her best to get me to the party and to have fun. Just then Luke came into the dinner room with his arm round Emma. She was giggling and was snuggled close to him. Everybody stopped eating as they got further into the room. First, they looked at them as they walked and then they turned round to look for my face. When they found it, they looked back at Luke and Emma, making sure that they knew what they were seeing. Emma and Luke didn't take any notice of the people looking at them. They just went to the table by the window where I used to sit there with Luke. They sat down; Emma nearly sitting on Luke's lap. People started talking to each other quietly again, I could hear my name being said, as well as theirs. We were known around the school as being together, so everyone know that this was wrong.

I looked at Rose. "Nobody knows." I said sarcastically.

"Look I am sorry about Luke, I really am. But you still coming to my party aren't you? Please I need you there." Whined Rose. I looked at her sympathetically. I knew what she was saying would sound selfish to other people, and people would want to know why I am friends with her. But this is the first party she has thrown without her parents being there and she wanted to show people she can do it. That she can have the best party in the school.

"OK. I'll try and have fun, but I can't promise anything." I said finally giving in. I know how much this party means to her and when is my turn to throw a party; I would want her there too.

"Good, I know you will have fun. I might even invite Luke's new neighbour; Elizabeth I think someone said her name was. It would be nice for her to make friends from school; I wonder what she looks like and if she will be in our class? She is about our age apparently."

I suddenly remembered Luke's new neighbour, her eyes flashing in my mind. I was so caught up with Luke and Emma stabbing me in the back, I had forgotten about her.

"Is it possible for someone to have your eyes?" I asked suddenly "I don't mean looks like your eyes; I mean actually have the same eyes as you."

"I guess, but only if you die in an accident and they get given to someone as a donor organ. Or there's an eyes stealer out there and they get you while you are sleeping?" She looked at me with a bit of a smile on her face, "Why?"

"Luke's neighbour has the same eyes as me. And I mean exactly the same eyes. Same colour, same shape, same shade, everything. No one have got the same eye colour as me anywhere."

"Your probably just seeing things with everything that was happening with Luke and Emma. She's most likely got a really dark eye colour, or maybe it was just the light you saw her in." Replied Rose with some of her logic.

"Yeah, maybe you're right, maybe it was just my mind playing tricks." I answered back not really believing what I was saying. I know what I saw, I know they were the same. "Do you think people will be asking me about Emma and Luke? Asking me what happened and stuff? Gossip of the year isn't it as nothing else is happening at the school at the moment." We got up and headed out of the room, it was nearly empty as people were heading to class.

"No they won't say a word about it, I'm sure." Replied Rose. "They're not like that; they will respect you and leave you alone. Most people know what it feels like to be betrayed." Just as she finished speaking a small year 9 boy came up to me. I think I might have seen him before somewhere.

"You're Luke's ex-girlfriend, aren't you? He doesn't like any more, he never did like you." And ran away laughing towards a group of friends who were waiting nearby.

I looked at Rose "No one's going to be asking me stuff huh! I bet you they'll keep reminding me about it all day and every day after that." I signed.

"Look one year 9 boy is not everyone, it's not the whole school. Look, he might just be a friend of Luke or Emma. So of cause he'll take their side and not yours that it's, don't worry about it. People won't come up to you much, it they do I will stop them."

"OK if you say so. I'll forget about it and carry on today like nothing has happened. But the second someone comes up to me. I'm gone." We walked to our next class, which was English with Mr Star. When we got there everyone was already sitting down, they all turned to look at me and Rose and then they started whispering to each other. I could hear mine; Luke's and Emma's names being thrown around by everyone. Rose took my arm and led me to the back of the classroom. This should stop people from looking at me, I am glad I picked it at the beginning of the year. Just as we were about to sit down, Luke and Emma walked in, Luke's arm still around Emma, are they now super glued together. Suddenly everyone stopped talking as they walked towards us, face full of thunder. I couldn't work out at first why they were looking at us like that or why they were coming towards me. Then I remember that me and Luke used to sit together at the back all the time. They must want to sit in the same place as me and Emma.

"You are sitting at my table." Sneered Emma when she got to us. Before I could say anything, even though I didn't know what I was going to say, Rose butted in.

"It not your desk Emma, it's Ingrid's it has been since we started school. So you have no right to sit here. I'm her *friend* so I can sit here as she wants me too. Sit back at your own desk."

"Yes but don't forget it's mine as well since the classes were merged, and I don't want you to sit here. I want Emma to sit here with me. So you." Luke pointed at me, "move and find somewhere else."

"Why don't you shut your mouth and keep out of this." Rose shot at him.

"Why don't you leave my *boyfriend*." She snared the word boyfriend "alone." I felt scared suddenly, I was letting my best friend fight my battle and it sounded like it was going to turn nasty. I didn't know what to say or what to do. Apparently nor did Luke because he wasn't saying anything now either.

"You are just jealous; you need to beg boys to go out with you. You change your mind every day about who you want to go out with, who you want to be seen with. You get them to spend all their money on you and then you drop them, because you're a..." She didn't finish what she was saying because Rose grabbed her brown hair and yanked half of it down as hard as she could. This put Emma into fighting mode, she started to fight back, knocking Rose onto the ground. Rose and Emma started punching and scratching each other, rolling around on the floor, knocking into tables and chairs. People moved out of the way taking chairs and tables with them to give the two girls more room to fight and allow people to stand around shouting, 'Fight, fight, fight.' Luke and I just stood by the side of the room with the rest of the kids. Neither of us saying a word or do anything to help the people on are side. Emma was on top of Rose pulling a fist full of hair when Mr Star walked into the classroom.

"What's the hell is going on here!?" He bellowed "Why is everyone out of their seat?" Nobody moved a muscle, no one wanted to mess with him. Even Rose and Emma had stopped fighting when they heard him. He walked over to Rose and Emma who were picking themselves up off the floor, brushing themselves down, trying to make sure their clothes looked straight. "Well!?" He shouted, his face turning red. They both started talking at once, shouting over each other trying to be heard, so that they could get out of trouble. He held his hand up to stop them speaking. That didn't work and they carried on bickering between themselves. "QUITE!" He demanded. Both girls stopped talking immediately and looked at him. "OK, let's try this again. But one at a time and slowly, alright? Let begin with who else, is involved?"

"Ingrid." Spat Rose the second he finished speaking to them.

"It was Luke as well." Rose cut in before sir could start shouting at me. You could tell he was about to by the way he turned to look at me.

"Right. Why don't you four go to Mrs Wednesday office so that she can sort this out, I will join you there after I get the rest of the class settled down and working. They aren't fighting in the middle of my classroom."

"Yes sir." We chanted in union. You could see in each other eyes, that we were glad that we got the other pair in trouble, but mad that we were here too. We walked out of the classroom, Luke's arm being back around Emma shoulder again.

"Why did you do that for me?" I whispered to Rose, loud enough so that she could hear me but quite enough that Luke and Emma couldn't. They were talking to each other ahead of us and I knew it was about us and the fight.

"Because you're my best friend and Emma needed to be brought down a peg or two because of what she did. Emma shouldn't have said those things or done the things she has done." We stopped talking as we walked into Mrs Wednesday office. No one dared to speak among themselves near her. She was on the phone to someone; it was probably a parent judging by the way she was shouting. So we just stood there, none of us saying a word. None of us looked at each other at all, we all just stared at her on the phone. Mr Star came in just as she slammed the phone down. "Ah Mr Star, what can I do for you? You're not usually here during lesson time." Asked Mrs Wednesday. Mrs Wednesday was our new headteacher. Our old headteacher, Mr House, left last term due to health problems. Everyone was sad; he was one of the best teachers around.

"Well Rose and Emma were fighting on the floor," He pointed to them as they stood next to each other just behind him. You would have thought that the messy hair and cuts gave them away as neither of them straighten themselves out enough. "And I've been informed that Ingrid and Luke were also involved somehow. Although when I came in, they were only watching like the rest of the class." He pointed us out, whom else would we have been though as we were also standing in her room. She looked at each of us in turn looking deep into our eyes. I don't like her, no one in school does, not the kids anyway, because she looks down at you like you're not even human. Not like Mr House, he would sit you down and talk to you make you feel like you matter. She stands over you and looks down her nose at you, just staring with her stormy blue eyes, like you just came up to her and killed her cat or something like that.

"Well what happened?" She asked. Her voice sounded like she wanted a fight just like Emma and Rose did.

All at once Rose and Emma started talking like it was the start of a race and Mrs Wednesday has just fired the starting gun. First blaming each other saying the other person had started it and how it wasn't their fault. Then Emma tried to get me into trouble saying I hit her first and Rose tried to drop Luke in it. Saying he would hurt us if we didn't move and made the first move. Lies on both sides. "Quite both of you." She shouted because Rose and Emma started fighting among themselves again. Emma looking like she was going to make another pass at Rose, Rose looked like she was going to tackle Emma to the ground. She looked at Luke and me who were still frozen to the spot. Neither of us had moved whilst Emma and Rose had been fighting among themselves. "Why don't you two tell me what happened, since you both seem to have just stood there saying nothing. What's wrong? Cat got your tongue. From what I can understand from these two, through all the shouting, lies and everything. You two were not in the fight or at least not the fight with fists anyway but with words. Am I right?" Luke said nothing; he just kept his eyes forward. I looked down at my shoe and rubbing it into the carpet, not daring to say a word. If I told her, Luke and Emma would make my life a living hell, telling everyone that I was snitch to everyone. But if I don't tell, Mrs Wednesday will do it instead, probably making me stay behind after school for months, phoning home, sending letter etc. Either way I be dropping my friend in trouble all because she wanted to help me. "Well?" She asked and I could tell from the tone of her voice that she was getting impatient. You could tell she wanted to get this sorted out quickly, which everyone knew wouldn't happen. When none of us spoke she walked over to the window and looked out of it. At what I don't know because it only looks out onto the back fields, which were empty as everyone were in class. "Well since I don't know who started it and who is to blame for the fight."

Rose opened her mouth to say something. "No Rose, you will listen." Mr Star said who must have notice she was about to interrupt what Mrs Wednesday were saying. She closed it again with a small snap.

"As I was saying." She continued, giving a Rose a look to keep quiet. "Since I don't know who to blame because everyone is pointing fingers at each other, I will be expecting all four of you to arrive at my office every day at precisely 3:35 with work to do for an hour and half detention. This shall last for the next 5 weeks, Monday till Friday. If you don't bring any work to my office, then I will find you something else to do for the time in the detention."

"5 weeks you must be joking. I'm not coming." Emma wined loudly. I think she meant to have thought it and not say it out loud for everyone to hear.

"No, I am not joking Emma. Mr House was too soft on the pupils in this school. If you started fighting in class when he was in charge all you would have gotten was a quick telling off to not to do it again and that would be it. Give you a cup of tea and some cake if you asked for it nicely. But that's not the case with me; I am going to show people that if you break the rules, there will be consequences. Every day of detention you miss, a week will be added, if you arrive late a week will be added and if you fight in detention a week will be added. Now go back to Mr Star's class, you will work hard without speaking and you will be separate until I decided you can behave yourself."

"But miss..." Emma started.

"No buts, do you hear me? You will not be sitting next to Luke, and Rose won't be sitting next to Ingrid either. I've heard the latest gossip about this group, and I will see you on Monday for your first detention, now go."

Mrs Wednesday sat down her at her decks and turned her back on us all.

We all walked out of the room, cursing Mrs Wednesday in our heads. I wanted her dead, I wanted her dead for how she is treating us. I knew I could tell Rose anything, however I knew one thing I could never tell Rose. That I wanted Mrs Wednesday dead and that feeling felt good and natural to me. The feeling of revenge.

Chapter 3

"I can't believe we got 5 weeks detention for an hour and half all because of Emma and Luke." Rose wined from her bathroom. After Mrs Wednesday told us what was going to happen, Mr Star took us back to our class in silence, everyone being too mad to talk. We were all placed in different area around the room. Emma was sat by the door at the front, which you could easily tell she hated it. Rose was sat on the same row but at the back of the room where she was planning to sit in the first place. I sat on the last row as far from the door and Emma as I could get. Luke had to sit right in front of the teacher at his own table. Sir had to put in another table so he could keep an eye on him. He said that he was older than us all, so he should know better. We know that this layout will be the same in any lesson we were in as I knew Mrs Wednesday will make sure all the teachers are aware of this arrangement.

It was now 10 past 4 and we were at Rose's house. I was helping her find some clothes for her party. She can never decide what to wear, she has so many dresses and things to choose from. She had already tried 6 different outfits in the last 10 minutes, she didn't think any of them were right for what she wanted. I'm glad Rose convinced me to come to the party now, the house looks great and I needed to take my mind of Luke and

Emma. We decided not to bring up the Luke and Emma situation when we got to the house; we were having too much fun to spoil it with them. Rose must have worked really hard to get everything right; the front of the house was covered in bright lights threaded round the trees and on the rails leading up the door. Rose had moved all the stuff in her living room to the edge so that people could use it as a dance floor. For music, I would love to know how she did it, she got a live band S.O. RULES, the most popular band ever, everyone knows them and loves them. All round the house there are lights, speakers and party decorations, even the bathroom has speakers and lights in, it was unbelievable.

"What are you wearing again? You can get changed while I get ready if you want?" Came Rose's muffled voice from within the bathroom.

I stood up and picked up the bag with my party clothes in. I had brought my black glitter dress, it was perfect. It went over my right shoulder and had three red stripes cutting diagonally over from the left to the right. The bottom came halfway down my calves and was pleated with red silk on the inside giving me room to move my leg around. I had brought a pair of my black shorts in case my dress lifted which I could wear underneath. On my feet I was going to wear my shin length boots that again had three red stripes on them to matches my dress. I got changed in the spare bedroom, which is the room me and Rose would use when I would come over. When I came out of the room zipping my boot up, Rose was finally ready and standing in the hallway. She was wearing a simple cream white dress that spread out at the bottom. The dress stopping at her knee and it was pared up with a pearl white fluffy sash that matched perfectly. She completed her dress with crystal slipper-like heeled shoes that looked like they came out of a fairy-tale book.

"Nice shoes, when did you get them?" I asked trying to figure out which of ex's gave them to her. They always buy her shoes as she not a jewellery person and everyone knows it.

"My mum gave them to me because of my good school report." Rose replied doing a spin to show them off.

"Be careful, you might lose them if your mum finds out about your fight with Emma." I smiled knowing that her mum would actually take them back to the shop and make Rose buy them back with her own money if she wanted to keep them.

"Yeah I will hide them before she finds out don't worry, I got a plan." Laughed Rose, "I'll hide them at your house and say I don't where they are. I don't think my mum won't look there as it too simple." Both of us started laughing at this.

The bell at the front door rang, making us bother stop laughing at once. Rose looked up at the clock, it read 4.25. The party doesn't start till 7:00. People shouldn't be arriving till 6:45, 6:40 at the earliest. I was only here because of what happening with Emma and Luke. Otherwise I would have been at Luke house till that time as well. Rose slowly walked to the door and opened it, peering through a small crack.

"Oh my god." She screamed throwing the door wide open and hugging the person at the door.

I smiled when saw who the girl standing was, standing on the doorstep was Rose's older sister Lily.

Lily was 19 and has been at university for the last year and has been living away from home. This is the first time either of us had seen her in ages. She looked different from how I remembered her. Her hair had been cut short, instead of down her back like the rest of her family. It was now just above her shoulder and getting slightly longer as it comes round the front of her head. It had also been dyed chocolate brown with a fuchsia pink fringe. Not the blonde she had last saw her. She looked like she lost some weight but looked much stronger than before. She was wearing a purple low-cut sleeveless dress and a black leather jacket with black high heels. "What are you doing here?" Rose beamed happily; her eyes were glowing with pleasure.

"Do you really think I'd miss my little sister first parent free party for anything." Lily replied happily, messing Rose's hair a little. She knew what Rose thought about freshly styled hair and didn't want to mess it for real. She walked into the hallway and looked around the room.

"Hey Lily." I said from the stairwell not knowing exactly what else to do.

"Hey Ingrid. How are you? It's been a long time." Lily replied giving me a hug. "Oh, I'm sorry about Luke by the way. If you want some sisterly advice, forget about him and Emma, they're not worth it." I guess nothing stays secret around here. Then again Lily knows Emma older sister as they are both studying the same things. She would have told Lily about her sister and Luke the second she found out.

"So how was uni?" Asked Rose, knowing that Luke and Emma were the last people I wanted to talk about.

"It's great, I'm sharing my room with these two girls, Ruby and Becky. They are really fun to be sharing a room with. I get given so much work to do now, I don't get to have as much fun as I used to. I'm not much a rebel anymore which our parents will be happy about." We were now in Rose's dining room. The dining room was quite big with a table that could fit 8 people and they also have a massive TV hidden in a cupboard on the wall opposite the door. A massive sofa sitting across from where the TV was placed. The dining room was the most used room in the house to hang out in as it had everything in it that was needed. "Oh, I just remembered. I got a DVD we can watch before the party; you might like it Ingrid." Lily said going back through to the hallway where she dropped her bags when Rose jumped on her. "Ruby is a lot like you Ingrid, and she said you might like this."

"This is so great. My first party and my sister is here." Rose beamed as she smiled at me. I smiled back at her. Rose seemed happy about her sister being here with her. I always wish I had a sister like Lily instead of Ben. Someone I could talk to and share my secrets with and share things with. Not a brother who I don't have anything in common with. Then again if anyone went after Ben I would stand in their way and fight for my family. Lily came back in with the DVD, I looked at the cover and smiled, it was a vampire film. Ruby must be a vampire and horror lover. Lily put it on, and we all sat down and started to watch it. After a while Lily and Rose started to talk, catching up on what they had both been doing in the year that Lily had been away. But, I was too interested in the movie to listen to what they were actually saying. The DVD was about this vampire girl, whose parents were killed so she was put into an orphanage and raised with no knowledge of where she had come from or why she is there. One day she finally snapped because she was being bullied continuously by other girls who are at the orphanage with her. This forced her to find out what she was; a killer, she ended up killing everyone who had ever did her wrong. The teacher who made her look stupid all the time, even when she knows the answer. Kids who would trip her up when she walked past and people like that. It ended with everyone being killed and she leaves the orphanage to find a new place to set up a home. A place where she controlled everything about her life and to start again. I like vampire films that end with the vampires winning and not killed by a slayer.

When the DVD ended, I notice that the dining room was now empty, Lily and Rose had left without me knowing. I left the room and found them in the living room, talking to the band who must have arrived while I was in the dining room. They just finished setting up the equipment and were joking around about lyrics and things.

"Hey when did you leave? I asked when I got to them.

"Oh when the vampire girl was killing the teacher in the school." Rose replied before turning back to the conversation with the band, about what songs they were planning on performing. I was shocked that they even left the movie. They left just before the best part of the movie; I had been imagining it was Mrs Wednesday she was killing. The doorbell rang and Rose went to answer it, I checked the clock, it was time for the party to start.

After that we had no time to relax, lots of people kept coming in and soon the house was full. It was time to have fun and forget all today trouble. Rose was trying to talk to everyone and making sure everyone was happy, she was actually a fairly good hostess. Everyone loved the band and the music and how it was everywhere in the house, begging Rose to tell them how she have gotten the band to play at the house. Most people have tried to get them to play at their party, but they were always too busy to do private house party. They even asked me, but I don't have a clue how she have gotten them to the play at the house as I not had a chance to ask myself. I was so happy that no one said Luke or Emma name. No one tried to give me sympathy or anything, ask me what happened and get all the detail. I didn't have time to think about them as I was too busy dancing and having a laugh. The doorbell rang again; someone went to answer it and they came back with a pile of pizzas. Everyone cheered and went to grab some slices. I wonder who order it and paid for it as I knew it wasn't Rose. There must be a small group as there was a least 15 boxes. Rose came towards me with some pizza in her hand, meat feast, my favourite.

"Wow, you've done an amazing job." I beamed at Rose and I meant it. She really had done well with the party.

"I know, everyone keeps saying that it's great and they want to know how I got the band to come."

"How did you get the band to come and play? I know lots of people have tried."

Rose pointed to her sister who was talking and giggling with the lead singer. "He couldn't say no."

"Ah" Understand what she meant. I smiled to myself, wondering what half the girls are going to say when they find out the hottest boy in the band is taken. It was about 11.30 when people started to leave saying they have had a fun time and it was one of the best parties. By 11.50 the places was empty as they last of the people left closing the door behind them. Because I was sleeping over, I needed to help with the tidying up which I tried to get out of but failed to do so.

"I wish they were a machine or something which could tidy up after you." Moaned Rose looking at all the mess. The chairs needed to be moved back to where they came from in the house. There were pizza slices that had been dropped on the floor as well as other food and drinks, someone of it going deep into the carpet. There were also boxes and cups all other the floors and sides that need cleaning up and put into the bin.

"Why don't we just do it in the morning, it too late to do anything now and we're all tired." Said Lily looking at the clock with the hands pointing to midnight.

"Yeah." We all agreed, it was definitely too late to start tiding up. We walked upstairs quietly as everyone was too tired to even talk.

The doorbell rang suddenly, it echoed in the silence house. We all looked at each other, no one should be ringing the bell this late. Lily went to the door, signing for me and Rose to stay on the stairs.

"Who is it? What do you want? My parents are here and we're not alone, they are calling the police as we speak." Her voice trembled as she grabbed the golf club their father kept near the door for when he goes away for the night. He had for the last four years but it have never been needed.

"Hello Lily, glad you are back. Come on open the door. I really need to talk to Ingrid and Rose, come one please." Came a voice that was as welcome as a toad in soup. It was Luke.

"You are not welcome here Luke. Get lost and leave Rose and Ingrid alone." Shouted Lily angrily. Great I thought to myself, why couldn't I ever fight for myself? Now Lily was fighting for me. Who will be fighting my battles next? Ben? My parents? A dog? Just then the door burst opened; we must have forgotten to lock it after the last person left the house.

"Get out." Screamed Lily making a grab for the golf club she dropped, but Emma had already grabbed it.

I guess she knew about it as well and where it was hidden. Lily, Rose and I backed into the living room with them both following us through the doors. I dared to look around the once crowded room. Not really wanting to take my eyes off Luke and Emma for too long, wishing everyone was here still and it wasn't just us. I looked at Lily and Rose and say they were doing the same thing and I knew they felt the same, I knew they wanted the room to be full again.

"What do you want Luke?" Sneered Lily. I was surprise she still had the courage to carry on fighting. Then again Lily have always been the strong one out of us all. Then again, I didn't have any fight in me to begin with.

"I want to talk to Rose and Ingrid." Luke answered.

Me and Rose looked at each other. No way would they do all this just to talk to us.

"Why do you want to speak to us?" I nervously asked.

"We" Spat Emma "want you two, to go to Mrs Wednesday and say the fight was entirely your fault and it had nothing to do with us. That we should not be punished and that we shouldn't be stuck at school with her for weeks and weeks." My mouth fell open, I couldn't help it and I knew Rose was doing the same. They were doing all of this, banging into the door, not leaving and grabbing the golf club, just for that. Because they don't want to say stay behind after school for a few weeks.

"Why should we? You've come into my house, threatened us with a golf club and you think we're just going to do everything you say." Rose shouted, getting madder now that she knew the real reason why they were here.

"Look." Luke butted in. "I got plans, and they don't involve Mrs Wednesday or you two. Not anymore." He looked at me with a smirk. "So, are you going to do it or what?"

Lily started swearing at Luke and Emma demanding that they get out of the house right now before she calls the police.

I looked at Luke, trying to see where this new Luke had come from. The person I was looking at was not the person I fell in love with. The person I thought cared about me. It was then I noticed something tucked into his belt, Rose eyes widen when she saw it too.

It was a knife, and from the way Lily was still going on, I don't think she noticed it. Or if she had she wasn't afraid of it.

Luke saw us looking and smiles, showing his teeth in an evil grin that sent shivers down my spine.

"Emma." Emma looked at Luke when he said her name, "Tie Rose and Lily to a chair and hold onto this for me." He gave her the knife from his belt. "I'll try and get Ingrid to agree, I normally can. There are also some, weird things that I have seen that we need to talk about." He took a step close towards me, a sinister look on his face that spelt trouble.

"NO!" Rose scream running forward, lunging herself at Luke. He just pushed her away like she was nothing and she fell backwards, hitting her head on the coffee table as she went down. The blow knocked her out leaving her unconscious on the floor.

"ROSE!" Shouted Lily crouching by her sister side, protecting her from Luke and Emma with her body.

Emma had the knife in her hand and put it to Lily's throat. Emma looked like she wanted to use it and it didn't matter on who. Lily looked away, hiding her face in Rose clothes. You could hear her crying lightly. All the fight she had was now gone as she knew she needed to protect her sister with all her power.

Why were they doing this? This has gone beyond of just asking us to go to see Mrs Wednesday, people were now hurt and weapons were involved. With Rose, Lily and Emma out of the battle, this left with just left me and Luke standing.

"Now here what's going to happen; I ask you things and you give me the truth. Then you are going to speak to Mrs Wednesday. That is the only thing that will be happening tonight." Luke tone of voice terrified me.

I was going to replied something to him when the lights went off and it suddenly went pitch black. I looked out of the window and I spotted that all the other house lights were still on, so it can't have been a power cut.

Was it just this house with all the light off? Before I had a chance to work out what was happening, everything started to go blurry and things were starting not to make sense. Things looked like they were happening in the wrong order, everything was getting mixed up and wrong. I tried to open my mouth to speak when I felt a pain in my body that I had never felt before. The pain burned through my body like fire, every inch of my skin felt like it was burning, as if needles were being stabbed into me. I felt like I was being burned up from the inside and I had no idea why.

I looked over at Luke, I could only see his face through the burliness, and I saw it was set in horror. His eyes were wide with fear and panic. "Luke. Luke!" Emma was screaming but it sounded muffed like it was miles away. I couldn't work out where she was, I had no idea where Rose and Lily were.

The pain suddenly stopped, and I started to black out, all I remember was hitting the floor before everything went dark. When I woke up, I opened my eyes and I saw myself standing over me like an out of body experience as I was looking into my own eyes. Suddenly I realised I wasn't looking at myself, I was looking at Luke's neighbour Elizabeth. I tried to shoot up, to ger away from her when realised that she was holding me down. I was starting to panic that I was trapped when I realise that she wasn't doing forceful, she was doing it like she was protecting me.

"Don't worry Ingrid, just close your eyes and go back to sleep. Don't worry, everything is going to be fine. You need to trust me and not tell anyone I was here." She said, her voice was calm, hypnotizing almost. I found myself doing what she asked and I closed my eyes again. I find myself not caring what was going to on; I just listened to her voice and feeling safe with what she was telling me. In the background I could hear other voices, but I was already too far gone to work out whose voices they were. It sounded like I was under water, but I could still hear Elizabeth voice as clear as anything. "It's going to be OK, everything going to be fine." Her voice started drift away like the other sounds. "Soon you will know the truth."

Chapter 5

I opened my eyes again, half expecting to see Elizabeth above and for me to still be on the floor at Rose's house. However, all I could see was a long thin light above my head, I had to blink a few times as the light blinded me slightly.

I moved slightly, and I realise I was in a bed and not on the floor. But it was not my bed because it was too hard and the covers that covered me where thin and itchy.

"I think she is waking up." Came a voice so quietly, I knew it was not me they were talking too.

It was then that I was aware of other sounds in the room, the loudest one being a beeping noise from a machine. I turned my head and saw that it was a heart machine and the voice belonged to my mum.

It then dawned on me that I must be in a hospital, that's why the bed was so hard and why there was a heart machine attached to me. I tried to remember how I got here, but all I remember was Emma and Luke barging in and Elizabeth... Elizabeth telling me it was going to be OK. That I needed to go to sleep and soon I will know the truth. But what truth was she talking about? I turned my head and saw my mum and my dad were both sitting next to my bed. There were no once else in the room apart from us three.

I saw my mum's eyes were watering as she spoke. "Ingrid thanks god you are awake." My mum shot up and gave me a slightly too tight of a hug.

I pulled away so I could breathe again. "What happened? Where are Rose and Lily?"

I knew Rose had been hurt by Luke and Emma, but I have no idea what they did to Lily once I black out.

"Don't you remember?" My dad asked.

I lied and shook my head as I wanted to know what Emma and Luke has been telling people.

"After the party you, Rose, Lily, Luke and Emma were all tiding up in the living room. Emma and Luke decided to help tidy up, even though they were not staying at the house as the house was such a mess. It was before midnight when 2 strangers burst into the house with a knife. One of them grabbed the golf club Rose and Lily father keep for protection. The police think they must have saw it and took a chance and grabbed it. They made sure everyone was unconscious before they took everything in the house of value. Jewellery, money, game consoles even the TV from all the rooms." He stopped briefly before he spoke again. "You don't remember any of the things I'm telling you, do you?" Asked my dad as I could hide the look of confusion on my face.

I shook my head again, but this time I wasn't lying. "No I don't remember of this. How did the police find us?" I asked wondering how Emma and Luke attacking us got change to 2 people stealing from us and attacking all 4 of us. Did I fake the memory to blame Luke and Emma? Did dream the whole thing up as I slept because of what they did to me? Maybe Elizabeth wasn't even there at all and her speaking to me was just in my mind?

"A girl called Elizabeth was walking past the window and saw the people attacking you. She got help and raised the alarm. She saved you and made sure everyone got help. However, the people who did attacking ran off before the police got there. They say Elizabeth just move next to Luke a couple of days ago and she was exploring the village when she came across the attack. It's lucky she walked past as no one knows what could have happened if she didn't. No one knows when someone might have found you otherwise."

I looked away from my dad and past him out the window he was sat next too. I saw the sun was shining through which seem a world away from Rose party. Now that Elizabeth name has been said by someone else, I know what I remember really did happened. That I was right to suspect Luke and Emma, and now Elizabeth was involved in it to. But why did Elizabeth make up a story that helped Emma and Luke escape with what they did? Why did she help me if she was on Luke and Emma side? Nothing was making sense no matter how much I thought about it.

"Are you OK love?" My mum said bringing me back to the present and out of my mind. She sounded panicked like she thought something could happen at any moment. "I'm just tired, I am going back to sleep." I lied; I just wanted to think, to be left alone for my brain to work out what happening.

"OK love." My dad kissed me on my forehead, took my mum's hand and left the room, closing the door quietly as they could behind them.

The second I was alone, my body started to slow down, it turned out I really was tired. I wanted to think but I fell asleep before I could sort anything out in my mind. No matter how hard I tried to fight it, I ended up losing the battle and sleep took me over. When I woke up again, I saw it was now dark outside the window. The only light in the room where from the corridor outside the door and a streetlight from the outside world. I don't know how long I been asleep for if it was late at night or early morning or even a different day.

I knew there were no point in being awake as there wasn't anything, I could do at this moment, so I closed my eyes and tried to force myself to go back to sleep. It was then that I realised something, someone else was in the room with me.

I sat up quickly in bed, my eyes scanning the room quickly. I then saw her sitting on a chair at the bottom of my bed. Elizabeth and she was smiling at me.

"Hello Ingrid. How are you?" She asked getting off the chair and standing next to my bed by the window.

"Who are you? Why do you look like me? What are you doing here? Why did you..." All the words were spilling out of my mouth without stopping.

"Ingrid." She put her hand to stop me, "Slow down and I might be able to answer some of your question. First my name Elizabeth as you already know as people has told you my name a few times. I live next door to your ex- boyfriend from what been happening and what I heard. Why I look like you its more complex and I can't answer that one yet. You need to know some more information which should let the answer fit into place easier. There is a better place I can explain that to you which is not this hospital." She looked at her feet then back at me like she was trying to think of what to say next. "I'm here because I need to talk to you. I need to show you what you are, and I need to explain to what happened at the party."

"Yes, thanks for being nosy with me and my ex's. Like you said I know your name and..." I stopped dead something suddenly clicking into place. "What do you mean what I am?" I asked just realising what she had said. "What do you mean what I am?" I left it hanging in the air.

"It's hard to explain as I know you won't believe me when you first hear the truth."

"What truth? Why do you keep going on about the truth? Just tell me Elizabeth, stop with all the riddles and secrets. I just want to know what's happening. I just want to know what going on"

"Look..." She started putting her hand in her pocket when there was a sudden bang at the door. I turned around and looked at the source of the sound and I saw it was a nurse standing by the door. She must have knocked into the door while doing checks. She looked apologetic and she walked away. She didn't say anything with Elizabeth standing behind me. Maybe she used to seeing two people in a room and she doesn't realise there only meant to be one in this room. I turned back to Elizabeth when I froze. Elizabeth was gone, where she was standing a moment ago was now empty.

I got out of bed and walked round the room to study it. She was nowhere to be seen and there were nowhere for her to hide. The room I was in was a medium size, wasn't too small you were cramped but not big enough for 2 beds. My bed was in the far corner next to the window, the door was opposite the window, so it faces the side of the bed. The room was bare with the only furniture being 2 chairs and a table that wheeled over the bed. Nothing else, nowhere to hide, nowhere for Elizabeth to be.

A nurse came in suddenly from the door, making me jump as I wasn't expecting it.

"Hey, I didn't think you be up and out of bed. It's 3:30 in the morning, you need to go back to sleep. Then again you been asleep for the last 12 hours, so you must be wide awake now." She said sweetly. "I only came in to check on you to see if you are OK as you under my care."

"How many ways are there to get out of this room?" I asked. It didn't matter what she was saying to me about me sleeping and going back to bed. I needed to know where Elizabeth went, I needed to finish speaking to her. I didn't want to sound rude or anything to her as she was being kind. I just needed to know the answers.

"Why? Planning to escape out of the hospital, are you?" She laughs slightly. "Well I am sorry but there is only one way out of here and that's the way I just came through. I am sorry but there no secret passage or anything like that. I wouldn't think of using the windows as they child locks are on. So there no escaping for you till the doctors say you." She smiled like she wanted me to laugh. You could tell she was really trying hard to help me.

"Oh OK." I tried to smile back, but my brain was too busy working overtime to make my smile more real. I don't know if she could tell if I was faking it or not.

"OK well you go back to bed and try and rest some more." She walked out of the door and left me alone after giving me a smile.

I stayed standing in the middle of the room as I knew I wasn't going to go back to bed. Even though the nurse tried her best, she didn't really help with how to leave the room without anyone seeing. I couldn't really tell her about Elizabeth dis-appearing from the room. She wouldn't have believed me, not with what she said about one way out. She would think it was in my mind and Elizabeth was just part of my mind.

I looked round the room, trying to figure out what to do next. I knew I couldn't stay in the room and do nothing, that was out of the question. A thought came to me about Elizabeth and where she could be. If Elizabeth came to see me, then she might have gone to tell the others about the cover stories. I knew what my dad thought happened was a lie at the party, maybe she with them now. I knew Rose got hurt so she would be at the same hospital as me as it was the only close by. Lily would be with her sister as I knew she wouldn't leave her side now she back. That is the most logical place for everyone to be.

I opened the door and stuck my head out looking down the corridor to make sure no one was around. I closed my door quietly, so no one would hear and see that I was sneaking around. I check the door number and saw it read 56 so I knew what room to head back too once I saw Rose and Lily.

As I got to the end of the corridor when a thought hit me. I was in a 3-way corridor with only numbers on the wall and I had no idea where anyone was. How was I going to find my friends in this place?

I couldn't go up to someone and ask them for Rose's room number. I was meant to be in bed and not standing in the corridor in the middle of the night. I was still standing in the corridor when I saw the nurse who spoke to me came out of the door next to me.

"Oh" She jumped back when she looked up and saw me. "What are you doing out here? You frightened me. I told you to go back to bed and sleep."

"I need to talk to my friends now please. And before you say anything it can't wait for tomorrow or later or whenever." I was starting to get confusing with what time of day it was now.

"Well" She thought for a few moments." OK, I know who you are talking about as you all came in at the same time. I know the 2 sisters Lily and Rose are awake as I just came past their bedroom and I could hear talking coming inside the room. I am not sure about the other 2 you came in with, Emma and Luke. I have not checked on them yet, so they might be up and awake or still sleeping." She started to walk down the hall and I followed her nearly tripping over my own feet.

"Luke and Emma?" I asked with confusion. Why was there in the hospital? With what they did shouldn't they be in the police station and not the hospital? "What wrong with them, why is everyone here?"

"Yeah Luke and Emma are here, but like I said they might not be awake. Then again maybe the whole group is awake and not going to bed like they are being told too. But I do I hope they are not walking around and things. I mean they both got some ribs broken, bruises, cuts and all sorts wrong with them. They lost some blood due to all their injuries, so they needed to be given some. However, I know that wouldn't stop some people from having a walk about in the middle of the night. Rose had a head injury so that was the main problem with her as that is not healing correctly. Your friend Lily is harder as she is not telling people what her injures are and what is wrong with her. Out of everyone you were the luckiest one. There wasn't a single scratch on you at all or any injury that we could find. The only reason you are here is because when the police and ambulance found you, you were unconscious on the floor with everyone else. That does means you will be going home either later today or tomorrow. You won't be in no longer than that, I don't know about any of your friends." She stopped outside a door and I nearly walked into her as I wasn't really paying attention. I was too busy listening to what she was saying. I could hear voices coming from inside the room and I recognize the voices belonging to Rose and Lily. I was so glad to hear their voices as it meant that they were OK.

The nurse knocked on the door and I opened it as she walked away. I walked into the room and saw that it was the same layout of me. The only different being that the room was bigger, and it had 2 beds in instead of one. I saw that Rose and Lily were sitting on the same one and were talking to each other.

Rose looked up and she smiled.

"Ingrid." Shouted Rose coming towards the door and gave me a big hug. "You awake, how are you feeling?"

"I'm fine, the nurse said I will be gone today or tomorrow." I said to Rose once she released me from the hug.

"That's good. We have not been told anything yet about when we are being discharged." Lily said more to herself then to me as she got of one bed's and went to the other one.

I sat on the empty bed with Rose and Lily stayed on her own. "Do you remember what happened after the party? My memory a bit fuzzy in places and I am not sure on some bits about." I asked wanting to know what they remember and what they don't remember.

"Yeah, but like you I only remember small bits. I remember we were thinking of tidying up but decided to leave it as it was late. I remember Luke and Emma were there when we were at the bottom of the stairs."

"Then what happened?" I asked eagerly. Rose remember Luke and Emma being there. That means that they must remember them attacking us as well.

"Then I remember a couple of random people burst in from the door and attacked us all. We were in the living room for some reason when it happened. I remember something to do with a golf club and a knife, I think the golf club was the one we have by the door." She shook her head as you could tell she was thinking hard. "I can't remember anything else. Do you Lily?" Rose looked at Lily who was sat up looking at us, she shook her head but didn't say anything.

"Have..." I started asking when someone knocked on the door and interrupted me from speaking.

All are heads looked at the door when it opened, and I saw Luke and Emma standing in the doorway. I couldn't believe how much of a mess Luke and Emma looked. They both had cuts and bruises on their faces and arms. They looked pale and I remember the nurse said that they needed to give them both some blood. You could tell how they were standing that they had some bruise on their body and broken ribs. You could see that breathing was hurting them and Emma finished the look with a blacken eye. Why did they look so bad, what happened to them?

"We are so glad that you awake, we need to ta..." Luke stopped talking when his eyes fell on me. I could see his eyes darken. "Never mind, we speak later."

He slammed the door shut and I could hear them leaving the hallway as quickly as they could with their injury. No one spoke till the footsteps went quiet and the hospital became silent again. I looked at Rose and she looked at me with the same confuse look on her face. That was not normal behaviour. I looked at Lily but for some reason she didn't meet my eye. Her face told me that she knew something, but she wasn't going to share it with anyone. Did she know what happened to them? Does she remember the same things as I do but not saying anything?

I was about to ask again what happening when a doctor walked into the room.

"Ingrid there you are, I have been looking for you. You need to go back to your room and stay in it." He said looking at me. "And I mean stay in your room, the hospital is not a place for people to explore at all time of night."

"But..." I started to protest I still needed to talk to Rose and Lily.

"No buts, if or so what. You need to go back to your room with no excuses. I have talked to your parents and you can go home later today. But before you can go you need to go back to your room and sleep as is still so early in the morning. I let you say goodbye to your friends first, then I will expect you to be back in you room fast asleep when I check on you in 5 minutes." He then left the room without a second glance.

"He's a nice doctor, you are so lucky." I rolled my eyes and Rose laughed. "I wonder when you be going home as I'm going later on today?"

I decided I wasn't going to listen to him and stayed sat on the bed with Rose. I will go when I find out what happening and not a moment before. I notice Lily was still looking away and wouldn't meet my eyes, this time Rose noticed her doing it.

"Hey Lil, are you OK?" asked Rose using Lily's nickname. She sounded worried as her sister wasn't normal like this. I was worried as well as she was acting differently than she normal does.

"Nothing is wrong with me. I'm just tired that's all as it been a long day. I'm going to sleep now. Ingrid," She said my name like it was poison and looked at me for the first time since I been there. "Needs to go like the doctor said. It's early in the morning and everyone needs to sleep." The way she said it made it clear I wasn't welcome here. She laid down and turned her back away from us. What did I do to her?

Rose just shrugged. "Maybe she has a point, I'm getting tired now. And I don't think the doctor will be happy if he notices that you are still here and not in your bed." She walked to the door and I followed her as I knew there wasn't any point in me staying. "Don't worry about Lily, she just hates hospital and doctors. That's why she is being so difficult to everyone. Don't worry it's not just you, even though I must admit she not normal like this even with hospital. I am slightly worried about her, but she must just mad because 2 strangers ruined my party and trashed our parent's house. I know she must hate herself because I'm her younger sister and I got hurt when she was there. Aren't older sibling meant to protect the younger ones. Sibling always look out for each other, no matter if you fight, scream or say you hate each other." She looked sad for a second and I knew understood what she was saying. Me and Ben always fight, and I know we will also will. But I know no matter what I will do my best to protect him from anyone and everyone. The feelings Lily must be feeling after not being able to do that for Rose.

Rose looked up again and smiled at me slightly. "Look she be fine once she calms down and we get out of here. See me later before you go please, or you won't hear the end of it I promise." She laughed slightly and I left, I heard the door close behind me.

I stood in the hallway for a few moments and thought about what I just heard. I couldn't understand how my ex and someone who meant to be my best friend who attacked me turned into 2 strangers attacking us. Why won't Lily tell Rose what happened? She knows something, she knows something isn't right but she not saying anything.

I started to walk back to my room thinking to myself about all the questions I had because of what I heard and saw. Why did Luke and Emma go to Lily and Emma's room? They seemed to be acting nice before they saw me. They wanted to speak to Lily and Rose for some reason but not me? What happened to them and why were they hurt like that? They attacked us, not the other way round. Lily knows something but not telling any of us.

I stopped in the middle of the corridor when another thought struck me. How much have they forgotten? Does Rose remember the fight at school and what happened before the party or is that a blank as well? Is

Rose going to go back to school and wonder why she's being made to stay behind after school for 5 weeks? If that does happen then Mrs Wednesday going to make her life hell by thinking she is being cheeky by pretending not to know anything.

I was about to start walking back to my room again when another thought hit me. What if none of this was real? What if I am in a coma like you see it on the TV all the time? That I was asleep, and this was all a dream and nothing that has happened since before the party had not happened. Luke and Emma never betrayed me, and everyone was still good friends. That would explain about Elizabeth appearing and dis-appearing all the time. Why she looks so much like me? The first time I saw her was when I was at Luke house, that means it must have happened before that. It was the only thing that makes sense with everything that has been happening. I kept the thought of this being a dream in my head I walked to my room, thinking all the way to wake up. I felt happier now I knew what was happening, glad that soon everything will be back to normal as soon as I wake up. Once I got to my room, I looked round thinking of what I was going to do now. I have no idea how you wake up from a coma dream apart from what I see on TV and they are always different. I looked around the room and I spotted something on the chair that 'Elizabeth' sat on. I walked over to it and saw that there a locket was laying on it.

I picked it up to look at it as I was curious about what it was. The locket was small and an oval shape which wouldn't be too obviously if it worn under a top. The locket looked like it was made of gold and it was encrusted with deep red rubies that went all around the edge of the locket. In the middle of the locket the letter I B was engraved.

I saw that there was a catch on the right side and I slowly opened it even though my body suddenly felt on edge for no reason. In the locket there was a photo of a family. The women was wearing a floor length dark red dress with wide shoulder sleeves, the man was wearing a black two-piece suit with a red tie that match his partner. In their arms were twin's babies both wearing short black dresses with red roses round the waist that matches the red of the parents. Each of the parents had a child in their arms and they were all smiling and laughing.

I closed the locket again and put it back on the chair where I found it. I went outside into the hall to look at the door number to make sure that I didn't accidently go into someone else room as they all looked the same. It was definitely my room, so I didn't make a mistake.

I went back to the locket and looked at the photo again but this time in more detail. Trying to figure out who could have dropped it, a doctor or someone seeing if I was OK while I was out of the room.

I felt my body freeze when my eyes fell on a certain part of the photo. I felt my body go cold even though the room suddenly felt so hot suddenly.

I closed my eyes wishing I was wrong with what I was seeing, I looked again hoping it had changed somehow. It hadn't. I stood there looking at the photo, so many things going through my head I couldn't keep up with them. It's was all a dream, none of this was real. I was in a coma and none of this was happening.

This locket was not real, nothing that has been happening have been real. It doesn't make sense, the photo doesn't make sense, nothing wasn't making sense. I started to have trouble breathing, my breaths were getting heavy and faster as the thoughts kept going round and round in my head. I started to gasp for air, my lungs were feeling like they were on fire and they weren't letting any air in or out. I couldn't stay in the room anymore, it felt like I was in a prison cell and I was trapped. I needed to get out, I needed to get some air. I turned around on the spot and ran out of the room and down the corridor as fast as I could. Nurses and doctors just stood there in shocked as I ran past them, none of them really trying hard to stop me. I guess it's not normal for a young female to be running down the corridor this early in the morning.

I saw the front door and sprinted to it and out of the hospital as fast as my legs could take me. I didn't stop running once, only getting faster and faster with each step I took. I ran past my parents who I saw where just entering the front door as I ran out of the hospital. I heard them shouting after me, telling me what I was doing and to stop running and to speak to them.

I didn't stop running. I couldn't stop running. I needed to get away. I never wanted to stop running, but I had to because I couldn't breath and each breathe was hurting. I started to feel dizzy due to lack of oxygen getting to my lungs and I knew if I kept going, I was going to pass out. I wanted to escape but I couldn't as my body couldn't cope anymore. I stopped to catch my breath, my lungs welcoming the air. When I looked down at my hands, I saw I was still grasping the locket tightly in it. I never dropped the locket before I ran. I wanted to drop it as soon as I saw it. I wanted to leave it in the room and never looked at it again, but I couldn't leave it. Something in my mind told me not to and that took over every part of my body and mind. I opened it again, my hands were shacking and looked into the eyes of the family in the photo. Staring at their cold black eyes, the eyes I see every time I look into my own.

Chapter 5

"And where do you think you're going young lady?" I heard my mum shout from behind me in the kitchen. I stopped just at the front door, my hand nearly touching the door handle; I thought the coast was clear for me to leave. I dropped my arm and turned around; my mum was standing in the kitchen doorway. Her arms were crossed across her chest and she had an annoyed look on her face. This won't be good. "Well?" She asked, her voice louder and sharper than before. "Come here." She led me to the kitchen, and I knew I had no choice but to follow. "When we tell you to stay in the house, we mean stay in the house. That does not mean going towards the front door every time me or your father have our backs turned. Now stay there." She pointed to the corner of the kitchen.

She turned around and started to look through the fridge. While she worked round the kitchen, I could feel her eyes on me to make sure I didn't move. I stood there for 15 minutes when she said I could go. She thinks making me and Ben stand in the corner will help us be good. It might have been a good idea when we were younger, but it doesn't do much now that I am older.

I sighed as I left the corner as I knew my mum would be keeping an extra eye on the door making it nearly impossible for me to leave the house. I went to my room as there wasn't anything else for me to do and sat on my bed. My eyes scan the room but there wasn't much to look at. My room had a single size bed in it with dark purple covers which match all my poster. The posters I use to cover the walls to hide the light paint colour which my parents painted it. I had some shelves on the wall next to the door with some photos of family and friends, I had my favourite horror books were slotted in between the photos. The only other furniture in my room was a wardrobe where my clothes and random things had been places in and a shelf which had all the family DVD's on that somehow ended up in my bedroom. That was it. There was no TV as my parents took that out, leaving a part of my wall bare. They made sure to take most of my things out of my room to punished me. I sighed again and laid back on my bed, there wasn't anything else to do in here. My parents made sure of that.

I haven't been out of the house for the last 2 days. I was a prisoner in my own home, in my own room. My parents found me in the park, sitting on a bench with the locket in my pocket. I had somehow managed to force my eyes away from the photo, but I wanted it to be near me still, so I placed it in my pocket. My parents told me they'd been looking everywhere for me and even the police were involved. they only found me in the park by chance. They had been heading to the school as for some reason they thought I be at the school at that time in the morning. My parents know I use the park as a shortcut to get to school and other places, they were trying to recreate the steps I must have took.

When they found me, they took me straight home and got a doctor to come to the house to see if I could stay there. I don't think they wanted to give me another chance to run if I go back to the hospital. They made me stay in the living room till he came; both watching every move I made. I moved, they moved, it looked a bit like a stupid dance we were doing. I couldn't even go to the bathroom without my mum standing outside the door to make sure I wasn't climbing out of the bathroom window or something.

When the doctor came and saw he me, he said he had no problem with me stay at home as I was going to be discharge that day anyway. When he said this my stomach dropped as I knew my parents would make sure I didn't leave the house ever again without one of them being with me. So far, I was right about that and every attempt I have made to leave the house has been stopped by one of my parents.

I got off the bed and went to my wardrobe and opened it. I pulled out a shoe box that I hid at the back of the wardrobe on the bottom shelve. In the shoe box I hid the locket so that my parents didn't find it. My parents never thought to check my pockets when they found me. I don't think they would believe me if I told them that I found the locket on the chair after Elizabeth came to see me. A girl that has more questions than answers and somehow vanishes into thin air. I am not even sure of what the story is myself, never mind trying to explain it someone else.

I made sure to hide the locket the second I was allowed in my room and out of my parent's line of sight. Since I been kept locked in my own house, the locket seems to keep my mine balance. When I am alone, I get the locket out and sit on the floor to look at it. Every second I spend looking at the photo of the family and the kids, the same feeling come over me. The same confusion about how they have the same eyes as me, eyes, I have never seen on anyone else. But the feeling on confusion was also mixed with comfort, a feeling I don't understand. Why would the eyes make me feel safe, shouldn't it be the opposite affect?

There was a knock on my bedroom door that made me jump, brining me back into the room and out of the photo. I put the locket quickly in the shoe box and shoved the box back in the wardrobe. My mum came in just as I got up and was walking towards the door. I was glad she didn't catch me with the locket otherwise I would have needed to explain it.

"Ingrid love, can I talk to you please?" She asked, sitting on my bed so I had no choice but to talk to her. I recognise the tone of voice; a tone she was using she has been using it since I been back home. I sighed, I knew I couldn't just walk out of the room with her in it, so I sat down on the bed next to her to save her following me round the house. Since I got back, she has been trying to talk to me all the time. Something she never wanted to before I got attacked. She always asking me why I ran out of the hospital? Why was I avoiding her and dad all the time? Why have I been acting strangely since I got back? Why was I trying to leave the house and not speak to them? Why I seem to be acting like I was someone else?

The only answer I would give her is that nothing is bothering me. I am fine and if they can leave it at that.

"I think it will be a good idea if you go and stay with your Auntie Bee and Uncle Ted for a bit. I don't like you being here with everything that has been going on. I want you to get away from this place and get better. Something has made you change if you want to admit to it or not. I know that a new place will help you get better and go back to normal. Get away from everyone and come back as a happy girl." She smiled at me.

This shocked me; this wasn't the talk I thought she was going to have with me. It took my brain a few seconds to make sense of what she had just said. What she wanted me to do.

My Auntie and Uncle lived in Texas USA, a whole another country away. I can't go, I wanted to stay here and find out what has been happening. About Elizabeth and what she knows about me and the party.

"Why do you want to go all the way to Texas?" My voice came out harsher than I meant it to. But she wanted me to move to a different country, away from my friends and everything I know. By the way she was talking, it didn't sound like mum, dad or Ben would be sitting next to me on the plane. "I am not going to live in the US. You can't make me; you can't force me to go."

"Because" her voice was stern. Her tone was strongly suggesting she wouldn't be taking no for an answer and I had no choice in the matter.

"You need to get away from this place and what been happening. Because you are not yourself and don't say you are because you're obviously are lying. Me and your dad thinks that it's will be a good idea if you went away and spent time with other people. You need to get away from Luke, Emma and whoever attacked you. You are going to go to your Auntie and Uncle's, and you are going to stay there till you are back to normal. We are doing this to help you as we care about you. So don't take that tone with me and the matter is now closed."

I opened my mouth and closed it again as I didn't know what to say, how to respond to what she was saying to me. I couldn't go, I couldn't go to live with them. We hated each other. They hate me, and I hate them simple as. They hate the clothes I wear, the make-up I put on, when I go to sleep and the places I like to go to. Basically, everything that makes me, me. They try and force me to wear white shorts and yellow tops when I stay with them. Their daughter wears the shorts and tops, but they like looking like they are playing tennis all the time. I have no idea why they want us all to look the same, like we are perfect clones.

Their daughters are called Molly and Sue, Sue is 13 and Molly is 14. Due to the small different between their ages, they look and act like twins when they are not. They dress the same, speak the same, so many people think they are twins. When they are near any adults, they act like angels, making sure they keep them wrapped round their fingers. Making sure they can get away with anything they want. However when we are away from the adults they turned into devils and make my life hell. They make it their mission to get me into trouble, they wind me up again and again, making sure they click all my buttons so that I snap and get caught by my parents. They also make sure that it looks like I started it and they are the innocent party to it all, making my life a living hell.

An example of this was when I was forced to go out with my family for the 100th time. They wanted to go for a walk for my Uncle's birthday and I had no choice but to go with them. We were in the sun for nearly 2 hours and most of that was spent with my Auntie telling us about the plants and trees we were seeing that could put anyone to sleep within minutes. There was a river next to the path that we walked down as it was a place that they like to walk all the time. When I asked why we were here, everyone kept telling me it was beautiful and perfect place to walk. All I saw was water and path that seems to never end.

Ben has been walking next to the river when he fell in after tripping over something. Molly and Sue helped him out straight away being the angels they are because their parents were around. I just stood there laughing my head off; Ben was soaked to the bone and dripping wet, he looked like a drown rat.

My parents glared at me. "Why can't you be like Molly and Sue? They help people and don't laugh at them. It's not nice to laugh at people."

Molly and Sue smiled at this and the adults carried on walking. I stuck my tongue out at them behind their back, which Molly and Sue told them about. Snitches.

When I decided to walk next to the river away from the group, Molly 'accidentally' knocked into me, sending me into the water. By accidently I mean she made sure that no one was looking, she went sideway into me to get me into the water.

"Oops, sorry Ingrid. I didn't mean to knock you into the water" She smiled at Sue and she smiled back. The adults and Ben laughed when they saw me soak to the bone. I could feel my face was bright red. What happened to, 'it's not nice to laugh at people'.

This annoyed me as I hated when people laughed at me, so I decided to fight back. I reached up and grabbed Molly. She was still standing near me laughing and had not bothered to move out of the way. This caught Molly off guard and from the look on her and Sue's face, this was not part of the plan and she fell in the river next to me. She now looked like a drown rat.

"Ingrid, leave Molly alone she only 14." My dad said, he stopped laughing but, he still had a smile on his face which he was trying to hide and failing.

I put on my sad and innocent face on. "I didn't mean to dad; I was just trying to get up. I didn't know she would fall in." I looked at him using all my acting skills that I have.

He just smiled. "That's OK. Accidents will happen. Come on you 2, get out the river before you catch your cold."

I got up out of the river and walked past Sue who were helping Molly out. "Bring it on."

I don't know if the parents know that there is a rift between us and that we were making life difficult for each other. We would break something and then blame the other person. We would lie and say that the other people hurt us and things like that every time we are together.

I looked back at mum bringing myself out the memory. If I go to my Auntie and Uncle in the US, then they would have the upper hand, I would be on their turf. If I go, I wouldn't be able to find out who Elizabeth was and about the locket and the people in it. If I go, I wouldn't find out what happened at the party with Emma and Luke. There to many reasons why me leaving this place was not a good idea, too many questions that needs answer which will only be possible if I stay here.

I won't go.

I can't go.

"I am not going." I said looking straight into her eyes, I was not backing down. "You can't make me; you will need to drag me there kicking and screaming."

My mum stood up suddenly, making me jump as I didn't expect her to do this. "We will carry on this when your father comes home, then I will see you try and talk back to him."

She walked out of the room slamming the door with a bang, my shelves wobbled a bit on the wall.

Great I thought and laid down on my bed.

My dad was the only person who can get me to back down from something, he always could because he was my father. If someone could get me on a plane to the US, is was him.

I needed to find Rose and talk to her, I need to tell her about Emma and Luke. She doesn't know what they are really like, to warn her about what they could do, what they did do. I need to tell her about Elizabeth and the party and all the other crazy things that been happening in my live. I needed help; I couldn't do this on my own, I needed someone by my side. I have no idea how I could see Rose; I couldn't leave or go anywhere because my mum and dad are making sure off that. They won't let me leave the house; they always got their eyes on the door. If I go to the door, they follow me. In move, they move, it's like having a human shadow.

They took my mobile phone off me and now keep it on them at all time. They got my laptop; tablet and they always have the house phone with them. If the phone rings then I can't answer it, it must be them. If the phone call was for me, then I would need to speak to them on loudspeaker in front of them. They wanted me to be trapped in the house like a prisoner. At least in prison they can use phones and have more freedom then me. I bet they make sure my Auntie and Uncle will keep me lock up per my parent's order if they get me to their house.

I walked to my door and locked it shut, they will need to break the door down to get me out of here. I am glad that my parents didn't take it off, it must have slipped their mind as it keeps me in the house and not out.

I laid back down on my bed and took a deep breath to clear my mind. I need to think of an escape plan, I need to think of a way to get out and get back to the hospital to see my friends. To find out what's been happening to me.

The only time I will be able to leave the house is when I go to school. But Rose is still in the hospital and I have no idea when she be out and back to school. I wouldn't be able to leave school during lessons as the teachers makes sure that you never leave the school grounds until it home time. Knowing my parent's they would drop me off at the gates, watch me go into the building and do the same when picking me up.

I looked out of the window and then it hit me. The oak tree, my night-time escape plan, why can't I use it now? If I was quick, then I could go before my dad comes home and catch me or speak to me about America. My head was so messed up I didn't notice the big obviously escape plan outside my bedroom window. I then realised that my shoes were downstairs and not in my room. I couldn't climb down the tree without my shoes as I would end up cutting the bottom of my feet. I unlock my door and went down quietly to get my shoes, They were at the bottom of the stairs, out of my mum sight which is a good thing. I was just about to grab my shoes and pick them up when my dad came through the door.

Busted, I dropped my shoes back on the floor.

"Good, you are home darling." My mum was standing in the kitchen doorway, has she been there all along? "Ingrid doesn't want to go to her Auntie and Uncle in America and when I told her about is, her responds was to back chat me."

"Really? Why?" My dad asked looking at me.

He seems shocked. He looked like he thought I would be jumping up and down. All packed and ready to go right this second.

"Well it just..." I started. I didn't know what to say, getting caught was not part of my plan. What could I say? Luke and Emma were the people who attacked us at the party and not 2 strangers which is what everyone think. The person who raised the alarm looks like me and spoke to me in the hospital and somehow disappeared after. I found a locket in the room which has a photo in with people who have the same eyes as me. That there is something happening which is linked to me and I am determined to find out what it is.

"Well?" My mum said folding her arms, "We are waiting for an answer."

"It just..." I started to say, trying to rattle my brain for an answer. What could say that wouldn't get me into any more trouble or make them think I was crazy?

Just then the phone rang next to my mum, saved by the ring.

"You wait here young lady" My mum said pointing at me. She went to answer the phone, she said hello and didn't speak for a few moments. She turned around and went into the kitchen, closing the door behind her.

I kept my eye away from my dad. I couldn't look at him. If I did, he would get me on the plane within the hours as he knows all my weak spots. I tried to hear what my mum was saying on the phone. Why did she go in the kitchen? Is wasn't something that she normal does, but my dad didn't seem to mind about it. Shame I could only hear one side of what was being said.

"No, I don't know. All I know she was there when it happened. She called the police so of course she was there."

This made me listen even harder to what was being said. Who is she talking too? Who is she talking about? Has something else happened while I was in hospital or is it to do with me?

"Maybe she made it happened? Maybe it was her who did it? Look just do your job and sort it out. That's is what you do, that is your job." I heard her end the phone call.

I looked at the wall, pretending that I had not been ear-dropping.

"Who was that?" I asked when she walked back into the hallway, putting the phone back in the stand.

"Just someone who was trying to sell doors. Normally cold caller stuff."

I looked at her, trying to stop my mouth dropping open. No way was she talking to someone selling doors. She knew the person and it sounded serious if it involved the police.

"Now love." I looked at my dad when he started talking. "Why can't you go to the America? I thought you like going there and spending time with family. A chance to see another country."

"No I don't like it there and you know I don't. Anyway, why are you trying to send me away when I have my exams to do here. You love it when I have exams to do as you get to plan my study day out from the minute, I wake up till the time I go to bed."

The one thing my parents love it making mine and Ben life hell when it comes to school and teaching. I think it has something to do with my mum being a teacher before she stopped when she had me and Ben. I'm surprise my mum have not made the house into a study hell yet she... I suddenly remember that I never told my parents about the exams yet. I been denying there was any exams to stop her making my life hell with studying. I looked at my mum knowing that I had dropped myself in it and how much trouble I knew I be in.

"Since when have you have exams been coming up. I been asking you about them for weeks and you told me that you have not been told yet? When do these exams meant start?" I was right, mum sounded way angrier than before.

"Months and in a few weeks." I simply said answering both her questions.

We got told 3 months ago about the exams which were happening in around 7 weeks.

"Well then." My mum looked at me, shaking her head slightly. "You are going to have to miss them because you are going to your Auntie and Uncles. I will call school and tell them you won't be here in a few days. I can see if we can work it out so you either take them in America or do them when you come back in a few months."

They want me to go in a few days and she wants me to be there for a few months. I looked at my dad with my best pleading eyes that gets me out of trouble and get him on my side in fights. They are wanting me to leave way sooner than I thought, I needed my dad to help me stay and be on my side.

"Look honey." My dad went passed me and put his arm round my mum. "Let Ingrid do her exams here. She's settled and she knows what she is doing in them. Then after she done her exams, then we can talk about her going to the US again. You want her to do well in her exams and you want her to have the best chance in them. And I don't think she can travel far distances yet, not so soon after being discharged from the hospital. She has only been at home for two days, give it some time before talking about this."

After a few minutes of my mum thinking she sighed in defeat and I knew that I won this battle for now. But I knew once my exams are done, there won't be anything that would stop her from putting me on that plane herself.

"OK you are staying till you have done all your exams. But since I have only just found out you have exams coming up, you can go upstairs and get you schoolbooks and do some revision. I have not seen you do any sort of studying at all and I expect high marks from you."

She walked away from me and into the other room, she was annoyed but she knew she couldn't do anything about it.

I smiled at my dad who smiled back, he followed my mum into the dining room and I went towards my bedroom.

I opened my door and I grabbed my books from the side. I could still hear my parents talking downstairs to each other. I was about to leave the room when I stopped, thinking I heard something. I turned around and saw my bedroom was still empty. I don't know what I was expecting to see but I could have sworn I heard something.

"Ingrid hurry up." My mum shouted from downstairs.

"Coming." I forced my eyes away from my room and let my room.

"What kept you so long?" My mum was standing at the bottom of the stairs with her arms crossed.

I walked down the starts as I answered her. "I couldn't find my books." I walked past her and towards the dining room. Won't she give it a rest? Why can't she leave me alone for 10 minutes?

"Well if you tidy that thing you called a bedroom them you would be able to find your things, won't you? You can do it tomorrow if it so bad you can't find your books." She followed me into the dining room.

I groaned when I saw what she did to the table. Laid out on the table was every colour of pens, pencils, rulers, calculator everything that my parents could think off. This was going to be an awfully long day.

My mum sat next to me all through me studying, making me go through everything in the books, even things I don't even need to know for the exams or ever. I was glad when it was time for bed, which was a first for me. I nearly ran up the stairs to get away from her and the books. When I got to my room my eyes flicked towards the wardrobe and I froze.

The door to my wardrobe with the locket in was slightly open. I swore I shut it correctly when my mum came in. Otherwise she would have comments on it as she hated it when we leave any doors open, even if the doors were in our own rooms.

I went to the wardrobe and was about to shut it when a thought hit me. The locket. Is it still in there? Had someone found out about it and took it? I opened the door quickly and grabbed the shoes box the locket was in. I had no idea why I suddenly felt so protected off it. I grabbed the shoe box and I was glad that the locket was still laying inside. I needed to be more careful with the locket and the wardrobe. I can't rick my parents looking in it and finding it. I made sure the wardrobe was closed and got ready to sleep.

As I laid on my bed trying to get sleep, my eyes kept going towards the wardrobe. Making it impossible to sleep no matter how hard I tried.

I was going back to school tomorrow and I knew what was going to happen when I got there. People are going to ask me what happened, wanting to know all the details. This types of things don't normally happen in a place like this. Everyone will want to know the answers to who attacked us and how was everyone? Why did they attack us and who did we think they were if we had any ideas?

How was I going to answer any of the questions without making it sound like I have gone crazy?

'Oh, my ex-boyfriend and ex-friend are the ones that attacked everyone at the party. However, I don't know what happened after they came into the house because the room went black and people started screaming. To make it more confusing a creepy girl called Elizabeth was there, but no one knew about her because she is new to the area and it seem that I am the only one that have seen her. But if you ask anyone else in the group about what happened at the party their answer will be different because everyone else thinks something else happened. The reason they remember something different is because of something that Elizabeth did. I have tried to find this out by asking Elizabeth, but she doesn't like to give a straight answer to any question.'

I sighed to myself knowing how crazy everything sound. I have no idea how I was going to survive school tomorrow.

I gave up sleeping and sat up in my bed. I felt hungry and got off my bed, I might as well do something as I wasn't going to go to sleep anytime soon. I went to my door so I could go downstairs to get something to eat.

My parents should be asleep by now as it was past 12:00 so they won't hear me. They hate it when I get food in the middle of the night, I sometime get some food before sneaking out.

I open my door and was about to leave my room when I heard my mum and dad talking in their bedroom. So they have not fallen asleep yet. I stayed as still as I could, I didn't want them to hear me and catch me sneaking around.

"She can't stay here; she has to go to America. She needs to be gone from here." I heard my mum say to my dad.

Cheers mum, thanks for wanting to get shot of me. I felt my blood run cold with my dad reply.

"Look, if we send her away then Elizabeth will follow her, I know she will. We wouldn't be able to stop her from there. That why I said for her to stay, we have better control then."

Elizabeth? Do they know that Elizabeth keeps following me? Do they know what really happened at the party?

"Look my sister knows the truth, she been able to keep an eye on her over there. If Elizabeth decides to follow her, then she will be able to handle her."

"Yeah well I think Molly and Sue has somehow find out the truth. Or haven't you notice what they've been doing whenever we see them. Blaming her for things she hadn't done, getting her in trouble and ganging up on her."

"That just children being children, Ingrid does the same thing to them. I notice that myself and already checked with my sister what's the story behind that."

"And what if it not. I'm not going to risk it she is not going. We can deal with everything here, we started this, we are going finish it. End of conversation."

Everything in the bedroom went quiet and there wasn't anything else to hear. I closed my door quietly, so they wouldn't know I had heard them. I suddenly didn't feel hungry anymore. I sat on my bed, my head swimming with what I just heard. Elizabeth said something about the truth before I blacked out the second time and again at the hospital. Now my parents are talking about both the truth and Elizabeth. So they know about Elizabeth and they know that something was happening. But why would Elizabeth follow me to America if I went? Why did it seem like my parents were afraid of something when it comes to me and Elizabeth? What was the truth that everyone knows about, but I am connected to?

I needed to know what the truth is.

Chapter 6

I woke up with the sun shining on my face after one of the worse night sleep I ever had. I kept running things in my mind, making it impossible to drift off to sleep. My alarm went off at 7.30 and I groan out loud, school was going to be hell. Because Rose was in hospital, I will need to face the entire school on my own. I don't know if I would be able to do this without anyone.

I got off my bed and went to grab my school clothes off the end of it when I sighed looking at the clothes and seeing my party clothes next to it. Last night during my reversion hell with my mum, Lily and Rose parents came and dropped off the clothes I had worn to school the day of the party. I just dumped them at the bottom of my bed as I couldn't be bothered to put them away. I sighed again, I felt sorry for Rose's family; I know loads of things were happening at their house at the moment and this would not be helping. Both of their children were in hospital and their house have been trashed and broken into. Lily had only just come home from university and it wasn't even a day before she got attacked. Rose was having her first party to show she could look after herself and she got attacked in her own home. A place which is meant to be safe, a place where bad things shouldn't happen. When they came here yesterday, they both had dark shadows under their eyes, which meant that they weren't sleeping well. I bet it was weird in their house right now, no more talking or life in the house. There morning was no longer busy getting Rose up and making sure she is ready for school, calling her to get out of bed and making sure she doesn't forget anything. I wonder what it was like for them when they first look round the house after the attack as we never cleaned up after the party.

I forced myself out of my bed and got dress in my uniform which were a pair of pinching, black leather shoes that makes me look like I'm wearing cowboys' shoes; a set of tight and uncomfortably black trousers that have no pockets to put anything in. To finish off my school uniform is a plain white, constructive blouse with 3/4 sleeves and a dull steal black tie that must be wore just above the belt. The only good thing about the uniform is that you can wear any dark belt, so I wear a dark purple one with random black crosses on it which no one can tell me off for.

I went down 25 minutes later to face hell as that how long it takes for me to get ready. I kept stopping and sitting on my bed, thinking off my friends and what I was going to face when I got to school. When I finally got to the kitchen, I found my mum sitting by the table; and she was smiling. Something she is not known for is smiling. What did I do? She never smiles in the morning; she always running around the house trying to get me and Ben out of the door in time. I can't remember the last time I saw her sitting down in the morning on a school day with a drink in hand.

"Hello dear. How are you?" Her smiled widen when she finished talking, taking a sip of her drink.

Had she been brainwash or something in the middle of the night? This was not normal behaviour.

"I'm OK. Why?" I asked suspiciously, not knowing what she was up to.

"I was just wondering if you wanted to stay at home today, instead of going to school? Have a few more days of to recover." She replied, her smile never leaving her lips.

That settled it, she has either been cloned, banged her head and now can't remember how she usually act, or she has been brainwashed. Mum has never let me, or Ben stay home from school. Ever! The only time we would be allowed to miss school would be if we are cold stone dead and even than I'm not so sure that be enough.

"No thanks, I rather to go to school." I answered for the first time ever.

I grab my toast and walked into the hallway before she has the chance to say anything else that was not in her nature and freak me out more. Why was she in such a strange mood? Just as got into the hallway the post came through the door, I was about to open the door and walked pasted the pile on the floor when something caught my eye. Among the dull white and brown envelope was a black one that had fancy red writing on it. I got curious and picked it and I saw that it had my name written on it.

I wonder who sent me this?

"Have you decided to stay then?" My mum asked walking into the hall and spotting me.

"I'm going." I said quickly stuffing the envelope into my pocket before she sees it and makes me open it. Or take it off me and she opens it while I'm at school as she might think I am planning something. With everything happening at the moment, the opening seems more likely.

Once I stepped outside, I took a deep breath of freedom. I was not an outdoor person during the day, but I miss the air outside the house. The only good thing about my mum being weird is that she wasn't taking me to school in the car which is what I thought she be doing. It means I get to enjoy freedom between my house and school and then back again. I got to the crossroad when I realise that I had been on autopilot and was heading to Luke's house. I turned on my heal and went the opposite, I groan out-loud not caring if anyone heard when I realised, I was walking towards Rose's empty house. This was going to be a very long day if I can't even get the school without messing up.

I got to school 20 minutes early then I would normal as I didn't go to anyone houses. I normal get into school with minutes before the bell goes. I didn't know what to do with the spare time. I stood by the gate for 5 minutes trying to figure out what I was going to do, when I spotted Mrs Wednesday coming towards me.

I did not need a lecture from Mrs Wednesday this early in the morning.

"Ingrid, I am glad you're here. How are you?" She smiled at me.

"I'm fine." I reply with a bit of hesitation. Now I was confused, what the hell was happening? I know I been attacked but this was beyond weird with both my mum and Mrs Wednesday smiling at me. Has it been 2 days or 2 years since I been away?

"Can you sign in with your tutor and come to my office please?" She asked still smiling at me. "I need to talk to you."

I nodded as I didn't know what to say, and she walked away without saying anything else. I saw people staring at me when they saw Mrs Wednesday smiling at me and being kind. They must be thinking the same thing as me and tying to work out what just happened. After I saw that people were not going to stop looking at me, due to the party and Mrs Wednesday I went into the main building and went to the girl's toilets to stop people from staring. You think I be used to that from the last time I was at school?

I stood by the sinks splashing some water on my face, trying to work Mrs Wednesday out. Maybe Mrs Wednesday was only being nice to me outside, so when I go into her office, she can kill me. Try and get my guard down and sneak up from behind to get me.

I sighed and looked at myself in the mirrors that were above the sinks. Even with everything that been going on, the breakup, the attack, the locket, the lies and everything else that been going, I still look the same.

Same long black hair reaching pass my shoulder, same almost translucently pale skin. Same facial structure, mouth and noise. The same dead, black eyes that could go right through someone.

I shuddered as I looked into my eyes, remembering the locket and Elizabeth. I still can't work out what they both got to do with me. Why we have the same eyes as at each other, eyes that I have never heard anyone else having. I don't know how long I stood in front of the mirror, just staring at my reflection. Trying to find out an answer to any of the questions I have going through my head by staring straight at myself.

I jumped when the bell went, bringing me back to the real world. Have I been looking in the mirror for that long? It seems that I am going into my own world more and more trying to figure out what happening. I sighed, grabbed my bag off the sink as I walked out of the bathroom. Time to face the devil in hell and everyone else in the school. As I walked down the corridor, I saw everyone pointing at me and whispering, just like when they found out about Luke and Emma. Will I ever have a normal day in school without anyone looking at me and pointing? I am starting to forget what it was like not to be stared out.

I found my tutor and told him I was going to see Mrs Wednesday. He said that was fine and he will see me in a bit because Mr Star was off, and he be taking my English class. I went to Mrs Wednesday's office and knocked on the door. The sound echoed in the empty hall, everyone else were in class and I was alone. "Come in." A voice said on the other side of the door. I opened the door and saw Mrs Wednesday sitting on a chair next to her desk, she was looking through some paper on her table. "Hello Ingrid." She smiled at me again, it looked weird on her face. It doesn't look right on her. OK I thought, she going to kill me now. "How are you today?"

"I'm fine." I said again, still waiting for the killer blow and the roof to come down with her shouting.

"Good, I'm glad. I was just worried about you after the attack. I'm sad that Rose is still in hospital. If you need to talk you know where I am. You can go back to your lesson now. I just wanted to make sure you were Ok after coming back to school only days from coming out the hospital. If you need to spend some time out of your lesson, you can spend some time in my office and away from your peers."

My mouth fell open, that was it. She wasn't going to shout at me, I don't what about what as I haven't done anything wrong but that never have stop her in the past. Had an alien taken over Mrs Wednesday body and turned her into someone who doesn't hate kids. I turned to leave the room when Mrs Wednesday spoke again. "Oh, Ingrid one more thing." I wanted to laugh, I knew it, she hadn't turned nice, she was only playing with me, she was going to kill me after all. I turned back to her waiting for what she had for me. "You don't need to come back to me for your detention, OK. Not till the others are better and everyone are 100%." I notice that the smile never left her face while she was speaking to me.

OK now I was scared. I turned back around and walked out of the office, closing the door behind me. That was weird, I don't know if I like Mrs Wednesday being nice or not. Or if I like my mum suddenly being nice and smiling all the time either.

As I walked in the empty corridor my phone beeped in my pocket. My mum gave it back to me that night so she could keep track of me while I'm at school. Even here I can't escape her completely, she texted jump and I texted how high or else. However I need to give it back to her when I get home and she decides when I can have it and when I can't, so she still have all the control.

I look around to check that the coast was clear before I took my phone out; phones were banned in the school building and I didn't want a teacher to take it off me. I saw that I had a message and it was from Rose, I forgot to text her when I got my phone. Glad she thought to text me first.

After School Come And See Me Please :)

I smiled; I hope my mum lets me go. I got all day to think off a reason why I should go. I did the whole study thing yesterday so that should work in my favour. If not, hopefully the happy mood means she will allow me to see her for at least an hour or so. I sent a text to my mum to ask if I could go and see Rose, saying that it will only be for a short time and dad can pick me up if he wants or even stay in the room. I hope she doesn't like the idea of the last bit as I won't be able to ask

Rose things if I have his eyes at the back of my head. After the I sent the text, I put it back in my pocket and walked to my lesson. Once I walked into the classroom everyone stopped and looked at me. While I'd been in Mrs Wednesday office, everyone had got to class and settled down waiting our tutor to turn up to cover the lesson. I felt like I was frozen to the spot at the front of the classroom. Every time I moved everyone else followed me and I felt trapped.

I heard the door behind me open.

"Ah, Ingrid you're here. How are you?" My tutor said walking past me. Good timing sir, couldn't you be here before the students, so I wasn't standing at the front of the class like an idiot?

"I am fine sir." I replied, wanting it to be the last time I have to say it, but knowing that it won't. Everyone will be asking how I am and of course what really happened.

"Good, good. I am going to be doing English with you today as Mr Star is ill."

Everyone turned to sir and groaned, this gave me time to escape to the back of the classroom and sit down without people watching. This time I didn't have Luke or Emma coming towards me wanting to fight. Sadly, I didn't have Rose here defend me or keep my company. Even before this Rose always made me laugh when we sit next to each other, making silly comments about everything. The table felt big and empty on my own.

"Today Mr Star wants you to write a story about anything. Friends, family things like that. But you must write in detail, the person reading it must be able to see what is being written. It needs to be the best you can do as it becomes a part of your coursework."

I like doing this type of work, me and Rose would always work together, it would always be a monster in a garden, a mixed of our favourite things. I signed missing her again and wonder how I was going to cope with everything without someone behind me to back me up. I made the decision that I was going to write a story to cheer Rose up. I know she hates hospital and she could stick it up on the wall to make it a bit more homey. It makes me feel like I am doing something at least instead of moping at school.

Sir handed out the paper we would be writing on, when he got to me, he asked,

"What are you doing yours on Ingrid?" I notice he only asked me and not anyone else.

"I'm doing mine for Rose. I will most likely be doing mine on gardens because, that what Rose likes. I want to try and cheer her up because I know she hates being stuck in one place."

"Good." He seemed surprise. "So I don't think there be any werewolf, ghost, death, blood, monster or vampires in I then. Mr Star shown me some of your work."

"You forgot coffins," I said sweetly as I could. "And I could add them in if I write it right."

Sir muttered something as he walked away. I smiled to myself, I know Mr Star shows my work to my tutor and I know they both say that I describe the death and monster too much. I don't get that, if you are writing a story, you got to write it in as much detail as you can. I thought with him and Mr Star being English teachers, they would understand it all.

I looked out of the classroom window and saw 3 birds flying around a tree just outside the gate. This gave me an idea for what I could write about.

Me, Rose and Lily are birds and we are flying in this garden, we can make flowers grow and trees blossom. We help animals in trouble and keep the garden full of life. Sir came to me halfway through the lesson just as the bird me saved Rose from falling out of a tree as she broke her left wing saving a hedgehog.

"How the story going Ingrid?" Sir asked standing over me. I hate it when teachers do that, it makes you feel small and weak. I notice that he was only asking me again.

Sir picked up my story and started to read it. Don't bother to ask me if you could read it. I thought as he grabbed the paper. At least it gave me time to look around the room. Even though people were doing their work, I could see some of them turning around for a second, then turn back quickly when they saw that I spotted them.

I sighed, even right at the back of the classroom I still got people looking at me.

"Are you OK Ingrid?" Sir said looking at me when I sighed.

"I am fine sir. Do you like it?" I asked so he could go and stop leaning over me. Doesn't he know that kids hate it when teacher lean over students?

"It's good, no monster or anything like that which is new for you. But did you really had to describe how a cat killed your little brother? Thinking about it, did you really needed to kill your little brother?"

"Yeah, I did. It adds dept to the story. Anyway, you always told us to put detail in our work and what you told us 1/2 hour ago, so I did."

"I didn't mean that type and you know that." Sir put my work on the desk and carried on walking round the room. Thank god he got the message.

I finished my story a couple of minutes before the bell went, finishing with the birds go to sleep and have a nice long break. Sir took my work and photocopy it and collect it with the rest of the classes. So Mr Star got one to mark and for my coursework and I have my own copy for Rose.

As I walked to my next lesson, whispering following me like a shadow. I was glad when I got to class, even though it was maths which was my worse subject. The only reason I was glad was because there would only be 27 eyes on me and not a hundred in the corridor. Me and maths never get along as no matter what sir says, I only see numbers that I can't make behave.

I sat at the back of the class again but, I knew there would be no point, people will still find a way to look at me. Not even sir could stop them looking at me when he had his back turned. Sir came in just as the second bell went, I hate it how teachers can come when the bells go, and students can't. We should make them stay behind after school and do our homework like they do with us.

In sir's hand was a stack of paper and everyone knew what they were before sir said the word. Tests. Sir stood front of us with a smile on his face, he loves giving us tests to do and make sure we don't know it coming. "You are all going to be doing test up to your exam. One lesson will be a test and the next one is marking the test. This shall be repeated till the day before your exam."

Everyone groaned when sir said this and he started to hand out the test paper, saying if anyone spoke or look around there will be trouble and we know he meant it. Great I thought, so I get an hour without people talking or looking at me, but I need to do a test to get some peace.

When he got to me, he stopped. "Ingrid, I had you mother on the phone to me earlier."

Great what did she say, why was she calling the school? Did she wanted to make sure I turned up at school?

"What did she say?" I asked.

"She told me you did this at home with her while you were off the last 2 days. Because of that, I am expecting high marks from you." He then put the test on the desk and gave the rest out.

Why did she ring up school and told my teacher that I'm suddenly great at maths? Has she done this for all my teachers? Now because of her I am expected to get high marks in the tests. I have more chance of having tea with the queen then that happening.

I somehow managed to get through the test knowing that I failed it completely. I had no idea what I was doing and just guess most of the answers. Because I know I failed it, I am going to have both my mum and my teacher biting my head off and making my life hell because of it.

The rest of the day passed in a blur with everyone talking about the attack and who could be behind it. Everyone kept looking at me, asking me what happened, why we were target and who did I think did it? It felt like I could never escape the questions or the stares of everyone. Question I was trying to find the answers for myself.

During dinner I went to the girl's toilets and ate in there, not the cleanest place but at least I wasn't sitting on a big table on my own with everyone watching me. Knowing my luck, I would choke on my food while everyone watched and spill drinks all over myself.

I just left my last lesson when my phone beeped again. I thought it was Rose, remanding me to come and see her. She knows what school was like, it could make you forget Christmas and your own birthday.

I looked at the ID and saw that it was an unknown number, coming up as private. I stopped suddenly making someone bump into me from behind, I didn't take much notice to who it was. I shouldn't have an unknown number as I make sure that if I give my number out, I get their number back. I click on the message that the number sent, even though every vibe in my body was saying get rid of it and forget it. It could be a virus or something like that, it could mess up my phone and delete everything on it. However I found my finger clicking the message and the message opened on my screen.

It said in bold letters, screaming from the page was the message:

DON'T GO. SHE KNOW'S THE TRUTH

GO HOME INGRID, PLEASE TRUST ME

Chapter 7

After I read the message, I put the phone back in my pocket not knowing what to do. I was about to turn around, not sure on what I was going to do when the text message finally sank in.

'She knows the truth.'

Who knows the truth? What is the truth that people suddenly seem to know about? Why don't I know about the truth as I am somehow linked to it and it seem to be following me? I shook my head trying to sort out my thoughts. I need to find answers, I can't have this going around my head any longer otherwise it will drive me insane.

My mum texted me back just as the bus came and I got on. The text read I could go and see Rose if I were only there for an hour and no longer. However, my dad or she MUST pick me up. I need to text them when I'm coming out of the hospital and wait for them outside on the bench. I sighed; they'll never let me have freedom again because I ran away from the hospital. If only they knew why, but I couldn't tell them. What could I say to them that won't make them send me to a mental hospital? I texted Rose I was coming, I got a text back saying hurry up, that she was bored and hates being in hospital.

I looked out of the window when the text message leapt back to my mind.

'Don't Go She Knows The Truth.'

Did they mean don't go to the hospital? Don't see Rose and Lily? Do they know something, but they aren't telling me? I shook my head, trying to get the idea out of my head. Rose doesn't know anything, if she did, she would have told me, we never keep secret from each other.

The bus turned a corner and drove pass Luke and Elizabeth house just as I looked out of the window and away from my phone. Luke house still looked the same, same warm orange brick, same terracotta roof tiles. Each window had a set of brightly coloured curtains, sky blue, lust red, snow white and ivory. The front door was a cream coloured and had a stain glass poppy in the centre of the window. Their front garden was full of flowers that was so bright you could see them at the bottom of the street. There was a rainbow of colour edging the garden making it look inviting and homely and the tree in the middle was blossoming with light pink cherry blossom.

Next door looked completely different making the houses look odd next to each other. I was surprise to see how much it changed in so little time. All the life in the garden had died since Elizabeth and her family moved in, all the once beautiful plants had blackened and dried up. The once green grass was now full of fallen petals and the apple tree was full of rotting fruit, some laying at the base of the tree. It looked almost forgotten and that no one cares about the garden anymore. In the window it seemed as if they had put up black-out curtain from the war, from outside you couldn't see in and it look like no light could get into the house. The front door was similar to Luke's but was coloured ash grey and rather than a sweet poppy it had poisonous nightshade in the stained glass, something that I knew had just been added to the house. The bricks had become a faded charcoal colour and the roof tiles had gone from the simple terracotta colour to a darker Indian red, the house looked evil and it filled me with dread just looking at it. I had to turn my head away from the house and looked straight ahead.

The bus stopped just outside the hospital and I got off looking up at the hospital, remember the last time I was here. I walked towards the hospital door just and was stopped just before I went in by a nurse who walked past me and stopped me.

"Hello Ingrid, what are you doing back? You're okay, aren't you?"

I looked at her blankly. How did she know me? Did my parent speak to her to keep an eye on me while I was here?

"Oh, you might not remember me; you asked me if there was another way out of you room so you could escape and see your friends. Well, you did escape, didn't you?" She laughed.

Now I remember her. She never did explain how Elizabeth could've escaped without anyone seeing her. I used the door; I know she didn't.

"Oh yeah, I'm fine thanks. I am just seeing my friends." I smiled; tired of telling people I'm fine all the time. Will people every stop asking me? How long will it take for people to back off? She smiled back and walked away when a thought struck me. She was in the room with me, before the locked appeared. "Wait." I shouted running after. She stopped ad looked at me in shock. I bet she hadn't expected me to suddenly run after her. "This might sound stupid and I bet it will but, did you leave a locket in my room that night, when I was there with you or when I was in my friend room?"

"A locket?" She asked confused. "No, why did you find one? If you did, you need to hand it into lost and found. You can't keep it if it's not yours. If you want, you can hand it to me, and I can make sure the owner gets it back."

Something deep in me told me that I shouldn't give the locket it to her; I should keep it.

"Don't worry, I hand it in myself. I promise."

She seems to believe me as she walked away from the hospital. I walked into the hospital before she took me to the lost and found herself and watch me give it in. I went to Rose and Lily room, glad that I remember where it was. When I knocked on the door and opened it, I notice that there was only 1 bed in the room and Rose was now on her own. Rose saw me at the door and came over and gave me a hug.

"Where Lily?" I asked sitting on a chair which now replace Lily's bed.

"The doctor said she needs to have her own room because she is going home soon, and I'm still stuck here." She said sitting on her bed facing me.

"Who kicked up the most fuss out of you two?" I asked guessing it was Rose, she normally does when it's about her sister.

"Lily did, which shocked everyone. Even my parents are getting worried about her and with everything that been happening. She is starting to act like someone completely different, she even threw some punches at one point."

"Really?" I was surprised too. Lily was normally the quite one. If there was a fight, she would stop it and get them to shake hands and make up, all this without a punch being thrown. "What did she say, why was she acting like that?" I asked, wanting to know what made Lily kick off the way did.

"Nothing that made sense. She just kept saying she needed to be her to keep me safe. To make sure that 'she' doesn't come back to see me, to hurt me. From what I could make out from what she was saying is that 'she' didn't have time last time to hurt me. But Lily know 'she' will this time if I'm alone and she not here to stop her."

"Who 'she'?" I asked, wondering if it could be the same 'she' that the text told me about. Did Lily mean Elizabeth? "What does Lily mean, 'she' didn't hurt you last time?"

"I don't know. I think she on about the people that attacked us at the party. Maybe she thinks that they will find us here and finish us off or something. That the only thing that make any sense. When I did ask what she was talking about, she just said talk to Luke and Emma, that they can explain it more."

"Luke and Emma?" I half shouted in disbelieve. "Why talk to Luke and Emma of all people? They are the enemy." How could Lily speak to the people who put her sister in the hospital? Why is she treating them like a victim and not the attackers? Even if she doesn't remember the party, she must remember them betraying me and Rose?

Rose just shrugged her shoulder almost as confused as I was.

"I don't know why either? That all she said to me when I asked, she won't say why Luke and Emma can help. I even asked if she knows why they ran away when they came to see us the last time you were here."

The face of Luke and Emma face when they saw me with Lily and Rose flashed in my mind. Remembering how rough they looked and how for a split second how dark Luke's eyes became when he saw me.

"Have you spoken to Luke and Emma at all since I left here?" I asked trying to keep calm about Lily speaking to them and the way she been acting.

"No why would I after what they did? They are both back stabbers and I don't know why Lily would speak to them either. I just don't understand any of this."

"Mm, me neither." I replied trying to figure it out myself.

"Talking about things I don't understand, why did you run away from the hospital? Your parents asked me if I knew where you went. You were about to go home, so why would you escape in the early morning. Come on Ingrid, you can tell me the truth."

Should I tell her? Can I trust her? I shook the thought from my mind. I know I can trust her, she's my best friend. What reason have I got not to trust her?

"You know Luke's have a new neighbour?"

"Yeah, I was going to invite her to my party, wasn't I? But when I went to call for her during my free time, there was no answered. As far as I know, no one has seen her except you when you were talking to me about her eyes."

"Well, she came to see me and started ranting about what I am and about the truth. Then I found something which freaked me out...."

"Wait. You found something and got freaked." She interrupted. "It must have been bad for you to freak out. I mean you're the type of person who, if you found a severed head, you would pick it up and have a closer look at it. Anyway I don't think Elizabeth can come and see you. Not unless she sneaks in and somehow got past a number of doctors and nurse in the middle of the night without anyone thinking it was strange and ask her who she is. Anyway how would she know where you were, she couldn't walk into every room asking for you could she or ask a nurse without someone asking questions? You might have thought you saw her due to the medication you might have been on. Or you could have dreamt it and thought you were awake during the time." Rose smiles and I forced a smile back.

Rose can make anything make sense; however I know that Elizabeth came and see me, I know that I was awake. And I know what I saw was real.

I was about to start talking again when there was a knock on the door stopping me. I need to tell Rose about the locket, but I don't want anyone else to know about it. I don't know who I can trust or who knows what is going on. The door opened and the doctor that looked after me and who told me to go back to bed came in. I saw that he had a clipboard in his hand and was smiling as he saw me.

"Ingrid, what a surprise. How are you after your great escape?" He laughed at his own joke.

"I'm fine." I sighed, really getting annoyed about being asked it all day.

"You're getting bored of saying I'm fine aren't you." Rose guessed with a smile on her face.

I smiled at her again "Yeah. I don't know what going to happen to the next person who ask me that." I winked at Rose who laughed.

"Well I won't ask again so I won't be that person." He smiled as he checked Rose over and looking at his clipboard.

"When can Rose come home again?" I asked the doctor, wanting my best friend home and school again so I won't be on my own anymore.

"Not for another week I'm afraid. The cuts on her head aren't healing correctly. They keep re-opening and not clotting right. Once they do, she will be allowed home." He finished checking Rose over and left, smiling at us as he left.

"Great." Rose laid down on the bed. "Another week stuck here. I can't believe I'm going to say this, but I want to go back to school."

"Do you remember what happened at school? Before the party?" I asked wanting to know how much she remembers.

"Do you mean the fight and Luke and Emma betray against you? Or the 5 weeks stuck with Mrs Wednesday for doing nothing? Why has she forgotten, and we are free?" She chuckled.

"No, she hasn't forgotten I'm afraid. We are still in trouble for the fight." So she remembers the fight and me and Luke breaking up. Then another thought struck me if she remembers me and Luke breaking up then....

"Why was Luke and Emma at the party? Why were they there when the attack happened? My dad said they were there when we were tiding up but why would they be there at all after everything they did?"

"I.... "She stopped thinking hard. "I don't know, I can't remember that part of the night. Never mind, there probably been a reason for them to be there. They might have come to the party and we didn't see them till everyone left. There were a lot of people there, it would have been easy for them to get lost in the crowd."

So they are gaps in the story, why I am the only person who see the gaps? Why is it I know what really happened and what does it mean?

"How school without me anyway?" Rose asked bringing me back to earth and talk about something else apart from the party.

"What? Oh, it's the same, still boring. We're mostly doing test for the exams, which my parents have only just found out about them, so I'm in trouble there. Wait, I nearly forgot, I did this for you in English; our tutor took over because Mr Star was ill." I gave her the story I wrote, she read it and laughed out loud.

"That's really good. I bet sir made a comment about the cat eating you brother?"

"Yeah, he said I shouldn't describe that bit in so much detail and if I really needed it in. Which I don't get, because he always says to write in detail, so that people can see it in their mind."

"I know right." Rose laughed and I joined in, it felt good to laugh again.

Just then Lily just walked into the room. She gave me a look that I didn't understand at first and then I realised it was anger and fear. If was the look that made you want to dig your own grave and get in it. I looked at Rose to see if she noticed, but she just went to her sister and hug her. Lily was still looking at me with that expression. Why was she looking at me like that? What have I done to her? Does she think I have something to do with the attack or something?

"You just miss the doctor coming in to see me." Rose dragged her sister to the bed and sat on it together. I stay sitting where I was, not really moving. "He says I can go home next week once I'm better. What about you?"

"I'm going home tomorrow, but;" She put her hand on Rose shoulder, "I'll come and see you every day. To keep you safe."

"Good because I would probably go out of my mind if you didn't see me. Anyway, why do you keep going on about keeping me safe? Who do you think is trying to hurt me?" Rose asked, keeping her eyes on Lily.

"I spoke to Emma earlier and..." Lily started.

"EMMA." Rose shouted in shock moving away from her sister slightly. "Why where you speaking to her after what she and Luke did to Ingrid? I got 5 weeks detention because of them. Why would you want to speak to them of all people?"

I wanted to know why Lily was speaking to them when she knows her sister hate them?

"If you let me finish the I will explain." She shot Rose a look. "I was talking to Emma to find out how long she will be in hospital for. They might have done some bad stuff, but no one deserve to be in here. Especially since they not only monster that's here."

What is she on about they're not the only monster that's here?

"And?" Rose said her voice still filled with shock and anger at her sister's betrayal. She doesn't seem to have notice that last bit of what her sister said or not care about it.

"She and Luke aren't going home for 2 weeks, well maybe earlier for Luke. He was less hurt than Emma, the doctor said he could be out in less than a week if he feels up for it."

"Good they are still stuck here; they deserve it after what they did to me and Ingrid. They made our life hell and you don't seem to care about that."

Lily just looked down and then at the door and not answering her sister. Was she was waiting for someone to walk in? Luke and Emma maybe?

"I've got to go." She gave her sister a kiss on her head. "I need to pack my thing up before tomorrow." With that she walked out of the room, not even looking at me as she went.

"Why would she talk to them? My own sister? Ingrid, I feel like I been stabbed in the heart." Rose said in disbelief waving her hands around a bit overdramatic.

"Maybe she wanted to find out how long before our freedom is taken away." I wanted Rose to not feel bad about her sister. Rose just looked at me when I said this. "Mrs Wednesday said she won't do the detention until all of us are well and back at school." I smiled "The longer they're in here, the longer the freedom we have."

"Is Mrs Wednesday okay?" She replied, "It sounds almost like she is being nice."

"I don't think she is OK. She was being nice to me all day. She hasn't shouted at anyone once or anything like that. Get this she has been smiling all day at me."

"Nice and smiling. Mrs Wednesday is smiling and being nice." She sounded as though she was in shock.

"Yeah, I know. I was in disbelieve when I saw it. I thought she was going to kill me." Just then there was another knock on the door. "Your popular, aren't you?" I said smiling at Rose who smiled back. Glad she was happy again.

The doctor head peeped round the edge of the door. "Visitors need to go now, sorry."

I looked at Rose. "I'll come again tomorrow; I promise."

"Good, I won't be happy if you don't." She smiled. "I'll keep texting you over and over again until you come."

I chucked, we said our goodbyes and left. I walked past the doctor and walked down the hall, texting my mum to pick me up. I knew if I didn't, she would have a fit and not let me see Rose again. I then remember that I didn't tell Rose about the locket. Damn, I forgot. I started to tell her, but the Lily came and started to act all weird. I'll do it tomorrow when people won't keep coming in all the time. I looked up and saw Lily looking at me the same expression as before. She was standing by the front door and I needed to get past her to get out, so I tried to act normal as I can.

"Hello Lily. I'm glad you are going home tomorrow. Shame Rose, Emma or Luke can't. I would hate to have stuck her for a long time." The only reason I said Luke and Emma's name was because Lily have been talking to them. Maybe she doesn't care what they have done. Even though she doesn't know half of the things they did at the party.

When I went to go thought the door, Lily move in-front of me to stop me from leaving.

"What are you doing Lily? I need to get pasted" I asked trying to get pasted her.

Lily looked straight into my eyes, like she was trying to look in my soul.

"I saw what happen at the party. I saw what really happened. I know what you are Ingrid, I know the truth. You better stay away from Rose or I will tell everyone."

Chapter 8

My alarm woke me up again at 7.30, it took me a while to work out what the noise was. After Lily told me she knew the truth she simple walked away like nothing happened. I was about to shout after her when my mum suddenly arrived outside the hospital to pick me up. It was too quick for her to have come from home, so I know she must have been waiting outside the hospital. I should have guess that she was going to do that with how she bene treating me since I been back home. When got into the car I kept a look out for Lily, but I didn't see her as my mum drove away.

On the drive home I didn't say a word, I kept replaying the scene between me and Lily in my head. Trying to work what she meant when she said she know what really happened at the party. Does she know it was Luke and Emma? If so, why was she being so friendly with them and what did she mean she knows the truth? Did something else happened at the party that I am not aware off?

"What wrong Ingrid, I never known you to be so quite?" My mum sound concern and her eyes kept looking between me and the road.

I replied to her in a flat tone. "I am fine, I am just not feeling that well. I didn't like seeing Rose in hospital like that." I suddenly started to feel tired, the events of the last few fays catching up to me, making me both mentally and physically tired.

When I got home, my parents asked for my phone which I handed over without any problems. The only thing I wanted was to sleep so once I gave it to my parents I went straight to my room, asking my parents not bother me so I sleep. To my surprise neither of them did check on me, which I thought they would do to make sure I was not escape during the night. Although this was probably the only time, they didn't need to worry about me leaving during the night as I feel asleep within minutes of closing my eyes.

I shut off my alarm and forced my legs to move and I got out of my bed. I grabbed my school top and put in on to get ready for another say of hell at school and it was the only second day. I was about to put on my trousers when I saw something sticking out of one of my pockets. It was the letter that came yesterday, I folded it so that I didn't feel it during school or when I saw Rose at the hospital. The red letters seem glow in the morning light, locking my eyes on my name written on it.

I quickly put the rest of my clothes on and sat on my bed with the letter in my hand. The letters seem to be glowing more now that the envelope was in my hands. I heard my mum downstairs telling my dad off for something, which meant I have at least 10 minutes to read it undisturbed before my mum started to shout me.

I opened the letter, hands trembling slightly as I read the words that were written.

Dear Ingrid,
I tried to tell you the truth when you were at the hospital.

You need to know the truth and you need to know it soon.

I tried to show you the locket, but then the nurse came in, so I left it for you.

It's important that you know what is happening around you.

Meet me at the park that you use at 8.15 on Tuesday morning.

Make sure you bring the locket; I know you have it.

It will help to explain things a bit better.

Please trust me Ingrid.

Elizabeth B

Today was Tuesday, that means she want to meet me this morning. I sat on my bed, staring at the letter in my hand. The words moving around the page, the black writing against the white page. Can I trust it, can I trust the words? The words trust me Ingrid was the main words that stood out on the page. The same words the text used. Does this mean Elizabeth sent me the text, that she had my number? Was Lily the she that she was talking about as Lily even said herself, she knows the truth? But how did Elizabeth know this? I got the text before Lily even spoken to me.

"Ingrid! Come down now!" I jumped as my mum shouted from downstairs. I looked at my clock and the numbers 7:50 was displayed. Where did the time go, have I been staying at the letter for that long? I got off my bed and grabbed all the things that I needed for school and put the letter in my pocket. I was planning on getting rid of it without my mum finding it when I stopped halfway out of my bedroom. I felt my eyes going towards the wardrobe where the locket was hidden. This could be my only chance to find out what's been going on. To find out the truth that everyone else seems to know.

I needed to know what was going on. I went to the wardrobe and grabbing the locket from the shoebox. I made sure everything was closed and before leaving my room and heading downstairs.

"What kept you?" My mum asked standing at the bottom of the stairs, arm folded. Has she become glued to that spot or something? "You're 10 minutes later than normal and you would still be in your room if I didn't shout you."

"I couldn't find any socks and I was on my way before you shouted me." I walked past her and went to the kitchen, hoping she couldn't hear anything in my voice as I could hear the nerves in it.

"I was down before you." My brother smirked, already eating his breakfast at the table.

"Shut up." I snapped I didn't have time for Ben to wind me up.

"I don't understand why you don't get up earlier, so you don't need to grab breakfast and rush to school or go to someone house." My mum said walking in behind me. "And don't shout at your brother because he is right. You took longer today, which means you're going to be in more of a rush."

"I don't like hanging around in the morning." I grab some toast and the when the phone rang in the hallway.

"Stay." My mum pointed at me. I was tempted to reply with 'woof, woof' like a dog. She closed the kitchen door and I heard the phone being picked up. Why does she keep doing that? I walked towards the door to listen to what my mum was saying. The last time she was on the phone, she was up to something and lied about who she was speaking to. She knows something about Elizabeth, and she knows she link to me. What else is she keeping hidden?

"What you are doing?" My brother whispered as he got of his chair.

"I give you £5 if you turn around and denied anything if asked." I replied with a whispered knowing he would do anything for money.

"£10." Ben challenged.

"Fine whatever." I don't have time to fight with him. My brother smiled and turned around, looking in the cupboard for something. I would have said I pay him £100 as long as he didn't tell mum what I was doing.

I lean closer to the door so I could hear her more clearly.

"Look, Ingrid got locket, my husband saw it when I kept her out of the room to do some schoolwork." I felt my body go cold. "We knew something was going on, she been acting weird for days now." So that explains why wardrobe door was slightly open. He must have looked when my mum was making me study. "When Ingrid goes to school today, I will go into her room and get it to send it to you. We couldn't do when we found it in case Ingrid happened to have gone upstairs and caught him." There was a pause, "Why? Because I don't want her to know the truth, she can't know the truth. You have no idea what would happen here if she ever found out. I know she doesn't know because it would have been hard to miss if she did. Look trust me on this. Goodbye." I heard her put the phone down and quickly stood by the table as she walked back into the room.

"Come on Ingrid, you need to get to school, you have exams to think about. And you are getting up early tomorrow, so you don't need to rush out of the house like normal."

"You the one who told me to stay, it's not my fault I need to rush now." I grabbed my school bag and walked out of the door, trying to act like I didn't hear her on the phone.

After what my mum said on the phone, I was more determining to see what Elizabeth had to say. I headed to the park which I normal would when going to school as halfway down the alley was a turn which was a short cut to get to school. It was handy when you are running late, and it means you don't need to go along the busy main road.

While I was walking down the path, my head was swimming with thoughts trying to make them make sense. My mum and dad know about the locker and my mum was going to get it right now. They both know about Elizabeth, but they are keeping it away from me. Why would they do that, why are they keeping the truth away from me? Why can't I know the truth?

I got to the turning and stood there looking road to school and the park which you could be seen from the turning. I could just turn right, go to school and forget about everything. Put the locker in a random bin or give it to someone and carry on like normally. Or I could head forward and know the truth, finds out what is going on?

I walked forwards and headed to the main park opening the gate that attached to the fence that circled the park. I sat on one of the swings that were in the middle of the park and looked at my watch. It was 8:15 already so Elizabeth should be here by now. I looked around and saw the park was still empty. I decided to wait 10 minutes and if she not here by then, I will go to school, get rid of everything to do with her and pretend that nothing have happened. Go back to normal and forget about everything that's been happening.

I started to swing lightly, looking at my feet as I drag them lightly on the ground. While I was lightly swinging, I thought of all the questions I needed to ask her and make sure that she answers them properly and not keep me going in circle and speaking in riddle.

Who was she and how come she seems to know a lot about me? Why do we have the same eyes? What is the truth that everyone knows but me? Why is she covering for Luke and Emma, why did she make a cover story about the party? Why would Elizabeth want to protect them?

I stopped swinging thinking of my parents. How does my parents know about Elizabeth? Do they know that she been following? Why are the keeping the truth from me if they know what happening?

"What you are thinking?" Said a too familiar voice next to me.

I fell off the swing and quickly look to where the voice came from and the other swing. Elizabeth was on the 2nd swing, swinging lightly like she been there the entire time. She was wearing plain black legging which went with the flowing black skirt and short sleeve dark red top. The shirt was blowing in the wind as she swung. "Are you OK?" She sounded concern and she stopped the swing with her feet.

"I'm fine, even though its none of your business." I got back up and sat on the swing trying not to wince. There were only concrete under the swings, so if you fell there were nothing soft to land on.

"I know you not Ingrid, I can hear it in your voice. You don't need to lie to me, you can trust me." She made it sound like I should know this already. She stated to swing again slightly, keeping her eyes on me.

"Why should I trust you, what have you done to make me trust you. I don't know who you are or why you here. You haven't given me a single straight answer to anything I asked you once." I snapped as she spoke in a matter of fact tone in her voice.

"Good point." I saw her eyes flicker slightly, like what I said had hurt her.

I move my eyes away from hers as they were making me unconformable, there were too much like mine to look at them for a long time. We both fell silence for a few moments.

"What do you know already?" She broke the silence, looking forward as she swung lightly.

I started swinging lightly as well, keeping my eyes forwards as well.

"I know for some reason we both look similar and that we have the same eyes. I know Luke and Emma attacked me, but you told my parents someone else did it. My best friend sister hates me since the party, and I suspect that you tried to warn me about her. For some reason everyone suddenly going on about 'the truth' and yet no one is letting me on the secret. And now on top it all that, this morning I heard my mum going on about this," I took the locket out of my pocket and showed it to her. "And she keeps talking about you to my dad and is planning to snoop in my room for this today while I am out."

"Wait, what?" Elizabeth suddenly put her foot out to stop swinging and looked at me making me stop as well. "Are you saying she knows about the locker and me?"

I could see that her eyes were full of panic now. "Yes, both my parents know. I first heard them talking about you when they were talking about sending me away and that you would follow me if they did. Then I heard my mum talking on the phone this morning about the locket."

Elizabeth jumped off the swings and started to pace in front of me. "They can't know we are here, I thought I was careful enough. I thought they wouldn't figure who I was. If my grandparents find out about this there will be hell for everyone. They will never let me have the life I want again, they never let me have any freedom. I found you and got my grandparents to move here. But I never told them the really reason why I wanted to move here of out of all the places. All I said was that I wanted a quite village and not a noise city and this place was the first one that I found." She stopped and looked at me, making eye contact and making sure that I couldn't look away even if I wanted too. As she stared at me, I could see her eyes were indeed were full of panic but also control. She made me feel like a deer in headlight as she spoke direct to me. "Are you sure you want to know the truth? Do you really want to know what happening? Because when you know the truth there no turning back. No matter what happens or how hard you try, you can never be the same again. Nothing will go back to normal."

I just stared at her not saying a word, trying to work out what she was saying, I couldn't figure out what she was meant at the beginning about moving here, finding me and her grandparents. But the bit I did understand the questions at the end. Do I really want to know, even if it means nothing will be the same in my life? This could be my only chance to find out what is happening, but can I trust her? I looked at Elizabeth and found myself nodding, not trusting my voice to speak.

"Follow me then." She grabbed my hand and pulled me off the swing.

I stumbled a bit as she started to drag me to the edge of the park. She opened the gate on the other end of the park and pushed me through it. Grabbing my arm and pulling me out of the park area. It took me a few seconds to realise where she was taking me. She was taking me towards the woods that were beyond the park. I stopped in my track, catching Elizabeth off guards and forcing her to stop as she still had hold of me.

Elizabeth turned to looked at me in confusion. I stood next to her; my eyes glued to the woods. "What is it, why have you stopped?"

"Because we are not allowed in the woods. Its closed off to everyone and the police arrest anyone who goes near it." I said my eyes scanning the area around the woods.

A couple of years ago 2 teenagers were found murdered in the woods and they never found out who did it. It remains unsolved to this day even with the police still searching and trying to find any clues. The teenagers were a boy and a girl both age 18 and they were lovers. The boy was a runner who broke every record that the school had, records that have not been broken since. He and his girlfriend were planning to go to Spain so he could go to a sport training school out there. His girlfriend was a writer and she was always seen with a notebook and pen on her, if she saw something that took her fancy then she would write about it. She used to always wear black with a colour as it was the only thing that suited her, but she made it look great each time, she was well known for it at school. They both looked like a perfect couple, they had everything planned and they knew what they wanted to do. Everyone was shocked when they were found killed in the woods, no one can think of a reason why they would have been murdered. Both of them had been stabbed with some sort of weapon and the male body got burned after, they needed to use his teeth to work out who he was. The girl body hadn't been burnt so that helped to work out who she was with. Due to the murder people say the woods are haunted and that at night you can hear them screaming for help. Adults don't want kids to go in there as it is a grave for the young kids, and they shouldn't be playing near it. They even got police to keep an eye on it at night as that when most kids would dare each other to go in. My parents said if they ever catch me or Ben in there then we can kiss are social life goodbye for the next hundred years. "The police will catch us if we..." I found myself saying, more to myself then to Elisabeth.

Elizabeth cut me off before I finished speaking.

"We not going where the kids were killed and found. And the police aren't here till the middle of the night around 2 and 3 so you don't need to worry about that. The police aren't that good around here." She smiled looking round the park. Her smiled froze on her face, her eyes fixed on something in the distanced.

"What?" I said in panic, my eyes following her line of sight. However all I could see were a couple having an early morning picnic and a mother with 3 kids, a baby in arms and 2 toddlers who were running around near her. That was all, the park was empty due to the fact everyone was at school or work. Those who skip school don't tend to be at the park till 11.

I scan the park again in case I missed something, but I couldn't see anything that would make Elizabeth stop talking and have the scare looked that I could see in her eyes.

"Ingrid please listen to me. When I say now, you must run into the woods with me. Keep close to me and don't fall behind or let them catch you. Don't turn around no matter what you hear or see."

I nodded, panic raising in me. What the hell was going on?

"NOW." I turned and took off towards the woods, keeping close to Elizabeth as she was in the lead. We were running nearly the same speed with me on her heels, I could have reach out my had and grabbed her if I wanted too. Suddenly I could hear footsteps coming from behind us, someone was chasing us. Someone else was in the woods with us. This made me run faster as I now felt even more scared. Suddenly Elizabeth stop, nearly making me run into her. I stopped with her, but she just pushed me forward, "Keep running, don't stop Ingrid."

I started running forward again, leaving Elizabeth behind. After a few minutes running I stopped, suddenly afraid as I looked round the woods. I just realised how deep I was in the woods and I had no idea where I was. I was alone in the woods, woods I wasn't meant to be in, in the first place. I kept turning in circle trying to figure out which way to go, becoming more lost with each turn. Suddenly I felt a hand on my shoulder, and I let out an ear piecing scream that echoed in the empty woods.

"Sshh Ingrid, it's me. It's OK its only me." Said the owner of the hand.

I turned round and saw Elizabeth standing there smiling. I couldn't help but give out a sigh of relief.

"Thanks for giving me a heart attack while lost in the woods. What happened? Who were chasing us and why were they chasing us?" My heart was still beating fast in my chest as I spoke.

"No one for you to worry about, it's been sorted. Come on."

She walked past me, and I followed her, glad that at least she knew where we were. We walked in silence with Elizabeth leading. We came to a clearing which had been cleaned of trees which only left a grass area.

I looked around the area, trying to see why she took me here and not speak to me on the swing. She walked across the clearing and I notice that there was a hole in the middle of the clearing. What the hell? I walked towards the whole where Elizabeth was standing next to it. I carefully looked down the hole, but the only things that greeted me was darkness.

A thought then hit me; "Are we going down there?" I looked at Elizabeth and my eyes glanced down the hole again, moving slightly away from the edge so that I didn't fall it by mistakes.

"Don't worry it safe so you don't be scared."

Before I could even open my mouth to reply to her she grabbed my hand and jumped down the hole. It only took seconds before we hit the ground, but it seemed a lot longer before we landed. Elizabeth kept me steady when I landed and made sure that I didn't hit the ground hard. I knew the hole was not meant to be jumped down and if Elizabeth wasn't there would have been a high chance of breaking my ankle.

There were a couple of candles in the room that were lit, I turned to Elizabeth as she went around the room lighting more candles and lighting the room up more.

"You OK?" Elizabeth asked as she turned to look at me the candlelight leaving part of her face in the shadow still.

I didn't answer her, my eyes looking around the room in amazement. The only light source were black, purple and red candles of different sizes were place all around the room. The room had very little furniture in it, the main piece was table with lots of photos of all sizes with candles on, however these candles were white. There were a couple of chairs scattered randomly around the room, the shape of them being covered by red cloth. The ceiling was covered in of lots of long empty light fitting each one covered in cobwebs. The walls were painted black with a red mist pattern, the only wall that was different was a fire brick red feature wall. Is was this wall that the table with the photos on were stood against. One of the black walls had letters sprayed on it with the same red letter as the accent wall.

I couldn't understand what the word said as it wasn't in a language that I recognised. From where I was standing in the room, I could see 3 doors connecting to the room. 2 of the doors were fully closed and the other one was slightly open which I saw lead to another room.

While looking around the room I heard a bang and my head shot straight up to the sound. I could see a panel covering the hole that was in the roof till it completely covered the hole and hiding the sunlight. The candle lighting the room even more now there were no natural light.

I heard Elizabeth laughing and I looked at her and she was smiling. I notice she was standing next to a rope that connected to the panel in the roof. She must have closed it. "It's an underground bunker, it was used during the war. But once the war ended, it got forgotten and now I use it as a hangout."

"I would love to have my room like this, but my mum liked everything to be cream and plain. The whole house is light and bright and things like that. So I just cover it with horror posters in my room which she has no control over." For some reason I feel like I can tell Elizabeth anything and she won't judge me.

I heard a phone ring in the room that had the door open. Elizabeth head turned towards it and then back at me. "I manged to hook the old system back up for certain things, I'm good with them type of things."

She went to the other room and the door closed slightly behind her. I didn't follow her or tried to listen to her phone call like I did with my mum as I felt I didn't need to with her.

I stared to move round the old bunker as I love exploring old places and I wanted to see what could be hidden in an old war bunker. I went towards the close door that I could see as I wanted to see what was behind it when something caught my eye on the table of photos.

I turned my head fully towards the table so I could look closely at the photo that I noticed. I felt my heart suddenly speed up in my chest, my breathing getting deeper and faster. I found my legs moving towards the photo and I picked it up as my hand shook. I shakily got the locket out of my pocket with my other hand and somehow manged to unlock it after a few attempts, nearly dropping it in the progress. I held both photos in my hand and compare them, they were the same, it was the same photo. I looked at the table and took notice of some of the other photos that were on the table. My blood froze when I saw the 2 photos on either end of the table. One was off Elizabeth wearing similar clothes she was wearing now. The other one was of me from the last school picture day, the one that was only a few months ago.

I heard a noise from behind me, I slowly put the photos down and locket down. I turned to around and I saw Elizabeth standing behind me with a concern look. I saw her eyes looked behind me at the photos that had clearly been moved and back to me. She swallowed; I could see her trying to think of something quickly.

"Who are you Elizabeth?" I demanded wanting answer now more than ever. "I am tired of all these games that you are playing. I am tired of being messed around by everyone and no one telling me anything. Every time I have asked you anything, you don't tell me a straight answer, you give me riddle and expect me to answer them. You tell me to trust you, but you not given me a reason to trust you. I don't even know why I trusted you enough to follow you to this abandoned place. A place that have photos of me in it and the photo from the locket you given me of people I don't know. You need to start answering me Elizabeth and you need to tell me the truth."

"Ingrid you need to trust me ple..." Elizabeth started but I didn't let her finish as I knew she wasn't going to give me the straight answer that I wanted from her. To repeat the same thing about me needing to trust her.

"Trust you, how can I trust you. You have a photo of me from my school, you were at my friend's house when we were attacked. You were at the hospital where you vanished, and my best friend sister now hates me. You are making everyone think that something else happened at the party instead of what really happened. I know you where the person who sent me the text, telling me not to see my friends. My parents are worrying about me because of you and thinking of sending me to another country. You are not giving me a single reason to trust you, a single answer to any of the questions I have asked you."

"Ingrid, you need to understand, it's not as simple as you are making out to be. It's not as simple to explain everything that you want to know." Elizabeth went to grab my arm, but I pulled away from her and moved away from her.

"Elizabeth tell me right now or I tell everyone what I know, that includes this placed and anything else you have hidden in here." I started to walk towards the door that I saw before, trying to find the way out of this place that I know must be somewhere here somewhere.

"Ingrid you must stop, you don't know what you are doing." You could see tears starting to form in her eyes, you could see that she was trying her hardest to make my listen. But now I have become tired of the games and didn't care about the tears.

"THEN TELL ME WHO YOU ARE THEN." I shouted at her, starting to lose my temper, my hand on the closed-door handle and ready to open it.

"I AM YOUR SISTER." She screamed back in response.

My hand dropped from the handle in shock. "What did you say?" I felt all the fight and the anger leaving my body. I took a step closer to Elizabeth "What did you just say Elizabeth?"

She swallowed "I am your sister, that is who I am Ingrid. I am your twin sister."

Chapter 9

"You are lying." I said shacking me head I took a few steps back hitting the wall behind me. "That's not true, that can't be true."

"For god sack Ingrid open your eyes and look at us." Elizabeth grabbed me and turned me around, opening the door I was trying to leave by. I saw that it was some sort of cupboard and not a way out like I thought. She opened the door full and I saw a full-length mirror was on the back of it. "How else would you explain what you see now?"

I looked at me and Elizabeth in the mirror and for once really looked at her and myself. It was then that I notice how much we really did look alike. I got to focused on her eyes that I didn't notice anything else about her, not in detail. We both had the same pale translucently skin that made them nearly see-through. She reached up and took her down so that like me it was down her back. This meant that I could see that it was the same length as mine and it went past her shoulder. The dark hair helped frame her face made it plain to see that everything from her mouth, noise and facial structure were exactly the same. The eyes I already knew were the same stood out on both of our faces making it more noticeable. Apart from the different clothes we were wearing and the jewellery, we were indeed the same.

I open my mouth and closed it again straight away, having trouble to find the words. I wanted to say that it wasn't true, that she was lying, and we were not the same. Yet I knew deep down she was telling the truth about me, that we were somehow twins.

I turned to look at Elizabeth as she closed the door. "How do you know all this, and I don't? How am I just finding out all of this now? Why didn't our mum tell me she had another child? That she had twins am I am one of them? Does anyone else know about you, does Ben know he got another older sister?" I suddenly had loads of new questions that I wanted to know the answer to.

"I know because I live with our grandparents and I was brought up with it." Elizabeth answered, not answering most of the questions I asked.

"I still don't understand the locket and the photo inside. Why do you have the same photo on the side? Speaking about photos, why do you have a photo of me?" I couldn't stop the questions from falling out of my mouth even if she didn't answer the ones from before.

"Yeah I bet the photo of you is hard to understand. I couldn't not have one of you as we are family. It's scary how easy it was to get it; I just sent a message to your school saying you lost your copy and they sent another one to me. I made it out like it came from you which is not that hard being twins and they believed it. The locket I gave you is one of two. We both got given them when we were born, the photo were put in the locket a month later." She replied showing me a locket that was around her neck that had been hidden under her clothes. I saw that it was the same as mine, the only different was hers had an E on it and mine had and I. That must mean that the letter I on mine means Ingrid and the E on her means Elizabeth. "I made sure to keep yours safe for you so that I can give it to you when you finally know the truth. For when you finally know who you are."

She looked down at the table of photos which we were now standing next to. I didn't realise we had been moving towards it. I looked at it in more details as I wasn't focus on the photo of me. It was then that I notice the pastel flowers that was laid across the table and the table had white candles with roses caved on them and not the dark candles that covered the rest of the bunker. I then notice that all the photos apart from the one of me and Elizabeth had the 2 people from the lockets in them. There were in photos on their own, with each other and with groups of other people. Each one of them had them smiling and happy.

It was a shine.

"Who were they?" I wondered looking at Elizabeth.

"They are family." She couldn't hide suddenly sadness in her voice and sat down on one of the random chairs. She wasn't looking at me, so I sat on another one near her. I didn't say anything as she bent her head, you could feel the pain she was feeling. After a few minutes of silence she sat back up straight and look at me with a small smile. "I'm sorry, it hurts when I think of them, even after all this time." She shook her head and smile at me a little bit more. "What do you want to know? I will tell you everything that I can tell you."

"Why didn't our mum tell me about you? Why is this such a secret they wanted to send me away to keep it that way? How come we have we not bumped into each other before if you live with our grandparents? I know I haven't seen them since I was 5 but I'm sure I would have noticed some sort of clue about you from other family members."

"She's not your mum." Elizabeth voice was low and full of anger. "They are not our family"

"What do you mean she not our mum? Of cause she our mum, she gave birth to us. They still family."

"SHE IS NOT OUR MUM." Elizabeth shouted standing up, making me jump and stand up as well. "Your mum as you call her and her husband, your 'dad', killed them! killed our parents." Her voice was getting louder and full of hate. "They took you after killing our parents as a prize. A prize that they could raise in their own image. To get you ready, ready to train you so you to kill us when you old enough. A secret weapon against us." I stood in front of her in dis-believe about what she was saying. Does she hate the fact I'm living with our parents and that why she saying all this? Saying that they weren't our parents. I know they our parents due to a school project meant I needed my birth certificate and I saw it. There were photos all over the house of me growing up from when I was I young baby. I believe her about being my twin sister, so why she is doing all this now? "But it's too late for them now." Her voice full of amusement now. "You are starting to remember your true nature. It won't be long before they know they have no control over you, that they never really did no matter how hard they tried. They already starting to guess that something is wrong, they already know something happened at the party with your friends."

"Wait what?" I needed to interrupt her when she started to mention the party. "Elizabeth try and calm down, you are not making any sense. What do you mean they already know something happened at the party with my friends? You mean the party that Luke and Emma crashed, and you made it out like they were innocent? Why are you speaking like our parents are killers? You need to stop talking in riddles and tell me what you are going on about."

She walked towards me, "Are you sure you want to know? It will change everything." Her voice was just above a whispered and full of promise.

"I told you I want to know everything." My voice matched the volume of her whispering. I shook my head and spoke in my normal tone. "I have just found out I have a twin sister who I never knew about. A twin who is speaking like our parents aren't real and they are killers of some sort. I somehow doubt that anything else you have to tell me can shock me anymore."

"You want to bet." She looked straight into my eyes and I saw her pupils started to become wider till all her eyes were solid black. I tried to blink but I suddenly couldn't move, it felt like my body had become frozen in place.

"What's goi..." I couldn't speak, why was it cold. I notice I was starting to see my breath with each breath I took.

"It's a trick from our people, a trick that can help explain everything. I am going to show you what happened at the party. Show you what you did and make you remember what really happened that night." Her voice was fading, and the room was becoming darker. There was a suddenly bright light that made me blinded me. I opened my eyes and I was suddenly standing in Rose's house during the party.

"ROSE." I saw Lily crouching by her sister side. I blinked again, trying to work out what was going on here? I saw Luke standing in front of me with Emma standing with him. What did Elizabeth do when she looked into my eyes, had I been right and everything with her was all in my mind.

I heard Elizabeth voice in my head speaking to me. It sounded like she was standing by my side, but I was standing on my own. 'You are remembering what really happened that night without the black out. Everything you did, everything you thought. You shall remember it all and I can try and explain as much as I can at the same time."

"Are you going to go to Mrs Wednesday or not?" Luke sneered. I was glad that I was right about Luke and Emma being the ones who attacked us. Since this was the second time, I been here I already know what was going to happen. The lights were going to go out, Emma would shout and then I would collapse. Maybe I would finally find out what happened after I collapses and what really happened to Luke and Emma? How they got the injures and why Lily hates me so much?

Right on queue all the lights went out and I felt my head turn to the window without me doing anything. I felt like a puppet having my strings pulled by an unseen force, no matter how hard I tried I couldn't stop my head from turning. As I looked out of the window, I suddenly spotted Elizabeth walking towards the house, so she was at the house.

'I was walking to speak to you as I knew you be there.' I nearly jumped out of my skin when Elizabeth voice came in my head. 'I was going to tell you about me as you saw me in the window. I didn't know what I was going to say though, I was just going to think on my feet. I didn't know you were going to get attacked, I would have stopped it if I knew. I knew you two had a fight, I heard it through the walls, but I didn't think anything like this would happen.'

She was right, I don't think anyone could have guessed what Luke and Emma would do this. I felt the fire going through my body again, the pain was so much I could make a sound or scream. I'd forgotten how much it hurt, how the fire felt when it went through my body.

I turned to Luke and I saw his face was full of horror, my screaming must have scared him. But as soon as the pain started, it faded, and the pain was gone completely.

I saw Luke's face calm down and his face turned back to normal. I then realised that he wasn't even looking at me, he was looking behind me at a door that leads to the garage. Wasn't he worried about me screaming? Did I even scream out loud or was it all in my head? The room was dark with a small amount of light coming from a distance streetlight, casting shadows on everyone faces and the walls.

"Luke, Luke." I heard Emma shouted. But it sounded different this time, it was closer and clearer than what I remember.

"Calm down Emma." I saw Luke look towards Emma, "It's only a power cut, we haven't been caught. We would have heard them come in and why would they wait so long to do something after turning the lights off. Be calm, we are safe." He turned back to look at me, his face looking even more evil in the limited light.

I couldn't remember Luke saying this, my mind must have blocked this out. Why would it block out Emma and Luke talking about the lights?

"If it's only a power cut, then why are the streets lights on and other people houses lights on? It seems this is the only house that's in the dark." I saw Emma was looking out of the window, I notice that I couldn't see Elizabeth anymore through the window.

"What? Are you sure?" Luke walked towards Emma and the window. "What is going on?" He sounded confused, even I was trying to make sense of the lights.

Emma whispered to Luke. "I don't know, maybe with the party it tripped a fuse or something." Just then all the lights came back on in full forced. It blinded me for a split second and I stumbling back slightly. I could just see Luke shielding his eyes and blinking. "It must have been a loose wire, dodging wiring." He laughed and smiled at Emma.

Emma looked at me and smirk. "Ahh look at the scared Ingrid, she not as brave as she thought she was. I never knew she could look worse than she does normally. We haven't even touch her yet and she looked like she been in a fight."

Luke was smiling as well. "I always told you she was a freak among her family. I don't know how they put up with her."

What were they talking about? I haven't moved from this spot apart from moving my head and a small stumble. Nothing has changed since the light went out, nothing that would have changed me.

Slowly my brain kicked in with the answer, the pain happened. The pain which came from nowhere must have done something to me. I felt my head turn to the mirror which was next to me. I tried to stop my head from turning, I didn't want to know what they were on about. I didn't want to see what I now looked like.

I felt my body freeze when I saw myself in the mirror, somehow the light being off and the pain have made me changes, has made my features have changed. My skin has someone how become paler and transparent, making my bones pop out of my checks. Yet it made me look stronger and more powerful, not weaker and frail. Because of my skin being paler, it made my hair look darker and bolder than it was before, making it almost blend in with the darkness.

But the obvious difference was that my eyes were nearly pure black, the white outline of my eyes had become dark. I kept staring into my eye, getting lost in the darkness of them, wondering how deep they went.

I want Luke and Emma dead; I wouldn't care if their heart stopped beating in their chest and stay silence forever.

I was shocked with the thought that went through my head. I didn't know if it the version of me at the party or the version from the den. Each one frightens me in their own way. I suddenly felt like I was watching myself, getting lost in the thoughts of that night and not being able to think of anything new. Losing all control of my body and my thoughts, going back to the thoughts of feeling of the night of the party.

"Of course she scared, we are all scared. Just leave us alone, just leave us." Lily sounded worried and she was nearly in tears.

I had forgot she and Rose was in the room. I forgotten anyone else was in the room at all with me. I notice Lily was still by Rose, I don't think anything will get her away from her sister side.

"Yeah well." Emma was the one who answered Lily. "She is meant to be the sad freak who is meant to likes scary things. Likes the dark and the horror that can be found anywhere. This is who she is meant to be, but she the one that looks the most scared at all of you. She a fake, when things get real, she goes pale with fright and looks like she going to burse out crying. She thinks we going to let her run to her mummy and daddy and get them to fight her battles. Tell them that her bad friends have been mean to her, calling her names."

Luke was now the one speaking, targeting me direct. "You can never fight your own battles can you Ingrid? There is always someone else fighting for you and risking themselves for you. You will never fight you own battles; you just roll over instead." Luke seem to be trying to hit every button with me, but I felt nothing with every word he said.

"Your wrong, I can fight my own battles. I don't need anyone to stand up for me." I have no idea why I said that it came out before I had a chance to stop it. But I didn't care as for some reason as I felt it was true.

Emma just smiled, not caring about what I said, she nudged Luke and he looked down at the knife that was still in her hand. "We are going to sort her out like we planned. You can get whatever information you want from her, and then get I can get her and Rose to do what we want."

"I will never do anything you say or tell you anything that you ask." I spoke in a matter of fact tone.

Emma eyes shift from Luke to me in disbelieve, her eyes narrowing slightly. "You are even more of a freak if you want to make people think you can hear them whispering. That you know what going on or you...."

Even though Emma voice was full of venom still, there was also a hint of uncertainty in it. But I can't understand why. "No, you are just a liar and a freak with no friends. You hate the fact that Luke picked me and not you. That he like someone who is normal and doesn't lie all the time and try and make themself the centre of the stage and have all eyes on you."

What did she mean about me making people think I can hear them whispering? No one in the room was whispering, they certainly weren't whispering. What was Emma talking about?

"I don't know what you are on about Emma, but I am not a freak and you are the one that lies all the time. You make up stories to make yourself look better and everyone knows it. You fall over and cut your leg; you make it out like you broken everyone bone in your body fighting a monster. You are a traitor as you don't care about anyone else but yourself, even those you meant to care about. You are the type of person who would sell everyone in your family for the right price if it helps you with the simplest of things." I was feeling the anger building up inside me and I could now hear the venom in my voice.

I saw Emma's hand tighten on the knife as she lifted it up to chest level. "You will pay Ingrid for everything you have ever done. For being a freak and making out that you are better than everyone else, that you are something else. For making it so hard for me to have what I want by standing in my way."

I saw Lily trying to get up when Luke grabbed her shoulder, keeping her on the ground as she struggled to get up.

"You are in so much trouble." Luke had a huge smile on his face. "It your fault for messing with my mind, for making me see things that aren't real."

I didn't have time to worry about what Luke was talking about because Emma started to head in my direction, I took a step forward towards her.

I needed to focus on Emma first, I deal with Luke later. "Like I said Emma, I really wouldn't do that." I sneered at her, shocked of how my voice sounded, the cruelness and anger that was in it. But I didn't care, the only thing I cared about what dealing with these and getting rid of them. I saw in the corner of my eye Elizabeth was by the front window behind everyone and looking into the room. I narrowed my eyes; I will deal with her when I am done here. I don't who she is, but she is not wanted here. I could feel the power inside me building up and going through my body and mind, taking control over all my nerves and muscles. The main focus I had was to get rid of everyone in this room who have hurt me. The people who were hurting me as I will defend myself from anyone at any cost.

Emma took a lunge at me with the knife and started to swing at me, but I just kept dodging with each swung she made. Every time Emma missed, she became even more anger, I just had a smile on my face loving every moment of it. During all this Luke just stood there, blocking Lily from helping me but this meant that he wasn't helping Emma himself.

Emma suddenly let out a loud screamed as she brought the knife straight down towards my chest. This movement caught me off guard for a split second and I only just stopped the knife millimetre from my chest by grabbing her wrist in a vice like grip. I felt the strength leave her body, her face full of panic and fear. I saw Luke over Emma shoulder and he looked like he suddenly wanted to be anywhere else but here. I saw him letting go of Lily shoulder in shock and talking a small step back. This meant that of Lily wanted to move she could, yet she stayed where she was on the floor, just staring at me and Emma.

I looked at each person in the room, starting with Emma and ending with Elizabeth who was now stepping back from the window, her eyes wide with cautious and uncertainness.

"You think that you could beat me, you think you can win," I lean closer to Emma ear and whispered just to her. "You can't win against me anymore; I am the strong one now."

I could feel Emma shacking through her wrist, I could hear her trying not to whimper out loud. I just smiled, loving the feeling of being the one on top in a fight for once. I let go of Emma wrist which dropped liked a stone to her side automatically, she looked like she lost all function in her body.

I felt the corner of my mouth curl up in a smirk and I saw Emma eyes widen slightly more. I took a small step backwards and used all my strength and kicked Emma straight into her ribs. I was now glad that I had shorts on under my dress as it lift slightly as I put all my power in my kick so that it made a solid contact. When my foot hit Emma ribs the sound of the breaking echo in the now dead silent room. Lily start to gag and couldn't look in my direction, Luke face was set in horror and he looked like he was going to be sick himself. Emma dropped to the floor like a dead body, curling up in the smallest ball she could and holding her sides. Emma mouth kept opening and closing in a silent scream of pain, for everything she done for me I was glad she was hurting. I walked forward, making sure I kicked her on the way past while she was on the ground. Lily was now screaming and crying, looking in my direction again.

"NO, EMMA." Luke seem to have movement back in her body as he ran toward me with a clenched fist. He was no longer bothered about Lily or Rose; he was only bothered about me and how much pain Emma was in. How nice of him, trying to protect his girlfriend from the monster. I knew he would never do anything like that for me, wouldn't fight someone for me. He swung at me and I ducked out of the way, he went to swing for me about when grabbed his neck as he moved to through the punch. His hand stayed in the air frozen in place, I looked past him when I heard a noise from the direction of Lily, she now crying uncontrollable with her face buried deep into Rose clothes. She was starting to wind me up with all the crying and noises she was making. I looked back at Luke, his skin going white with fear. I felt the feeling of the fire and power going through my body again, yet this time there were no pain with it, and it made me feel alive, more alive than I felt in a long time.

Luke closed his eyes and his breathing was getting faster and heaver. "Ingrid I'm sorry, please." He was now begging me, oh how the mighty have fallen. "It wasn't meant to go like this."

Of course not, when this was all plan, I bet you didn't think I fight back for the first time in my live. I loosened my grip slightly on his neck, I still had control, but he could move a bit more freely. With his new limited freedom, he moved his face away from me and towards the wall with his eyes closed, you could hear him whimpering over Lily crying and screaming. I found my eyes locked onto his neck and I could have sworn I could see his pulse becoming more clearer and clearer the more it beat. I felt my teeth starting to tingle and ache in a way that made it feel like I could feel them growing. Before I could or have the power to stop myself, I bit down into his neck and I found that my teeth went through his neck like knife through butter. I found myself coming to my senses of what I was doing, that I had just bit Luke and my teeth was now in his neck. I wanted to stop, to remove my teeth from Luke neck, then I realise I was drinking the blood that was coming from Luke neck. But as the blood slide down my throat and into my stomach, I found that I was getting lost in the taste of it and the flavour I found myself drinking deeper. The blood tasted sweat and the most refreshing things I ever tasted, and I never wanted it to end or for it to stop flowing. It felt like it was taking control of my body and my mind, soothing the fire that I felt was racing through my body with power.

I became blind again when the bright light returned, making everything turn solid white. I blinked and found myself standing back in Elizabeth den. I found trying to catch my breath, trying to figure out what has happened, what I remembered happened. I sat down on a chair that was behind me, finally having control over my body and mind again. Elizabeth grabbed a chair and sat in front of me, I saw she had a concern look on her face, her eyes never leaving my face.

"I... Luke... Party" I whispered trying to put the puzzle together in my mind, so many images and memory going through my mind.

"That wasn't all that you did." Elizabeth spoke softly to me. "Once you finished feeding from Luke, you kicked him away from you with good distance. The strength of your kicked made sure to break some of his ribs in a few places. Even with everyone you did to Luke, he was still alive and breathing. You didn't drink enough for his heart to stop beating in his chest. Emma was still on the floor curled up; she didn't move while you were attacking Luke. You picked her up by her hair, making her scream in even more in pain. You made her look deep into your eyes, made her feel the fear before you bit deep into your neck. You would have finished drinking her if it if it weren't for Lily screaming at you, because halfway through you dropped her to the floor before you were done. You made sure to stand on Emma as you walked towards Lily, you certainty wanted to make sure she was in pain. It was while you were walking towards Lily with you face covered in Emma and Luke blood that Lily fainted. Rose didn't wake up till she was in the hospital, so she never saw anything at the house. Emma and Luke were starting to fall unconscious at this point, I didn't realise how weak some people minds were."

The more Elizabeth spoke, the more I saw the memory in my mind. Remembering everything I did, the power I was feeling.

Elizabeth coughed and carried on speaking. "It was while you were walking towards Lily with the evillest look on your face that you fainted. If not, I don't think anything would have stopped you from attacking Lily and Rose, even if they are your friends or not. The power and the change were too much for you, it shouldn't have happened this soon for you. But you were in danger and you needed to defend yourself, your body responded the way it needed to. Lucky the door was still unlocked and opened which meant I was able to get into the house and made sure there was no blood on you. That wouldn't have been good being found with people's blood on your face by anyone. You were only out for 10 minutes before you woke up and saw me and we spoke. The police and the ambulance came a few minutes later to help you and everyone else. They saw me there, so I needed to think of a lie to tell them, I needed to think fast on my feet. Sorry if I dropped you in it in anyway. I did try and warn you, I sent you the text to stay away from Lily. I got your number of your phone; you really need a password on your phone. Lily saw everything that happened, she saw you biting Luke and Emma. You need to start trusting me when I tell you things, you need to start listening."

"I... You...We..." I mumbled, still trying to force words out of my mouth, trying to speak. All the memory's going through my mind, remembering everything that Elizabeth unlocked in my mind. I couldn't get my mind wrap round everything that been happening, things that only happen in movies, in books. "It can't be true."

Elizabeth grabbed my hand and I looked me in the eyes, I back into her eyes, not being afraid of them anymore. "You know it true Ingrid, deep down you know what your heart and mind is telling you. You've remembered everything, you know everting that happened that night."

"I bit Luke and Emma and drank their blood." I took a moment before I answered and said the words, I been thinking out loud. "I'm a vampire, we are vampires."

Elizabeth only smiled in with respond, her teeth catching the light of the lit candle burning around us.

Chapter 10

I wrapped my hand around the warm cup of tea, taking a deep needed sip. My head had finally stop spinning with what real happened at the party. I knew what I was told, and what I saw was the truth and I know what I really was. We moved away from the main room and was now in a side room that was connected to the main room. This room was bigger than the main room but was still lit by candles that had places around the room and had the same colour walls as the main room. This room had everything in that you would in a house, you could live in this room with no problem. I was sitting at a small square table with a dark green tablecloth that didn't seem to match anything else in the den. The chair I was sitting on and the chairs that were stacked up in the corner were made from dark wood with plain red cushions on the seats. There was bed in the corner of the room away from the door with the same colour red of the chair cushions. At the base of the bed was a bookcase that was filled full of books of all shapes, sizes and colours. Next to the door was the kitchen area, a small camping gas stove with the kettle on top and cups around it.

"How did you even find this place; how did you know this existed?"

I couldn't stop looking around the places, it looked like a place you would explore in the dark and scare each other with horror stories.

"I found it a month ago before we moved here, I found it on the villages old map by chance. I figured out it could be useful in different ways, some alone time when our grandparents are on my back, away from slayers if they come for me or when I just want some me time. When I first found this place, everything was turned off and it was empty. We got water here, but no electric hence all the candle. I manage to get the furniture from my grandparents when we moved, they got new furniture for the new house, so I kept the old stuff, surprising they didn't notice it missing. But I like it, it's my place to escape too when things get too much. The fact that is old and abandoned fits the vampire part of us well."

I smiled at her, twisting the locket with my fingers as it hung around my neck. I knew I would need to hide it under my clothes when I wasn't with Elizabeth. I knew it would be hard to explain it to people about the twin bit, never mind the whole bit about me being a vampire and biting people.

"How can we be vampires? How is it possible that we are vampires?" I asked, needing to know as much as possible, wanting to know as much as possible.

"What do you mean how is it possible?" Elizabeth sat across from me at the table with a smile on her face. "It possible because it is, it's the same answer as if you asked a human the same question."

"Ok, fair point. I do have some other questions about me being a vampire if I can ask?"

Elizabeth smirked. "Of course you can ask, I grew up with all this. All this is new for you and I bet you have so many questions you want to know the answer to."

"How come I can do things I know vampires aren't meant to be able to do? I mean I can go out into the sun; I can eat garlic and I can see myself in the mirror. I can enter people houses without needing someone to invite me in and last time I checked I don't have fangs coming out of my mouth."

"Well," Elisabeth pulled a disgust face and lent back in the chair. "Only you eat garlic as I can't stand the taste. What you read in books and see on TV is different from what vampires are like in real life." She got up and grabbed a book from the bookshelves and put it front of me. "This might help you with some of the questions."

"What is it?" I asked peering at the cover of the book to see what it was. It was an inch thick A4 book made from black cloth that looked quite old as the material had stated to fray at the edges. There was a deep red border round the edge of the book and in the top corner nearest the spine there was a small bat with wrings following the border round. It had the same strange word written on the front as on the wall next door at the top of the book in red. Under the writing was an image of a figure with dark violet almost dragon like wings. The figure itself was too shadowed to make out any sort of specific detail features.

"It's a book about vampires. About our people." Elizabeth smiled pushing the book closer to me.

I picked it up to have a closer look. "Why do I need a book? Can't I search the answer online? Or ask you or even our grandparents. I know I not seen them in so many years, but I bet they love to see me know all grown up."

"No." She lowered her eyes, no longer looking at me. "You won't be able to meet them, not yet. Especially with our grandad, we need to be carefully with meeting him."

"What do you mean?" I was confused. "Why can't I meet our grandad yet? Why do we need to be careful when I am his granddaughter?"

"Our granddad is old fashioned and strict. Very Strict in fact. You never grew up as a vampire, so as far as he concerned you not a vampire and you no longer part of this family. In his eyes you need to prove who you are and to be honest I don't know how long that will take or what it will take. Our grandma is different, she wouldn't care if you have been living in a zoo all these years. But that doesn't mean she won't reacted and go against you if you suddenly turn up on their doorstep. Basically, study the book and learn everything in it. Prove our grandparents wrong, prove that you know what it takes to be a vampire. Do that first then we can see what else we need to do once you know the basic stuff."

"Ok, I will study the book. You sound like my teacher at school." I put the book in my school bag when I suddenly realise something.

School.

"Wait, what time is it? How long have I been here?" I asked in panic, somewhere in the den I heard a clock strike 4. This made me jumped up out of the chair, "Oh my god." Have I really been here that long? "I need to get home before my par..." I stop mid-word, remembering something that Elizabeth had said to me before, only just taking notice of what she was said before. I looked at Elizabeth who was now standing by the table, her eyes were lowered again to the ground. It made it look like she knew what I was thinking, to what I was about to ask. I got so caught up with being a vampire and Elizabeth being my twin that I didn't take any attention of what she said about my parents and what they did. "Earlier you said that the people I'm living aren't my parents, that they killed them and took me as a prize. What did you mean by that?" Elizabeth shift her eyes to the side but still didn't look at me. "Elizabeth please, you were shouting early about how they killed our parents. You already told me about me being a twin and a vampire, so what else is there that can shock me?"

Elizabeth lifted her eyes up, finally looked at me. "The people you have been living with for years, the people you have been calling mum and dad, aren't you parents. They killed our real parents and took their place in your life." Her tone and eyes were both full of anger. I made myself keep my eyes locked on her. "When they killed our parents, they took you with them as a prize. A vampire baby. You were with our parents at our house when they came. You were ill so I was at our grandparents, they didn't want me to catch it and both of us being ill. The people who took you weren't aware that you were a twin, it was only recent that they found out about me. We used to live in a city which made it easy to blend into with the crowd and there were so many people there no one took any notice of us. Being vampires, you don't really want people to ask questions you can't answer. However, someone found us who knew what we were and by chance knew the Jones, they didn't realise who the Blazes were. Blazes is our family name and is your real last name. I knew what the Jones did to our parents and I manage to get the address of the person before he got dealt with by our grandparents. They didn't know I found your information and address after all these years. I have been trying to find you for ages, to bring you home. But it's hard when you don't want people to ask questions and I didn't know much information on the slayers apart from what I been told. I couldn't ask our grandparents too much personally information or they might be able to figure out I was up to something. I used us being caught as a reason for us to move to a different place and start again. So I picked the village where you were living so that I could find you and for you to find out the truth. I told my grandparents I was tired of living in a city and wanted a village life. The Jones didn't know you were a twin till we moved here, that was when they realised, I exited. The surname Blaze is and will always be burned into their mind since they been bringing one up for years and years. So, when they heard that a family with the surname Blaze were moving into the village and there was a child the same age as you. Well it didn't take them very long or to many brain cells to work out who I was or why I was here. That why they probably wanted to move you away from here, away from your real family and kind. The people you are living with are vampire slayers."

I found my hand reaching for the locket and holding it tightly in my hand. I closed my eyes, trying to work out everything she was telling me, what I saw and what I have heard. I always knew I was different from the rest of my family; it has been a running joke with me and my friends for years. I don't look like any of them and I don't act like them. They somehow knew things about Elizabeth that they shouldn't possibly know. They been acting differently since she been here, they wanted to send me to a different country which they have never thought of doing before all this. The only reason for this is that they knew about Elizabeth before I did. That they know what she was and what I was. Even though part of me didn't want to believe it, that I had been living a lie and with killers. But I knew what Elizabeth was saying was the truth, that the people I had been living with killed my real parents and replaced them in my life. Making me believe they cared about me when they stole me from my own family.

I still had my eyes closed when I gently felt a hand touching my shoulder, I opened my eyes and saw Elizabeth next to me smiling. The smiled told me that she was going to be there for me, and that everything was going to be Ok. I could help but answer back with my own smile.

"Come on" Elizabeth gestured with her head towards the door. "You need to go before you get find out that you have not been in school. We can't have anyone finding out you been here with me all day."

Elizabeth went back to the main room and I followed her without hesitation. Once we got to the main room, she walked towards the other door that was in the room, the one that didn't have the mirror on the back of it. This door led to a small corridor with a wooden ladder leading upwards and out of the bunker. Elizabeth went to the ladder and stated to climb up, looking back at me with a smile and started to climb higher. I followed her up the ladder where she stopped near the top, I saw that it looked like I had been blocked by something and we couldn't go any further. This didn't seem to matter to Elizabeth as she pushed the roof and it opened to the outside. She climbed out and helped me out when I got to the top, the bright sun blinding me slightly, having gotten use to the dark and the candlelight. When I got out of the hole, Elizabeth put the cover back over the hole so that it was completely covered. Unless you knew it was there, you wouldn't have thought a moment ago there was a ladder that led to a secret bunker was hidden there.

Elizabeth smiled when she saw me looking at her. "This is how people meant to get in and out of the bunker when it was used. You are not meant to use the hole in the roof like I do, but I find it quicker than the ladder." She laughed and I joined in with the laughter.

"Can I come back tomorrow? I need to come back tomorrow, I still have so much I want to know. That I need to know about vampires and our family, I feel like I don't know anything anymore." I pleaded with Elizabeth.

"I don't think that would be a good an idea, you shouldn't come back tomorrow. You need to go to school tomorrow and you need to stay. If you come here again tomorrow and keep coming here, you are going to get caught. The slayers are going to figure out that something is wrong, that you are hiding something. If not the slayers then the school are going to be asking questions, they going to make phone calls and send out letters and you won't be able to explain why you are absent. What excuse can you say that won't get you into any more trouble? An excuse for you to miss days of school and yet you are meant to be heading to school every morning? Even missing 2 days in a row is going to get your school thinking and we need to be careful with the slayers, they not as dumb as they might appear to be."

I tried to think of anything that I could say that would allow me to come back. That would allow me to keep missing school and to come back to the den. But I knew what Elizabeth was saying made sense and I knew if I didn't go to school tomorrow then Mrs Wednesday would call the slayers. After fighting so hard to stay in school, I knew nothing I could say would make any sense and it might end up with them talking about sending me to America again. "OK, I can see your point about missing school. But what can I do then? I can't sit back and do nothing after finding out I been living a lie all my life can I?"

"I know it going to be hard Ingrid but that is what you need to do." Elizabeth answered "But you can't make the slayers aware that you know about them. Keep a low profile and study the book, it should help answer some of your questions about vampires. If you can't figure something out, then you just need to ring me, and I will help. I can let you know when it safe again for us to meet up again, we need to make sure no one see us together. You never know who you can trust, it only takes one person to make one comment and we could get find out."

"Erm my par... The slayers," I re-worded quickly, "Have got my phone and keeps the house phone on them at all time. So, I don't have any way of speaking you or for you to contact me."

Elizabeth shook her head with a knowing smiled on her face. She put her hand in her pocket and pulled out a phone that looked the same as mine back home. She handed me the phone with the same smile on her face, "Yeah I guess they would take your phone off you after you ran from the hospital. I made sure to get the same one you had so it didn't look out of place if someone saw it. Just be careful if the slayers see it and they still have your real one on them. Keep it hidden but close by so we can keep in contact with each other. You can only call and text one it, it not set up for anything else."

I nodded, hiding the phone from view in my inside pocket. Knowing what could happen if it gets found. I turned to get ready to leave when Elizabeth spoke again. "One more thing, don't go and see Rose at the hospital anymore."

I turned back at Elizabeth in shock. "Why? She my friend, I'm not going to abandoned her. Expectedly not while she in the hospital because of everything that happened."

"Come on Ingrid, think about it from another point of view. Lily knows you are a vampire; she saw you biting people and drinking their blood. She is not going to let you go near Rose quietly after everything she saw at the party. I've not had chance to see how much Luke and Emma remember. Sometime biting people stops them remembering things, but that is not always the case. So please Ingrid, you need to promise me that you are not going to go back the hospital. I knew Rose is your friend, but I need you to keep safe. Please." Elizabeth pleaded up me.

"OK Elizabeth. I promise I won't go to see Rose. I stay away from the hospital and I won't go back." I lied without needing to think.

No matter what Elizabeth said, I wasn't going to stop visiting Rose. I have known Rose for too many years to give up on her now, no matter what danger I might be putting myself in.

"Get home and try to act normal. Read the book and learn what you can about vampires. But be careful, anyone could be working for the slayer and I mean anyone. Being a vampire mean be killed or kill."

I looked past Elizabeth into the woods, remembering the people chasing us when we first came to the park. "The people who was chasing us were slayers weren't they? Did you kill them?" I asked, putting all the puzzles together with what Elizabeth was saying.

I looked at Elizabeth who looked like she was going to hesitate for a split second before she spoke. "Yes they were slayers and they work with the people you live with. They were in the park when we arrived, they were the people who were having the picnic. Unfortunately, there are multiply slayers in the village, but I am not sure who they all are. I am surprised the slayers chasing us where even near the woods after the public mistake they made. Most vampires know about it as they nearly expose the slayers to the world.

"What do you mean expose them? What public mistake did they do?" I asked, noticing she wasn't answering the question I asked.

"The same reason why you didn't want to come into the woods. The slayers that were chasing us where the same ones that killed the kids that were found in the woods. From what I heard the slayers were new to the village and they didn't know who were vampires and who were not. They thought the kids were vampires and tried to ger rid of them but failed. Slayers don't care how old you are, whether you an adult or a teenage they will try and kill you. Slayers are everywhere, in all jobs and places which means they can cover things up like an accidently murder. That should show how dangerous slayers are which include the people you are living with. They don't really care who they kill as long as they don't get caught and they get the vampire they are going after."

"Did you kill them?" I re-asked, my voice shacking a bit. "Did you kill the slayers that were chasing us? And what happen to the slayer that found you in the city, what did you mean he was dealt with. Does that mean you killed him as well?" I don't what answer I wanted to hear, which answer would make me feel safer.

"You don't need to sound so worried; I didn't kill the slayers that were chasing us. I trapped them somewhere so someone I know can deal with them later. The one that found us in the city, my grandparents did kill them yes. Go home, I need to stay here and sort some stuff out."

I nodded with mix feeling, still not sure how I felt. I still had more questions that I wanted to ask, but I knew I didn't have time.

"Let me know when I can come back here, I still got more I want to know." I said with a small smile as I walked away from Elizabeth and back into the wood.

I felt weird walking in the woods knowing what I knew about the murders, I was half expecting to see the slayers trapped in the woods somewhere. Yet I didn't see a single person in the woods or as I walked home. I manage to get home around the same time as if I did go to school, which was good as I meant I didn't need to explain anything to anyone.

I walked through the door when I heard Mrs Jones voice from the kitchen. I felt sick hearing her voice now I knew the truth. Know I knew that she wasn't my really mother. "How was school? What was you doing today?"

I noticed that there was something in her voice, something that was different and wrong. Have I been caught somehow; does she know something? I knew that tone meant she was far from happy.

"It was OK, we mostly did tests. I think I done well on them all." I called back, heading upstairs as quickly as I could.

I knew that this was the best places to head when she had that tone in her voice. Exactly now I was aware the real connection between us.\, knowing who she was.

"That's good, I expect good grades. You need to drop your bag in the hall, go upstairs to get changed and come back stairs. Quickly. I need a word with you and Ben."

I then saw Mrs Jones came out of the kitchen covered in water and flour, meaning it was stuck in all her hair in clumps. Her voice was full of anger, not surprising given she looked like she was half yeti or something with all the flour over her.

"What happened to you?" I asked trying not to laugh at her, but I knew I had a smirk on my face which I couldn't hide.

It looked like she was about to shout at me when Ben walked through the front door. He didn't even bother to hide his laughter, he just burst out laughing in front of her.

"You two upstairs get changed and then come back down. You have TWO MINUTES." She yelled the last bit and me and Ben took off running upstairs to our rooms. The laughing escaping me as I went up the stairs joining in with Ben's laughter.

Ben went into his room and I could still hear Ben laughing loudly through the walls as I went into my room. I took Elizabeth's book from my bag so I could hide it when a pocket side book fell out of it.

I picked it up of the floor and saw a message written on it.

Translator, so you can understand the book. Elizabeth B

I smiled; Elizabeth must have slipped it in without me knowing.

"1 MINUTE." I heard a shout from downstairs, the voice was becoming more inpatient.

I put the notebook and the big book under my pillow so no one could find it by mistake. I got changed quickly and ran downstairs before the countdown ended

I went to the kitchen where Mrs Jones and Ben was. Ben was sitting at the table with a smile on his face still, so I sat down next to him as I had no idea what else to do. Mrs Jones was still covered in flour and still looked annoyed was standing by the table with her foot tapping on the floor.

"Ingrid, you're not seeing Rose or Lily at the hospital at all. Ben, you're not going on the X-Box, computer or anything like that for a month either. Neither of you are allowed out of this house nor is anyone allowed in without my express permission. I don't care what you have had planned, set up or there something you must do or the world going to end." She stated before me or Ben could say or do anything. "You are both grounded and that is the end of story."

"Why." Benn complained like a spoiled child." I didn't do anything and that's not fair. Ingrid is already grounded so that's not going to make a different to her is it. I feel like I am getting the worst end of this punishment."

"Wait, I didn't do anything either. I need to see Rose, it's not fair to leave her on her own when she in hospital. I can't leave her there on her own she going to think I've fallen out with her." I wined with Ben.

How can I see Elizabeth when I am allowed? How was I am going to see Rose no matter what Elizabeth said.

"Well, one of you put the flour trap in the shower, so when I open the door and got into the shower, I ended up being covered in wet flour. And because I don't know who done it, both of you are in trouble. So, unless one of you tells me the truth, I'm not going to change my mind and the punishment stands."

Ben groaned, got up from the table and went upstairs, stamping on each step as he went. I didn't hear the door slam from his bedroom like I thought I would with all the banging.

Mrs Jones turned her back on me and was trying to get the flour out of her hair over the sink. I didn't say anything else to her and I got up and went back upstairs like Ben.

At the top of the stairs I saw Ben waiting on the landing, that explain why I didn't hear his door banging. I saw his face was full of anger and he was blocking my way to my bedroom. What was wrong with him? Why did he look anger at me? I didn't have time for any of this as I wanted to read some of the book before tea.

"Hey, Ben you are blocking the stairs, can you move please? I want to get to my bedroom I have things to do."

"You did it." His eyes narrowed at me. "You need to go to mum and tell the truth now. That you set the flour trap and I had nothing to do with it. I am not being punished because of you."

"Why would I do something a 5-year-old would do? You the person in the family that play pranks on everyone, not me. I am not going to admit to something I didn't do. Now get out of my way Ben, I am not playing this game with you." I pushed passed him and went to my room, closing my door behind me.

I sat on my bed when the phone Elizabeth gave me beeped. Thank god it didn't go off while I was downstairs. I need to think of a story in case that happened as I am not meant to have a phone on me.

I got my phone out and looked at the message from Elizabeth:

Sorry, I had to do the flour trap. I knew you were planning to visit Rose no matter what I said to you. I'm trying to help you, please remember that. Sorry.

"For god sack" I muttered a bit loud to myself. Ben must have saw Elizabeth set the trap, he thinks it me who did it. That explain why she didn't walk with me through the woods, she was setting the trap to stop me from leaving. I wanted to be angry at her, but I knew why she did it. She knew I wasn't going to listen to her, that I was going to see Rose, even if it meant me putting myself in danger with Lily being there. I was safe in the house if I didn't let the slayers know that I have found out the truth. If I keep my head down and mouth shut, then I will be safe for a while.

I put the phone away and grabbed the books from under my pillow.

I looked through the pocketbook to see if I could see what the word said on the front and the word on the wall. I found it and smiled;

Vampires.

Of cause it's going to say vampire. It's a vampire book, given to me by my vampire twin, who told me that I was a..... vampire. It wasn't exactly going to say elves or fairies on it. I couldn't help but shook my head with how obvious it was.

I never was good at learning new languages, so translating the first page was difficult.

Vampires aren't born with their full powers; they get these when they are 18 years of age. Until this time, they can go into the sun, they will still have a reflection in mirrors and go near garlic and crosses without harming themselves. Under 18's can drink both human and animal blood, but they won't have either the fangs or the blood craving that come with it. They will be able to use some of their capable super speed and heightened senses to help them to survive until the age of 18.

So, I will get my fangs in 2 years and I should be able to do other things now that normal human can't. I was glad that I didn't have the blood craving as that didn't sound like a good thing, at least I had a few years to prepare.

I carry on with the rest of the page to see what else I could learn.

However, if a vampire is in a life-threatening incident or feel like they are in one, then they will develop their fangs early to defend themselves. It is normal for people who develop their fangs early to forget about the reason around it and remember it later with time. Once a vampire has developed their fang, they keep them and use them like any other vampire over the age of 18.

I shuddered at the memory of my teeth going into Luke's and Emma's neck. Look likes I won't be waiting till I am 18 before I get my fangs. Glad I remember with Elizabeth help and not on my own, I don't know how I would have cope if I had to do it all on my own.

I heard Ben's door open and footsteps going down the stairs, but I carried on reading the book, too deep into it to stop now.

However, there are side effects of getting your fangs early. The main one is that they will become more aggressive towards any humans. They will have blood craving that only human blood can satisfy, and they will begin to have more access to their vampire skills that they can use to help with their craving and to survive. They will still be able to go into sunlight, but they will find it irritating and uncomfortable. They will also find it hard to sleep in beds and will only find comfort in coffins. They will feel more tired and become more active once their fangs have started to grow,

I don't mind the sleeping in a coffin bit, I think it would be great to sleep in one. However the blood craving was starting to worry me, expertly now it was on about needing human blood to be able to cope with it. It sounds like it might hurt a bit, I don't mind pain, but it doesn't sound like it be a walk in the park. I don't mind not going out in the sunlight as I hate it, anyway, might make going to school interesting.

"Ingrid come down." I heard Ben shouted from downstairs, I could hear the smugness in his voice. I looked at the clock and saw that it had took me ½ an hour to do one page. I put the book back in its hiding place and went down the stairs. I found him and Mrs Jones in the kitchen still, Ben having an evil smile on his face and she had her arms folded over her chest. Seem like Ben snitched and said that I did the flour trap. Great, can't really tell the truth and say it was my twin sister, could I?

"Ben said he saw you setting the flour trap. Is this true? Come on Ingrid, don't lie to your mother, you've been brought up better than that." Her eyes were telling me to tell the truth, that I shouldn't lie to my mother.

The problem was that she wasn't my mother, she killed my real mother and replaced her, making me believe I was someone else. That I was something else.

"It wasn't me who set up the flour trap. I've been at school all day and you saw me come through the door when you were already covered. Anyway, how can Ben see who set the trap when he came in last, shouldn't he have been in school during the time it was set?"

I knew the answer to the last bit. Mrs Jones always goes next-door for lunch and has done for years, and Mr Jones always works early till late, so the house is empty during lunch time. Ben uses this so he can leave school when he is not meant to and spends his lunch time in the house. He normally uses this time to play on his computer and things and gets back to school before anyone notice he is missing, and people come back home. I only found out this information by chance because I was sent home from school for being ill and caught him in the house. I knew Ben wouldn't risk dropping himself into trouble and let everyone know about his lunch time activities if he needed to explain himself fully.

"That is a good point Ingrid." She looked at Ben, but he wouldn't meet her eyes and didn't say anything like I knew he wouldn't. When he didn't say anything Mrs Jones carried on speaking. "Well in that case both of you are still grounded for the month. And don't try and drop each other into more trouble or worse is yet to come for that person. It's time for tea, your dad is not eating with us tonight so it just us 3. Then I want both of you in bed after tea and you will stay there till morning."

She turned her back on us so she could get the food out of the oven and Ben has his back turned from me and was looking out of the kitchen window. This meant that none of them noticed the evil smirk on my face, I might not have set the flour trap, but I was enjoying the outcome of it. I wasn't normal a bad person, I normal kept my head down but something in me told me that is not how a vampire act. I felt like I needed to do bad things, that I had the power to do it and nothing could get in my way. All the things I thought of doing to those who done me wrong I could do. It was going to be fun being a vampire and being bad. I was too busy thinking to take much notice to what I was eating, I could be eating wood and I wouldn't have notice. Thinking of all the things I could to people who have done me wrong, Mrs Wednesday, Luke and Emma.

After I finished eaten, I went upstairs, I couldn't help smiling to myself on the way up. I didn't even try to fight it like Ben was doing downstairs. For the first time ever, I wanted the next day to come quickly and for school to begin. I wanted to show everyone who Ingrid Blaze really was and what happens when you mess with a vampire like me.

Chapter 11

It felt wrong staying in bed all night; I couldn't fall asleep fast like I wanted to. It felt like my body would suddenly jump out of the bed and window and hang out in the dark without me being able to stop it. To explore the darkness and the night where I belong. When my alarm finally went off, I leaped out of bed and turned it off. I looked at my school uniform that was at the bottom of my bed, thinking what could do with it to show a different side to me. I could hear Mrs Jones coming up the stairs and into her room. I knew I couldn't do anything while I was in the house as it might make Mrs Jones figure out that something was wrong. I put the clothes on as normal so that I wouldn't get caught, making sure I had the phone Elizabeth gave me was hidden on me. I went downstairs alone while Mrs Jones and Ben were still in their rooms. I walked into the kitchen, smiling at myself with some of the ideas of what to do to my uniform, having fun planning it all. I was about to grab some toast that was on the side when Mr Jones came through the front door suddenly, looking around the hallway. I couldn't help but jump as he is normal gone by now and I didn't expect him to suddenly come through the door like he was on a one-man mission.

"I thought you meant to be at work." I found myself asking walking to the of the kitchen.

"I am meant to be at work, I am meant to be there now. But I can't find my work bag, have you seen it? Is the leather one, I swore it was in the car or at work. Or maybe I left it here without thinking?" He kept moving coats and bag in the hallway in a panic.

I shook my head, "No I haven't"

I knew what bag he was talking about as he always takes it to work with him. I always wanted to have a look in it, but he never let me or Ben near it. Knowing now that he was a slayer, maybe it was a good idea that me and Ben have never looked in it.

"Honey." He shouted upstairs. "Please tell me you have seen my bag or have it?"

"You mean the leather one?" I notice her voice had a hint of something in it. Panic maybe? Maybe that means there was something important in there? "No, I haven't seen it. You need to ask Mark for some spare things as he normal have some. But you need to make sure you report it missing so they can try and find it."

He groaned in response and got his phone out of his pocket. I didn't hear him speak on the phone as he walked back out of the front door and closed the door before he started speaking.

I grabbed the toast and took a bite out if it when I heard footsteps rushing down the stairs. Ben came rushing through the door and jumped. Most likely because he didn't realise I was standing by the side.

"What are you doing down here already?" He quizzed. "What are you up to? I am the one that is normally down here first."

I just smiled and didn't answer him.

"Ingrid." Mrs Jones walked into the kitchen. "What a surprise, I was about to shout you to make sure you were up. Is this the same Ingrid from yesterday or do we have an imposter living with us?" She laughed. "Or are you listening to me for once about getting up early for school?"

I just smiled at the joke. I didn't want to say anything as I didn't know what would come out of my mouth. I wasn't the same Ingrid anymore and she was the imposter that was living in the house. But I knew I had to keep up the appearance, or I would put Elizabeth and even myself in danger.

"What was dad shouting about?" Ben asked as he looked in the fridge, I knew he was looking for bacon because the only thing else in there were milk and salad.

Mrs Jones also figured this out. "No bacon," She slammed the door, nearly hitting Ben in the face. I would have laughed if she did. "He was looking for his work bag Ben. Have you seen it anywhere?"

"Nope." Ben said, grabbing some toast off the side. His voice showed he wasn't listening to what was being asked.

"Don't be in a mood Ben, you know my rules. On school day you can have toast, cereal or porridge, nothing else. Weekend is when you can have bacon and things like that."

"Yeah, yeah I know about the breakfast rules." You could tell he didn't really care and that he would stay in a bad mood all day no matter what. He dropped onto one of the chairs and put his headphones on.

I shook my head and headed towards the front door with some toast in my hand when Mrs Jones shouted after me. "And where you are going young lady?" I stopped and turned to face her as she was standing in the kitchen doorway. "You woke up early, so there no need for you to rush off. Is there?"

"I'm going to school early because I want to catch up with what I missed while I was in hospital." I said knowing that this should stop her from bugging me and let me leave the house. Any other day she be shoving me out of the door early, when I do try and leave early, she wants to stop and ask questions.

"You only missed one day." She said crossing her arms. "And you were at school yesterday, you should have caught up on everything things."

"I didn't have time to do it all." I said walking out of the door and closing it behind me before she could say anything else.

I pretended that I was going to school till the coast was clear, then I turned my on my heels and went the other way. I had things I needed to do before I got to the school gate. I didn't go to the park either remembering that Elizabeth said about being careful when seeing her, even though part of me wanting to go back to the den. Instead I went to the shops instead, I needed to pick up some new extra things for my uniform.

Once I finished with all my preparations, I arrived at school 20 minutes after the bell went. Mrs Wednesday was standing by the gate like she does every morning. She was taking names of students coming in late, so she can deal with them later. "Ingrid Jones you're la..." She stopped speaking in her tracks. "INGRID JONES!" She shouted at the top of her voice in shock.

I smiled to myself at the reaction as it was how I wanted people to react when they saw me. I had brought some purple hair extensions, which real stood out against my natural black hair. I was wearing dark purple lipsticks, 2-tone purple and grey eye shadow with heavy mascara and thick eye liner. I had the button on my collar undone, this meant my tie, which I made thick and small where low on my top. I had on my black hooded jacket with a simple white revered cross on the back which I took from my house in the morning. I had changed my trousers to a medium length circle skirt on with high heeled black boots which the school banned months ago. I finished the look of with a skull belt and earrings with the locket showing slightly but remaining mostly hidden. "What do you think you are doing?" She demanded. This is the side of Mrs Wednesday I know, not the all smiling happy one that I saw last time I was at school.

"I am walking into the school 20 minutes after I'm meant to. I will do exams which I will fail and get a job that I will hate every second off. I will be blaming it on you as my teacher you are supposed to guide me to what is right. Which is something you have never done for any child as you hate us as much as we hate you."

I then walked pasted her smiling, her face was set in shock and you could see her mouth moving but no words were coming out. I don't think she expected that type of answer to come out of my mouth.

I walked into my history class as I missed morning tutor, which was a shame but at least it will make afternoon tutor more fun. Our teacher wasn't in class yet but everyone else was, everyone stopped their conversation and took a double take when I came in. But I didn't care I walked pasted them with my head held high, went to the back of the class with a smile on my face. I was glad people kept turning in their chairs to look at me and was whispering to each other about what they were seeing. It made me feel strong and more in control then the last time everyone kept staring at me, this time I wanted them to.

Mr Rode our teacher came in just before the second bell went, he stood in front of the class and looked round. He didn't say anything when he saw me, he thinks personal expression should be welcomed in school. You could come to his lesson in PJ's or a Halloween mask and he wouldn't say a thing. Not the reaction I wanted.

"Sorry I'm late, had to get a video link off one of the other teachers for us to watch. But first things first, homework in please, come on hand them over." Everyone started moving their chairs and getting homework from their bags and pockets. We were supposed to have done a 4-page essay on the Tudors. I did mine before the party with Rose and it been in my bag for the last few days. However I saw it when I went to the shop, so I made sure to rip it into small pieces and put it in the bin with other schoolwork that I had done.

Mr Rode got to me. "Where's your homework Ingrid?" He stretched his hand out to me.

I smiled sweetly at sir. "It grew legs and jumped out of the window when I tried to put it in my bag. It landed in a puddle outside the window and a car ran over it and it died. So sad, bye bye homework, rest in pieces."

Some of the classes snigger, even sir laughed at my comment.

"Funny Ingrid, hand it over so we can watch the video. We are all waiting." His hand was still outstretched, waiting for the homework.

I dropped the smile, tired of playing.

"I didn't do it because I don't see the point of writing about people who died years and years ago. If I wanted to do that, I go to the funeral home and write death certificates. It would be funnier and better than being in this school."

Everybody froze, even sir looked like I just smacked him in the face.

"Right." He took a deep breath and lowered his hand. "After this lesson, you will stay behind, and then I can talk to you about your lack of homework and sarcastic comments."

"I can't sir, or I'll be late for maths." I answered back. "Can't be late for maths, can I?"

Mr Rode just turned around and walked towards the front of the class without saying anything else to me. The look on his face suggested that he was doing his best to stay calm; no teacher want to lose control in front of their class. "Right class, while you watch this video, I want you all to take notes for your coursework, OK? It needs to be at least 2 pages long with all the dates which you will need to remember."

Everybody but me nodded at sir as he turned the light off. Mr Rode turned the video on, and the rest of the class took notes on their paper. I doodled my name all over my pages in different font style as I have no interest with doing the coursework or taking notes.

Mr Rode turn the lights without warning and before the video finished. This made most of the people in the class including me close our eyes due to the suddenly bright light.

"OK class, before you go, does anyone need any help with anything they'd seen or heard?"

"Sir?" I put my hand up, sounding innocently as I could. If only I was. "I've got a question about the video."

"yes Ingrid?" Sir sounded relived that I was sorry for what I said and done. Shame he was very wrong about that.

"I was just wondering, what was the video about? I was doodling and didn't watch any of it. I've got no notes or dates for my coursework, might have well not have turned up today." I leant back in the chair and put my feet on the table with the biggest smile on my face.

Everyone looked at sir to see what he was going to say and how he was going to react. They knew that I was pushing all his buttons and they wanted to see what he would do. They wanted a reaction as much as I did, by the way his face was turning red, he was trying his best not to explode.

"After. School." He spoke each word on its own, "Come. Back. Here. For. An. Hour. Detention." He took a deep breath to get back into control. "Then you can explain yourself."

The bell went but no one in the room moved, their eyes glued on what was happening.

"I can't sir; you must give us 24 hours' notice before I can stay behind after school. Anyway I got plans after school, so I will see you tomorrow. If I can be bothered to come school in the first place." I smirked and walked past him; I saw his mouth drop open in surprise.

I could hear students behind me laughing and snickering, didn't hear anything from my teacher. I wonder if he is still standing in the middle of the class with his mouth open. I smiled to myself, it was fun being bad in school. I walked into my maths class and went straight to the back, thinking of what I could do to disrupt this class. My maths teacher is known to have one of the shortest tempers in school, so this one will be very straight forward and enjoyable.

The phone in my pocket beeped and I knew it was a message from Elizabeth.

I guess you going to be bad in school, it's normal behaviour for vampires to be bad. Have fun but remember not to do anything dangerous or get caught by the slayers.

I couldn't help but smiled at the message, she always seems to know what I'm thinking or doing.

Just then the teacher came into the room. I put my phone in my pocket to stop him from taking it off me, this is the only way I can keep contact with Elizabeth, and for her to keep in contact with me. I know he give the phone to the slayers and not back to me. That was something I couldn't risk it, or everything would be exposed.

"Right then clas..." He stopped mid-word when he spotted me sat at the back of the class; I stuck out like a sore thumb with my 'new' uniform among the sea of other student's uniforms.

"Ingrid Jones! Take those things out of your hair, wipe off your make-up, re-move your jewellery and put your jacket and shoes on my desk. What you are wearing is not school uniform, so don't argue with me."

Everyone looked at me, waiting for me to move. Waiting for me to do what I been asked to do. But I didn't, I just sat there looking at sir, not breaking eye contract with him. He had no control over me, no human can tell me what to do. Not anymore "I won't continue the lesson until you do it Ingrid. That means the rest of the class will have to wait." I still didn't move. I just crossed my arms and smiled at him. Sir groaned and started to handing out the test results from 2 days ago. "Where were you yesterday?" He asked when he reached my table. "You missed class and there was no note of why you were absent."

"I was sick sir. Sick of work. Sick of school. And sick of you." I leant back in my chair, putting my feet on the edge of the table.

Sir muttered something I couldn't catch, and he dropped my test on the table in front of my feet. I put my feet on the ground so I can look at the test paper. 90/100, I was shocked on how well I did. At least this might keep the slayers off my back for a sort while. Any letters the school give me about today, I can just throw in the bin on the way home.

"Right today's lessons..."

"Sir, sir." I shouted out, waving my hand in the air and interrupting him. "You said if I didn't take off my jacket and things you wouldn't start the lesson. I haven't done them yet, so why are you starting the lesson?" I asked in my most innocent voice.

"After school..." He started.

"You need to give me 24 hours." I played back.

"Tomorrow." Sir was really starting to lose his temper.

"I can't sir. Busy with history." I could see I was hitting all the right buttons now.

"THE DAY AFTER." He bellowed. "YOU WILL BE COMING HERE FOR DETESTATION NO MATTER WHAT. SO GO STAND OUTSIDE THE DOOR AND WAIT THERE UNTIL I SAY SO. MOVE!" I got up and walked towards the door, smiling at sir as I did so. I made sure it was a biggest cheesiest smile I could do. "I SAID NOW. GET OUT."

I banged the door behind me, I leant on the wall opposite the door so I could see if anyone came out. Finally, maths was fun. I could hear sir shouting in the classroom at those inside about their test results. Asking how none of them had manage to get more than half marks in their test. Saying how the worse behaved person in class today, aka me, had the highest test in class. He then seemed to calm down and asked if they knew what was wrong with me. No one had an answer for him, of course no one could of guess my whole life had been a lie. Or that I had a whole other family I never knew existed and I was a vampire.

After about 15 minutes my teacher came out to see me, as I was re-applying my eye shadow and lipstick. "Ingrid." He sounded calm now. I didn't like that he was calm, it was no fun. I needed to change that before he went back into the classroom. "I know it's hard for you because Rose isn't here and everything that is going on with Luke and Emma. That you must feel so alone at school. But you don't need to change to get other people to like you and be your friend." He smiled. "You should be yourself and people will like you for who you are. Not someone you are trying to be. This look and your attired it not you who you are is it?" He smiled trying his hardest to be nice to me.

"Sir," I smiled back. "I've got other friends apart form Rose and I am not trying to make people like me. I don't care if other people like me or not. It hasn't been that hard without Rose because I speak and see her all the time. She has only been in hospital a few days and she be out soon enough, so I won't be alone at school. Emma can go and jump into a lake for all I care because of what she did. Luke is lucky he not getting buried in a stranger's garden. You are telling me to be myself, well this is the real me. This is who I really am. If you didn't dress like someone from the 50's then maybe other teachers will talk to you. Then you won't need to eat on your own in the classroom every lunch time. You could eat in the staffroom with the rest of the teachers and have your own friends. Maybe you should focus on yourself and leave me alone."

Sir didn't respond and just turned around and went back into his classroom. His face becoming red again and he was no longer calm. I just stood by the wall with one of my feet on it, just thinking of other things I could do in school today to cause problems.

When the bell went for the end of the lesson, I walked back into the classroom to grab my bag which was left in there. When I went into the classroom, Jake stopped me at my desk before I could grab my bag. Jake is one of Luke's oldest friends, but we have never even said one word to each. What does he want with me now?

"Ingrid, I don't know what is wrong with you, but how you are acting now is ridicules. I know you upset about the Luke and Emma situation. And I am sorry about them and I know I should have told you about them before..."

"Wait you knew about them?!" I interrupted him disbelief, I didn't think anyone knew about Luke and Emma before they came to school. How dare he. "Of course, you knew about them." My eyes narrowed.

"You're one of Luke's oldest friends aren't you. I bet you even helped him hide it from everyone. Hide it from me. Bet you love laughing behind my back with Luke and Emma."

"Look, don't be like that Ingrid. Would you even have believed me if I'd told you? Hey Ingrid, guess what Luke and Emma are stabbing you in the back and are seeing each other. I don't think the reply I would have got from you would be, thank you Jake I believe you, would you?"

"How do you know what I would have said? I might have believed you; you could at least have tired telling me about them." I could feel the anger starting to build up inside me even more. How dare he not tell me about Luke and Emma? He had no right to keep that secret from me. He is no better than Luke and Emma. He made me feel like such an idiot in front of everyone I know. And now he is standing in front of me and speaking to me like he was a friend or something.

"Ingrid, you might be mad at Luke, Emma and now most likely me. You might think this will make it better but..."

"Why don't you just shut your mouth?!" I snapped at him; I was getting tired of hearing his voice. "You had no right to keep that secret from me. You have no right to stand there telling me what I should or shouldn't feel nor how I should react. You can't control me; you can't tell me what to do and expect me to listen." I picked up my bag and the test and stormed out of the room. I heard him sigh as I left.

How dare he? How dare he tell me what to do? How dare he not tell me about Luke and Emma? He knew, he knew everything about them and did nothing. I thought I was going to explode with all the anger I was feeling, I needed to do something, I needed revenge. I stopped in the hallway and sent a message to Elizabeth, asking her if we could do one certain thing to do. Due to the amount of kids in the hall, I knew I wouldn't get caught with my phone.

'I want to go out hunting, I want to kill. I know who I want to be my first human.'

I saw Jake leave the classroom with other students. My first kill.

Chapter 12

I got a reply from Elizabeth during English after I got sent out for not handling the work out when asked by Mr Star. I had a fight with him about it and throw the papers all over the classroom. He even threatened to get Mrs Wednesday to come to the classroom. I challenge him to do it and walked out of the class when I knew he wasn't going to get Mrs Wednesday.

The message I got from Elizabeth was not what I was expecting;

Maybe, only if I think you're ready for it. Not before, they can't be any emotions.

I read the message a couple of times, trying to make sense of it. Emotions? Does she think I will kill someone and regret it? That I will feel guilty after and do something stupid? I won't regret killing Jake after finding out everything he had done to me. I feel no emotions towards him.

By the time school ended, I had been sent out of all my classes, been sent to Mrs Wednesday 3 times, got given 7 more detentions and I had 6 letters in my bags to give to my 'parents', all of which I binned on the way out of school. I lost count on how many people asked me what was going on and why I was acting the way I was. I never answered any of the people that asked, no one would have believed me if I did tell them.

I took the shortcut home which I normally wouldn't do, so that I could clean myself up and look like I did when I left. I didn't want to get caught yet by the Jones's or give them any clues of what I am if they spot the new me.

I got to the house and opened the front door, making sure I had hidden everything in my bag. Before I could shout out anything, a voice greeted me from the kitchen. A voice that did not belong to the slayers.

"Hello dear, you home earlier then you mother said you would be." I froze with my foot hanging in mid-air.

I slowly walked to the kitchen with caution, fighting the urge to run back out of the door. I got to the kitchen and saw Bee, the person who was meant to be my Auntie, but I knew the truth. She was sitting at the table with a cup in her hand and a massive smile on her face when she saw me. I smile I knew I shouldn't trust.

"What are you doing here?" I half shouted at her. I'm not going with them to the America, I thought Mr Jones sorted it out so I can stay here till after the exams. I can't leave Elizabeth here alone with the slayers.

"Ingrid don't talk to your auntie like that" Mrs Jones came in from the back garden. "Your family have come here all the way from America to see us. Anyway, don't forget after the exams you are going over there for a bit, so you need to start being polite to them."

I'm not going to America with them. You are only trying to get rid of me, so that you can go after Elizabeth. Bee and Ted know that I was a vampire, they are more likely to kill me once they had me in their home.

"Where is everyone else?" I asked, I didn't like the idea of not knowing where all the slayers were. They could be near Elizabeth; she could be in danger.

"Ben is still not back from school yet, your dad at work and Ted, Sue and Molly have done some shopping to help your mum." Bee answered. "They are helpful like that, they do little jobs round the house, even though they are still young." She smiled at Mrs Jones which said a lot of things.

That her children were better than me and Ben and they were perfect. The look that Mrs Jones gave back to her agrees with her and how me and Ben will never be as good as them. It was a looked that got shared so often they might as well be saying it out loud.

I snap when I saw the look they shared; I couldn't stop what I was thinking from coming out of my mouth. "Yeah, I completely forgot, they are little angles, aren't they? They do nothing wrong and never will. They are always perfect, yeah right. They are the devil children of the group, not me like everyone think. But you are too blind or stupid to see that. Or you just don't even care that they are both spoiled brats who gets away with everything!"

"INGRID JONES, HOW DA..." Mrs Jones shouted before I slam the door cutting of her voice.

I leant against the door took a quick deep breath to calm myself down and went to my room. I need to keep control of my temper more if I am going to stay hidden. It's fine at school, but it more dangouses here. More chance of me getting caught and found out. I went upstairs to my bedroom and close the door behind me. I was glad that I didn't hear any footsteps following me up the stairs which meant no one was following me. I sat on my bed with my legs crossed and tried to learn some of the vampire language. I kept writing my name and other commons words repetitively till I could do them without the notebook. It took longer than I thought as it didn't look like a real word and I had no idea how to say it. My guess vampire uses this language so that human don't accidently find the book and know all the vampire secrets and weaknesses. I heard the front door bang open and I could hear Sue's and Molly's voice raising from downstairs. I got up quickly and locked the door before they could come into my room and catch me with the book. I was glad that the locked stayed on the door and no one thought to take it off, it meant I have a barrier between me and them. The second I sat on my bed, Sue and Molly started to bang on my door.

"Ingrid, let us in." I heard Molly whine from the other side of the door. She hates it when there a door and she can't get through it.

"We want to play." Sue joined in with the whining.

After years of being in the US with them, I have gotten good at blocking out their voices. I kept my focus on the trying to learn the language, I didn't want to risk sayings something I might regret later.

After 20 minutes of them whining at my door, they shouted

"DAD!"

"What is it darlings?" I heard their dad shouting from somewhere downstairs. He must have come in at the same time at Sue and Molly.

"Ingrid won't let us in her room so we can play with her." They both said together, their voices getting higher and higher.

I hate it when the do that. They think they sound sweet; I think it sound like a cat have just been stood on. There are meant to be 13 and 14, but they act like they are no older than 5.

"Hold on, I am coming up." I heard their dad reply.

I heard footsteps quickly coming up the stairs. They got their dad wrap round their little fingers; he will do anything for them to make them happy.

I heard a knock higher up on the door, so I knew it was their dad doing the knocking.

"Ingrid dear, it's your nice uncle. Can you open the door so the girls can come in and play?" He was talking to me like I was 5, not 15. It made my skin crawl all over with how sickly and sweet he sounded.

"No. Go away I am busy." I answer back, putting the book back in its hiding place just in case they manage to get in. I was half expecting the knock the door to suddenly come off its hinges.

I heard voice coming from the other side of the door but couldn't hear what was being said. It was most likely Ted talking to Mrs Jones about me, I heard more footsteps coming up the stairs once the voices stopped.

"Ingrid. Come down we're going to play a game." Mrs Jones said through my bedroom door. "Now please."

I groaned to myself recognising the tone in her voice. The tone that meant I needed to go downstairs or so she WILL take the door of it hinges. She done it before with Ben's door once so I wouldn't put it past her. I left my phone under the pillow with the book in case it goes off while I am in the room with everyone. I open my door and jammed it shut from the outside, no one can sneak into the room without me catching them. I went down to the living room and everyone was smiling when I walked in.

"Good, you're down. Now we're going to play a family game." Mrs Jones walked forward so she was standing in the middle of everyone.

A messed-up family with killers, vampires and slayers I thought to myself, forcing a smile on my face.

"Can we play twister?" Sue said with a smirk on her face.

"Let play Monopoly instead." Molly said looking at Sue mirroring her smirk.

"No Monopoly twister, I know what you are both thinking." Their mum stepped in before anyone else could.

"Wwwhhhhyyyy?" They both complained at the same time.

I smiled for real this time. I like it when they don't get what they want.

"The reason why is because the last time you played that with a friend, she ended up eating a hotel. And I ended up having to explain to her mum why her daughter was in tears when she was got picked up."

The smile on their faces seem to grow as their mum was telling the story.

"What about Cluedo?" I suggested out loud.

I wanted to get this over and done with and go back upstairs and away from everyone. I felt on edge being in the same room with everyone, like I could get attacked at any moment by anyone in the room. Everyone looked at me in surprise when I spoked up. I guess they didn't expect me to be so 'open' to the idea of playing games with them.

Mrs Jones was the first to speak. "That is a good idea Ingrid, we haven't played that in a while." She walked out of the room and I smiled knowing why we haven't. Whenever me and Ben play, we both cheat and end up auguring till it nearly end up in a fight. After a while Mrs Jones got fed up with out fighting and hid the game away, we tried to find it again but failed.

"Ingrid and Ben, please don't cheat and hurt each other please. It is only game; it doesn't matter who win." Mrs Jones said walking into the room with the banned game in her hand.

"Why would I hurt Ben? He's my little brother and my only sibling." I smiled innocently.

"Yeah you would. You are evil and liar and never take responsibility for anything. You don't care about anyone in the family." Ben tried to say under his breath. He didn't do that good off a job as EVERYONE heard him.

"Ben don't say that about your sister." Mrs Jones spoke in a sharp tone, not taking any notice of where she was placing the game. It fell of the edge of the table, making the pieces go everywhere but no one took any notice of the spillage.

"But mum she is." Ben fought back, something which he doesn't normally do. "I saw her put flour in the shower and..."

"This has been sorted already. We are both in trouble and you think doing this now will get you out of trouble." I taunt Ben, being bored with playing happy family and I wanted to see how far I could push Ben.

"I know that." Ben shot at me.

"Then why are you talking about it now then." I shot back at him.

"STOP IT BOTH OF YOU." Mrs Jones yelled over us.

"WHY?" Ben shouted back at Mrs Jones making everyone jump. Ben has never shouted at his mum before, no matter how mad he been in the past. "I saw her do it. I saw her set the trap; she should be grounded not me. She gets away with everything because she the eldest. No one listens to me when I try and tell them, I know she is guilty."

"How do you?" I challenged him, wanting him to drop himself in it. Come on Ben, open your mouth and dig your grave.

"I saw her because..." You could see Ben mind trying to think up a story.

"Yes?" Bee quizzed standing next to her sister with her arm crossed, getting involve with the drama.

"I'm going to be Colonel Mustard." Ben grumbled in defeat, grabbing the game of the floor and picking up the fallen pieces.

"You never said how you saw Ingrid. How did you see Ingrid set a trap?" Sue asked Ben. She never knew when to drop something, for once I am glad of it.

"Just forget it will you." Ben snapped at Sue. He was starting to lose his temper again and I knew I could make it worse for him.

"Ben don't snap at Sue like that. She only 14 and she was only asking a question that everyone is thinking."

"Don't act like you care, I heard mum talking about you shouting at Aunt Bee. You kept Molly and Sue out of your room just 5 minutes ago."

"Well I am sorry." I forced myself to say through gritted teeth. I cough to clear my throat. "I had a bad day at school, I didn't expect Auntie Bee to be in the kitchen. I was just shocked of seeing her there and I took my anger out on her. I didn't mean to keep Sue and Molly out of the room, I had a bad headache from working so hard at school and I fell asleep on my bed. I only heard the door when Uncle Ted knocked on it and woke me." I forced at smiled at the adults in the room.

"Well this seem like a different Ingrid from the one that came into the kitchen. I am glad that you have apology and I accept it. I know how hard school must be with your exams, you mum explained that's the reason why you can't come to ours straight away." Bee smiled at me and I was starting to feel nausea with all the smiling.

I could see all adult's smiles were as fake as mine and they were only pretending to be part of one big happy family.

"Talking about school." Mrs Jones put her hand in her pocket and pulled out a letter.

My heart stopped beating in my chest when I saw the school logo. When did the school send a letter? Do they know how I been acting today, that I was different? I had to stop myself from bolting from the room in panic, being in a room full of slayers suddenly stopped being fun when everyone could suddenly be exposed. I forced myself to listen to what Mrs Jones had to say. "It came this morning with the post about Ingrid mock test. Not 100% but it says she got the best in her class." Mrs Jones seem to be beaming that her daughter, the one that was always in trouble was doing good at home and in school.

I smiled back at her but not for the same reason. I felt my heart starting to beat normal again, I thought for a second that I had been caught. I notice that I had moved slightly without realising and was now nearer to the door. I don't know if it's a good thing that my mind is on flight mode and not fight mode when it comes to slayers.

I was so focus on the slayers that I forgot that Ben was in the room till he spoke up. "What do you mean she been good since she left hospital. You haven't taken your eye of her since she been back. So clearly there something in your mind that says you can't trust her. How do you even know that letter even real anyway?" Ben demanded, he can never back down from a fight for too long before he got to get involved again.

"What do you think I did? Stole some paper from school, fake it and sent it to the house?" I shot back; I knew I could handle myself when it comes to Ben.

"Ben, I mean it. You need to stop this now." Mrs Jones stood in-between me and Ben, "You both need to behave, you are embarrassing me." Mrs Jones put her hand in her pocket, and I saw her pull out my real phone. She put her hand out towards me with the phone in it. I hesitate for a second before I took it off her, not trusting her action. "It for the results, I am taking a chance on trusting you again."

"That's unfair, you are giving her phone back when she meant to be grounded. Why does it seem like she getting a better deal than me? Why can't you see she is lying to your face and you are believing her?" Ben asked bitterly moving back from his mum.

"Why wouldn't she believe me? I've done nothing wrong unless you can prove otherwise." I hope deep down that he didn't have any prove of Elizabeth being in the house, I didn't know if the slayers would see it was Elizabeth and not me.

"Come on Ben." Mrs Jones was starting to sound worried and deep down so was I. Ben was acting angry towards everyone which even I knew wasn't normal for Ben. "What wrong with you? You've have changed ever since Ingrid went into hospital and come back home. Did she scare you when she was in there? Are you scared about being attacked? Or did you think that your sister was going to be stuck in the hospital for weeks?" Mrs Jones asked walking towards Ben and putting her arm round Ben shoulder. You could see in her face that she seems generally concern about Ben.

"No she didn't scare me." He spoked coldly, his eyes trying to stare deep into mine. "I wish she was still there and wish she gotten even more hurt." His voice was getting louder and louder, pushing his mum arm off his shoulder. "I wish she never came out of the hospital. She has ruined everything I had plans and she is making everything worse being here. She is evil but everyone is too stupid to see that."

"BEN." A voice roar from behind us, everyone in the room fell silent you could hear the clock ticking in the room.

I turned around like everyone else in the room and I saw Mr Jones behind us in the doorway. I saw Ben eyes widen and all the coldness leave his body and replace with regret.

"Yes dad." The coldness had left Ben voice as well.

"Say sorry to your sister and go to your room." His voice was stern and set.

Ben didn't move, he just lowered his eyes to the ground.

"SAY SORRY TO YOUR SISTER AND GO TO YOUR ROOM. I don't want you downstairs till tomorrow no matter what. How dare you say that? HOW DARE YOU? You know what it was like for me and your mother when Ingrid was in hospital. When the police came to the door and said Ingrid and her friends have been attacked. Say sorry and GET UP THEM STAIRS." He bellowed. I took a step back from him, I never seen Mr Jones this angry before. If he is this angry with his son, how bad does he react when it comes to vampires. "Ben." Mr Jones voice brought me back to the present.

"I'm sorry Ingrid." Ben huffed. He made no effect to hide the fact that he wasn't sorry.

Mr Jones pointed to the stairs without speaking. My eyes followed Ben as he went up the stairs. He made sure to stamp on each step and slammed his bedroom door with full force.

"Are you OK Ingrid?" I took my eyes of the stairs and looked at Mr Jones.

I tried to find any sort of emotions in his eyes as he spoke, but I found nothing. Any I did found I could see was fake, he was acting the part of being my dad.

I nodded as I didn't know else to do. One thing I knew is that I wanted to get out of this room and back in my bedroom. "Yeah I'm fine. I am just going to my room for a bit to do some revision. I'll get some food later, I'm not very hungry."

I walked past him and went up the stairs before anyone could say anything. As I went up the stairs, I could hear the adults in the living room talking again. There were on about Bee and Ted going to a hotel to sleep due to the tension in the house. They had to get up early to get a plane back home tomorrow. Thank god they were only hear for one day and I don't need to think about them till after my exams. Look like family night is over without a game being played. I unblocked my door and went into my room without turning my light on. I closed the door and locked it at the same time as I heard the front door closed. I turned around and put my hand over my mouth to stop me screaming out loud and bring people running. Someone was sitting on my bed. Someone was sitting on my bed in the pitch black. I saw they had the vampire book in their hand. I knew the door was blocked still when I came in, so how was it possible. Does Ben know I was a vampire, is that why he was acting the way he was?

I scrambled for the light switch, I couldn't find it at first and I was starting to panic. I found the light switch and I turned it on, flooding my room with a bright light.

"Did I scare you?" Asked Elizabeth with a small laugh as she got off my bed. It wasn't Ben with the book, for a split second I thought I had been caught.

"Could you make me jump any higher?" I checked I locked the door as I walked towards her, so the slayers didn't catch us. "How did you even get in here anyway; the door was jammed shut?"

"I used the window as you never lock it, like I use the roof instead of the ladder when it comes to the den." Elizabeth mouth went into a smirk. "I will admit it not the first time I done it. I had to wait a few days after you came back from the hospital before I could check. Nearly got caught by you, but I learnt some good trick."

I suddenly remember the noise I heard in my bedroom when I got back home from the hospital. It was Elizabeth, I thought I heard something that day.

"Should I be worried that you can appear in my room without me knowing."

"Trust me, I can do worse than suddenly appearing in a room." Elizabeth voice was steady as she spoke, making me not want to ask what she meant. "You need to hide the book and the phone in a better. I found it on my first look, which means that the slayers will find it without any trouble.

"I wasn't planning on keeping them there, I just shoved them there out of sight. I got a better place to put it."

I took the book and the phone of her and she watch me as I pulled my rug to one side. I could see the confusion in her eyes, as I pulled one of the floorboards up and laid it on the side. I broke the board a couple of weeks ago and kept it secret in case I needed to hide anything from anyone. I place the book in the gap, making sure everything was back in place after. I hid the phone in one of my inside pockets, you wouldn't know it was there by looking at it.

Elizabeth didn't say a word while I was hiding the book, she just had an impress smile on her face. When I was done, I stood up and Elizabeth spoked "Ok I give you points, that is a good place." I smiled and I sat on my bed, Elizabeth sat next to me with her legs crossed under her. "I here to speak to you about your text. I thought it be better to explain it in person then by text."

I nodded, Jake face appearing in my mind, the anger building up in me again.

"Can I ask you something first? About you and drinking blood? About how it works if…"

"If I wasn't the one that was attacked, how I drink blood? Do I get my fangs when you get yours as you were the one that got attacked? Your life was the one that got threaten but mine wasn't? Elizabeth figured without me asking.

I simply nodded my eyes not leaving Elizabeth.

"Like the saying says, it's a twin thing. In the vampire word when something happens to one twin, it happens to the other. You get a headache for no reason; you feel mad at nothing or you suddenly got a bolt of energy from nowhere. We are linked from the moment we were born to right this second. So because you are getting your fangs, I will get mine at the same time as well as other skills that link us. And I know who you want to kill tonight as well."

"How can you know who I want to kill?" I answered my own question before Elizabeth could. "You been followed me to school, didn't you?"

Elizabeth nodded, "I wanted to make sure went to school and not at the den. I wasn't planning on keeping an eye on you the whole day, but I got curious on what you were going to do as I saw your new look…. And I heard what was said to you in the classroom. About your ex and you text me straight after. I didn't need to work hard to work out what you were thinking and planning. I was standing by the school gate away from any windows, so no one thought it was you. I heard everything that was said between you and I would be mad as well. I would be planning the same things as you."

"So can we go hunting tonight?" I ask eagerly, glad that Elizabeth would be thinking the same as me. I needed to get out of this house, I needed to get away from the slayers. I hated being nice to them and pretending like I don't know anything when I know evening.

Elizabeth shook her head keeping her head low.

"Why not?" I snapped back, immediately regretted it after.

I opened my mouth to say sorry when Elizabeth put her hand up stopping me.

"You don't need to say sorry, like I said I know how you feel. But I have my reasons which you need to listen to and try and understand them. You are mad and like most things, doing thing when you are mad is never a good idea. You might end up regretting it later and there be no turning back. We don't know what blood would agree with you as not every vampire can drink all blood type. The last thing we need is you getting blood poisoning and getting sick. You don't even know how to hunt; you can't go up to someone and ask for them to open a vein for you to drink from."

"So...." I knew this was leading somewhere, but I could see where if I wasn't allowed to go out hunting.

"So tonight we are going back to the den to fine out blood you like. The blood will be both human and animal."

"Animal, I didn't think we could drink animal blood? The book said that on human blood can take away blood cravings." I questioned.

"You right that human blood is linked to the blood craving, but we do still drink animal blood. I grew up with it as part of my diet and it can be handy when you don't have access to human blood. If you get hurt, then human blood will heal you better then animal blood and not every animal blood taste nice. Cow's blood is my favourite blood." Elizabeth shift so was fully facing me.

"So we are we going to a farm for blood?" I was still clueless with what Elizabeth was planning.

"No, we are going back to the den where I have cups of blood set up. You can try small amount of blood, so we know what you like and what you don't. I got most of the blood from my grandparents blood supply for the taste test." She lowered her eyes and I caught something was wrong.

"But you don't have all the blood." I felt a deep sense of fear in my stomach

"No we don't have any AB- Blood as only 1% of the population have it, so it hard to find. It's the only one that is missing and there a limited supply in this village." She raised her eyes and took a deep breath. "Ben and Sue are blood type AB-, one of them need to die for their blood."

Chapter 13

"We need one of them for blood?" I manged to repeat after a few moments of silence, justifying my sense of fear. I wanted to drink blood, to get revenge but Sue and Ben were not on my list. The get on my nerve and we fight but they were too young to die. "How do you even know what their blood type is, you never met them?"

I got off the bed and went to the window, the dark street empty below me. Elizabeth remained sitting on my bed.

"I can smell their blood, something you can try and learn tonight. Vampires have a high sense of smell and hearing which we use to hunt. I don't want to go out of the village to look for blood and there aren't many people in the village whose blood we can us. Because this is a small village, you know everyone whose blood we can use."

"Why Sue or Ben? Can't it be an adult? They are only kids."

"Them being children might help us as it be easier to deal with them than a fully grown adult. But part of me wants to use them so the slayers know what it like to lose someone they love. It's up to you who we use, you the one who will be drinking the blood as well."

I looked at Elizabeth, thinking of an answer. I could see Elizabeth was hurt; she has known the pain of lose all her life. Too have the power and knowledge to cause pain to those who have cause you pain. An eye for an eye, the only thing that was stopping that was me. Could I agree to use Ben or Sue, to take away someone from the slayers like they did to me?

I opened my mouth, even though I didn't know what I was going to answers. I was saved by my real phone beeping in my pocket, saving me for now from an answer.

I took the phone out of my pocket and I was so happy to see that it came from Rose. I clicked it without hesitation:

Hey, how come you haven't been back to the hospital? I have not seen Lily since you were here, it seems like you have both disappeared. Have you fallen out with me? Because Lily was acting weird? I need to see you; I need to speak to you about Luke and Emma. Somethings is happening that doesn't make any sense. Please.

I looked up from my phone and saw Elizabeth was standing in front of me. I didn't even notice or hear Elizabeth moving, I knew she had read the message from Rose.

"You can't go to the hospital and see her. The slayers aren't going to let you leave because they have grounded you. I don't think you getting caught escaping again is going to go down well, you can risk them catching on."

"Why do you want me to stay trap in this house? A house which is own by our parent's killer. The only reason why I am grounded is because Ben saw you set the flour trap."

"I know and there is a reason for that. Between Lily and the slayers, the slayers are the safest at this moment. The slayers are not going to suddenly attack you in the open, not with their son being in the house. I have no idea how Lily will react to you near her sister. I'm sorry but you can't go to the hospital to see Rose."

"Yes I can and I am." I snapped, not caring this time. "I know Lily knows I am a vampire or at least that I attacked Luke and Emma at the party. I have no idea how much Luke and Emma knows but even I know that's a bad idea if they know anything. She mentioned

Luke and Emma in the text which means that something has happened. And I don't know about you, but I think I might remember something like someone biting my neck"

Elizabeth opened her mouth and closed it again without saying anything. She looked at the door and back at me with a sighed in defeat.

"You're right. We need to find out what Luke and Emma know, I forgot about them. We need to get you ungrounded first and get you to the hospital."

"I'm going to the hospital to see my friend, not to get information out of her." I wasn't going to use Rose for anything.

"I know you worried about your friend, but I am worried about you. Keep the phone I gave you on you. You might have got your real phone back, but that won't stop them checking it." She handed me the phone that I left with the book.

"How do you know I got the phone back? You didn't sneak downstairs, did you? Never mind me being careful, what would have happened if you got caught by any of the slayers?"

"I never left your room, I heard everything from here. Vampires have got good hearing; we can hear people and things that are far away. You will be surprise what skills you will developed now that your fangs are coming in, how all your senses will improve and develop more. From hearing, seeing, smelling and even speed."

"Sense that will help me hunt and kill, to drink human blood." Part of my stomach dropped as I spoke.

I wanted to drink blood; I suddenly didn't like the idea of killing someone so close to me. Even with Elizabeth idea of revenge and eye for an eye with the slayers.

I don't know if Elizabeth finally figure out what I was feeling, or she could see something in my face.

"I got an idea how to make it easy for you. There only a small number of people who I can use for blood. Unfortunately because it's a small village, you know everyone or someone who is linked to them. So pick a number and hopefully you will never find out who they are. I will try and keep you distanced from the killing. The only thing you need to do is pick a number between 1 and 6."

"I pick 3."

I didn't want to take long thinking about who I had just sentence to death for their blood.

She nodded and I went to leave the room to face the slayers. I knew I didn't need to ask her to hide as I knew she had already left the room through the window. I knew Elizabeth could look after herself with the slayers, I needed to learn to be able to look after myself when it came to them.

I walked down the stairs and took a deep breath when I got to the bottom. I could hear the TV playing in the living room and I knew that the slayers were in there. I walked in and the Jones turned the TV off when they saw me.

"Ingrid, how are you? Are you OK with everything that happened earlier with what Ben said?" Mr Jones stood up and walked towards me as he spoke.

"Yeah I will be fine, don't worry." I walked pasted him and towards Mrs Jones. "Mum." I had to force the word out of my mouth. "I need some fresh air; can I go to and see Rose at the hospital please?"

"No you can't go and see Rose. I still don't know who put the flour in the shower and I said you can't go out."

"I know you told me I couldn't see Rose, but I need to see her. She thinks I have fallen out with her as I've not seen her at all like I promised. Lily has stopped seeing her, so she is all on her own now. I hated being in the hospital and I know if I were there, Rose would see me every day after school. You know I couldn't have put the flour in the shower, you saw me come through the front door and it's not like I could leave school in the middle of the day. I need to get out of this house, I need to clear my head after everything that been happening. Please."

She looked at her husband who had now sat down next to her. Her smiled at him and he smiled back with a small chuckle.

"Well OK, you can go and see Rose." I smiled in victory and was going to walk out of the room when she spoke again. "But your dad will drop you off at the hospital and pick you back up again straight after. Just make sure Ben doesn't find out I back down with you, we wouldn't hear the end of it otherwise."

I ran out of the room and grabbed my things before they changed their mind. I was by the car when Mr Jones came out and I jumped into the passenger seat as soon as the car was opened. I kept my eyes out of the window as I watch the sun go down, it didn't realise how late it was.

"You sure you OK after what Ben said?" He asked after 5 minutes, breaking the silence in the car.

"Yeah I'm fine." Saying those words again were as hard as it was a few days ago at school. I kept my eyes on the window, not wanting to look at him.

"Ingrid, can you look at me please for a moment?" I forced my eyes away from the window and looked at him for the first time since I got into the car. "Ingrid I am worried about you and Ben. He shouldn't have said those things to you, but both of you have been acting strange. You know you can speak to me and your mum about anything, you don't need to keep any secrets from us. We care for you both the same, you are my children."

He smiled and I simply nodded and went back to looking out of the window. His words going around my head, that he cared about me and I don't need to keep secrets from him. My whole life was full of secrets and lies, everything I thought I knew turned out to be untrue. Why would he care if his own flesh and blood hated the monster that lived in the house? I thought he would be proud of Ben and how he been acting.

He pulled up outside the hospital and I got out of the car as fast as I could. I was starting to feel claustrophobia and I needed to get out of the car so I could breathe again. I took a few steps forward when I heard the car window open behind me. I turned and Mr Jones lent across the passage seat so he could speak to me.

"I pick you up in 20 minutes. It can't be any longer or Ben going to figure out that we have gone. OK?"

I nodded and walked straight towards the hospital before I could be stopped again. Glad I got to Rose's room without anyone stopping me or asking questions. I remember where Rose room was from last time, so I didn't need to ask anyone for direction to get there. I walked into the room without knocking, shock when I saw a doctor was with her. I stood by the door as the doctor had a needle in her arm and was taking blood from Rose.

"Are you OK Rose?"

I don't know why I should be surprise that a doctor was seeing Rose as she was in the hospital. But it looked like they were doing more test, which means she won't be out of the hospital anytime soon. It would have been good to have a second person on my side with everything that has been going on.

"Yeah, I'm fine. I am so glad that you came. Ow" She looked at the needle that was still in her. My eyes were still locked on her arm and the needle. "Don't worry about the needle. They just need to do some more test; I am getting sick of test in this place. I am even being made to do school test as I am being tested myself." She laughed and I felt more relax as I walked towards Rose and sat next to her on the bed.

I suddenly became aware of a smell that was in the room. The smell was sweet, and I suddenly realise how hungry I was as I haven't had anything to eat in ages. The smell reminded me of fresh baked goods, I looked around Rose's room for where the small was coming from. The smell was making me even more hungry and I was going to nick what smelled so good. However as I looked around the room, I could not locate where the smell was coming from.

"Put a tissue on your arm, if it doesn't stop bleeding in 5 minutes, shout me OK?" I heard the doctor say.

I looked down at Rose's arm he removed the needle from her arm. A small amount of blood came out of the small needle mark. A dreaded feeling crept over me as it dawned on me what the smell was. It was Rose's blood. Her blood was the scent that was making me hungry, I felt my eyes lock onto the blood as it ran down her arm slightly.

"Yeah I will." Rose replied as she grabbed some tissue and put it over the needle mark, however this didn't stop the blood coming through.

I forced my eyes on Rose's face, glad that Rose didn't notice me staring at the blood. I tried to focus on Rose as she was fiddling with something next to her and not on her blood. I could feel the blood craving starting to creep into my mind and body. It felt like someone was stabbing my stomach with sharp sudden pain coming from nowhere then going again and coming back. It was becoming hard to focus on Rose as my eyes wouldn't stop being blurry and I could feel my throat starting to burn and become dry.

I swallowed to try and take control over the dryness of my throat so I could speak

"So why do you need more test?"

I was grateful that Rose didn't seem to notice that I wasn't acting like myself.

"It's nothing major, they think the bleeding to my head might have caused me to have anemia. It's annoying as it makes me tired all the time and I can do without the headaches when I am trying to do schoolwork."

I nodded and smiled at her, the blood craving becoming weaker. The pain in my stomach was becoming less painful and less frequent. My eyes were becoming sharper and my throat was becoming less dry and I found I could speak easier.

"Has your arm stop bleeding yet?" I asked, knowing that it had as I could no longer smell the blood.

She looked at her arm and removed the tissue.

"Yeah it has, I can get rid of this then." She chucked the blood cover tissue in the bin and I stopped my eyes following it.

"So why haven't you been down?" She asked. "Have I done something wrong the last time you came to see me?"

"What no. I was grounded, I am still grounded. There was a flour trap in the shower and my mum." I tried to not make it obvious that the word mum was hard to say. "Got caught in it and covered."

Rose smiled and I was glad to see her happy. "Let me guess who the guilty one."

"It wasn't me, for once I am innocent." I did a cross over my heart with a smile. It was my secret twin sister I thought to myself, making my smile more genuine.

"You? Innocent? That makes a change. You are normally the one that causes all the trouble."

"No I'm not." I pushed her slightly and she returned the favour by sticking her tongue out. It felt nice to do something so normal after everything that's been happening. I leant back slightly with my hand behind me on the bed, glad that I don't need to feel on edge while I was here.

"Out of everyone in our group, I am the most innocent." The happy feeling left me when I remember the only reason why Elizabeth allowed me to come to see Rose was to find out about Emma and Luke. "Rose?" You could hear the change in my voice. "Why do you want to talk to me about Emma and Luke? I thought you wasn't friend with them, I thought you hated them?"

Due to everyone thinking it was someone else attacked us, was Rose now friend with the people that actually attacked her.

"What no, not after everything they did. No I am not friend with them." Rose sounded almost offended. "I've not spoken to them since they been here. I am only speaking about them because of what they said to the police and…"

"The police?" I interrupted her, sitting up straight. "What about the police?"

Elizabeth never mention anything about the police and I never thought to ask about them.

"The police have been speaking to everyone about the attack. But for some reason, Luke and Emma have changed their story about 2 people coming to attack us."

"What do you mean?" I was really starting panic now; I could feel my breathing getting faster, but I didn't care. "When did the police came? What do you mean Luke and Emma change their stories about the attack?"

Have they told the police about me? Are me and Elizabeth in danger of being found out?

"The police only came yesterday to speak to us, it took them long enough. The police were saying that they thought it was strange how two strangers burst into house where they were loads of people who have all just left. That out of all the houses on the street, they only target a house that had teenagers and no adult. It seems like good timing and the police think the timing was too good.

"What did you say? What did Luke and Emma say?"

I was now worried and scared. How could me and Elizabeth prove to the police that it was 2 strangers and not me?

"I told them the truth. I told them that I don't know why two strangers would attack us. That they must have took a chance and attacked the house. I don't know why and isn't that the police job to find out. I remember the front door opening and that all. That what I told the police when they asked, that I don't remember any of the faces of the attackers."

"And Lily?" I asked, I had no idea which side Lily was on as she knew about me and she didn't hide that she didn't want me anyway near her sister.

"She said the same thing to police as me. That it was 2 strangers who attacked us after the party. The strange things was the way she said it, it was weird. I heard her by chance, and it sounded like she didn't believe in the word she was saying. Like she was a robot and she was programmed to say it."

"What about Luke and Emma, what did they say? You said that they change their stories?"

I was glad that I didn't need to worry about Lily, at least not for the time being.

"You not going to believe what they said to the police. They told that it was a vampire that attacked us. They were saying how they are real." She hesitation for a second. "and that the attacker is someone in group. Ingrid, they told the police it was one of us."

I felt my body go ice cold with fear and I could feel my body starting to shake. Luke and Emma remember everything I did.

"What did the police say when Luke and Emma said it was a vampire, that it was one of us?" I put hands in my lap to stop it being noticeable that I was shaking.

"They think they are still in shock which is why they think it was a vampire. The weird things is, is that they are not ruling out the possibility that it was one of us. I told them it is ridiculous to think it was someone at the house. Haven't the police spoken to you yet, I thought with you being at home you would have been the first to have been spoken to?"

"No I have spoken to the police yet. Maybe they came here because most people are here."

The longer they take to see me, the more time I have to speak to Elizabeth. I thought to myself, I have no idea what to do with the police. I tighten my hand together more in my lap, Rose seem to not have notice me acting strange.

"Maybe they come and see you tomorrow or the day after. Just tell them the truth and you should have nothing to worry about."

"Yeah, they might come in the next few days. I know I have nothing to worry about." I knew as I was saying the words that me telling the truth would not be possible. How could I turn around to the police and tell them what really happen? That Luke and Emma attacked us. That I was a vampire and I bit Luke and Emma after they attacked us. That my twin sister was in the window watching it all and was the one who made up the cover story. Even thinking it sounded it crazy, never mind saying it out loud to the police. "Why hasn't Lily been to see you?" I wanted to forget about the police, I needed to forget about the police. "You said that she not been to see you either. Why is that? I thought with how she was acting last time she was here; she be camped outside the door."

"I thought she be doing the same things. My parents have come and see me every day, but Lily hasn't seen me since you were here last. When I asked about her, they said since she came out of the hospital, she locked herself in her room. She hardly leaves her room unless she is getting something to eat or drink. When my parents manage to speak to her during a trip out of her room, she was acting so cryptic with them. She said she was going to stay at home for a few weeks, maybe months till she knows for sure. She wouldn't explain any more than that and locked herself back in her room. My parents think she in shock still like Luke and Emma. They think she scared that if she leaves to go back to school, the people will attack the house again."

More likely she scared of me and what I am. I was fully aware why Lily was acting weird and why she won't go back to the university. Rose talking brought be back to what she was saying and out of my own mind. "The main things that stand out about Lily is the type of food she keeps eating is strange."

"What do you mean the type of food she is eating is strange?" Now she got my attention.

"Well, all the food she is eating at the moment has some sort of garlic in it. If it doesn't have garlic in it, then my parents said she will add it to it.

"What do you mean? Why is she doing this?" I could hide the panic in my voice now. I knew that garlic is known to effect vampires and I know Lily knows the truth about me.

"Like I said, everything she is eating have garlic in it. Do you know what I think Ingrid?" She was suddenly serious.

I felt the cold fear came back into my body.

"What do you think?"

"I think she thinks the attackers were vampire. That she has the same fear as Luke and Emma."

"Why would she think that? Why would any of them think it was a vampire that attacked us?"

How can't Rose hear the panic in my voice? Why is everyone suddenly talking about vampires?

"I think the people that attacked us were dressed up as vampires. They hid their faces with masks or something so that we didn't know who they were. Because they were in shock, their minds believed that they were real vampires. Maybe their brain is trying make sense of everything, but it is really tricking them. I think we not been affected by it because we are always watching horror movies all the time. What do you think?"

"Yeah that could be what's happening with everyone. I don't remember anything to do with vampires or anything to do with the attack to be honest."

"That's the same as me then, that will be a very short statement." She smiled reassuring.

I tried to return it, but I don't know if I made it seem real. I was still panicking; I knew I needed to speak to Elizabeth before the police came to see me. I had no idea what to say apart from the basic information I got told after I woke and what other people had said.

I opened my mouth to ask more questions about what she said to people as I wanted my story to be like hers. The doctor walked in without knocking before I had a chance to say anything.

"Sorry for walking in, I didn't realise your guest was here still. Rose I'm just updating you on your blood. You will need another single blood transfusion, however because you and your sister have the rare blood type of AB-. We need to wait till the blood comes from another hospital before you can have it as you have had so much already. So they will be a delay in your discharge am afraid." He left with an apologetic smile and closed the door behind him.

Rose groaned and laid down on the bed, sticking her legs up on my lap.

"Great, I need to stay here because my blood is so rare, there not a single drop left in this hospital because of how much I have already had. Great, just when I thought I could escape out of this place like you."

She laughed but it sounded wrong, like I was underwater and the sounded was getting lower and lower. My head was spinning making my stomach heaving. Rose and Lily had the blood that Elizabeth needed. Elizabeth would have known that I wouldn't pick Lily or Rose by choice, but did I pick them by mistake? Have I sent my friend to her death by my twin? I know knew who 4 of them were, Rose, Lily, Ben and Sue. Who was the 5th person who had the blood we needed; would I feel more or less guilty if Elizabeth killed them?

"I need to go." I said suddenly, I jumped off the bed and pushing Elizabeth leg off me. "I need to leave now I'm sorry." I nearly lost my footing as I took a few steps forwards.

"What?" Rose sat up. "Why?" She wined. "Where are you going?" She looked hurt as I stood in front of her.

"I'm sorry Rose, I'm grounded remember. I am only allowed here for 10 minutes and my dad is outside waiting for me. I don't think he be very happy if I leave him out there and he freezes to death. Don't worry I will hopefully see you tomorrow." If you are not dead by the end of the night because of me. I walked out of the room, but then ran down the corridor. I didn't care if people were looking at me. I needed to find Elizabeth, I needed to know who I killed. Why didn't I think about asking who the people were who were on the list? I could have just sentence Rose and Lily to death without realising.

I ran out of the hospital door and froze, my legs feeling like jelly. Standing at the bottom of the hospital path was Elizabeth. She was staring up at the hospital windows, the window that lead into Rose's room.

Chapter 14

"Please tell me you not here to get Rose's blood?" I begged her as she stood there in silence. "I don't want you to kill Rose or Lily. I want someone else if it them." I took a few steps forwards till I was in front of her face.

"You don't need to change your mind, it not your friend or your sister. So you don't need to worry about your friend. It's not any of the slayer's family either, so they don't get to know what it like to lose someone they care about."

"Why are you here then?" I was somewhat happy that it wasn't Rose or Lily. However due to the size of the village, everyone knows everyone. "Who is it then? Who are you going to kill?"

Elizabeth opened her mouth but then suddenly looked behind her and down the road that lead to the hospital. "He is coming, we can't be seen together. Meet me at the den at midnight. I can example more than."

She took a quick look up at the hospital window and walked off into the darkness. The sudden bright lights of the headlight blinded me for a second from the side and I took a step back.

Mr Jones car pulled up in front of me, he rolled down driver window.

"What are you doing out early?" He seemed surprise to see me outside the hospital already. "You still have 10 minutes before you needed to come out. I was going to let you stay out later if you wanted. I was just going to say to your mother that you got stuck in traffic." He laughed slightly at his own joke as I got into the car. "The doctor was with her and doing test, so I wasn't allowed to stay long." At least what I was saying was partly true."

"OK, maybe next time you can stay longer." He seemed to have believe me and he started the car and started to drive home.

I kept my eyes out of the window and not say anything to Mr Jones as he drove. Who at this moment was Elizabeth targeting due to their blood? Why the more I think about it, the less I feel bad about it? I thought I feel some sort of guilt, but by the car pulled up outside the house, it was completely gone.

I walked through the door and went straight up the stairs.

"I am tired, I'm going straight to bed."

Neither of them said anything and I got back to my room without any problem. I didn't know what to do while waiting for midnight, I kept pacing the room and ended up laying down on my bed. I needed to speak to Elizabeth about what is going to happen tonight, about the person who going to be killed. Will they be missed? Will anyone notice them gone? Why do I not care about who being killed, a human life?

I turned my head and looked at the rug in the middle of my room. I can't rely on Elizabeth for everyone question I have. I need to show her that I can think for myself and read the book and learn for myself.

I swung my feet off my bed and opened the floorboard and got the book out. I sat on my bed and checked each page till I find the page I needed. I found it near the beginning of the book.

Blood drinking

You don't need to be 18 to be able to drink blood and you don't need to have your fangs to drink blood either. Fresh blood is better for vampires and most blood from outside the source can only last up to 24 hours depending how it is stored.

All vampire can drink human or animal blood, however human blood has better benefits then animal. You will heal faster with human blood, be stronger than those who drink animal and your senses will be more heighten.

Before you drink any type of blood, you need to find out what blood agrees with you. A high dose of blood that doesn't agree with you will make you week and vulnerable to any form of attacks. If you drink a blood that doesn't agree with you, then you will ill straight away. However if you are not ill, then you can carry on drinking that type of blood.

"At least that example why Elizabeth won't let me kill Jake yet." I find myself muttering to myself. I carried on with the reading, wanting to know more.

Some rare vampires can only drink one type of blood while some can drink all types of human blood. As a vampire age, their tolerance to blood changes and they may find out they can drink more blood or less blood then when they first tried them.

Vampire don't feel any emotions from the human they are feeding from. Depending on how the vampire have been brought up, they may feel emotions to a human if the blood has been spilled and not drank from. This is rare and they must be some sort of connections between the human or their family. Once a vampire starts experiencing blood craving, they will find that any emotions connected to human will start to fade. This means that they may find themselves caring about humans they know but stop caring about strangers and people they have strong feeling of hate for. This will fluctuate for a while before it settles and there is a very little connections between human and vampires.

I closed the book and looked at the cover, taking in all the information. I don't care about the person who Elizabeth killing because they are a stranger to me. They might always be a stranger and I will never feel anything. Soon I will stop feeling any type of emotions for all humans which made me feel strange and I don't know if I like the idea of not feeling anything. I don't care about not feeling anything for a stranger, but I still want to care for my friends. I don't know if I want to be the vampire that can drink one type of blood or any type of blood.

I felt my body freeze when I suddenly heard footsteps coming up the stairs near the top.

I chuck the book under the pillow again and turned off the light. I stared at the door and listen to the sound outside of it. The footsteps got to the top of the starts and I heard them heading towards my door. I laid down with my back to the door and place the cover over me. I could feel my breath getting faster as I heard the steps getting closer. I cursed myself that I didn't lock the door when I got back to my room, suddenly realising that the slayers could have suddenly walked in while I had the book out.

I heard my door open and I had to force my breathing to slow down as the hallway light lit up part of my bedroom. I kept my eyes staring at the wall and I could see the silhouettes of the slayers against my wall. I saw one of them taking a small step forward before going back to standing in the doorway.

"She fast asleep, thank god." I heard Mr Jones whispered. He must have been the one that step into my room briefly. "I didn't think that would have after everything that happened earlier with Ben. Do you think Ben has found out the truth about Ingrid? About what she really is?"

My breath caught in my throat for a second before I made myself breath normally again, I didn't want to get caught awake. Does Ben know I am a vampire? Is that why he was saying all those things to me earlier?

"No, Ben doesn't know anything, and he won't for a long time. He just mad at the world at the moment. He just been having problems at school and I don't think me grounding him and treating Ingrid different since she been back. He could have snapped at anyone, Ingrid just got caught in the middle." Mrs Jones whispered back. "You need to relax."

I had to stop myself sighing in relief, I was glad that Ben was still in the dark with everything that is happening.

"I will be more relax once Elizabeth been dealt with. She nearly got close to Ingrid at the party and we can't risk that happening. We might not be so lucky next time if Ingrid sees her, she will ask questions she mustn't know the answer too. Once Elizabeth is gone with the rest of the Blazes, we can go back to hiding Ingrid. We made the mistake of not knowing that Ingrid was a twin, but that will soon be corrected."

The slayers closed the door, putting my bedroom back into darkness and I heard their footsteps walking away. I stayed frozen under the cover, not be able to move any part of my body. There were going to kill Elizabeth. They were going to kill Elizabeth and our grandparents. I forced my body to move and pushed my covers off me and onto the floor. My eyes fell on my clock, the red-light flashes 22:30 in the dark room. It wasn't time to meet Elizabeth yet, but I couldn't stay in the house knowing she was in danger. She needed to know the slayers are going to go after her and everyone else in our family.

I made sure to hide the book in my floor and used pillows and blankets to make a dummy to replace me in bed. I didn't want the slayers to check up on me and notice the bed was empty. I didn't want to risk locking my door in case they knock the door down and then I will be in trouble.

I climbed out of my window, keeping an eye out people as I knew I could get caught any second. I made it out of the house without being seen and headed straight towards the park and the den. I had to keep an extra eye out for people, so I didn't get caught as there was still so many people out and about. It was completely different from when I am walking around at 2 in the morning, it felt crowed somehow and I felt more exposed.

I got to the park gate at 10.45 and I notice that there were still people there. I saw that there were all teenagers and there were all by the swings and messing around on them. I put my hood up and tried to hide my face as much as possible and walked on the side of the part furthest away from them. I didn't want any of them to see my face, I didn't know who I could trust, and I don't want anyone to know I was here. There have been a set of slayers based at the park before and there could be more. However when I got to the edge of the park and away from them, curiosity got the better of me and I turned around to see who were at the park.

My eyes fell on one of the teenager lads that was standing on one of the swings and was trying to swing. All the anger I felt before came flooding back into my body. Jake was one of the people at the park. I found myself taking a step forwards, not caring who else was at the park, just that Jake was one of them. I wanted the power from the party to come back so I could bite him.

Not caring if I became ill from his blood. I can never forgive him for embarrassing me in front of the whole school, for keeping Luke and Emma a secret from me.

I suddenly felt someone grabbing my arm from behind. I swung round with a fist but dropped it when I saw it was only Elizabeth.

"What are you doing here so early? It not midnight yet." She didn't seem to care that I could have hurt her when she grabbed me like that. Even though I know with the skills Elizabeth have, I would be the one be in the floor not her.

I opened my mouth to explain what I heard from the slayers when I spotted something on Elizabeth sleeve. Blood, fresh blood.

Elizabeth seem tense when she followed my eye line and relax when she looked at her.

"Ow, don't worry, its only cow's blood. I got thirsty setting everything up and had a sneaky taste." She smiled and I couldn't help but laugh. Only Elizabeth could make a conversation about blood sound normal. Elizabeth smiled and walked towards the wood and I followed her. "So why are you here so early? What happened at the hospital? I didn't have time to ask you before the slayer came."

We got to the wood but this time I had no problem with walking in. Between the house and the woods, the woods felt safer.

"Rose said that Luke and Emma told the police it was a vampire, and..."

"I know about the police. I heard one of the police officers talking to Luke's mum about it. A friend of mine was at the house when they came, he said he will sort them out while he here."

"Wait, what friend?" I don't know why I should be surprised that Elizabeth had friend. "Is he a vampire like us or a human?"

"He a vampire, his family is close to ours so it's not unusually for him to visit for a few days. He normal hides at ours if he is in trouble which he gets into a lot. He said he said he will stay to help with the slayers, he worried about me being with you all the time as you grew up with the slayers. He was the one who called the den when you were there, he knew I was alone and wanted to make sure I was safe. He very protects of me as our grandparents grew up together, he is a good vampire to have on your side in a fight."

"I heard the slayers talking about you and our grandparents. They were saying they want to make sure you were dealt with as you and…"

"That they want to kill me and wipe out the Blazes. I can figure that out already by their history. While I been keeping an eye on you, I been keeping an eye on the slayers and what they been saying to each other. Which when you are not in the house, tends to be about killing me and our grandparents."

"Do they know that they are in danger?" I asked, still worried about Elizabeth being in danger as she doesn't seem bothered about what I heard.

"Our grandparents, no and they still don't know about you yet. I don't know how to explain to them that I made them move here for you and that you back in the family."

We got to the clearing and Elizabeth opened the panel to the den. She looked at me, "You coming?" and jumped into the den.

I followed her and jumped down the hole without any hesitation. I was starting to like this way into the den. The den was just as amazing as the first time I came here. The only different this time however was that there were 2 long tables with cups full of red liquid. I knew straight away it was blood in each cup. I saw the cups were sealed and looked air tight. I knew that the cups much be deigned to keep the blood fresh and useable.

I had a closer look at each cup and saw that each cup had a peel-off label. The cups I were looking at had animals name on. Cow, swan, dog, rat, bear, fox, deer and rabbet. I notice that each animal had 2 cups of blood each. Some of the cups didn't sound bad, however some of them I would never have thought of drinking.

I slowly walked towards the other table, knowing what type of blood was on this table. Each cup had the blood type written on it, there were both negative and positive of each blood type. My eyes fell on the AB- cup and I saw that it was the fullest.

"Do you have any questions before we begin?" I notice that Elizabeth was standing by the animal blood, I was too busy looking at all the blood that I forgot about her.

"Yeah. A couple. Can we drink all animal, I mean swan and rats blood doesn't sound very nice?" I asked in disbelieve. Rats blood doesn't really sound that nice and it wouldn't be the first animal I would fancy drinking.

"Vampire can drink all mammal blood; some are just harder to get then others. I couldn't get every animal in the world in the den, so I got the ones I thought would be the most helpful. I would be careful with swan, it a nice taste but you don't want to get caught trying to get it."

"And rat's blood?" I can't see rat's blood tasting nice.

"Rats blood not my favourite's blood, too cold and dull for my likely. It's helpful if you stuck anywhere and there's nothing else to drink. It does tend to be a last resort. Anything else, anything to do with the human blood? I thought you would have more questions."

"A couple. Since you done the drinking stuff before, can you drink any blood type or are you stuck with one type? And what happens to you once my fangs start to grow as mine will be coming in early because of what happened at the party?" I was more curious about her fangs then her blood drinking.

"Nice to see that you have been reading the book, it will help you a lot with the whole vampire things. To answer your first question, I can drink all type of human blood. You are right that you will have your fangs because of the party. Well I got mine for the same reason, it's a weird twin thing that happens with vampires. Once one twin gets their fangs, the other one gets theirs as well. It should only take a couple of days before our fangs are fully grown. You might notice them growing slightly so I be careful around the slayer. Once they are fully grown then you won't notice anything different with your teeth till you need to use them. But I do have a question about something at the hospital. How did you know Rose's blood type? You seem certain that I was coming for her blood." She asked with curious look on her face. "I know something happened in there. When you came out, you had a look about you. A thirsty look."

"She was having some blood taken and I could smell it. It hurt like hell due to the blood craving and you right, it made my thirsty." I was hard saying the words out loud. That I was thirsty for my best friends' blood. "I couldn't smell Jake's blood for some reason. He was at the park with his friends. That's why I didn't hear you come up behind, I was too busy focus on wanting to kill him."

I looked at Elizabeth and I saw she had a bit of a smirk on her face. This made me annoyed.

"Why are you laughing? I could have done something stupid to Rose and then what would have happened?" Why did she think this was funny?

"I'm not laughing at you because of Rose. I should have told you something like that might have happened if you come near fresh blood. I was smirking because I keep forgetting how naïve you are still when it comes to vampires. You can't rely on blood scent to know what someone blood type is, you need to learn about human national scent as well. People are not going to help you with identifying their blood type by bleeding before you bite them. We can work on that after we drank the blood if you want to?"

I let out a sigh, I couldn't stay mad with Elizabeth. She grew up with this all her life, it must be weird for her to explain all the basic things to me. I know it's going to be hard, but this was my life, my real life. I needed to learn everything there was and I needed to learn how to survive this world.

"Yeah that sound like a fun idea."

I smiled at her and she smiled back. "OK first we going to do animals blood, starting with cow, my favourite then we will move onto the human." She picked up both cups and passed one to me. "What can you smell? Really focus on the scent."

I put the cup to my nose and took a deep sniff. I couldn't compare the smell to any type of human food, I couldn't say that it smelled like a summer BBQ in a cup or something sweet. I could say that it had a meat smell to it, but that was all.

"Meaty." I laughed

Elizabeth joined in with the laugher. "You will get better at it. Cheers." Elizabeth raised her glass.

"Cheers" I clicked her cup.

I closed my eyes and drank all the blood in one go.

The tasted was like nothing I ever had before. I can't describe the taste if someone asked me to or relate it to anything just like the smell. It was so refreshing and made me feel so full. I can see this being my favourite one like Elizabeth.

"I can see why you like cow blood so much."

"Yeah I really like it the taste. It nicer from the source. I teach you that later in your training. After we done all the blood tasting, we can do the basic stuff."

"Like high hearing, moving fast and suddenly appearing in people rooms you mean?" I laughed and Elizabeth just shook her head with a smile on her face.

The swan had a sweet taste to it, but deer was the sweetest out of them all. The rabbit tasted like you think rabbit should taste. The bear had a spicy flavour to it which I find strange, but it beats the salty taste of dog. The worse one was the rat's blood. It was sour and bitter; I don't know if I would rather starve then drink it again.

Once me and Elizabeth drank the blood, I found myself standing in front of the table with the human blood on. I found myself staring at the dark red liquid, a small bit a doubt in my mind. Drinking animal blood is not unusual, people do it with stake and other meat all the time. But with human blood is difference, it was too close to home. A doubt like a small candle flicker in a dark room. I force my eyes off the blood and looked at Elizabeth, I needed to get past the doubts of drinking blood.

"OK. With human blood it is harder to tell the different between each type. Even harder when it comes to positive and negative types of blood." She handed me the cup with the label A negative on and I took it. I kept my eyes on Elizabeth as she got her own cup of blood.

"Ready?" Elizabeth asked, she looked like she was having second thoughts with me drinking the human blood.

"Ready." I closed my eyes and drank all the blood in one. The taste was stronger than I expected it to be. I thought it would taste of metallic and salt, but I couldn't have been more wrong. It was sweet and I felt like ever part of my body was on fire. But it wasn't the painful fire that I felt from before, it was a powerful fire. As the blood when down my throat, I felt my mouth watering for more. I can't remember tasting anything so strong yet so delicate before. I opened my eyes, not knowing if they have been closed for seconds or minutes.

"Do you think human blood is better than animal?" Elizabeth couldn't hide the smile that was all over her face.

"Do I really need to answer that?" I found my smile matching Elizabeth's.

"Not really." She passed me the A positive blood, the smile still on her face. "Try and focus on the flavour of this one. There only a slight difference between the flavour of negative and positive blood."

I drank the blood in one go and the taste was just as amazing as the negative version. The positive blood had a stronger blood to it, and I could taste a hint of salt in this blood. However the salt wasn't an unpleasant addition to it, like when you add salt to your normal food. The blood gave me the same feeling of power and I felt like I could take on the world and win.

"Can you taste the difference in the blood?" Elizabeth asked, I forgot she was in the den with me. I keep getting lost in the blood that I am losing focus with everything around me.

"A bit of salt and a stronger taste." I put the cup next to Elizabeth's and smiled at her.

"Not bad for a newbie. It's not going to take you long to learn everything about vampires." Elizabeth smiled in return.

She handed me the next blood which I took with no hesitation. I don't know why I was so worried about drinking human blood. Both the O positive and A positive had a slight iron taste to it. It wasn't the most pleasant taste, but I knew being the most common blood type, I will need to get used to it. The negative version on the bloods had a spicy flavour to them which had a nice kick to it. It made me feel all warm inside and it was pleasant feeling. B positive and negative had a sweet taste to them, the flavour reminded me of warm drink like hot chocolate. I can just image me drinking the blood on a cold evening indoor. The AB positive blood had a taste that I couldn't describe. It had a slight sweet taste to it but not in a desert way and a bit of an earthy taste to it.

I put the cup down and I was glad that none of the blood had made me sick. I stood in front of the AB negative blood; my eyes glued the liquid inside. Even from a distance I could smell the blood, the memory of Rose in the hospital coming back to my mind. The smell making me feel thirsty and my mouth dried. It was like I haven't drank anything in day.

"Are you Ok Ingrid?" Elizabeth took a step towards me, concern in her voice and her face was full of regret. "You don't need to drink the last one if you want. I know you thinking about Rose." She reached her hand out to grab the blood, but I got the cup before her.

"No, I'm fine. I am just being silly. Let finish this and if we have time, we can do some skills. You still need to teach me how to appear in people bedroom without them knowing." I smiled at her but we both knew it was fake.

I closed my eyes and took a deep breath before downing the blood. Out of all the blood that I have drank. AB negative tasted the best. The second the blood torched my tongue, I felt shock going through every nerve in my body. I felt like I could take on the whole world and nothing would stand in my way. I looked at Elizabeth we the cup still in my hand. I felt my hand tightening on the cup. I didn't want to admit it or say it out loud. I knew that I would do anything to feel this power again.

"We need to tidy everything up before we do any skills training." It took all my strength to place the empty cup on the table. Either Elizabeth didn't notice how I was acting with the blood or didn't want to say anything about it. "Let me get a box to put everything in. Relax and make yourself at home, this place is just as much as yours as it is mine." She smiled as she left to go into the second room.

I sat in one of the chairs looking around the room, there were 3 doors that lead from the main room. One lead to the side room, one lead to the ladder out of the den and the last one lead to a cupboard which had the mirror on the door. There wasn't anything new that I didn't notice the first time I came to the den. I leant back in the chair slightly when I notice something hidden in the corner of my eye by the shrine. I got out of the chair and walked towards the photos to have a closer look. There was a thin crack going up the wall and I notice that it went across the wall and back down. It then dawned on me that I was looking at a hidden door. It was painted the same colour as the wall, so it was almost invisible to the naked eye. Now I was standing close to the wall, I could see that there was a small handle about the size a £2 coin behind one of the photos. I turned around slightly to sit back down on the chair, but my curiosity was getting the best of me. I carefully moved the shrine away from the door outline, making sure that none of the photos moved or got knocked over on the table. I didn't want to break anything that belonged to Elizabeth or our family. I reach my hand out and place it on the handle and the coldness going through my body like an electronic shock. As I felt the coldness of the handle, I had a suddenly feeling of dread taking over my body. That what was behind this door was forbidden and I didn't want to know what was behind it. Yet I couldn't stop my hand from turning the handle and the door unlocked without any problem. I had to take a deep breath, my eyes on my hand on the handle, the feeling of dread becoming worse. I lifted my eyes up as I opened the door and I close it fast, stepping back from the door my eyes locked the handle. The door blending back in with the wall around it.

I turned around and saw that Elizabeth was standing behind me, an empty box in her hand. I knew Elizabeth know what I saw in the cupboard, that she could hear my heart pounding so loudly in my chest.

Elizabeth smiled. "Sorry I took so long; I couldn't find the box. Forgot I folded it up and put it behind the bed."

I remain standing there not saying anything but find myself smiling back at Elizabeth. Either Elizabeth didn't notice me looking in the cupboard or she didn't care what I saw. I was waiting for my brain to panic, to be scared of Elizabeth in some way, but I wasn't in any way or form.

"Are we going to get the cups cleared up so we can go?" I asked taking the box off Elizabeth and walking towards to cups.

"You need to go back home." Elizabeth spoke behind me.

I spun around on my heels and saw Elizabeth standing behind me.

"What?" Was all I manage to say. Was Elizabeth mad at me because I was snooping around in the den? Have I spoiled everything by seeing something I wasn't meant to see? "Why what's wrong?"

"Don't worry, nothing is wrong. Have you not noticed the time? You need to get up soon for school, even vampires need some sleep to function. We can't have you falling asleep in class and risking the slayer being called."

She took the box back out of my hand and started to place the cups in it.

I looked at my watch and saw that it read 03:05. This couldn't be right? I couldn't been at the den for this long and not notice? Could I?

"When can I come back here?" I looked up at Elizabeth who had somehow packed up all the cups within a few seconds.

"Soon don't worry, you head back home on your own and I finish sorting this place out." Elizabeth smiled and I found myself relaxing and becoming calmer.

I left the den by the ladder and walked through the woods, the darkness not doing its normal jobs of clearing my mind. The thoughts of what I saw going through my mind. Why didn't Elizabeth say anything about the cupboard? She knows that I moved the shine and that I saw what was in the cupboard. Why wasn't I panicking about what I saw? I saw who Elizabeth used for the blood, who she killed and bled. I looked and I saw that I was somehow outside my house, I don't even remember doing the journey. I looked at my watch again and I saw it only took 5 minutes to walk back home. I wonder if any of my other vampire skills are going to come through.

I climbed back into my bedroom by the tree, my mind now focused on what I saw in the cupboard.

The person Elizabeth killed, the blood still flowing slightly from the throat. The face frozen in fear and the eyes stuck open in horror. A face I have seen every day for months, the face of Mrs Wednesday.

Chapter 15
I was shocked on how quickly sleep overtook me when I got to my bed. I thought after finding out that

Elizabeth killed my head-teacher and I just saw her body, that I would be tossing and turning all night. I don't even remember my head hitting the pillows and I didn't even have any nightmares about what I saw. Instead I had thoughts about how easy my life was now that she was gone. I don't have detention anymore for the next 5 weeks, for something that wasn't even my fault. Because of something that Luke and Emma did, because they betrayed me and stabbed me in the back. Rose was going be kept behind with me for standing up for me, for being my friend and doing what she thought was right.

I didn't have any bad feeling for her, I am a vampire and she was human. And in my new world, human mean blood and food. The memory of how nice her blood tasted and how it made me feel, the power it gave me. Just thinking about her blood made me thirsty again, remembering how much I wanted more. There was no way of getting away from it, I liked drinking her blood and I would do anything to have that taste and power again.

It wasn't like anyone was going to miss her, to mourn her death. No one liked her and school will be better place without her. We might even have a nicer teacher to replace her as our head-teacher, someone the kids like and respected. The only family that she has ever mention was a husband. A man who must be as mean if he was with someone like her. Everyone will now be happier and better off because of what Elizabeth did.

I pulled myself out of bed once my alarm went off, feeling groggy due to the lack of sleep. Elizabeth was right about me heading home to get some sleep, I feel like my body weighed a ton. I got changed into my uniform, making sure all my extra things were hidden at the bottom of my bag. I had some new ideas to try at school to cause as much trouble as I can.

I grabbed my curtain and pulled it slightly open when I froze, my hands locked onto the curtain. My eyes glued to the places outside my house that was normally empty, apart from this morning the place now had an empty police car. I knew it was here for me because it was the only car this side of the street. I forgot to ask Elizabeth what I was meant to do with the police when they come and see me. I took a few deep breaths to calm myself down, but it didn't help in anyway. I forced my hands of the curtains, my eyes never leaving the police car in the street. I was a vampire, the policeman was human, I shouldn't be afraid of him. No matter how many times I repeated the sentence in my head, it didn't make me feel calmer.

I slowly walked down the stairs, taking each step one at a time. My body and mind wanting to run back up the stairs or out of the front door. I got to the bottom of the stairs and Mrs Jones was standing by the kitchen door. I had no chance of running now and I knew I had to face the policemen. I took a small breath in and walked towards Mrs Jones, keeping my face straight.

"Morning Ingrid, did you have a nice sleep?" She smiled at me as walked pasted her and into the kitchen. The first thing I notice was the policemen sitting at my kitchen table. "Ingrid, this is CID Cole, he is here to speak to you."

I looked at the person sitting on the table, taking in every detail of him. He looked more like a banker then anything to do with the police. He wasn't as big as I thought he be, he was no taller than 5ft 7 and he looked like he not eaten in days. However he looked strong enough to take anyone and anything down. The black suit and blue tie with the short brown hair didn't really help with the banker look.

"Hi Ingrid, it is nice to meet you." He stood up from the chair, holding his hand out for me to shake.

I felt like I had no choice but to shake his hand back. "Hi, it's nice to meet you too." He must be able to feel how much I am shaking.

Mrs Jones walked pasted us both and stood behind Officer Cole near the sink.

He nodded and sat back down in the chair and I sat on the chair that was opposite to him. I placed hands in my lap, twisting my fingers around each other and trying to breath normal.

"You don't need to look worry Ingrid. I am just here to ask you what happened at the party. I already spoken to everyone else who was there that night. Do you remember what happened that night? The night you were attacked?"

I just nodded my head slightly, not trusting my voice yet. Trying to think of something I can say to the police, something that wouldn't let slip what really happen. The only story I know is the one that Mr Jones said when I first woke up in the hospital and what Rose and Lily said. If I agree with them, then maybe they won't listen to what Luke and Emma said and it will all go away.

"What do you remember?" He asked again leaning back in the chair slightly, his eyes never leaving mine.

"I remember going upstairs with Lily and Rose after the party had ended. We didn't want to tidy up, so it was decided to do it in the morning. We were just walking up the first few steps when two people came bursting through the door. The next thing I remember was waking up in the hospital." I kept my eyes on the Office Cole as I spoke, not wanting to give any clues that I was lying.

"What about Luke and Emma, they were there weren't they? You've not said anything about them yet." He raised an eyebrow. "Only Rose, Lily and yourself."

You could see where this was going, and I knew that there were holes in the story I was telling. I knew I needed to keep a few steps in front of him otherwise I would get caught out. "Yeah, I know that, but they weren't staying behind like I was. They were only there to help tidy up as the place was such a mess. It was late and they were leaving when the attack happened." I hope that this new information was close to what everyone else had said.

"OK. One more question I want to ask you before you go to school. I promise I won't keep you any longer, however I will need to speak to you again." He leant forward and put his hands on the table, I could see that his eyes were trying to read my face. Why were you the only one at the party to have no injuries? Lily had bruises like someone was holding her down. Rose had her head split open and lots blood because of it. Emma and Luke were in pieces after the attacks, they had the worst injuries out of everyone in the group. Broken ribs, cuts, bruises and other marks. On the other hand you didn't have a single mark on you. After the attack, the hospital found out that you had no injuries as a result. How would you explain that?" I force myself to keep my face straight, stopping myself from running out of the room in panic. I didn't think about everyone else getting hurt apart from me. It suddenly dawns on me how everything was staking against me. He carried on talking, not waiting for me to answer. "I don't know if you are aware of what other people have said, but you might be interested in what Luke and Emma said. They said that is was someone in the group that attacked them. Or maybe even be the one who let the attackers into the house." He leant back into his chair, his eyes never leaving mine. "Ingrid I am going to be honest with you, at this moment I think..." His radio beeped, stopping him in mid-sentence. It didn't matter in anyway; I knew I had been caught.

He clicked the radio and spoke into it. "Charlie, Oscar, Lima, Echo- 3247. Over"

A cracking voice came over the radio. "A body of a woman in her 30's have been found near the park. CID are requesting you to go to the crime scene. It's 15 minutes from your current location. Family have been notified as well and work placement. Think it's a stabbing to the neck Over."

"Message receive, I am on my way to the location now. Over"

"Keep us updated. Will send address by car radio. Over"

He stood up as Mrs Jones moved behind me, I hated her being so close to me.

"You must excuse me, but I need to deal with this crime." Office Cole said, moving towards the kitchen door and past me. I stood up and moved away from Mrs Jones so he could get past. "I might be back later today after Ingrid has come home from school. I will call you later to let you know. I will need to know more information about the attack."

Mrs Jones nodded. "Yeah, that sound fine. I understand that you are needed somewhere else. I will be out the next couple of hours as I am dropping Ingrid off at school and then I have some errands to run. I will be in after that if you do get in contact with me."

"Wait what? I can walk to school. I thought you were at least trusting me enough to walk to school. I don't need dropping off."

This was something new. She has never dropped me off at school before. How can I change into my clothes if I am in a car? A teacher could come up to her and blow everything I have done.

"Well they just found a body and you was attacked a few days ago. Do you think I be letting Ben or you out on your own? From now on…" The phone rang and I ran past everyone to get it, not letting her finish was she was saying.

The last few times the phone have rang and the slayers have gotten hold of it, it has been someone that knows about vampires or Elizabeth. I grabbed the phone of the side, nearly dropping it as I put it against my ear. "Hello." I answered breathless.

"Hello Ingrid, it's only Rose's mum. How are you?" Came the voice from the other end.

Part of me was annoyed that I didn't manage to catch the slayers out. "Hi, yeah I am fine, how everyone down your end? Rose said something about Lilly acting strange when I spoke to her before."

"I think she alright, to be honest she keeping to herself and we don't see her anymore. Anyway, I am only calling to speak to your mum. I just found out that school has been closed today and I wonder if your mum knows why? I work at the school and we haven't been told anything. Does your mum know why as she normal knows things like this?"

"I don't know, I will grab her for you." I put the phone on the side and went back towards the kitchen, knowing why school was not opening today.

"Rose's mum on the phone, she says school closed and she wonder if you know why. She can't fine any information."

I notice that Office Cole was still in the room and Mrs Jones was sitting in one of the chairs. I thought Office Cole was needed somewhere else, why was he still here? He knows too much about what really happened, I can't risk him finding anything else out.

"What do you mean school is close?" Mrs Jones stood up with force that I thought the chair was going to fall back. "You got exams coming up, so school need to be open so that you can study." She walked past me and closed the door as she left. I was now alone with Office Cole, the one thing I didn't want. I thought he was leaving to solve the crime at the park, why was he still here with me?

"Why do you think school is closed?" Officer Cole ask as the door closed.

I opened my mouth but stop for a split second. I thought I heard Mrs Jones put the phone down but I then her talking again.

"I don't know." I answered, my eyes looked onto the door. I moved them away and looked at him again. "Maybe there a bug going around or something."

That something being the Mrs Wednesday was lying dead in Elizabeth cupboard. I thought I heard the phone being put down again but I could still hear sounds coming from the hallway so she must still be talking to someone.

Mrs Jones suddenly screamed from the hallway, making me jump and spun around. Officer Cole ran towards the door and I followed close behind. I was half expecting someone to be in the hallway or something like that. But Mrs Jones was alone, she was sat on the floor with her back against the wall. The phone was still in her hand and her face was as pale as mine. Her eyes were wide open and looking ahead of her, not blinking as we went towards her.

I got the phone out of her hand and put it against my ear.

"Hello? Hello?" The line was silent, who every was on the other end was now gone. What was going on?

"What's wrong? What's happened?" Office Cole crouching down in front of Mrs Jones. I put the phone down on the side and found myself crouching down as well.

"After I spoken to Rose's mum, I rang the school directly. To find out why it closed and to give them a piece of my mine." I got up and leant slightly on the wall. I could have sworn that I heard the phone being put down a couple of times. She looked at Office Cole, her eyes full of tears. "The body at the park. It's the school headteacher, it's Ingrid's teacher. I didn't realise I was screaming till you came running in"

Mrs Wednesday body was at the park? Why is it there, why was the body in the open? What was Elizabeth playing at?

 "OK, I am heading there now. Ingrid?" He stood up in front of me. "Your mum is in shock. You need to make your mum some strong coffee and try and get her to lay down. After that I would recommend calling someone for her. You need to be a brave for your mum."

I just nodded my head. Biting my tongue with being spoken to like a 5-year-old again.

He nodded at me with and with a smile and walked out the house. My eyes following him as he left. He was talking on his radio as he walked, closing the door behind him. Thank god he was now out of the house, hopefully he's not coming back for a while.

"Come on." I turned my attention to Mrs Jones who was still on the floor. "Let get you to your room."

I helped her up and took her to her room. Her eyes were locked in front of her and she was making it harder to ger to her room. When I got her onto her bed, she finally spoke to me.

"Ring your dad, tell him to come home with Ben. I want everyone here; I don't want anyone outside. I want everyone home where they are safe.

"Where is Ben?" I asked suddenly realising that I had not seen him yet, Surely, he would have come down when his mum screamed?

"He already left for school because he got morning revision. Oh my god, he going to see the body." She sat up but didn't try and leave the bed. "He going to see Mrs Wednesday murdered body."

"Calmed down, you don't need to worry. Ben doesn't walk near the park the park to get to school. There is no reason for him to be anywhere near where the body was found. I will ring everyone now. I make sure everyone is back home soon."

She shocked her head. "Your dad doesn't have his mobile on him today. There is a number pinned up on the notice board. He needed to go to a new place today, you can reach him on that number." She laid back down on the bed and closed her eyes.

I walked to the notice board and saw the number that was pinned on it. I copy the number into my phone before picking up the house phone. I didn't want to use any of the mobiles in case the numbers could be trace or hacked.

I dialled the number and put the phone against my ear, the phone was picked up after a couple of rings.

"Hello?" A man voice answered that I didn't recognised, he sounded guarded as he spoke.

"Hello, who this?" I asked. "I'm looking for my dad. He gave my mum this number. He is supposed to be with you today."

"I'm Mark. Are you Joneses daughter, Ingrid? You sound just like him." I could hear him relaxing as he spoke. "Are you wanting to speak to him?" He asked.

Mark? Where have I heard that name before? When Mr Jones lost his bag, he was told that Mark might have some spare things. Was he a slayer as well? "Please, it's really important." I replied trying to remain focus.

"Of course, two seconds I get him. He just helping someone." I heard him place the phone on the side and I could still hear noises in the background.

I focus more on the sound; it was someone talking. I closed my eyes, using everything I had to hear what was being said.

"Help me please. No please don't he's my child. No" My eyes shot open, the sound becoming clear with each word. "Please don't kill us." I could hear the pain and terror in her voice.

"Hello?" Mr Jones voice came on the line, cutting of the cried off help I could hear in the background. I opened to answer him, but I couldn't make the words come out.

"Ingrid?" I could hear panic in his voice now. "Are you there?"

"Yeah I am here. You need to come home now." I took a deep breath, trying to control my voice. The sound of pain still ringing in my ears. "You need to pick Ben up on the way as he needs to come back here."

"Why, what happened?" He definitely sounded panic now. "Has someone hurt you or your mum?"

"Schools been closed. They think my headteachers been found at the local park. Ben left for school already and… and mum wants everyone home. She in shock and is not coping with everything that is happening. Can you make it home?" Please say no. After what I just heard in the background, I wanted him to stay as far away from me as he could.

"What? Oh my god. Stay where you are Ingrid, stay with your mum. I am leaving now; I am leaving right now. I will find Ben and I be home in no more than 15 minutes." He put the phone down before I had the chance to say anything. The phone beeping in my ear.

I put the phone down and went to the kitchen to make a strong coffee for Mrs Jones. I knew I needed to keep up the act of the loving daughter. I took it up to the room and opened Mrs Jones bedroom door. She was still laying on the bed and staring at the celling.

"I made you a drink." She didn't respond. "Everyone is on their way back home now." Still nothing. I put the cup next to her. "I going to do some work in my room." I left her on her bed and went to my room. I sat on my bed, trying to work out everything I have learnt. I grabbed a random notebook from my side and wrote everything down, trying to get everything out of my head.

Does Mrs Jones know that Mrs Wednesday was killed by a vampire? The body was found at the park with a neck womb. Mrs Jones will know that the park is a regular place for slayers and vampires. I don't know what happened to the slayers that were chasing me and Elizabeth, but they are most likely missing. I am 100% that Mark is a slayer, it's the only thing that make sense. I looked at the number which I had written down. Whose number was this? Is it a random number the slayers are using or is it linked to one of them?

The pen hovered above the page, the voice coming back into my head. The scream for help. Have the slayers killed another vampire? Is that what Mr Jones do when he leaves the house, finds vampires and kill them? Is that what he did to my real parents, my real mum?

I heard a car door slam outside, making me jump and come out of my own world. I shove the notebook under my pillow and looked out of the window. I saw Mr Jones running into the house, Ben slowly following him a distance away.

"Ingrid? Honey? Where are you both?" I heard footsteps coming up the stairs at great speed. I thought a heard of animals were coming upstairs he was making so much noise. I quickly stuck my head out of the door and put my finger to my lips and pointed to his bedroom door.

He looked towards his bedroom door when Ben came running up the stairs. "Have you seen the news?"

I left my room and followed Ben and Mr Jones down the stairs. We walked into the living room where the news was on the TV.

"This morning the body of Mrs Alex Wednesday, head teacher at the local high school, was found at the park." It flicked to an image to the park which was covered in police and cars. "It is believed to be a stabbing and her throat had been slit and her body was dumped on the swing at the local park. Her husband gave out this message to the public."

A man came onto the screen who he was standing outside a house. He looked in his late 30's and his face looked kind and gentle. Who was this person? He had brown hair that was bolding at the top and a small beard that was starting to turn grey in places. The main thing I notice was his eyes, not the colour or they size. But that they were full of love but full of lost and pain. 'Please." His voice matched the pain in his eyes, his voice already breaking. "Someone much knows what has happened to my wife. This awful thing that has happened to our peaceful family." He started crying and put his hand over his face. "She has never done anything wrong. She was a great wife, a great mother and a great teacher." He broke down in uncontrollable tears and walked back towards the house.

It went back to the news reader from before.

"Her husband has decided to show a video of his wife from 6 months ago. A video to show what type of person his wife was."

The next video was from a phone and it showed Mrs Wednesday. In the video Mrs Wednesday looked younger somehow then she looked at school. How could this video be from 2 months before she became our headteacher? She was smiling and laughing, something I don't think anyone at school have ever seen before. A girl around 6 years old came out from under a table. She had black hair that was in pigtails and pink flowers PJ. Mrs Wednesday picked her up and spun her around, both laughing and giggling. Since when Mrs Wednesday have a child? She doesn't seem to be a motherly type at all. Mrs Wednesday husband came in frame, in his arms was a boy who couldn't be more then 3. He was wearing blue PJ'S and his hair colour matched his dads and was flat against his head. Mrs Wednesday have 2 children? Mrs Wednesday took her son in her other arm and spun both her children around. Everyone was laughing and seem so happy.

The video ended and it went back to the newsreader.

"If anyone knows anything about this case, please call the number on the screen."

Mr Jones turned the TV off and walked out of the room, leaving me and Ben alone in the room.

I went to follow him out when Ben stood in front of me. I haven't really spoken to him since the night he said all those things about me.

"Ingrid..." Ben started to say.

"Ben, I don't want another fight with you. Not with everything that is happening."

"I know, that's why I am apologising. I sorry for what I said, I glad you back from the hospital. You are not making everything worse for me and you are not evil. I'm sorry." He smiled and went upstairs to his room, leaving me standing in an empty living room.

I looked back at the blank TV, still waiting to feel something for Mrs Wednesday. I slowly walked upstairs, thinking about the video I saw. Mrs Wednesday children will never know what happened to their mum, that's she was found dead on some swings and that it. At least I know how my mum was murdered by the slayers, they will never will.

I got to my room and closed the door, sitting on the floor with my back against the door. I kept thinking about the news, about Mrs Wednesday. Why did Elizabeth put her body on shown? Why didn't she keep her in the cupboard, I thought she wanted to keep a low profile? I got my phone out and text Elizabeth, telling her I needed to speak to her. I need to know what was happening, with her and the slayers.

I leant my head back against the door and closed my eyes. I wondered if Mrs Wednesday thought it was me when she saw Elizabeth? I wonder if she knew what was happening, that she was going to be killed?

There was a knocked on my bedroom door, making me jump. I got off the floor and place my hand on the handle.

"Who is it?" I asked with caution.

"It's Ben, please I need to talk to you." I notice that there was something in his voice. Fear.

I opened the door and saw Ben standing outside my door. His looked at me, tears in his eyes and I could see that he looked so scared.

"Ben what's wrong? What happened?" I was starting to panic now.

"I know who killed Mrs Wednesday. They are in this house, right now." He whispered back.

Chapter 16

"What?" I manger to choke out. My body going cold with fear. I notice my hand was shaking so I put it behind my back. "What do you mean there are in the house?"

"I think dad was the one who killed Mrs Wednesday."

I looked at Mr Jones bedroom behind Ben and quickly grabbed Ben and pulled him into my room. I closed the door and locked it before any of the slayers heard him.

"Ben what are you on about?" I asked, still panicking

He didn't say anything. He lifted his arm up and I noticed he had something in his hand.

Mr Jones leather bag. The missing one.

"Why have you got that?" I asked, taking the bag away from him. "What's inside it, Ben?"

"I took it so dad could stay home more, I saw it by the stairs and just grabbed it. I don't know why but I looked inside it and I saw…" He stopped and I saw tears going down his cheeks. "I'm going to Tom's house. I don't want to be in this house anymore. Not with a killer."

He unlocked my door and bolted from the room.

I heard his footsteps going down the stairs and out the front door with a bang. I remain frozen in the middle of my room for a few seconds, trying to work out what just happened. I looked down at my hand and saw that I was still holding the leather bag. I put the bag on the floor and closed the door quickly, making sure it was locked before the slayers saw the bag in my room. I turned and looked at the bag in the middle of my room. What was in the bag that scared Ben so much? To make him think that his dad was a killer. I got my phone out again, telling Elizabeth that I needed to see her right now. This was getting to big for me to deal with on my own and I don't know what to do anymore. I hid the bag under the floorboard as I didn't like the idea of being able to see it. Something about the bag made me feel uneasy.

I sat on my bed and took some deep breaths, trying to calm myself down. I looked at my phone, waiting for a reply from Elizabeth. There was a knocked on my door again, I looked up at the door, the phone still in my hand.

"Ingrid, it's your dad. Can I come in please?"

I quickly shoved my phone under the pillow, praying that Elizabeth doesn't pick now to reply to me.

I slowly walked to the door and opened it slightly. Keeping Mr Jones out of the room. "Hi, is everything OK?"

"Yeah, everything fine. Can I come in? I need to talk to you." I could feel the door moving forward slightly against me.

"What no, you can't" I put my foot and leg against the door, blocking his way into my room.

"Why?" He asked, his eyes narrowing. Does he suspect something about me?

"Because..." What could I say to stop him? My brain was going through excuses to stop him. "I just want to be on my own right now. I know you want to help, but I just need my own space. I need my own safe space with everything that has been happening in the last few days."

His eyes seem to soften slightly, and I felt him release the door.

"Do you have any idea what is wrong with Ben? He just ran past me and it looked like he been crying." He sounded worried.

I shook my head.

"He said he was going to Tom's house. It could be because he never knows someone who died and the shock of it all. He is only 13 after all. He just might need some space from the house. I might do the same later, it might help clear my head."

"That might be a good idea." He smiled and walked away.

I closed the door and put my forehead against the door, appreciating the coldness of the wood on my skin. I shut my eyes, taking a few deep breaths to help calm myself down but it wasn't working.

"Has something happened?" I heard a voice from behind me. Hearing that voice made me instantly calmer. I turned around and saw Elizabeth standing by the open window. "Ingrid are you OK?" She looked and sounded worried.

I opened my mouth to answer her when I heard the front door close from my bedroom window. I looked at Elizabeth and we both went towards the window. It sounded like someone was trying to sneak out, if the window weren't open, I would have missed it. I hid behind the curtain and saw that Elizabeth was doing the same with the other curation. I watched as the slayers walked towards the car with some speed. Mrs Jones seem better suddenly; I should have known that she was acting when Officer Cole was here. She was a train killer and a random body being found wouldn't have affected her like that in real life.

Elizabeth and I watched them as they drove away in silence with great speed.

"At least we can speak out loud, I thought we would need to whisper and keep an eye out for the slayers. So what's happened Ingrid, what's wrong?"

I took a deep breath and gave her the notebook.

"Why was Mrs Jones faking when she heard the news about Mrs Wednesday? Does she know the killer was a vampire or linked to a vampire?"

"The slayers will know it was vampire that killed your headteacher. That might be stupid, but they are not that stupid. Mrs Jones needs to be seen as weak and vulnerable at all time, staying under the radar. They can't act hard and solid when bad things happen around them."

"What's the number that Mr Jones wrote on the board. Who did I call?" I sat on the bed as I asked and Elizabeth sat next to me.

"The number is most likely a dead number. The slayers use them for a short time and then disconnect it and use a new one. Did the slayer who picked up give you a name at all?" Elizabeth put the notebook next to her and turned her body towards me slightly.

"He said that his name was Mark, he didn't give me a second name or another like that."

"I know Mark, he is a rubbish slayer. I have dealt with him before. He has been after us for the last 6 years and he have never been close. I swear he couldn't get a vampire if they were standing bang in front of him with open arms and they give him the weapons." She laughed to herself flicked through the empty pages of the notebook.

I closed my eyes, remembering the voice from the phone. I couldn't bring myself to write the words down. I opened my eyes and looked at Elizabeth.

"Elizabeth." I could hear my voice breaking already. Elizabeth eyes shot up from the notebook in panic. "I don't think that's true anymore. I…" I felt my voice getting stuck in my throat.

"Ingrid what wrong" She put her arm round me and I felt the tears starting to flow down my face.

"While Mark was getting Mr Jones, I heard someone in the background. It's was a woman who was begging for her and her child's life. It got me thinking about mum for the first time, wondering…." I couldn't finish what I was saying and a broke down in tears.

"Ow Ingrid." Elizabeth hugged me tighter. "Come here." She pulled me closer towards her and I found myself crying into her. "It's OK to cry. I still cry about them. They were our parents, our mother. All this is new for you, everything is happening at once."

I pulled away from her and whipped my eyes.

"What are we going to do about the mum and her child? We need to do something to help them. We need to save them from the slayers. We need to…." I found myself getting faster in speech and not being able to catch my breath.

"Hey calm down Ingrid, calm down." Elizabeth interrupted me, grabbing both my hands. "Take some deep breaths and breathe. I know we need to help them, but we can't go storming in without knowing thing. If we go in blind, then there is more chance of one of use getting hurt. Do you have any information on the slayers? Anything that might help us?"

My eyes flicked towards the floorboard and where I hid the leather bag.

"I might have something that belongs to the slayers." I got off the bed and went towards the floorboard. "Ben gave it to me before you came." I got the bag out and placed it on the floor. "It scared Ben so much that he ran out of the house. I've seen the slayers with the bag before. It must have something bad if it made Ben think it was the slayers killed Mrs Wednesday and not us."

Elizabeth sat on the floor next to the bag.

"Then we need to keep it away from the slayers if it can cause useharm. It might even help us know who we are dealing with." Elizabeth opened the bag and looked inside. She moved stuff around the bag before taking her hand out "And it looks like these slayers like uses old fashion weapons. That might help us, but they could still have stuff hidden we don't know about."

Elizabeth pushed the bag towards me, and I looked inside the bag. The first thing I saw was a carving knife in a silk box. I saw that the blade had a red stain all over it. If I didn't know who the bag belongs to, it looked like the knife could be used to carve wood. The knife had a wooden handle with crosses carved onto the handle. The blade was a few mm thick and about 5 inches long, I could see that it was made from silver. No wonder Ben was scared when he opened the bag and saw the knife. I took the box out of the bag and placed it on the floor between me and Elizabeth. Under the box were more weapons that look like it would hurt anyone if they were vampire or human. There were 9 stakes of different sizes like the one you would see in a vampire movie. I got a whiff of garlic coming from the bag when I moved one of the stakes and I saw some loose garlic in the bag. I saw that there were a range of crosses and silver chains of different thickness. I put the knife back in the bag and gave it to Elizabeth, seeing all the weapons made me feel uneasy.

She put everything back under the floorboard as she spoke.

"We need to try and workout where the slayers came from, where they are heading to now."

She stood up and pulled the rug over the floor and I stood up next to her.

"And how are we going to do that? Apart from which way the car came from, I have no idea where to look first.

"Do you remember my friend I mention a while ago?" She asked walking out of my room and down the stairs.

I followed her down the stairs closed behind her.

"The one who called you? The one who you said would sort the police out?" I grabbed Elizabeth arm when she got to the bottom of the stairs turning her to face me. "I had an Office Cole in my house this morning asking questions about the party. He only left when he heard about Mrs Wednesday body. Why did you do that to Mrs Wednesday body like that?

"I had no idea about that till I saw the news myself. That was my friend who did that, and I am sorry for that. I know we need to keep a low profile, but he just wants to wind the slayer up as much as he can. But we can trust him, and he will do anything to protect us. We will deal with Office Cole, it just complex as he has met my friend before. He used to be a policeman at his old village where Matt got into a bit of trouble." I let go off her arm, glad to know that Mrs Wednesday body being displayed had nothing to do with Elizabeth. "You don't need to worry about him."

Elizabeth turned around and walked towards the door and opened it,

"So what are we doing…" I started saying but stopped when I saw what was outside my house.

Where the slayers car was parked moments before, was now a black Bentley Sports car. Standing next to the car was a male who was 18 maybe 19 years old. I knew that he must be the friend that Elizabeth had been talking about. He was tall with broad shoulders, like he could take a car hit and the car would take more damage. He had dark black windswept hair which covered his right eye and as I walked closer, I could see that his eyes were dark brown, and I swear there was a hint of red in them as well. His skin was as pale as mine and Elizabeth and I knew he was a fully-grown vampire. He smiled, the corner of his mouth lifting enough so I could see a long white fang. He had dark trousers on with a zipped-up leather jacker which looked like would protect him from the sun. I looked at the sky and I cold that the sky was cloudy with no hint of sunlight. No chances of Elizabeth friend bursting into flames while he was with us suddenly.

"Hi, I'm Matt am a good friend of Elizabeth's."

He held out his hand and I shook it. His grip was strong, and he squeezed my hand harder than he needed to. Even though his words were friendly, the tone gave it away that he clearly didn't trust me. I was glad when he let go as I wouldn't be able to get out of his grip any other way.

I looked over his shoulder and I saw Elizabeth getting in the front passenger. She had apologetic smile on her face as her eyes flicked to Matt. She mouthed the word sorry before fully getting into the car.

"Hop in." He didn't look at me as his spoke and got into the driver seat. I open the back door on the driver side and got in. The first thing I notice when I got into the car was that all the seats were made of leather and the console looked like it belonged in a spaceship with everything that was on it. I looked out of the window and I saw that all the windowing, including the front ones were heavily tinted. I guess that there was something else in the window to stop sunlight from coming into the car and burning Matt as he drove around.

"How did you know we needed a car?" I asked Matt as he started the car. The car engine purred as we drove away. I knew he didn't like me, but I couldn't not speak to him for Elizabeth sack.

"I didn't know you needed a car. I was just coming over to try and figure you out, I don't trust slayers and you been brought up by them. I don't want Elizabeth or her family to get hurt as they have done so much for me. I saw Elizabeth go into the top window, so I decided to wait to see what was happening. I moved to the front of the house when I saw the slayers leave and waited for Elizabeth to come out. I heard you talking about needed to get somewhere which is linked to the slayers. So where are we driving to?"

"We don't know yet, we need to work that out." Elizabeth answered from the front of the car.

We stopped at some traffic light and I saw Matt reaching towards the glove box.

"Hang on, this might help." He pulled at a map and passed it to Elizabeth who passed it straight to me. "We might be able to work it out as slayers keep to a similar pattern. It best to use paper maps when it comes to slayer hideout. Slayers can easy remove building from new phone maps, but they can't do anything about pre-made paper maps." He kept his eyes focus on the road ahead as he spoke. "Slayers need a big place with lots of buildings or something, to hide things like a farm or something. Something out of the way but not too far that people ask questions." I scan the map trying to find anything that matched what Matt was saying. "Who this stupid idiot crossing the road?" I heard Matt say.

I looked up from the map and I saw Jake crossing the road in front of the car. He kept stopping after each couple of steps and looking at the unusual car.

"Just Run him over if you like, no one will mind." I said looking back down at the map. "No one will even notice that he gone." I felt the car creep forward slightly towards Jake.

"Don't you dare Matt." I heard Elizabeth threatened Matt started to laugh slightly and I found myself joining in. "Both of you, I mean it," This made us laugh more. She sounded like a mother telling her kids off. "We don't need another body linked to us; we already got a body on a swing to deal with."

I saw Elizabeth looked at Matt and he just shrugged his shoulder.

"Yeah well, I deal with the body in the park later, at least me and your sister is getting along. For the time being anyway." He looked at her with a big cheeky grin on his face. I knew Elizabeth rolled her eyes without needing to see it. I felt slightly more at ease with Matt as it seems like he was going to be at least civil with me at the moment as I don't want him as an enemy. "Anyway chill out, he's out of the road now." I felt the car pull away and carry on driving down the road. "So, why could I have killed him?" Matt asked looking in the mirror at me for the first time.

"He knew my boyfriend was cheating on me with my best friend. I want him dead, but Elizabeth is being unfair and said no."

He chuckled. "She definitely like you then Elizabeth when it comes to revenge."

I saw Elizabeth glare at him before turning around in the chair to face me. "Found anywhere yet?"

"Maybe." I gave her the map. "There is a farm about 10 minutes away. It looks the right size and it fit with everything else Matt said."

"Need to start somewhere. Even if it not the main slayer hideout, the slayers could still be using it.

Matt took the map off Elizabeth and followed it to a gate that lead towards the farm. The gate was a big steal one which looked look rusty and it would break if we torched it. It was protected by barbwire and it had more locks then what was needed on a gate. We all got out of the car and stood in front of the gate.

"How are we going to get through without someone knowing we were here and without leaving my car in the open?" Matt said as he walked closer to the gate.

"HEY." A voice shouted from behind us, making me jump out of my skin. I turned around with Matt and Elizabeth and we all saw a man getting out of an old car behind us. The first thing I thought when I saw him was that he remined me of a typical cartoon famer. The weird green hat which had some thin grey hair escaping from under it. The hat was the same colour as he green cloth jacket which he paired with brown trousers which were covered in patches. The only different between this man and a cartoon famer was instead a of a happy and smiley famer, his face was red, and you could see the anger in him.

"What are you teenagers doing on my land? Get out of here before I call the police. You are not allowed on my property."

Matt was about to open his mouth to respond when I took a step forward. Elizabeth might trust Matt but so far, he has not given me any reason to.

"Sorry Sir, I know we shouldn't be on your property. Me and my sister was playing when I got hurt, we tried to get back home but we become lost and we lost our phones. This gentleman found us and said he help us.

He not from here though so he doesn't know the area. We saw this road and we decided to follow it to see if it leads to someone who could help us. Can we please use your phone and then we leave? I promise. We didn't know what else to do.

His face relaxed slightly but I could see that there were fires in his eyes. He didn't believe a word that I said but he wasn't going to admit it out loud.

"I'm sorry, I didn't know you were hurt or lost. I have been having trouble with kids messing around on my land. I lost count the amount of times I come here and found the gate broken." He opened the gate and the noise was almost deafening with the rust "Go to the house, I will follow you up once I closed the gate behind us."

We got back into the car without saying and word to him and drove through the open gate.

"You need to explain how you thought of a story so fast." I could feel Matt burning into mine as we drove up a long lane." Matt said. "I've be caught lots of time and I have never thought of a lie that quick before and I got more experience then you."

"Me and my friend Rose love exploring different places. We have been caught a couple of times, so we have thought of a couple of excuses for why we were there for when it happens."

Matt made a noise from the front which I couldn't catch but I knew he wasn't happy with me. Elizabeth turned around again and gave me a reassuring smile. I smiled back and she turned back around to face the front. I looked out of the windscreen to see where we were heading, but the only thing I could see were empty fields with a ditch running alongside of the road. The car was silent as we drove up the road and after a couple of minutes, I saw a house coming into view. The house looked like it used to be a barn that had been made into a house with some of the walls being made from stones and the windows being wooden. It must have been done a long time ago as the house looked like it was falling apart, and it could collapse at any moment with the slightest touch. The windows looked rotten and some of them were coming away from the wall but only on the top floor. The roof was missing a lot of tiles and it didn't look waterproof in any sort of ways. The only part of the house that looked secure in anyway was the door which looked like it was made from strong mental which looked out of place with the rest of the house. This was not a house that someone could live in this for more than one night at a time.

We stopped the car in front of the house, and we all got out of the car. I looked around the area and I saw that there were a few buildings that was slightly away from the house.

"Matt." He looked at me and I nodded towards the buildings just behind the house.

"I will check them out once he out of the way. He most likely a slayer and I don't want to get caught snooping around by him."

I nodded as the farmer pulled up behind Matt car, he got out of the car and went straight towards the strong front door. We all followed him towards the door as he got a key out and opened the secure door which swung open without any trouble. The door opened to a hallway with stairs leading to the upstairs of the house. I took a step forward and looked round the almost empty room. The wall were bare stone with patches of wallpaper were on the wall was stained yellow with a dark strip pattern underneath it. There were no photos anywhere or personal items that made it look like someone lived here. The only things that stood out in the hallway was a wooden door that was under the stairs. It had a bolt that looked new as it was shiny brass colour which stood out against, the dark colour of the wood.

I took another step forward and Elizabeth and Matt followed behind me.

"What are your names?" I turned around and saw that the farmer standing by the door, blocking our way out.

"My name Rob, I'm just passing through, to get to my new collage." Matt lied. "These are Chole and Hannah. They introduced themselves to me already." I looked at Matt, why was he lying about our name?

The farmer nodded and walked to another room and came back with a phone in his hand. He held it out in front of him and I took it off him as he stood by the front door again.

"Call your parents and get them to pick you up. I don't care if you are lost or not, I don't like kids hanging around my property." He watched me as I type in random numbers slowly, leaning slightly on the door frame.

"So what's your name then?" Matt asked, I stopped clicking numbers and looked up at Matt and the farmer.

The farmer stood up straight and crossed his arms across his chest.

"Why do you want to know?" He sounded defensive and his eyes were locked on Matt.

"Because you know our names and we want to know who is helping us." Matt took a step forward not backing down.

"Bill." He looked at me and I took a step backwards away from him. "You need to call your parents now."

I looked back down at the phone and started to type in the numbers slowly again, wasting as much time as I could.

"Bill, nice name." I heard Matt say next to me. "Do you live here?" You could hear the smugness in his voice. "Doesn't look very good does it?" Matt knocked on the wall and dust fell around us, making me cough and stop clicking on the phone. "Look like someone would say this was a house when it was not." Matt smirked at Bill and leant on the wall facing him.

Bill didn't seem to notice that I stopped using the phone and seem now more focus on Matt now. I looked at Elizabeth in the corner of my eye in panic. What was Matt doing? Elizabeth looked at me and she appeared to be completely calm.

"Why would someone say they lived in a place when they don't?" Bill took a step forward into the house and away from the doorframe.

I took a step backwards, but I notice that Elizabeth didn't move an inch and Matt took a step towards him. "Why don't you tell me?" Matt smirked again and it looked like him and Bill was going to fight.

I was shocked when Bill started to chuckle. "You are very funny."

He turned on his heels and walked out the house, I heard his car starting and the ties screeching. I walked to the door and I saw Bill car heading down the path with speed away from the house.

"He knows we vampires." Elizabeth guessed.

"You think." Matt said. "I give him 10 minutes to either get weapons or get some slayers."

"Then why did your challenging him like that? Why did you lie about our names?" I demanded from Matt.

I knew I didn't have a plan, but I knew that winding up someone who might be a slayer wouldn't be part of it. I don't understand why Elizabeth doesn't seem to care about how Matt was acting.

"Well to begin with he knew that we were lying when we first spoke to him, even you should have known that. He knew we were vampires and he was just acting clueless to make us drop are guard. I lied about our names because I am known among the slayers and I guess we are trying to keep people clueless about you. I wind him up yes, but that does mean he is now gone, which mean we can search this place without getting caught. So" He clapped his hands." While your ladies check the house, I check the buildings that Ingrid saw out back. Shout if you need anything help." He smiled and ran out of the door, his footsteps dying away.

Elizabeth turned to look at me.

"Matt is not as bad as you think. He does things for a reason and it is always for the right reason. Just give him a chance and I will speak to him about his behaviour towards you. Like he said before, he is just weary because you have been brought up among slayers." You could see that she was tying her best to reassure me about her friend. But I don't trust him, and I know he feels the same about me. "Come on." Elizabeth grabbed my arm and went towards the stairs. "Let start upstairs and work our way down. We need to work fast as who knows who might walk through the door at any moment."

I nodded and she went up the stairs first and I followed close behind with speed.

We just got to the top of the stairs when we heard the front door open and a voice shouting out.

"Hello, Uncle Bill. Are you in?"

I found myself frozen at the top of the stairs, not even bothering to try and hide out of view. I knew that voice. I knew that voice very well. I slowly turned around and looked down the stairs and at the figure standing at the bottom.

The figure at the bottom of the stairs looked like they were frozen as well. I could see their breathing getting faster and faster as I could see them getting anger and anger.

"WHAT ARE YOU DOING HERE?" The voice sounded loud in the quiet house. "Where is he? What have you done with my Uncle?" I looked at Elizabeth and she had the same confused look on her face. "Answer me Ingrid." Luke demanded from the bottom of the stairs.

Chapter 17
"I WILL ASK AGAIN. WHERE IS HE?" He shouted at us.
"Not here." Elizabeth said walking down the stairs towards him and I slowly followed her. She seems to have gotten over the shock, but I suddenly felt afraid.
"Where is he? What have you done with him?" He took a step forward as Elizabeth got to the bottom of the stairs and I stood just slightly behind her, wanting to keep my distance away from him.
"You need your ears cleaning out. Like I said he is not here, not anymore. He drove off in his car not that long ago like he really needed to be somewhere. The way he was driving I would never have given him his licence."
"You are lying." His voice was low, and I could hear the hate in his voice. "I know that you killed him, you blood sucking vampires."
I felt body go cold stone with shock and fear. Vampires, Luke know about vampires.
I found myself speaking for the first time since I saw Luke in the house.
"What do you mean vampires?" I somehow manage to get the words out of my mouth.
"You know what I mean, there no point in pretending anymore."
I saw he reach behind him and pulled out a knife at least 6 inches long. I found myself frozen, my eyes locked onto the knife. "I know everything." He pulled the knife up and wasted no time in bring it down with force.

I closed my eyes and turned my head away, not wanting to see it coming towards me. I waited for the pain to come, to feel the knife cutting through my body and for me to fall to the ground dead. But nothing happened, the knife never came down on me. I slowly opened my eyes and I saw that Luke was frozen place, his face fall of fear. I looked at the knife that was still raised in his hand and I felt myself relaxing slightly.

Matt had snuck into the house without anyone noticing and now had a tight grip on the hand with the knife in and Luke's other hand was pinned to his side. I could see Luke's hand was starting to turn a bright red colour. I looked at Elizabeth and she was leaning against the wall with a massive smile on her face.

"Drop the knife like a good little human you are. Or I can break your hand and you can drop it that way instead." Matt smiled a big grin, tightening his grip on Luke's arm. It looked like Luke was trying to pull away from Matt before he slowly opened his hand. The knife hit the floor, the sound echoing around the silent house.

"Now." Matt stood face to face with Luke, his gripping the raised hand and keeping it above his head. "You are going to explain everything that you know." He smiled again but this time showing off his fangs and making a low threating growling sound. I found myself taking a small step backwards with the sound.

"I… I don't know what you are talking again. I… I don't know what you want with me." His voice trembled as he spoke. But I knew he was lying, and it seems like Matt did as well.

"Really?" Matt made his smile bigger and he flicked his wrist suddenly. "Human bones are so breakable." Luke screamed in pain, but Matt had him pinned so he couldn't defend himself.

The scream seemed to bounce of every wall in the house, the sound being almost deafening. The sound of

Luke screaming made me feel sick inside, I thought my legs were going to go from under me. Matt pulled Luke arm behind his back and locked them in place not caring how much pain her was causing him. I kept my eyes on Luke, shouldn't I be glad that he was in pain because of everything he did to me, for everything that he done to hurt me?

"Ready to start telling the truth yet" Elizabeth was the one who was now speaking. "You were speaking about vampires and you tried to stab us with a knife so if I was you, I would start telling us the truth."

Luke looked at me his eyes never leaving mine.

"My Uncle use to tell me stories about vampires as I grew up, maybe that why I fell for Ingrid in the first place. He believed vampires were real and living with the rest of us, I just thought he was crazy. He was in his early 20's when he first met a vampire with his friends and when he became a trained slayer."

"Is that what happened at the party? The reason why you and Emma attacked us." I found myself asking out loud and I needed to know the whole truth.

"Emma only attacked you at the party because I put the idea in her head. She only did it because of me and I knew because of the fight at school, she had things took away from her and she wanted to act out. I went to the party because I needed to get information out of Ingrid, and I knew she would have spoken to me face to face. I will admit, it went too far too fast. We never planned on Rose getting hurt like she did, that was an accident, but we knew we couldn't just walk away after that. The knife was there for show, Emma was planning on messing with Ingrid when she brought the knife down. Ingrid was the one who attacked us, we never laid a hand on her." Luke voice was almost calm as he spoke about the party, like he forgot that Matt was holding onto his wrists and trapping him.

"What information did you want form me." My voice was far from calm.

"About Elizabeth. I lied when I said that I hadn't seen the new neighbours, I saw her and at first, I thought it was you playing a trick on me. But then I realise that there was 2 of you, it wasn't till the party that I realise what it really was. That everything my uncle told me about vampires was true and I had been dating one without knowing it. When my uncle found out that I had been attacked, he came to see me at the hospital, and I told him everything that I knew. Ingrid biting Emma, that we had new neighbours that had someone else that looked like Ingrid and how she attacked us. He explained to me that Ingrid was a twin and a vampire, and so were my lovely new neighbours. About how the Jones's were trained slayers that took Ingrid when they killed her real parents and now Elizabeth was looking for her. He re-told me the stories about vampires and slayer, but this time I listened to him and believed every word he said. When I got out of the hospital, he showed me this place. He uses it as a hideout for new slayers to be taught the skills they need to defeat vampire. This is where he showed me what to do when I meet a vampire, how to wipe them off the face of the earth."

Matt and Elizabeth suddenly hissed at Luke, I jumped, forgetting that there were other people in the room with me and Luke. Matt arm jerked again but this time harder making Luke screamed and nearly falling to the ground. The sound bounces of the wall again and it went through me.

"Are you telling me that you have killed a vampire?" Matt hissed and flicked his arm again, hurting Luke even more. Matt's fangs were so close to Luke neck, you couldn't even get a paper though the gap between them. All the calmness Luke had was now gone and he looked scared and afraid, he closed his eyes and was trying to move away from Matt fangs, but he was trapped. He slowly nodded his head and I could see Matt fangs slightly scrapping Luke neck but not breaking the skin.

"Who and when?" Elizabeth stood toe to toe to Luke, leaving me standing on my own. She had her teeth on show, but even though she didn't have her fangs yet, the look on her face said she could do as much damage as Matt.

"I don't know the name. It was just women and she had a child with her. I don't know what happened to the child after the mother died. I just went home to tell my mum I was staying tonight here and left the other slayers here."

"You mean you killed the women today?" I felt my body go suddenly cold, putting all the pieces together in my head.

He just nodded his head, not saying a word.

Elizabeth turned to look at me and I knew that we were both thinking the same thing. The women who Luke killed might be the one I heard begging for her and her son's life earlier.

Matt eyes turned dark with anger, his eyes burning with hate. He moved his head back, his fangs ready to use on Luke's neck.

"DON'T." I found myself hissing at Matt, the sound was sharp and strong.

Matt jerked his head away from Luke's neck and Elizabeth even took a step away from me.

I slowly walked towards Luke, feeling like I was the one who was now in control. I could see that Luke was trying to move away from me, but Matt was stopping him from moving.

"Who else have you hurt? Who else knows about vampires? Lily? Rose? Emma?"

"Fair point, what happened to the other females from the party? You miss that bit out of your story." I saw Matt twisting Luke arm again and I saw Luke locking his jaw shut so not to scream.

"Matt you need to stop hurting Luke or else." Matt might be stronger than me, but at this moment I feel like I could take on anyone. "Let him go Matt and Luke you need to explain everything that you know."

Matt looked at Elizabeth and she nodded at him. Matt put his fangs away and let go of Luke arm but remain standing right behind him.

"Emma and Lily saw you..." His voice was back to the cold calmness as before.

"I know that Emma and Lily saw me biting everyone. What happened when everyone woke up and at the hospital?" I found my tone matches his calmness.

"Emma and I were in the same room together. I woke up first out of us both and I remembered everything I saw. When Emma woke up not long after, I asked her what she remembered. She had trouble speaking at first but then she admitted what she saw and felt as Ingrid bit her and drank her blood. Even though I have not spoken to my uncle yet, part of me knew that you were not human. We knew that we needed to warn Rose and Lily about you. At this time I didn't know how much they knew or remembered. We found out what room they were staying in and went to speak to them. However when we got to their room, you of cause was there so we couldn't speak to them. Lily found us the next day to speak to us, I was surprise when she came to find us. Turns out she knew the truth as well and guessed that we did. We worked out how much everyone knew, turns out Rose is the only one who doesn't know about the world around her. It was decided that Rose shouldn't find out what really happened luckily, she never saw anything that happened. When my uncle came to speak to me, he made sure to speak to Lily and Emma at the same time."

"So Lily and Emma know about me being a vampire?" The calmness in my voice was dropping.

Luke nodded. "And they are going to help me get rid of every vampire in this village."

Matt hissed again with his fangs, making me take a step backwards away from him. "I can guarantee that we will win the fight."

I opened my mouth to tell Matt to put his fangs away when a cried cut me off.

"Help. Someone pleases help." The voice sounded so small, so innocent. All our heads shot to the door where the voice was coming from, the door under the stairs. Luke stopped us before we had chance to check the house, someone else was here. "Please, can someone help me." The voice came from a child, a boy that sounded so scared.

I rushed towards the door, grabbing the lock at the top of the door.

"DON'T YOU CA..." Luke shouted making a run towards me. Matt grabbed his arm and put it behind his back with speed and jerking him back towards him. "LET GO OFF ME VAMPIRE." Luke started to kick behind towards Matt, but he dodged every time.

"Don't worry, you are going down there first human. If not, I will break you or worse." He looked at me. "No matter what anyone says."

I let my hand dropped away from the lock and took a step back away from the door. Matt forced Luke towards the door, he tried to fight every step, but Matt was too strong.

"Open the door now." Matt growled and Luke slowly unlocked the door, his hand shaking as he pushed the door open. The door swung inwards and darkness appeared in front of us. The stairwell was so dark, you could only see a few steps ahead before it went into darkness.

"Start moving." Matt pushed Luke down into darkness of the stairs and Elizabeth followed without hesitation. I stood at the stop of the stairs as the darkness swallowed them up and followed them a few steps behind. The steps were steep, and I was finding it hard to get down them without slipping. God know how Luke was finding the stairs with Matt forcing him down them with his arms locked behind his back.

"Can anyone hear me please?" The boy pleaded, he sounded so scared.

"Yes we can hear you." I found myself shouting back, "We are coming to help you, don't be scared."

When Matt got to the bottom of the stairs, I saw him stopping and so did Elizabeth, they looked like they were frozen to the spot. I got to the bottom of the stairs and saw what they were looking at.

The basement was one single room that was the same size as the house above. It looked like the walls and the floor was made of the same stones as the stairs. Even though the room was so big, the only thing it had in it was a single squared based cage. The base of the cage wasn't any bigger than a meter across and it was a couple of meters high. Sitting on the cage on the floor was a young boy around 5 years old. He had his back against the cage with his legs crossed in front of him. The young boy had dark blond hair that came just above his eyes which were a light brown colour. Even though his face was red due to him crying, I could make out some freckles on his cheeks.

I pushed past everyone and ran towards the cage and the child. Luke made a grab for me, but Matt grabbed his arms again and pinned them behind his back.

"Don't even think about it." I heard Matt hissed behind me, but I didn't take much notice to him.

"Please help me. I don't know where my mum is. I don't know where I am." The boy sniffed, but his eyes appeared slightly brighter than before.

"What is your name?" I asked, sliding the bolt open that was at the top of the cage. I notice it had been put out of his reach.

The boy sniffed again. "Danny."

"Hello Danny, my name Ingrid." I turned to the others who all remained in the same place. "This is my twin Elizabeth and her friend Matt. You don't need to worry about the other boy." I turned back to Danny who was still back of the cage.

"That's what you think." I heard Luke says behind my back. I didn't need to turn around to know that Luke yelping was Matt either kicking him or yanking his arm back.

Danny laughed a small bit and climbed into my arms, locking his arms around my neck.

"You don't need to worry anymore Danny, I got you. You are safe now." I turned to Luke and mouthed "Where is she?"

Luke looked behind me before dropping his eyes to the floor.

I looked behind me and made sure that Danny face was hidden in my shoulder. Just behind the cage was a pile of ash with a human skull on top of them. The remains of Danny's mother. Danny has been so close to his mums remains and didn't realise it. I could feel my heart getting stuck in my throat.

I look back at Elizabeth and Matt and I knew that they saw the skull. I looked at Luke and his eyes were still glued to the floor and away from everyone else.

"Where my mum?" Danny looked into my eyes and I felt my heart dropped a mile. No way could I tell him the truth.

"Come on, let's go and find her shall we." I told him, wanting to protect him.

I pushed past Elizabeth and Matt again and walked up the stairs with Danny, making sure his eyes never looked behind us. I heard Elizabeth following me and Matt forcing Luke up the stair.

When I got to the stairs with Danny I went straight towards the front door. I needed to get Danny way from this house, I don't know where but anywhere would be better than here. When I got to the door I turned around and I saw Matt pushing Luke towards the dining room and Elizabeth followed him. The opposite way out of the house.

"What are you doing?" I asked following them with Danny still in my arms. Don't they understand we need to get Danny out of here? The slayers could come back at any time, we don't have time to mess around here.

"Well unless you had your eyes closed back there, something needs to be done. Both of you take Danny to another room and stay there. No matter what you say, you are not part of this anymore."

He pushed Luke into a chair, trapping his arms behind the chair and making it impossible to move.

"What you mean by that?" I half shouted back, starting to lose my temper with him.

Who does he think he is? I don't care if Elizabeth trust's him, I don't even slightly trust him. There is no way I am going to let him control me.

"Sshh." Elizabeth took Danny from my arms. "You are scaring him; he's been through enough already."

She took him out of the room, leaving just me and Matt with Luke.

"Why are you being nice to the slayer suddenly? It's not like he a friend of yours." Matt challenged me. "He is a killer, you know that. You saw that with you own eyes, you saw the skull Ingrid."

I didn't answer him as I didn't know the answer myself. I know I should be like Matt and wanting to hurt Luke and cause him pain. But deep in down in me it didn't feel right, nothing that is happening now feel right. It doesn't feel human.

I looked at Luke, trying to forget Matt and making my voice strong.

"What happened with Danny's mum?" I heard Matt laugh under his breath. "Well?" I was trying to keep my cool, but Matt was not helping.

"The slayers you been living with had them here for me when I got here."

"You know about the slayers I live with?" I found myself interrupting him.

"Yeah Mr Jones told me about what he did to your parents and how they stole you. It was him who found them for me to practice with."

"Where did he find them?" I demanded from him.

"How I am meant to know? He just found them; I didn't ask for their life stories. I don't care who they were before, I just know that they are vampires and that enough for me." He started to smile and started laughing to himself. "You know what, the slayers had her pin to a chair like you are doing with me now. Weird that isn't it, how you are doing the same things? The only difference is that we made sure her legs were broken so she couldn't run away and used silver and garlic to make sure she was weak. Being my first kills, they didn't want anything to go wrong. I think the worst bit for her thought was when we took that kid away from her. The way she begged and screamed for him. The weird thing was I wasn't even nervous about killing her, I mean it's not she human. I was about to kill her when you rang the phone. Did you really believe a train slayer like Mrs Jones would be so scared about a body being found? She called not long before you to gives us a head up on what she was doing. Pretend to be scared, get Mr Jones back to the house and then get out of there without you knowing a thing. Clearly you knew too much beforehand for that to work. More than the other slayers are aware of. The slayers knew Elizabeth were to blame for Mrs Wednesday death and I knew you were linked as well even if they don't. Did you enjoy killing Mrs Wednesday as much as I enjoy killing the vampire. Did you taste her blood, was it better than mine or Emma's?" The smile on his face was getting bigger and bigger the more he spoke. "Her little boy looks a bit like Danny, what do you think? That what makes me and you the same. You took away Mrs Wednesday away from her children, and I have done the same thing to Danny. At least I don't leave mine in the open for the world to see, something her children will remember for the rest of their lives. At least we took Danny away, right out of her arms as she screamed. Your daddy stayed with me till I killed her before returning to the house. He wanted to watch my first kill and made sure it all went to plan. I got a long sharp stake, pressed it against her chest and pushed it all the way through till it hit the things that supposed to be her heart. I watched her with my own eyes as she turned into a pile of dust on the floor." He laughed.

"Why did you come back here after you killed Danny's mum?" Matt spoke, I forgot that he was even in the room.

"To finish the job." Luke spoke with no emotion.

"To kill Danny." I took a step back from Luke. I shock by his coldness of the idea of killing a child.

Luke leant back in the chair.

"Shame the Jones's didn't have the same idea I had."

"And what idea is that?" I heard Elizabeth voice from behind me.

I turned around and saw Elizabeth standing alone by the doorway.

"Where Danny?" I asked.

"He's safe." She took a step into the room. "I ask you again, what idea did you had that the slayers didn't?"

"To kill you and Ingrid while you were still young. To stop you from growing up and interact with people lives." He suddenly turned to me. "Allow me to let a vampire into my life. To fall in love with a monster that should have died with her parents. A monster I let near my mum and my brothers. A monster that has never been human, who would attack her own friends without a second thought."

"Shut up." I took a step towards him, sick of the things he was saying.

"Why, does the truth hurt? The truth about how you are a monster. You infect everyone's life around you; you are just a parasite that needs to be stop. You, Elizabeth, this idiot." He nodded towards Matt, "And even Danny. You belong in the ground like your dear old parents. All this which are doing proves how similar you are to me and your 'dad' when it comes to killing."

"I said shut up." All the anger I felt for Luke, all the lies, the betray everything I felt exploded inside me. I pulled Luke up, yanking him out of Matt grasp to his and Matt surprised. I pushed him against a wall, not wanting to listen to anymore. Luke tried to push me away, but I didn't move an inch. He kept struggling under my grip, trying to break free. "Don't you dare talk about my parents like that, don't you dare. I am nothing like you and I am NOTHING like the man I been calling dad all my life. I do not infect people around me, and I do not kill innocent people.

Luke stopped struggling and locked his eyes into mine, burning deep into them.

"I know what the eyes of a killer looks like, it's like looking into a mirror. But you right, we are not the same. You are worse than me because you are a vampire, a monster. And last time I checked; you don't know your real parents. They have been rotting in the ground for years and you didn't even know it."

"SHUT UP." I screamed in Luke face and I pushed him away from me. I watched as his head hit the chair on the way to the floor. The sound of his neck snapping made me freeze, my hands still stretch out in front of me.

I could hear Luke's heart getting slower and slower till I could hear nothing. I watch as his blood started to form around his head.

I've killed Luke.

I lowered my arms and took a step away from Luke body. This was not what I wanted, I wanted revenge, but not for someone to die. Not really. I thought back to Jake, about how I wanted him dead and how much I hated him. I was a monster.

I turned around and saw that Elizabeth was still standing by the door. This was all her fault; she was the one who made me into a monster. If she never came here, Luke wouldn't have seen her from the window and come to the party for answers. I wouldn't have attacked them, and nobody would have gotten hurt. Luke uncle wouldn't have filled his head with stories about vampires and Danny wouldn't have been brought to this place. He would have been at home with his mum, happy.

I looked back at Luke. I wasn't a vampire, I was human.

Chapter 18

"Ingrid." I heard Elizabeth speaking behind me, but she sounded like she was somewhere else. I kept my eyes on Luke's blood, lost in my own mind. I felt a hand on my shoulder, and I knew it belong to Elizabeth. "Ingrid, it's Ok. It doesn't matter, it just…" I didn't let her finish speaking, I didn't want her anyway near me. I pushed her hand off me and pushed past her, knocking her to the ground. "Ingrid, hang on." I heard her shouting after me, but I ran towards the door. I heard footsteps behind me, but I don't know who they belong too.

I flung the front door open and ran out, not knowing what I was doing or where I was going.

"Ingrid, stop now." I heard Matt shouting angerly behind me, he must have been the one following me.

"Ingrid." Elizabeth sounded worried but I kept my head down and kept on running. I kept running till I felt my like lungs were on fire and I couldn't move my legs anymore. I put my hand on my knee and took some deep breathes, trying to get air back into my lung. I looked up and saw that I was at the bottom of my road, I was nearly home. I was nearly safe.

I ran the rest of the way home and burst through the front door. The house was still empty, no one else was here but me. I saw the clock on the wall and saw that it only took me half an hour to get back home. I ran up the stairs towards my room and banged the door shut and locked it. I put my head against the door and suddenly found myself crying, I slid down the door and put my head in my hand. I didn't think I could make such sound, everything coming crashing down on me. I killed someone. Luke was right, I was a murderer. I do infect people around me, innocent people. I thought about Luke's mum, I have destroyed her family and there is nothing I can do to fix it. She has done so much for me and has helped me when I needed it and I took away someone she loved. No, I thought to myself, it was Elizabeth who took him away. She changes everyone around her, she is the one who infect people.

"Ingrid?" My head shot up towards the voice. She was here. I looked at Elizabeth was standing by my open window; I need to start locking that, I need to keep her out. "Ingrid, what's wrong, why did you run away like that?"

"What do you think wrong?" I shot of my feet and walked towards Elizabeth, the anger building up in me. "Why do you think I ran away from the house, from you." I was nearly to toe to toe with her now.

"I understand that you are upset, this is still new to you. But don't worry, you will get over this. He was human and that was all, our food, our prey."

I didn't realise how heartless and cold she was.

"They are not our food or prey, they are people." I didn't expect my voice to go so high or to get the word out. I took a deep breath, I didn't want to lose controls with her, that would mean she has won. "I didn't want him to die, I didn't mean for that to happen. If I could turn the clock back, there would be so much I would change."

"He didn't love you anymore?" Elizabeth spoke in a calm voice that was making it hard for me to stay calm.

"I know that, I know we weren't going to be best friends anytime soon. This is going to break his mum's heart and destroy his little brothers and it all your fault. You make everyone around you into killers and you don't even care about anyone." I didn't care that my voice was no longer calm, Elizabeth needed to know what she has done, she was the one that needed to know the truth.

"I don't make people into killers and I care about you." She sat down on the edge of my bed, her body straight and confident. "I don't make people do things they don't want to do, and I never made you kill Luke. That was not the plan, that was not what I wanted to happen. I understand how his mum would be feeling, but we can't do anything about that now."

"You don't understand any of this. You don't understand anything about being human." I said coldly. "You don't care about me and I don't believe you about killing Luke not being part of your plan. Like you said, he was human and your prey. You have never cared for anyone that was human."

Elizabeth took a deep breath and stood back in front of me, her face suddenly serious. "Last year, in the city before last, I had a friend that was human. We were such great friends, but she didn't know I was a vampire."

"What was her name?" I didn't believe what Elizabeth was saying but I wanted to know more.

"I can't remember her name, I have met so many people in my life, their names all become a blur. Even hers. I used to sneak her into the house all the time or I would sneak out. Watching movie, shopping, eating out and things like that. I do remember it was fun and part of me even miss it. I couldn't risk our grandparents knowing about her. She was human and they didn't like us to socialise with our food. Our grandma does seem a bit more relax surrounding things to do with human."

"She is not my grandma." I chipped in.

Elizabeth eyes flicked for a second, but she carried on with her story. "I was off school for few days; I was ill so had to stay at home. She got worried as I didn't tell her I was going to be off, so she came to see if I was OK. She snuck into the house one morning, everyone in the house was asleep. She cut herself on a sticking out nail on one of the sides, been meaning to sort it out for ages. She cut herself and she bled, and our grandparents smelt her." She smirked slightly when she said the word ours. "We don't need to sleep during the day, we just do it as it easier to keep out of the sun. They smelt the blood and came up to see what was happening. I dragged myself out of my bed, but they got her before I did. They were not happy that I broke the rules, I brought her into our house.

"Let me guess that this story ends with her being dead and blood being drank." I don't know if Elizabeth thought that telling me this story would make me feel sorry for her, but it was working the opposite way.

"Correct." The answer Elizabeth gave had no emotion in it at all.

"Did you drink any of her blood?" I demanded from Elizabeth.

"I had some a few days after, we left the city not long after that. For a short time I kept an eye on her family, so I understand how you are feeling about Luke's mum."

"No you don't, you don't understand. I didn't drink Luke's blood after I killed him like you did. You don't even remember your friends name." I found myself taking a step back towards Elizabeth.

"You will get over all of this, I had no choice but to get over it. Do you think I don't feel guilty for her death, that I feel bad? I knew it was my fault, or at least part of it. She was my friends and I brought her into my world. I used to think about all the what ifs. What if I told her that I was ill and not to worry? What if I even told her I was a vampire? What if, what if. Ingrid, this will destroy you if you let it. You need to move on and forget about Luke, I understand that it will be hard. I am not going to pretend that it's going to be easy and it will be done in 1 day. But Ingrid you need to remember that you are a vampire and we feed off humans to survive, we have no other choice. Unfortunately, that's is just something you will need to get used to, otherwise you are not to survive long in this world.

"I WON'T." I was surprise that I shouted the words out, the sound hurting my ears with the sudden loudness compared to how Elizabeth was talking. However I no longer care about staying calm. I no longer care if this meant that Elizabeth was the one in control, I couldn't hear anything else from her. "I won't forget Luke or what I done. I won't forget my friends and be empty and heartless like you. I will not let you make me into a monster like you." Elizabeth seem hurt at my words, but I kept going. "All this talk about what ifs are just words, and I don't believe you mean any of it. I am not going to drink, and I will not let you trick me into doing it again."

"I never tricked you into drinking blood and you can't walk away from who you are and pretend you are someone you not. You are a vampire and we are family, that is something you can never walk away from. The fact that you are still wearing the locket around your neck, proves all that."

The locket around my neck suddenly felt heavy and it felt like it was strangling me.

"You know what." I ripped the locket off my neck and slammed it into her hand. "Take it. I don't want anything to do with you or vampires. I want you out of here and to leave me alone."

"Ingrid don't do this. We are family and we need to stick together against the slayers. Otherwise the monster will win."

"THEY ARE NOT MONSTER, THEY ARE FAMILY." I screamed in her face. It was Elizabeth's turn to take a step back. "I have a mum, a dad and a little brother. No sister, no twin or blood sucking grandparents."

"Don't you dare say that." She hissed at me, her body going tense. "Don't you say that they are your family. Not after what they did to us, they are killers."

I laughed in disbelief. "They are killers." I echoed her words towards. "You killed Mrs Wednesday and it seem too good for it to be your first kill."

Elizabeth opened her mouth to say something when we both heard the front door open. I found myself freezing to the spot. Someone else was in the house.

"Ingrid." I heard Ben shouted upstairs. I felt my heart break as he sounded so scared. I was so focus on Elizabeth that I forgot about Ben. I opened my door and stuck my head out so that I could hear him better. "Mum and dad are back; they are wanting help with getting some things out of the car. I don't want to go out there on my own. Please come down."

"I'm coming, just stay there." I closed the door again and looked back at Elizabeth. "Get out of here right now, or I am going to my parents and telling them you are here. Don't think I won't do it." I threaten.

"You need to start calming down and start thinking straight again. You are either going to either say or do something you are going to regret."

I opened the door and left my room, not caring how Elizabeth were leaving my room I as long as she wasn't there when I got back. I closed my door and went to the top of the stairs and shouted down them to Ben. "

Ben come up here please, I need to speak to you for a couple of minutes."

I looked towards my door for a few seconds as Ben walked slowly up the stairs towards me. Was he so scared of me or something else? This is not the Ben I know or care for.

"How are you doing Ben?" I only just noticed how frighten he looked as he stood in front of me.

Ben looked down at his feet, rubbing it into a mark on the carpet.

"I'm scared, I am scared of everyone. I don't want to be here anymore. I can't be here anymore. I know what dad did and I am scared he is going to do it again."

"Ben looked at me." I placed my hand on his shoulder. No matter what Elizabeth said, I am Ben's older sister and I need to look after him. I can't make him think that Dad killed Mrs Wednesday when I know it was Elizabeth. "You have no reason to be scared of anyone, you have no reason to be scared of dad. You ran out of the house before I had a chance to speak to you. I know dad didn't kill anyone because he is our dad and I heard him and mum talking the night of the murder. Do you think mum wouldn't have notice if he suddenly left the house in the middle of the night?"

Ben shifted slightly but he kept looking at me at least. "What about the bag?" He asked but he appears less worried then before.

"It just his work bag that he uses when he is making things in his shed. He probable building something for us and don't want us to spoil it by being noisy. Do you really think deep down that dad could kill Mrs Wednesday and then act like nothing happened?" I hope he believes in what I was saying.

"No I don't think he could." He sniffed a bit and gave me a small smile.

"Kids are you coming to help us or not." I heard dad shouting from the front door.

"We are coming." I answered back.

Ben went down the stairs first and followed shortly behind him. I was glad that Ben seem calmer now and was no longer scared. We went outside and I saw dad and mum was standing by the car, they smiled as me and Ben walked out.

"Feeling better mum?" I asked smiling, glad that the smile was no longer fake.

"Yeah, I just been to the doctors to get some things for the shock. I'm a lot better now thanks for asking. After the doctor, me and you dad decided to do some shopping. We even got you both something as you have been so helpful over the last few days. You have done so much, even with everything that has been happening."

Dad gave Ben a box from the boot of the car and he opened it. Inside was army gear with fake guns, maps, clothes, everything a young boy need to pretend to be in the army.

"Cool." Ben face lit up and I was glad to see him so happy.

"There two sets in there, one for you and one for your friends. Just don't turn my garden into a real war zone."

"Thanks mum, thanks dad. Can't make any promises about the garden." He ran into the house, not caring about anything else in the car that needs taking in.

Mum and dad laugh just laugh. Even I had to smile on my face, I can just imagine what the garden is going to be like by the end of the week. Mum is not going to be happy for too long.

Mum stood next to dad and reach into the car and got out a shoe box. She handed the box with me and I looked opened it. Inside where a pair of black and gold high heels shoes with ruby going along the straps. I saw these shoes ages ago and asked for them then. However I was told I couldn't due to the price of them and I couldn't buy them myself.

I put the shoes down on the edge of the boot and gave both of my parents a big hug. I was glad that they hugged me back, it made me feel safe, made me feel this is where I belong. I didn't care if they weren't my birth parents. They took me to school every day and made sure I got home safe. They picked me up when I fall and made sure I was OK. When I cried, they dried my eyes and let me cry on their shoulder when I needed too. They watch me grow up and they protected me as much as they could. They were my parents.

We broke apart and dad shouted towards the house. "Hey Ben, come on, grab the food bags and take it into the house. You can put them straight into the freeze. We going to have a take-away tonight as a treat."

We heard Ben cheering in the house, and we all laugh again.

Mum handed the shoe box back to me and smiled. "Take them in your room and bring down a DVD we can watch as a family."

I nodded, as a family.

Ben came out of the house and I saw he was already wearing his new army gear.

"Why are you being nice?" Ben asked as he got to the car.

I gave Ben a look, why was he asking that? I was glad that they were happy, and I didn't want it to be spoiled by him asking stupid question.

"We are happy, because when we found out that Mrs Wednesday was killed, we realise how lucky we are that we are all safe and well. Let go in and order the takeaway I bet everyone is hungry." Dad said clapping his hands at the end, a big smile on his face.

We all grabbed a bag of food and took them in the house. I made sure the shoebox stayed under my arms.

I put my food bag on the side and went upstairs towards my room. I got to my bedroom and stopped, looking at my closed door. I took a deep breath and threw the door open; I was glad to find that my room was empty. I put my shoes on the side when I heard my phone beep and I knew before looking who the message was from. It came from the phone she gave to me.

I got the phone out and I was right, Elizabeth name was on my screen.

'YOU CAN'T RUN AWAY FROM WHO YOU ARE. WE ARE FAMILY AND BONDED BY BLOOD. THEY KILLED OUR PARENTS; YOU CAN NEVER FORGET THAT.'

Why won't she take the hint and leave me alone? I don't want anything to do with her or her world. I turned the phone off and took out the battery. I will not let her get into my head or get in contact with me. I hide the phone under the floor with the other one. She knows that phones number as well so I can't use that one either. I will need to try and get another phone with a different number somehow without anyone asking questions.

I left my room and grabbed a random DVD of the side, not even looking at what I was grabbing.

I walked into the living room and found everyone waiting for.

"Which movie did you pick?" My mum asked as I walked in.

I looked at the DVD as I didn't even know. It was The Railway Children. A very rare, non-vampiric horror DVD that I liked watching with the rest of my family.

I put it on and sat next to my parents on the sofa, feeling safe and losing myself in the movie.

At the end of the movie I looked towards my parents. They were cuddling each other, and you could see that they cared for each other. Why did I hate them? Why did I think they hate me? They made sure I was safe as I grew up, if they really hated me then they wouldn't have done that. They wouldn't have kept me safe for so long.

The film ended and it was Ben turn to pick another DVD to watch. Ben ran straight upstairs and came back within 15 seconds with the DVD hidden behind his back.

"OK." Dad spoke clapping his hands together. "What do you want to eat? "Pizza, Chinese or Indian?"

"Pizza." Me and Ben said together. I laughed and it felt good to be laughing out loud.

"Well you two seem to be nice to each other again." Mum said looking at the pizza menu she got from next to the sofa. "What are you up too?"

"We are not up to anything. We can be nice to each other without there being a reason." I smiled and took the menu of my mum.

"OK. We only having one large pizza, so what flavour are we getting?

"Meat feasts." I said.

"Plain." Ben said at the same time.

Dad laughed "Some things never change. We will get half plain and half meat feast to keep this rare peace in this house.

Mum picked up the phone. "Everyone alright for chesses garlic bread and chips?"

I took no notice that she was looking at me as she asked about the garlic bread. Has she always done that or was it because I been acting so differently lately?

"Yeah, we normally get that with pizza." I smiled, trying to act as normally as I could.

"I know." She smiled back at her. "Just wanted to double check."

"So Ben what film are we watching?" Dad asked, "As you still hiding it behind your back."

Ben smiled a big grin and he took the DVD from behind his back. Jaws. A film he would watch 20 times a day if he could.

"Put it on." Dad sighed rolling his eyes.

"What wrong with it?" Ben said all innocently as he put it in the DVD player. He had a big smile on his face as he spoke.

"What right with a shark killing loads of people?"

"What wrong with a shark killing loads of people?" Ben smiled back as he put the DVD in and hit play.

Halfway through the film, dad got up to answer a knock at the door and then shouted us a few minutes later. "Grab your food kids, you can eat in the living room for once so we can watch the film."

I got up and went to the kitchen.

"Ingrid you got the extra garlic bread, Ben you got the extra chips to make it fair. No arguing" Mum said, handing my plate to me

"Why does Ingrid always get extra garlic bread?" Ben wined grabbing his plate of the side.

"Because." I said taking a big bite of the extra garlic bread. "I do, so deal with it."

Dad laugh and kissed the top if my head.

Ben stuck his tongue out and walked into the living room with his food, I followed them with mine and sat down.

Ben played the film again, however I just kept staring at my plate. Thinking back more on my life as I grew up, looking at the extra bit of garlic bread. Ben was right, if there is any extra garlic bread, I am the one that normally have it. If we order any sauces it normally a garlic one and it normally on my plate whether I asked for or not. When either of my parents cut themselves, they always seem to show it to me first before they put a plaster on it. I looked round the room and saw a few crosses that we had on the side and I saw the cross on my mum necklace. How have I missed so many clues that something was not right, that something was happening?

I looked at Ben, he smiled at me and looked back towards the film. I thought back to the flour trap, Elizabeth could have done anything to him while she was here. She doesn't care who she hurts, and I would never have forgiven myself if Ben got hurt in anyway. She nearly destroyed my family from the inside and there would have been nothing I could have done to stop it. I bite a bit of pizza and forced it down so that no one would see that something was wrong. I looked at the TV and saw kids my age having fun and I thought about Lilly, Rose and Emma and how we are now. Both Emma and Lilly know about vampire and they remember what I did at the party. Rose is still clueless about what been happening around her and I was glad.

Luke…

I found my breath getting caught in my chest and I forced myself to breath as I thought about Luke. I could still see him lying on the ground in the house, blood flowing around his body. Is he still lying on the floor at this moment or has Elizabeth or Matt moved him? Is he going to be dumped in the open like Mrs Wednesday, is that how Luke mum is going to remember him? Dumped in the open for everyone to see? Or is something worse going to happen to him? There was a lot of blood and Matt was in the room as he bled, did he drink any of Luke blood? Or has Elizabeth gathered his blood and now has it in cups in the den? For what reason? Danny? The thought of Danny drinking blood of any sort nearly made me throw up. What was going to happen to him now? I left him with a bunch of monsters, who know what is going to happen to him now? Is Elizabeth and Matt going to bring him up evil?

Make him drink blood from early age and control him like Elizabeth tried to do with me?

The phone rang, making me jump and nearly dropping my food everywhere.

"I get it." I jumped up and went towards the phone, everyone else were actually watching the movie.

I got to the phone and looked at it for a few seconds. What if it was Elizabeth trying to get hold off me? She can't reach me through the mobile anymore and I don't think she be stupid enough to come back to the house and come face to face with me. I grab the phone quickly before anyone came out and asked why I wasn't picking the phone up yet.

"Hello?" I asked with caution, waiting for Elizabeth voice to be on the other end of the phone.

"Hello, Ingrid? Its Jake from school, you don't mind me calling you, do you?" Jake cheerful voice came from the phone.

"Jake." I forgot all about the Jake, the plan of me wanting to kill him and asking Matt to hit him with the car when he was at the lights. He has done nothing wrong to me and I had been planning his death. "Jake I am so sorry for how I acted towards you at school. I shouldn't have shouted. You didn't do anything wrong; you were placed in a difficult place and I know I didn't help with the matter with how I was acting." I apologised, feeling so bad with how I acted towards him.

"So does that mean you gone back to the nice Ingrid?" I could hear him smile as he spoke.

"Yes, I have gone back to the nice calm Ingrid, not the one that shouts at teachers or other students." I found myself smiling as well as I spoke. "I been dealing with a lot of stuff my end and it all just got too much. But I sored it all out." I hope I couldn't help but thought to myself.

"I'm glad to hear that. The way you acted at school was not you." There was a short pause before he started to speak again. His voice changing slightly. "I am only calling as there gathering at the park tomorrow for Mrs Wednesday. Most people from school are going and I was wondering if you were going to go? We could go somewhere else after if you wanted to. School is going to be closed for a few weeks for respect, so it be good to meet up." I could hear the uncertainty in his voice.

"Why does this sound like you asking me out?" I was taken aback by what Jake was asking.

"Well not at the gathering obviously, that would be wrong. Somewhere after I was thinking. Unless you want to stay at the park, I saw you there last night. You are a rubbish spy; I saw you with your hood up." He laughed a little. "What were you doing at the park late at night anywhere? I am sure I never seen you there before?"

I felt my body go cold, remembering what I did at the park last night. Wanting to kill Jake then and then without no hesitation apart from he was there. That I was at the park to drink human blood, including Mrs Wednesday. Blood that I enjoyed drinking and wanted more, and I didn't care whose blood it was. I took a deep breath to try and calm down, I didn't want to remember all the bad things I did that night. "I normally walk around during the night as I find it calming and relaxing. Now about going out…" I found my voice trailing off, the image of Luke on the floor flashing into my mind. I took a deep breath as I felt like I was going to cry down the phone. "I am not ready for anything like that at the moment."

"Yeah that's OK, I can understand. So how about we go as friends then, it might do you some good if you are dealing with a lot of stuff at home. Get out of the house for a while and do something different." Jake was calm as he replied.

I took a few moments to think about Jake offer. I might not be such a bad idea to go to the gathering with Jake. To do something close to normal and escape for a few hours, getting my life back under control. "Yeah, I go to the gathering with you as a mate. You can come to my house and we can walk up together, we could grab something to eat after."

"Yeah that great. I will see you tomorrow then. Bye Ingrid."

"Bye Jake." I put the phone down and for the first time in a while I felt relax and calm.

I walked back into the living room and I could feel how big the smile was on my face.

"Who was on the phone?" Dad asked raising one of his eyebrows. "You appear to be in a very happy mood suddenly."

"Don't worry. It was just someone from school. There is a gathering tomorrow for Mrs Wednesday to pay our respect. He is picking me up and then we going to grab something to eat after." I sat down on the sofa and picked at the topping on my pizza.

"Ow it's a he is it?" My mum smirked.

I stuck my tongue out of her.

"Don't panic, it is nothing like that. We are only friends. I know him through Luke." The second I said Luke's name, the good feeling suddenly left me.

I had forgotten all about him and what I done, for a short period of time, I had felt normal again.

There was a sudden loud banging on the front door. Someone was knocking on the door, a fast pleading knock that wanted to be let in.

The room fell into silent, the music from the end credits being the only sound being heard. Dad suddenly moved towards the door and everyone followed him, not wanting to be left alone in the living room.

I looked towards the door and my heart skipped a beat when I saw that is was Luke mum and Emma. I saw that they both had mascara running down their faces and the tears were still flowing down their cheeks. Mum pushed past everyone and ran full speed towards the front door. She swung the door open and Luke mum collapsed in her arm, her cries becoming louder. "

He is dead, he is gone." She screamed louder as she spoke.

"Dead? Who dead?" Mum looked at us and I saw the panic in her eyes.

"Luke." The word sounded like it got stuck in her throat and I felt the room suddenly go cold. She buried her head into my mum clothes that only slightly muffled the sobs of pain and loss.

I lifted my eyes up away from my mum and Luke's, but I made the mistake of catching Emma's eyes. She might have been crying, but I could see the fire and anger in her eyes. She knew that somehow; I was involved in Luke's death. And she was right.

Chapter 19

I put the cup of tea down on the coffee table in front of Luke's mum, after my mum added half a bottle of brady to it.

"Thank you, Ingrid." She placed her hand on my check, stroking it slightly. "You were so good to Luke; I can't believe he hurt you like he did. I know that wasn't the son I brought up, someone changed him to do what he did to you."

I saw Emma in the corner of my eye, sitting in the chair furthest away from everyone. I moved away Luke's mum; I didn't want Emma to say anything about what she knows about me. All the chairs were taken in the room, even with Ben being told to go upstairs. I sat in the middle of the room, feeling exposed to everyone.

"What happened?" My dad asked, my dad voice was soft and low. "What happened to Luke?"

I saw her eye filled up with tears and some escaping onto her cheeks.

"I went to my brother's house looking for Luke. He had only just come out of the hospital and I wanted him home where he would be safe. No matter what age he is, he was my little boy." The tears were now flowing freely, and she didn't even try to wipe them away. "He lives on his own in a remote area, I hate him living so far away from anyone. I know he been spending a lot of time with Luke, so I guess Luke would be at his house. I drove up to his house and I didn't realise how bad the house looked. It looked like it was going to fall with the next blow of wind, and I hate the idea of my brother staying there or my son. I got to the door and I saw that it had been left open and I felt my heart drop so far. I enter the house and the first thing I saw was the house had been destroyed inside and took everything that wasn't nailed down. I shouted for my brother and even Luke, hoping that they weren't in the house when it got robbed. I walked into the living room and saw the damage, but it was empty, so I went towards the kitchen and…" She made suddenly howl like an animal that was trapped in a cage. My mum sat next to her as she cried, trying to help calm her down and comfort her. "I found my boy, my beautiful boy dead on the floor. My brother came back and found me cradling him in my arms and called for help. His blood, there was so much blood and…"

I stood up quickly, make the room go quiet. I couldn't hear any more of the story; I couldn't be in the same room as Luke's mum anymore. Not after what I did to her family, to her son. I kept seeing the image of Luke's dead body in my mind and I felt like I was going to throw up. I headed towards the door and I could feel the room starting to spin around me. I got to the door and I put my hand on the frame before I felt myself falling towards the floor and everything going black around me.

I opened my eyes and I panic when I saw someone was leaning over me. I thought Elizabeth was leaning over me again, but I relax when I saw it was my mum. I slowly sat up and I saw I was now in my bedroom. My dad must have carried me up the stairs after I collapsed.

"I am so happy you are wake, you been out for nearly an hour. You don't need to worry any more, everyone has gone now. I am so sorry you heard all that about Luke. I should have sent you upstairs with Ben, I shouldn't have let you hear any of that story. I am sorry Ingrid, in should have protected you more." She brushed my hair away from my eyes and I suddenly lost control of all my emotions. I suddenly burst into tears, all the stress and secrets I been dealing with taking over. My mum pulled me into her arms, and she hold me as I cried into her shoulder. I felt like I was a little kid again, but for once I didn't care. "Sshh baby, it's OK, I got you. You can cry for as long as you want. I know this must be so hard for you. You knew him for so long and this is the first person close to you that have passed away."

He didn't pass away, I thought to myself, I killed him. The thought made me cry even harder and I felt my mum hold me tighter. I didn't want to stop crying, I wanted to feel the pain for ever. I deserve to feel the pain for what I did to everyone. Somehow the tears stopped flowing and I felt empty inside.

"When is his funereal?" I choked out, the words being just above a whisper.

There was a slight hesitation before she answered. "It's tomorrow."

"Tomorrow?" I moved away from mum slightly. "That's soon?" Why was the funeral happening so quickly?

"Yeah. Luke's Uncle Bill works for a funeral home, so he got it all done within a day. I asked about the police and she said that it was fine to have the funeral. Your dad and I are going, and even Ben said he will go. Will you be up for going?" She sounded worried and you could see how concern she was.

I nodded. "I want to go; I need to go."

I needed to say goodbye and to apologies for everything I did to him and his family.

I rested my head on my shoulder, she started rocking me and singing a lullaby I haven't heard since I was child and I used to have bad nightmares. I started to feel my eyelids getting heavy and I couldn't keep them open. I didn't want to sleep yet, I was scared what would happen if I closed my eyes, but I couldn't fight it and sleep overtook me.

The nightmare felt more real than any I had ever had before. I was back at Elizabeth den and it looked the same as the last time I was here. I was alone in the den, but I could hear Elizabeth and Matt laughing from somewhere, the sound sounded like it was coming from everywhere around me. I could feel someone eyes behind me and I spun around to see who was watching me. I saw Danny was sitting crossed legged on the table, empty cups scattered around him. I saw that it was the same cups I used for the blood test. I could see that there were traces of blood still in the cup, some of the blood dripping onto the floor. Even with Danny keeping his head down, I knew straight away that it was him. I can't believe I left him with Elizabeth, I should have grabbed him on the way past and run out of the house with him. I don't care how I would have explained it to my parents, Elizabeth and Matt could do anything to him and no one would be able to stop them. I took a step forward, getting ready to grab him and make a run for it when the floorboard creaked under my weight. Danny head shot up and my foot froze in mid-air, the sight making my body go cold. Danny had blood coming from the corner of his mouth and I knew the blood didn't come from him. He grinned at me, showing me his teeth and fangs and I knew I was too late. Elizabeth had gotten to him and turned him evil and there was nothing more I could do to save him.

I heard a door closing behind me, I spun round, and I saw Matt and Elizabeth standing by the door that lead to the woods. They were blocking the door and I knew I was trapped. Matt had the same evil look on his face, showing off his sharp fangs. Elizabeth stood next to him with her arms crossed her chest, a nasty smirk on her face.

"Look Matt it's the murderer." Elizabeth snared and I saw she had her own set of fangs. Fangs? Since when did Elizabeth had her own fangs? I ran my tongue over my own teeth, but they were all normal.

"I am not a murderer." I stood a step backwards, but I knew there was nowhere I could go as they were blocking the only escape way.

"But didn't you kill your boyfriend?" I heard the small voice say from behind me. I turned around and saw Danny jumping off the table. "You pushed him to the ground and made his neck snap in half. You killed him because you are one of us." He voice was small still, but I could already hear the evil in it.

"I didn't kill him." I found myself taking a step away from him, however this meant I took a step closer to Matt and Elizabeth. "And I am nothing like any of you."

"You did kill him. You killed him because he killed my mummy. Don't you want to protect me anymore." His eyes were tearing up; however it no longer looked right with his fangs and the blood coming from his mouth.

Suddenly, I felt a pair of hands grab me from behind and pinned my arms to my side.

"If you not one of us," I heard Matt whisper in my ear, the sound sending shivers all over my body. "Then you one of them. Which to us," He growled closer to my ear. 'Means food."

Without any warning I felt a pair of fangs going into the left side of my neck and I felt the blood leaving my body as it was being drunk. The pain was unimaginable, and it got worse with every mouthful shallowed. I tried to pull away, to make any sort of movement to get the fangs out of my neck, but the arms pinning me was making sure I didn't move a single bit. I felt a set of fangs going into my wrist, the pain shooting up my whole arm. I managed to look down with my eyes and saw the Danny was hungrily drinking from my wrist, some of my blood dripping on the cold floor. I tried to scream but the sounded got stuck in my front and I couldn't even make a whimper. I felt my tears going down my face, the pain was getting worse and I didn't know how much more I could take. I thought back to how I bit Luke and Emma and how much pain in put them through when I bit them and drank their blood. I didn't even think to how much I was hurting them. I felt the last pair of fangs going into the right side of my neck and I suddenly found my voice when I cried out in pain. I felt the tears coming more freely and I could hear myself sobbing. I knew they were going to drain me dry of my blood and there was nothing I could do to stop them. I felt my legs give up from under me and I crumbled to the floor. I thought that me collapsing would stop them from drinking from me, however it seems to make them drink even deeper and even faster. I could feel my head spinning and the room kept going in and out of focus. My eyes locked onto something under the table and I stopped breathing, the air getting trapped in my lungs. Under the table was Luke's dead body, his eyes wide open and staring right at me and I couldn't do anything to look away.

I sat up in bed, my heart beating fast in chest. I looked round the room and I could see daylight coming from my window. It was morning. I lay back down on my bed, trying to slow my heartbeat down and control my breathing. I could hear people moving downstairs and I was glad that I wasn't alone in the house. I heard a knock on my door, and I sat up in my bed as my mum walked into my room. I saw she was wearing an ankle length plain black dress with a plain black button jacket. Today was Luke's funeral.

"I got your clothes for you." She put the clothes on my bed and sat on the edge of it. "Are you sure you want to today? If you want, we can stay in together instead, just the 2 of us." She pushed my hair away from eyes and I could see the worried look in her eyes.

"I am going to Luke's funeral." I need to make this right somehow, I thought as I got out of bed and starting to get changed into my clothes.

Mum gave me a sad smile and left the room as I finished getting changed, wearing a similar dress to my mum but with a longer button jacket. I sat on my bed once I was done and looked out of my window at the weather. It was a sunny and bright day, with not even a single cloud in the sky to spoil the perfect weather. The weather felt wrong for Luke's funereal, it should be dark and gloomy with thunder and lighting. I stood at my window, the sun hurting my eyes and saw a few people enjoying the nice weather in the street. They were laughing, joking and having fun, it felt like no one should be happy on this day.

I went downstairs and saw that everyone else were already waiting for me. I saw that dad and Ben were both wearing a black suit with white shirts and sitting at the dining room table. The atmosphere in the house felt weird, no one was speaking to each other or even looking at each other. I felt alone in a house full of people on a day that shouldn't be happening. Ben should be in bed still, sleeping in late and mum shouting for hum to get up while baking things in the kitchen. Dad should be in the garage, trying to mend something that me or Ben had broken and tried to hide. And I should be hanging out in my bedroom with Rose, watching scary videos and trying to scare each other. We shouldn't be standing in the dining room, all wearing smart clothes and getting ready to go to a funeral.

I remember my dad getting the car keys and getting into the car, but everything else of the funeral was a blur. I remember seeing Luke's coffin at the front of the church and people crying around me, but I could only name a handful of people who were there. I saw Rose and I was glad that she was finally out of the hospital, but Lily kept her away from me. However it seems like Rose didn't seems to mind being pulled away from me every time I walked toward her. I tried to speak to Luke's mum while at the funeral, but Emma kept by her throughout the day. Every time I walked towards them, Emma would give me a look to stay away and would steer her towards other people.

The wake was held at the village hall and there were even more people there sharing stories about Luke's life. I kept away from the people in hall, finding an empty corner and watching the world go past. No one took any notice of me as I watched them, some talking in a low voice, other just nibbling the food while other you could see had been drinking and the volume of their voice increasing with each pasting minute. None of the people in the hall should be here, this day shouldn't be happening at all. More people came into the hall and the room was become more crowded and I was starting to have trouble breathing. I kept hearing beating noises; my mouth and throat kept going dry. I looked down to the floor, not wanting to admit what I knew it was. The beating sounds were the heartbeat of everyone in the room and I was becoming thirsty by all the people around me. I felt my body starting to shake slightly and I was starting to struggle to breath. I looked up for a split second and I saw Rose walking towards me, I felt so relieved that she was now on her own. However that feeling didn't last long as I saw her face was full of hate and betrayal. I opened my mouth to say something to Rose when she grabbed hold of my wrist and pulled be harshly into a bathroom nearby.

"What the hell Rose?" I snapped at Rose as she let go of my wrist and slammed the bathroom door. I looked at my wrist and saw there was already a red mark appearing. "What is your problem?"

"What's my problem? What's my problem?" She half shouted at me, taking me off guard. "I got one big problem with you. Like how you know who attacked us at the party but won't tell the police? You won't tell anyone what you know, not even me and I am meant to be your best friend. I mean I was the last person to find out that you knew this whole time about the truth. Lily knows, Emma knows, and even Luke knew before he died about you. I don't understand why you won't tell the police what you know, what are you hiding Ingrid?" She was nearly shouting now, and I could see the hurt in her face.

"You need to believe, the only thing I am doing it trying to keep you safe." I pleaded, glad that she was still in the dark about what really happened. "But I can't tell you what I know, but I need you to trust me, please Rose."

Rose scoffed. "Trust you? Are you serious?" Rose took a step towards me, "I will never trust you again. I told the police this morning that you are hiding something, I expect that they will be speaking to you again soon enough. Good luck trying to lie to them a second time." She turned and walked towards the door and placed a hand on the handle before turning back to me. Her face now set in anger and not hurt. "From now on Ingrid, stay away from me. Stay away from anyone in my family. I know Lily been acting weird because of you, you infect everyone around you. You are on your own from now on." She turned back to the door and pushed the handle down on the door.

"Rose please listen to me." I grabbed her free hand to stop her from leaving, I needed her to believe me.

Her other hand came off the handle and smacked me across the face. I stumbled backwards in shock, my hand going up to my check. Rose just smirked and walked out of the room, not even look back to see if I was hurt or not. The sound of the door banging shut made me jump, getting movement back in my body. I let out a gasp, not realising I had been holding my breath after Rose hit me. I look some deep breath, trying to calm down and get control of my breathing. I went to the sink and splashed some cold water on my face, the coldness making me feel better, even with the stinging on one side of my face. I looked in the mirror and I was glad that there wasn't any mark on my face, I wouldn't even know where to begin to explain why Rose hit me. I took one deep breath and left the bathroom and back into the main hall and into my corner. I saw Rose on the other side of the room with Lily, Emma had now joined them, and I could see Rose lips moving. I knew Rose was telling them about hitting me, about staying away from me and I knew Lilly and Emma were happy with this news. I forced my eyes away from that part of the room, I didn't want to get caught staring and a fight starting in the middle of the wake. I saw my parents were speaking to Luke's mum, my mum's arms around her shoulder. I notice Ben were standing near them with Jim and Tim. I could see Ben was trying to keep them busy and trying his hardest to help them cope. So many people lives had been affected because of me because I tried to turn my back on the family. I let Elizabeth get inside my head and changed me into someone I was not. A killer. I saw Jake walk towards Ben, he must have sense someone was watching because he stopped and turned towards me. Jake saw me and smiled a little towards me and I gave him a small smile back. At least I got one person who is there for me, I know he will run away from me like everyone else once he knows it was me who killed Luke.

I stayed in the corner for another 30 minutes before my dad came over to me. "

We are going now. We are dropping Ben off at Tom's and then me and your mother are going out. You don't need to come back with us. You can stay here, or we can drop you off somewhere else if you want?"

"You can drop me off at home, it be good to have some peace and quiet on my own." I knew there was nowhere else for me to go and I knew I couldn't stay at the wake with all the real grieving people.

Ben got dropped off first at Tom and then I got dropped off at the house. I watch my parents drive off before I went into the now empty house. I stood in the empty hallway, I closed my eyes and I took in the silence. I was getting used to being on my own, even in a room full of people. I went up the stairs so that I could lay on my bed for bit before I decided what I will do next. I opened my bedroom door and I saw straight away that Elizabeth was standing by my window again, only this time she had Danny in her arms.

"Ingrid." Danny face lit up and he got out of Elizabeth arms and ran to me.

I gladly picked him up and gave him a squeeze. I was so glad to see him, even with memory of my dreams from the morning going thought my mind. The nightmare was fake, an idea put into my mind by Elizabeth. Danny was just a lost little kid, who has had a lot of bad things happen to him in his short life. I clutch to him even more tightly; I didn't want him to go back to Elizabeth.

"I am surprised that you till care for him." Elizabeth finally spoke, still staying by the window.

"Why are you so surprise? He has done nothing wrong in all of this. Everything that has happened has been because of you. Every little thing is your fault." I didn't hide the fact that she was not welcome in my house.

"You can't blame everything that happened on me. In the house, there were you, me and Matt and everyone was involved in one way or another." Elizabeth snared back at me.

"Where is Matt?" I was so focus on Elizabeth and Danny I had forgotten all about him.

Elizabeth smirked. "Took you long enough to ask about him. I told Matt everything you said to me the last time I was here. He didn't trust you before and he doesn't trust you even more now. He sees you as a slayer, as one of them." I felt my body go cold with the words from my nightmare, Elizabeth kept on speaking. "I mean he could be anywhere, and you wouldn't even know. Near anyone that you say you care about." I could see that she was trying to wind me up, I wasn't going to let her win.

"I don't care what Matt thinks of me, or if he trusts me or not. If he wants to remain on this earth 'alive', then he better stay away from anyone I care about. I will fight him and kill him if needs be and any other vampires that tries and harm anyone I care about." Even as I spoke Elizabeth and I both knew the last bit was a lie. More chance of Matt killing me then the other way around. "How do you keep entering my house anyway, I have never invited you into this house?"

Elizabeth smiled and showed me her teeth. I noticed straight away that her front teeth had become sharper. Sharper than human teeth. I slowly rang my tongue over the same teeth in my mouth and I found they had become sharper as well. Elizabeth had fangs growing and so have I. I felt the panic go through my body, I didn't want to have fangs, I can't have fangs. "The entering rule doesn't work on me and it will take more to keep Matt out of the house." She had a smug smile on her face, and I hated it. "Come on Danny, we need to go." She held her hand out towards Danny.

Danny looked at Elizabeth and then me, sucking his thumb. "I want Ingrid to come back with us, she promised to help me"

I felt my heart drop a mile, Danny was scared, he doesn't understand what was happening around him. His mum was killed and the people who saved him were falling apart around him.

"You don't need to worry Danny." Her voice was soft and gently, full of confidence. A tone that didn't match the monster I know she was.

Danny took his thumb out of his mouth and got off my hip. I tried to keep hold of Danny, to stop him going back to Elizabeth. But he was too slippery, and he went to Elizabeth who lifted him onto her back without any trouble.

"I won't be back." My voice was filled with the same confidences as her. Elizabeth eyes burned straight into mine. "No matter what you do, no matter what you say; I will never be part of your world ever again."

I left my room and closed the door behind. I hated the idea of leaving Danny, but I knew I had no choice for the time being. I needed to stop Elizabeth, I know I needed to stop her coming back into my house, to stop her hurting my family. I went straight into the kitchen and opened all the cupboards, getting every bit of garlic I knew my parents kept in the house. I went straight back towards my room, a plan forming in my head. I knew I needed to keep the house safe and everyone inside. I know there was a way to keep Matt out of the house, there must be a way to keep Elizabeth out of the house as well.

I got to my room and I saw that it was now empty. Elizabeth was gone, but she took Danny with her. I should have walked out of the room with him when I had him in my arms, I should have done more for Danny. I notice something in the corner of my eye on bed, something that wasn't there before. The vampire book was now on my bed and on top of the book was the locket. I saw the locket was wide open, I knew that Elizabeth was trying to play mind tricks on me with the photo. I went to the locket and snapped it closed, none of Elizabeth mind tricks will work on me anymore. She can't use the locket or the photos against me, the people in the photos are nothing to do with me.

I jumped when the phone rang from downstairs. I put the garlic and the locket on the book and walked down the stairs. I stared at the phone as it rang on the side, trying to work out who was ringing without answering it. I picked up the phone on the last ring and placed it against my ear.

"Hello?" I answered, not knowing who I wanted to be on the other end of the phone.

"Hello Ingrid, it's only your mum. How come it took you so long to pick the phone up?"

I felt myself relaxing hearing my mum's voice. "Hi mum. Sorry I was watching TV. I didn't hear the phone ring at first."

"That just proves that you had the TV on loud. How many times do I need to tell you and Ben, next door doesn't need to be able to hear our TV?"

"I know, I promise to turn it down." I found myself rolling my eyes. "What are you calling for anyway?"

"Your dad and I are going to be away for a few days but it's nothing for you to worry about. Ben is staying at Tom's house till we come home. You can stay at Rose's house and we pick you up when we get back. With everything that has been happening, I don't want you to stay at the house on your own. OK?"

I took the phone away from my ear and thought hard. Should I tell her that I wasn't friends with Rose anymore? That I have nowhere to go and I will be home alone? I looked towards the kitchen and I saw a bit of garlic that I must have dropped on the floor. If I tell my mum the truth then she will make me go somewhere else. The house will be empty, and Elizabeth will be able to enter the house and do anything. She could wait for Ben or my parents to come back and do anything to them. I put the phone back to my ear before my mum got worried about me not answering her.

"Yeah that's fine. I will head over to Rose's house in a bit." I lied, my eyes not leaving the garlic on the floor. "I will see you when you get back, bye."

"Bye Ingrid, good night."

I hanged up the phone and put it back on the side. I went towards the kitchen and grabbed the bit of garlic that I missed. I went back upstairs and grabbed the rest of the garlic in my bedroom. I crushed the garlic in my hand, wincing slightly as the garlic must have gotten into a cut I didn't know I had on my hand. I put the garlic on all the handles on the outside and inside of the windows and the door downstairs. I don't know if it will keep Elizabeth out, but I know that I will keep Matt out or even hurt him if he tried to enter the house. I went back upstairs and went to my room and I was glad to see that it was still empty. I saw the book on my bed still and an idea came into my head. I picked up the book, something I thought I would never do again and sat on my bed. I fan through the pages, hoping that it had a page that I needed, a page that would help me. I found the chapter I needed near the end of the book.

How to kill another vampire.

Chapter 20

There are many reasons why a vampire may need to kill another vampire. This should never be done lightly as it can never be undone. There are many legends about how to kill a vampire permanent or slow them down, not all legends are true and will get you killed trying them.
The most dangouses ways to kill a vampire who is over the age of 18 is by sunlight- this will cause their body to become a light and burn, the fire being able to burn other vampire around them. Yet vampire can walk in the day if cloud or other objects blokes the sun and the day is dark.

I thought back to when I first met Matt and how cloudy that day was outside- I know I can use the sun against Matt, but that won't help me with Elizabeth. I rubbed my hand against my leg, the cut still bothering me. There must be something else that can help me in this chapter.

Only raw garlic will burn a vampire when it touches their skin, no matter what age the vampire is. If the garlic have been altered in anyway, then it can't be used to harm a vampire. Even if a vampire has garlic on them, simple washing it off can neutralise the burning. If they can't, then the garlic will continue to burn thought out their body and slowly kill them. Vampires who have gotten their fangs early will feel the burn and the pain with time, but it won't kill them.

I dropped the book and ran to the bathroom, suddenly working out while my hand has been hurting. It wasn't because I had a cut and the garlic went into it, it was the garlic itself. I shove my hand under the tap and kept it there till I felt the pain stop and the garlic traces was gone. I let out a sigh of relief, I knew I needed to be careful that I didn't do harm to myself when trying to deal with Elizabeth. I caught myself in the mirror and I slowly opened my moth to have a look at my teeth. I saw that I now had 2 teeth now that were becoming sharper, both my fangs were now growing. I knew I needed to deal with them once I shorted out Elizabeth, I couldn't risk my parents finding out that I had fangs. They would know that I had planned on becoming a monster and all the bad things that I have done. I slowly walked back towards my bedroom and sat on my floor this time with my back against my bed this time. I picked up the book and started to read again, there must be something else that can help me.

There are some legends among human and some vampire is that you can slow vampire down with rice or a knotted rope. They believe that simple throwing rice or a knotted rope will force the vampire to count each grain or undo every knot. This will not slow a vampire down in anyway and will lead to the other vampire being killed.

Any vampires that are over the age of 18 will need to be invited into a house which has humans living there. If a human within the house have been bitten by a vampire, then they can enter the house without being invited in. If a vampire lives among the humans, then vampires may enter the house at any age and doesn't not need to be invited in. Once a vampire leaves the house, then vampires will need to be invited in again.

"Damn it." I didn't realise that I had spoken out loud, realise what Elizabeth meant when she said it will take more to keep Matt out of the house. She knows that her and Matt can come into the house whenever they want while I am still living here. I had nowhere else to go, there is no way I can move out of the house and I knew my parents wouldn't let me leave even if there was a place for me.

Crosses will not harm a vampire in anyway and a vampire can look and touch them without worrying about any injures. Holy water will burn vampires of any age and it will make them weak enough to be killed, however holy water won't kill them outright and they can heal back from it. Holy water is the only water that can affect vampires, running water like streams and rivers have no affect with harming vampires.

One thing that can harm and kill a vampire of any age is silver, the silver does not need to be pure to work. Any type of silver that touches a vampire will make their skin burn and stabbing them in the heart with silver them permanently.

Another way to kill a vampire is a wooden stake through the heart. If the stake goes into any other part of the body, then the vampire will be able to remove the stake without lasting damage.

I leant my head back against my bed slightly, so there where ways to hurt Elizabeth, Garlic, Holy water, silver and stakes. I went to close the book when my eyes caught a couple of words.

Vampire twins.

I opened the book more and read the couple of sentences linked to the words.

When attacking Vampire twins, you need to be careful. When the vampires turn 18 or they get their fangs early, they will become more linked and it will not matter of the distance between them. If anything happens to one twin, then it will happen to the other one. This means that if one twin gets hurts, then the other twin will feel the pain to a degree. When attacking a twin, you need to be aware of the other twin is and doing. The reason being is that the twin that is not being attack can drink human blood and heal the other twin. Giving them strength to defend themselves and attack you back.

I slammed the book closed and slammed it on the floor next to me. If I hurt Elizabeth in anyway, then I will hurt myself in the progress. And Elizabeth has read this book like I think she has, then she can use it against me when killing people. I don't know what to do now.

I looked out of my bedroom door and I saw a family photo that was hanging on the wall. It was a photo of the 4 of use on holiday last year. My dad and Ben were both wearing bright red and green shorts. My mum was wearing a short pink flower summer dress and she was smiling normally. I had black shorts on with a dark red top on and I had my tongue sticking out. If I give up now, then Elizabeth and Matt will hurt then and maybe even kill them. I can't let that happen. I got off the flood and I heard something falling to the floor.

The locket.

I had forgotten about that, I picked it off the floor and put it in my pocket. I need to get it out of the house, I needed to deal with Elizabeth and be strong for my family. I went to the floorboard and got my dad bag out of the hole. I looked at the book and shoved that back in the hole, it might still be useful for information to use against Elizabeth and Matt. I opened the bag and got one of the stakes out, I didn't want to use the knife in case I caught myself on the silver. I knew if I did anything to Elizabeth, I would hurt myself, but it was risk that I knew I needed to take.

I put everything back under the floor and made sure that nothing looked at of place in the house. I know my parents said that they will not be back for a few days, but I could risk them come home early and see that I had put garlic everywhere. I left by the front door, making sure that the house was locked up and secure. I knew where I needed to go, I needed to go to Elizabeth's den as I know this is the most likely place for her to be. I double checked that the stake couldn't be seen in my inside pocket, I could risk anyone seeing it and calling the police. I still have no idea how I am going to deal with the police now that Rose have told them that I know something new about the attack. I looked down at my watch to see what time it was. It was just before 7:30 at night so I know that they should be few people at the park still. It might be helpful if Elizabeth tries anything, however she might use it to her advantage, and I can't stand to have anyone else's death on my hands. I was too busy looking at my watch walking down the alley that I didn't notice someone walking the other way till I walked straight into them.

"Hey watch it." I snapped at the person as I looked up at them, I then realise who it was. "Jake." I half shouted in surprise; I didn't think Jake lived anywhere near the alley.

"Hi Ingrid." He was calm as he spoked, seeming not caring that I just walked into him and snapped at him. I notice that he was still wearing the suit from Luke's funeral and it suddenly dawned on me that I haven't changed out of mine either. "I was just coming to get you." He smiled shyly looking at the ground. Coming to see me? Why would Jake be coming to see me? I then remember the phone call the day before about meeting up on the non-date. I was meant to be meeting Jake today for the gathering at the park for Mrs Wednesday. Jake must of notice my hesitation. "Look if you don't want to do it anymore..." He started to say before I interrupted him.

"I still want to go to the gathering. Sorry, my mind is everywhere with everything that happened with Luke." I gave him a small smile and I was glad when he returned it.

"Tell me about it. I know people have set something up for Luke at the gathering as well. Come on." He lightly put his hand on my arm and lead me down the alley towards the park. "So what happened with Rose earlier?" Jake asked after a few moments of silence.

I stopped, taking Jake of guard and making him stop with me.

"What do you mean what happened with Rose?" Did Rose say something to Jake when I left the funeral with my family?

"I overheard Rose telling Lily and Emma about hitting you while you were in the bathroom. Why did Rose hit you, I thought you were such friends, expertly with everything that has been happening?"

I looked at the ground and back at Jake, not sure about how much of the truth I could tell him.

"Rose thinks that I know who attacked us at the party. She has even told the police that I know something and now I don't know what to do." I know I couldn't tell him the whole truth, but I can tell him the basic. "She said that Emma, Lilly and Luke were aware that I knew something, and I won't tell the truth. She hit me when I tried to explain all this to her." I found myself tearing up when I realise how many friends, I have lost in the last few days, how alone I had become in the world.

Jake put his arm around me in a way to let me know that he was shoulder to cry on.

"I can't see you keeping something so big a secret. I've seen how you been since that attack and I know you would do anything to get the attackers found. And the police think they know who done it anyway and are leaving the village in a few days."

"What do you mean? How do you know about the police? Does everyone know?" I felt my heartbeat faster in my chest, moving back from Jake.

"No one else know this yet. I shouldn't know this, but I overheard the police talking to Luke's mum earlier this morning. Another witness has come forward and have told the police that Luke was involved in the attack. That he hurt himself so that people didn't investigated him too much and that they are not looking into it anymore." I could hear the sadness in his voice as he spoke about his late friend.

"What about Luke's death?" I don't know whether I was relived or not that the police weren't looking into the party anymore as I was as guilty as Luke and Emma.

"The police are not looking into that either. They said it was an accident, that he fell and hit his head on a chair nearby that he had been using. They think he must have been looking for something which was why the house was such a mess. Even Mrs Wednesday death seem to not bother the police anymore, just that they are looking into it, but they don't think they can do anything more with it." I could see that Jake didn't believe in what he was saying. "This whole village is making people act strange and no one understand why." He gave me a small smile. "At least you turned back to normal and not letting the village win."

I smiled back a little. "I am glad that you stuck by me, none of my other friend have, I don't know what I would do if I had to deal with this all on my own."

I saw Jake smile dropped and he looked to the floor. "I won't be here much longer.

"What do you mean?" I had a bad feeling in the pit of my stomach.

"Before I came to see you, my mum told me that I am going to live with my grandparents." He sighed, "They live over 4 hours away and my mum is not wanting me to come back to the village once I've gone. Too much is happening to people in this village. You got attacked, our headteacher was found dead on the park swing and Luke 'accidently' died in his uncle's house. No one knows what will happen next or when it will stop. My mum just wants to keep me safe, to protect me and that means sending me far away.

"When are you leaving?" I didn't even try and hide the sadness. Jake was the only person left who was standing by me, if he leaves, then I will be truly on my own.

"My mum is picking me up in a bit and driving me there tonight." Jake reach into his pocket and pulled out a piece of paper and gave it to me. I looked at it and saw that it had his name on a number. "It's my grandparent's number, you can call me whenever you want a friend to talk to. I lost an old friend in Luke and now I am losing a new one in you."

"Thanks, I promise I will call. You can help keep me grounded from the madness of the village" I gave him a reassuring smile and put the number safely in my pocket.

"Come on." Jake nodded down the alley and we started walking towards to park again in silence, neither of use knowing what to say to each other.

We got to the end of the alley that lead out to the park and I was shocked with how many people where there. It seemed like every student and teacher from the school were here, I even spotted Mrs Wednesday husband among the crowd. People were in small groups around the park but most of them were gathering around the swings.

Around the swings set where Mrs Wednesday body was displayed were flowers, messages, candles and even some teddies. On the swing themselves where massive photos of Luke and Mrs Wednesday. Mrs Wednesday looked young in her photo, like she did in the videos on the news, her children sitting on her lap in a garden. Luke's photo had him standing with his mum on the beach, a massive smile on both of their faces. Both the photos were swinging in a light wind, the candle flames dancing on their faces. My eyes kept jumping between the eyes of the photos, full of life and happiness that was took away from them. I didn't realise I had been holding my breath till I felt my legs give way under me and found myself gasping for breath.

I was glad when Jake caught me before I hit the ground and half dragged me back to the alley, "Come on." I try to force my eyes away from the photos, but all I could do is keep switching between the 2 photos.

"Ingrid" Jake stood in front of me, blocking the view of the photos. "Ingrid look at me." I looked at Jake and found tears going down my cheeks. The guilt of the part I played in both Luke's and Mrs Wednesday death. If it wasn't for me, then they would still be alive and no one at the park would be here right now. "Come here." He pulled me into a hug, and I accept it, glad of the human contact and the feeling of being safe.

I pulled away when I heard a car beep just of the alley and Jake phone beeped a few times. I looked at my watch and sawt hat we have been in the alley for nearly half an hour.

"That's must be my mum picking me up." Jake sighed as he looked at his phone. "Make sure you stay safe Ingrid." He smiled and I smiled sadly back at him as he walked away, leaving me alone in the alley.

I put my hand in my pocket to made sure I still had his number when my hand brushed against the stake. I got so caught up with Jake and the wake at the park, I forgotten the reason why I came here. To go to Elizabeth's den, to get rid of the locket and deal with Elizabeth, even if I hurt myself in the progress.

I got to the park and made sure not to look at any of the photos by the swings as I headed towards the woods. I couldn't risk losing focus and I didn't have Jake to support me through it this time. I got to the woods and turned back towards to the park to see if anyone had seen me going towards the wood. I couldn't risk anyone knowing where I was going or following me in and getting caught up in everything. I saw that everyone was at the park still, I then noticed that everyone at the park had they heads down in silence. I found myself bending my own head in respect for all the people I hurt because of my actions and the actions of Elizabeth. I lifted my head up after a moment and went into the woods, the sound of people suddenly clapping from the park soon disappeared as I got deeper into the woods completely alone.

I manage to find the clearing without much problem, and I saw that there wasn't a hole in the ground. I don't know why I thought it would be so easy for me to get back into the den. I went towards where I knew the hole was, there must be a way to open it from the outside. I saw for some reason that the panel hasn't closed properly, it seems it had caught on something and there was now a small gap. I crouched down and managed to get my finger in the gap and managed to move it enough so that the gap was now big enough for me to get through. I got the stake out of my pocket ready and took a deep breath as I jumped down into the den and landed on my feet without any problem. I hold the stake out as I looked around the den, noticing that all the candles where lit but it seemed like no one was home. I put the stake back in my pocket and took out the locker, putting it on one of the chairs abandoned in the room. I turned towards the exit when the shine caught the corner of my eye. All the anger that I had been feeling about Elizabeth suddenly took over my body. She killed Mrs Wednesday meaning that her kids will be growing up without their mother. She made me part of the mob that killed Luke, his family will never know what really happened to him. They think it was an accident and he was involved in the attacking his friends meaning that they will never be able to move on. Jake's mum was moving Jake across the country to keep him safe from Elizabeth, to keep him safe from me. She has destroyed

Lily, Rose and Emma life, making them scared of the world they live in, making them scared to leave their own bedrooms.

I found myself striding towards the shine, eyes of the photos watching me as I came closer. I can't believe I felt anything for these people, these monsters. I grabbed hold of one side of the table and smashed it towards the grounds, all the photos, candles and flowering flying towards the ground. All the photos smashed apart from the main one, it remained in one piece and facing towards me. I lifted my foot and stamped on it, rubbing it into the ground as I heard the glass break, the sound being so satisfying. It felt like someone else had took over my body as I found myself going towards the second room and destroy that room as well. Pulling the bookcase onto the floor, books being thrown across the room and some of them ripping. I empty all the cupboard of food and drinks and empty them all over the bed and the floor. The more I destroyed the den, the better I was starting to feel. Once I could break everything I could I went to leave the den when 1 door caught my eye and I knew I needed to check something before I left. I went to the door where the shine used to be and where I saw Mrs Wednesday body the last time I was here. I don't know why I wanted to look inside, but before I had any more time to think about it, I found myself opening the door to the empty cupboard. I took a step forward into the cupboard and saw that there wasn't a single drop of blood, I wonder how many times Elizabeth or Matt had needed to clean up after a body, it seemed to clean for it to be the first time that it has been done. I left the cupboard, not even bothering to close the door as I made my way out of the den. I couldn't wait till Elizabeth comes back and see what I have done, I hope it kills her inside and shows her that she has no control over me anymore.

I walked back to the park, it felt like a had a sudden spring in my step. I cut through the people at the park, noticing that Emma, Rose or Lily haven't turned up yet. I don't know what they would do if they saw me here with how they reacted to me at Luke's main wake. I was glad that no one see to have noticed me as I didn't feel like speaking to anyone at the moment, I just wanted to be on my own for a bit. I didn't want to go home to an empty house, so I just walked around a bit for about an hour, but then I started to feel cold, so I walked back towards the house to get warm again, realising how long I have spent out of the house.

I froze when I got to the path towards my house. The front door was wide open and was bent in the middle and all the windows on the ground floor were smashed. A feeling of dread took over my body as I slowly walked to my door, not knowing what I was going to find inside. I stepped into the doorway and heard the familiar sound of glass breaking under my foot. I looked and I saw the family photos from the hallway broken on the ground. I took a few more steps into the house, looking at all the damage in the hallway. All the photos from the walls had been ripped off and smashed on the floor with everything that were on the side that wasn't nailed down. I went into the kitchen and saw everything from the cupboard were smashed on the floor and even the table had been turned upside down and were missing 3 legs. I walked back out of the kitchen and was about to head upstairs when I heard a noise coming from upstairs, someone was in the house and I knew who it was. I got the stake out of my pocket and slowly went upstairs so Elizabeth didn't know I was coming for her.

I stood on the hallway and I could hear crying coming from my bedroom.

"Danny you need to calm down. I am trying to think, and I can't do it if you are crying. I know I scared you, but I need to think right now." Elizabeth voice was sharp and stern.

Danny was here, I felt my hand tighten on the stake more. I wasn't going to let Elizabeth leave with him this time. The ways she was speaking to him now just proves what type of person she was. I slowly walked towards my bedroom door, making sure that I didn't make a single sound as I reach the handle. I opened the door fast, not wanting to give Elizabeth any time to react. I saw Elizabeth head snapped towards me as the door hit the back wall as I took a step into my room. I notice that it seems like my room was the only one that has not been destroyed yet by Elisabeth.

"Ingrid." Danny ran towards me and I picked him up and gave him a quick hug. I put him down behind me, I didn't want him to be between the stake and Elizabeth.

Elizabeth just stood where she was, her eyes full of fire as she kept them locked on the stake facing her.

"I saw what you did to the den." She chucked something at the floor by my feet and it landed with a clatter. The locket.

I kicked the locket behind me as I took a step towards her, I wasn't going to pretend like I care about that piece of metal.

"I already figured that already by what you have done to my house. I hope it shows you that I don't care about you at all. I am glad what my parents did to your family and if you don't leave right now on you own, then I will do the same to you. Danny is staying here with me; I won't let you take him away this time." I promised her, standing my ground.

Elizabeth just smirked and shook her head, acting like I didn't say anything. Without thinking a made a lunged toward her with the stake in my hand. I was tired with her acting like she was in control all the time, that she was in control of me. Elizabeth took a step back and kicked the stake out of my hand, making it fly across the room. "Just leave me alone already vampire."

I put my hands on her chest and pushed he backwards, using the advantage of her not having her balance back from the kick. I didn't expect the strength that I had and the look on Elizabeth face I don't think she expect me to that strong either. I pushed her across the room, and something must have caught her foot and she went backwards and out of the open window. I saw her try and grabbed the window still to stop herself from falling but she missed. I ran to the window and she hit the floor with her feet in a crouch. Her eyes met mine as she looked up at the window, burning with hate and fire. She shook her head and turned around and walked away from the house and away from me. I let out a breath that I didn't realise I had been holding, I have finally beaten her. I turned around and saw that Danny was now standing next to me. I picked him up and gave him a squeeze to comfort me, I could feel him shaking as I held him as I walked away from the window. I suddenly heard some tires screeching outside and I turned back towards the sound. I saw a black van stopping outside the house and a group of 3 people grabbing Elizabeth and dragging her into van. Elizabeth eyes met mine as I stood back so not to be seen by the people in the van, they were full of terror and fear. I watch as the van speed away from the house and into the darkness. What did I just see?

"Elizabeth." Danny got out of my grip and stood by the window crying. "We need to help her; we need to save her." I stood in the middle of the room, staring at the spot where Elizabeth had stood. I could feel my heart beating so hard and fast in my chest with fear. "Ingrid?" I looked dan at Danny, his eyes red and puffy.

I thought back to what Elizabeth has done to me, to try and hate her and to walk away but I couldn't. All I could think about were all the good things that she had done for me. She helped me after the party, she made sure I wasn't caught for my part in what I had done. She has tried and kept me save from the police and people around me that could cause me harm. I looked back at the spot where Elizabeth stood, the scared look on her face as she was being dragged away. I knew deep down, even though I had just moments tried to stake her with a stake, I couldn't walk away from what I just saw. I needed to save Elizabeth. I looked at Danny, his eyes looking up at me. I needed help to save Elizabeth and the only people who I can think who might help, are the only other vampire in the village. Elizabeth's grandparents.

Chapter 21

I felt so bad as I got ready to leave the house and go to Elizabeth grandparent's house. I was starting to feel guilty for what I did as the den, to what I did to Elizabeth. She trashed the house only after I smashed up what could be the only things she has left of her parents. I put my hair in a tight bun and nicked a black baseball hat from Ben to wear. I wanted to look different from Elizabeth as much as I could, I couldn't risk Elizabeth's grandparents thinking I was her. I grabbed some of my mum's make-up, adding colour to my cheeks to my pale skin. I checked that Danny was calm and wrapped up warm before I picked him up and left the house with him, closing the door as much as I could. I slowly walked towards Elizabeth's grandparents house, Danny holding tightly onto my back. I don't know if I was doing the right thing or not, but I knew I had no other choice. I knew if I tried and find Matt then he would attack me without hesitant. I have not hidden the fact that I don't like him and the fact that I had put garlic around the house has made it clear on what I think about vampire. I got to the bottom of the street that lead to the house when I stopped when I saw movement outside Elizabeth's house. I then realise that it was Luke's mum and his brothers, it looked like they were packing their car. What were they doing? I looked at Danny and I knew I couldn't walk past them with him and walk in Elizabeth's house without them asking questions I couldn't answer.

I notice that there were some trees and bushes next to the road that were thick enough for Danny to hide within without anyone seeing him. I walked over there and took Danny off my back.

"You need to hide in here till the coast is clear. People are out on the street and they can't catch us going into the house, so you need to be brave and stay here." I gave him the locket from my pocket and placed it into his hand. "You can keep this safe for me till we can give it back to Elizabeth's grandparents, it will help you stay brave." Danny hand closed around the locket and I watched him go deep into the bush, making sure he couldn't be spotted by anyone walking past. I looked down to the road towards Luke house and took a deep breath. I knew that Luke's mum would ask what was wrong if she see me acting different, even though I could feel my whole body shaking, I slowly walked up the road and towards the houses.

I just got to the car and was about to open my mouth when Luke's mum turned around and jumped when she saw me. She shook her head a little and put her hand over her heart. "Ingrid you gave me a fright I didn't hear you there. Got your quite shoes on for your night-time walk?" She tried to smile but failed, her face was red and puffy, it looks like she was going cry at any moment.

"Yeah. I need to relax, and the house was feeling too stuffy. I didn't fancy going near the park where they are loads of people. What are you doing this time of night?" I looked into her car and I saw that everything in their house was now packed into boxes with labels on them. I even saw some boxes that had Luke's name on that were tightly packed up. I looked back at Luke's mum and I saw she was looking at the floor, she knew that I had worked it out. They were leaving their house, leaving their house in the dead of night like they had something wrong. "You're leaving." It wasn't a question as I already knew the answer.

She nodded before turning towards the house.

"Come on you 2, we need to go." She turned back to me. "We can't stay here anymore, not now Luke is gone. He died alone at my brother's house and I couldn't do anything to save him. The police have now decided that Luke was the one that attacked everyone at the party, and I won't stay here and see people options change on him. The police don't even seem to care about his death, saying it was an accident and that it is. I don't think they understand how empty the house it now without him, how quiet it has become since his death. I know people will want to ask me question about Luke, but I need to protect Tim and Jim from all this. This is why we are going now, before anyone has the chance." Luke mum sniffed a bit, trying to keep it all together.

"Where are you going to go?" I hated knowing that she feels like she need to move out in the middle of the night like a criminal.

"I am going to my mums to begin with, I am not sure where after that. I will call someone to put the house on sale once I get there."

I saw Tim and Jim walking out of the house, it was weird not seeing them running around and laughing.

She helped them into the car and then gave me a big hug and I found myself returning it. She pulled back and I saw her wiping her eyes. "I am glad that you came by Ingrid. Make sure to keep yourself save and everyone else you care about. Goodbye Ingrid."

She got into the car and drove down the road, not once looking back at the life she was leaving behind. I felt a cold wind going down my back and I looked at Elizabeth's grandparent's house, feeling like the house was watching me. I can't lose focus of why I was here in the first place; I need to focus on saving Elizabeth.

I walked back to where I left Danny, glad that he had stayed hidden.

"Danny, you can come out now." I whispered into the darkness of the bush. I heard rushing and Danny climbed out of the bush, I picked him up and places him on my right hip. "Come on Danny, we need to keep going."

I walked back the way I came in silence, keeping an eye out for any other people who might walk into.

I stopped when I reached the gate to the house, having a more detail look then when I went past on the bus. The fruit from the tree was starting to rot on the ground and not a single plant have survived in the garden, more petals falling onto the patchy grass. The path leading up to the door was made of stone and the garden has started to claim it back as roots and weeds grew through it. I tried to see if there were any lights in the house, but the blackout curtains made it impossible for any light to enter or leave the house. Knowing what lives in the house, the dread I felt looking at the house made sense and why everything about the house have changed.

I pushed opened the gate and walked up the path to the door, trying to make sure I didn't trip over any of the broken stones in the path. I got to the door and saw that it had been changed to a more solid sturdy one that made sure to kept people out who they didn't want in. I lifted my hand up to knock on the door when I realised, I had no idea on what I was going to say to them. I was coming here to ask them to help me after I got their granddaughter kidnapped and nearly attacking her.

I heard a bang coming behind me, I turned around and let a sigh of relief when I saw that it was the gate banging close. I must have forgotten to close it behind me, and the wind must have caught it, slamming it close. My eyes were still on the closed gate when I suddenly felt a hand grabbing me from behind and violently pulling me into the house. The door banged shut as I was pushed against it by my neck, hitting my head on it with enough force for it to hurt. I blinked the pain away trying to work out wat was happening and I saw it was Elizabeth grandfather that had grabbed me and was now holding me against the door. I notice that Elizabeth grandmother was standing just a few feet behind the grandfather, her eyes locked onto my face like a predator.

It felt like time had frozen as I took in the image of Elizabeth's grandparents. You could see that the grandmother used to have dark hair that was now starting to turn grey, it was short and messy in a wild look. Her eyes are the same dark colours of her granddaughter and her skin was so see through that you could nearly see her bones. The grandfather hair was the same darkness as the grandmother with less grey on it in a crew cut style. His eyes and skin matched those of his wife and granddaughter, and you could see that they were all related. They both had their fangs out, fangs that looked longer and more deadly than Matt or any vampire I have seen on TV. The women licked her lips, the hunger all other her face and the husband eyes were full of hate and thirst. I tried to look away as the women walked towards me, her eyes trapping me in place, ready for the kill. The growling she was making becoming louder and louder with each step. Danny screamed in my arms, I wanted to put him on the floor, to give him a chance to run but I couldn't unhook my arms to do it. He clutched hold of me tightly the sound of metal clattering on the floor, breaking the spell the grandmother had on me. My eyes looked towards the sound and I saw that Danny had dropped the locket. It hit the ground the locket bursting open for the room to see. The grandmother eyes shifted to the locket on the floor, the hunger look from her face disappearing instantly. The grandfather eyes never left my face and his hands stayed around my neck, not noticing his wife sudden change in behaviour. I could hear the grandmother saying something that I knew was the vampire language, I was too focus on the grandfather to work out what she was saying. The grandfather turned to look at her, the hand on my neck becoming tighter. The grandmother words became sharper and more forceful and the grandfather hand dropped away from my neck. I took some deep gulps of air, glad that I could breathe fully again. He stormed away from me and into a room connected to the hallway muttering as he went.

I heard a tap running and lots of banging from the room. I stayed where I was, not daring to take my eyes of the grandmother. She slowly walked towards me with more care this time, talking her time with each step she took. She slowly reached her hand and I jerked my head back in reaction as her hand came close to my face. The grandmother didn't take any notice of me moving away as she took off my hat and my hair came down around my shoulders. I found myself swallowing, what was happening? I saw the grandfather come back into the hallway with a bucket that he put onto the floor next to the grandmother, the water in the bucket splashing onto the floor. He still had a guarded look on his face as he took a step behind the grandmother. The grandmother picked up a sponge that was in the bucket and started to clean off my make-up on my face softly and with care. She was turning me back into my pale self, to someone that looks like Elizabeth, the one thing I didn't want to happen. With each wipe of the sponge, the grandmother eyes were becoming brighter and brighter. Once all my disguise was gone, she put the sponge back in the bucket and took a step back. "Ingrid."

I found my mouth going suddenly dry, my body going on high alert. I no longer have control of this situations, the whole point of me coming here was to leave Danny somewhere safe and leave for Elizabeth. I can't have them confusing me with their granddaughter, someone who I am not.

I saw the husband turn around and walked away, not even taking any notice of anyone in the room. His footsteps getting quieter and quieter as he went deeper into the house. I had to placed Danny on the floor, I felt my body starting to shake and he was becoming too heavy to carry.

"I not who you think I am." I found whispering. "How do you know who I am?" I licked my lips and spoke louder. "I know who you think I am, but I am not them, I am not a vampire either. I am just someone that Elizabeth knows, I am human."

"I understand that this might be too much for you Ingrid. I understand that everything that you have been told by Elizabeth has changed your life. The only reason I know all this is because Elizabeth doesn't seem realise how much we hear in the house when she is talking to Matt. I heard everything they said. About your friends attacking you at the party and you defending yourself. About Elizabeth sneaking off to see you and about the death of your friend at the slayers HQ and you running off. I don't where Elizabeth is now, Ingrid what is wrong?" She sounded worried at the end when I could no longer look at her in the eyes.

I took a deep breath, knowing that I needed to tell her the real reason why I was at the house.

"That's the reason why I am here. Me and Elizabeth had a fight, a really bad fight. Things got said... I said things that I knew I shouldn't, and I did things I regret doing now. I forced her to leave the house and someone kidnapped her and it my fault that she got took. That is why I am going after her, I just need someone to look after Danny and I don't know who else I can ask. I am part of the reason why he is here in the first place. I need your help to save your granddaughter."

I found myself holding my breath and looking at the floor after I finished talking, waiting for her to shout for her husband and attack me again for putting her granddaughter in danger.

"Explain." Was the only respond from the grandmother.

I lifted my eyes and looked at her. What did she mean explain? I thought I covered everything already. Did she mean explain more about Danny, did this mean that Elizabeth never brought him here.

"Luke.... my ex-friend killed his mum because of the slayers. There we no one else to help him but us, we couldn't have left him in that place. And there is no way I am taking him back there to look for Elizabeth which is why I need you to look after him."

I waited for some sort of reaction from Elizabeth grandmother, but she kept her voice level as she spoke again.

"Explain why." I was struggling to speak is disbelief, why did she kept asking why? Why didn't she just tell me what I need to know and look after Dany. "Why." Elizabeth grandmother kept on speaking. "If you are not a vampire or not connected with this family in anyway, are you going after Elizabeth? Why are you going into a dangouses place and risk getting hurt for someone it sounds like you turned your back on?" She smirked as she picked up the locket of the floor and walked down the hallway.

I opened my mouth to shout out the answers to her when I closed it again. Taking time to think hard. Why was I going after Elizabeth? I could turn around now and go back to my house, take Danny with me and think of a reason to why I had him. To go to bed and wait for people to come back home and pretend that everything that has happened in the last few days never happened? But I know I couldn't walk away. Deep down I knew the answers and I couldn't turn my back on her. I found myself walking down the corridor where the grandmother went, keeping a tight hold of Danny's hand. I walked pasted a few closed doors, trying to work out where the grandmother went when an opened door caught my eye. I walked slowly towards it, keeping Danny behind me; I still felt on high alert and I still didn't trust the grandparents fully. I looked into the room and saw the walls and floors were bare, the only thing in the room was an old chest. Kneeling by the chest was the grandfather, he had his back to me, and it looked like he was looking through the chest. Even with his back to me, it seems like he appeared sad and not like the angry man I met before. I took a step forward into the room and the floor groaned under my feet. I froze when I saw the grandfather back tense before he carried on looking through the chest. I turned to leave the room, feeling the threat coming from him when I felt his hand around my neck again, yanking me further into the room and turning me to face him. I tried to scream out for help, but no sounds could get past his hands and it was getting hard to get air into my lungs. I saw Danny curled up in the corner of the room, crying to himself and not knowing what to do. I saw the opened door behinds the grandfather, why wasn't the grandmother coming to help? I thought she wanted to help me to safe Elizabeth, or was she just pretending to care to get me deeper into the house and away from the front door? I felt my feet leaving the ground as the grandfather lifted me up by the throat, making it even harder to breath. He didn't care that I was trying to save Elizabeth, he wanted me dead and there was nothing I could do about it. He threw me onto the floor towards the chest, just missing it with my back.

I took some deep breaths as he towered over me.

"I don't care what my wife says or Elizabeth." He snared as he spoke. "You are a slayer, not my granddaughter. I will defend my family against anyone who put them in any sort of danger."

He left the room and closed the door behind him with a bang. I heard a key turning in the lock and I knew he was locking the door. I go up fast and ran towards the door as I heard his footsteps walking away.

"Hey let me out. Let me out of here, you can't do this to me." I started to kick the door, willing it to break open "I am trying to save Elizabeth, I am trying to save your granddaughter. Let me out of this room." I started to kick and hitting the door harder and faster, the sounds bouncing of the walls of the small room.

"Ingrid?" I heard Danny speak over the noise I was making, his voice sounded so small. I stopped banging the door at once, I had completely forgotten about Danny. I took a step away from the door, what was I doing? I was going to scare Danny and I knew I need to keep my cool. I turned to look at Danny and saw that he was standing the chest looking into it. "Why is there an unopened envelope in here with your name on?"

I walked to where her was standing and picked up the envelope. The envelope was yellow and brown in colour and it looked like it was years old. The paper felt cold in my hand, I saw my hand was shaking slightly as the fear of the unknown creeped into my body. I opened the envelope and pulled out a letter. The writing was small and neat, filling the whole of the A4 page.

My Dearest Darling Ingrid,
If you are reading this it means your father and I are no longer alive, and my parents have done what I asked and given you this on your 15th birthday. You are old enough to read this now and hopefully understand everything.
I hope that you and Elizabeth have grown up without getting into too much trouble with your grandparents. I know you might think that they are being unfair, but the only thing they are wanting to do is to keep you safe, to make sure you don't have your fangs. We want you to have a life with people and a childhood without needing to worry about things like blood and fangs- not till you are years older at least. If for some reason you and your sister do have your fangs, then I hope you still are good people in your heart and souls.
I need you to know that your father and I love you and we will always love you. You have always been the apple of your father's eyes, never wanting to get off his knees and laughing at everything. You have always had a strong link with Elizabeth, always seem to be by your sister side if she gotten hurt before anyone else. Staying by each other side since you were born, never wanting to be moved away from each other. I hope you are still looking after each other, keeping each other safe and standing by each other through anything and everything.

But I need you and Elizabeth to be careful and safe, I know there are a group of slayers out there after us. The reason they are after us is because we are vampires and they are going after are kind. I hate the fact that we can't protect you, that we can't protect our own children from the slayers that are coming.

But know that your father and I will always be watching over you and will always be a part of your life. Each one of us have a locket, it was links all of us together and means that we will always be together.

I miss you Ingrid and I will always love you.

Bye Ingrid, I know you will make me proud.

Your loving parents

Xx

I found tears going down my cheeks, no longer having the energy to keep lying to myself. I read the line about the locket again and found my hand automatic going towards my neck. I felt the bare skin under my hand, and I remember that I no longer had the locket. The last thing I had that linked me to my real parents, my real family. My eyes fell on the chest and I saw photos of my real parents and I remember what I did to their shine, my own parents sound. I felt sick to my stomach with guilt and I found myself collapsing to my knees, Danny coming towards me. I pulled him into a hug, not wanting to scare him with my crying. I knew I needed to be strong for me, but I no longer knew how. I had turned my back on my real family and tried to destroy everything linked to them because I got to scared of the truth. Yet Elizabeth stayed by my side and tried to keep me going, and I responded by betraying her and forcing her to leave me.

I stood up, wiping my eyes and taking some deep breaths. I need to rethink and stay focus. I felt something cold suddenly torch my skin around my neck. I looked down and saw the locket was hanging back around my neck.

I turned around fast and came face to face with my grandmother standing a foot behind me.

"Hello Ingrid." She smiled and I found myself hugging her, nearly knocking her over with the sudden movement. I was glad when she hugged me back in a tight squeeze. "I knew it was you once we removed all that make up and took your hair down." She pulled me away and wiped my tears with her thumbs. "You look just like your mother, and Elizabeth of course. I'm so sorry about your grandfather, he thinks you are an imposter and a slayer. He wants to protect his family he has here, from anyone who even thinks about hurting his family.

My stomach turned with guilt when I remember the stake and my plan on using it on Elizabeth. If she knew what I was hiding, then it wouldn't just be my grandfather attacking me.

"Come on child, don't have such a worried look on your face." She smiled and stood by the door of the room. I turned away from her and looked at the chest, thinking about the shine again. "We can look through the photos later and I can tell you more about your parents then." She left the room and I heard her footsteps going down the hallway. I felt Danny hand in mine, and I smiled down at him. I walked into the hallway and saw that there were multiply doors. "I am in here." I heard my grandmother shout from one of the doors and I walked towards the sound.

I stood in the doorway and investigated the room where my grandmother voice came from. The room was high and wide, the walls covered in dark red wallpaper with lighter red flowers on them. The floor had a dark black carpet that looked like you would sink into it as you walk onto it. The curtains were the same dark colour as the carpets which hung by a big bay window, they were thick enough to block out the sun during the day. The room was being lit up by the pale moonlight coming in from the window, candles like the one that Elizabeth had in her den and a fireplace that was on the other end of the room that gave part of the room a warm glow. The room had 4 dark purple armchairs that were placed around a dark oak coffee table. The coffee table oak match the bookshelves that were in the room and other small tables that were placed in different places around the room. The room was full of stuff that were places on the bookshelf and on the side around the room. There were books, old statures, old toys and electrics; things I have only seen in museum.

My grandmother was sitting on one of the arms chairs, she smiled as we entered the room. Danny ran straight to her and sat on her lap; I was glad that Danny seem relax with being in the house now. My grandfather had his back to the room and was looking into the fireplace, the flames were high and made him look more like a monster then before. He turned around as I took a step into the room, the flames dancing in his eyes as his eyes burned into mine. His voice was low as he spoke, his fangs out and ready to be used. "

I don't think you are my granddaughter. You are a slayer and nothing more." He took a step towards me and I forced myself to stand my ground. "You might have everyone else in my family tricked, but it will not work on me. You don't even know the first thing about being a proper vampire."

I remember what Elizabeth said about our grandfather not believing I am family because the slayers took me. Our grandmother has accepted me, but I knew I needed to work harder for our grandfather to accepted me. I took a deep breath, my heart beating so fast in my chest I knew he could hear every beat. I knew I couldn't let him chase me away from my family, I knew I needed to proof to him that I was a vampire. I closed my eyes and let the power in my body take over me, letting my vampire side take over me. I could feel my fangs growing, I knew they weren't as big as him, but they could still do some sort of damage. I opened my eyes and my grandfather took a step forward towards me, I mirrored him and took a step towards him.

"I am your granddaughter and a vampire." I kept my voice calm. "I have never been a slayer and I never will be one. I have not tricked anyone; people know who I am and have accepted me and I don't care if you believe if I am Elizabeth twin or not because I am. The bit about me not knowing about being a proper vampire, you couldn't be any wrong. I have tasted blood with the blood test, and I have bitten 2 people and drank from them. The reason I am standing here and listening to you denying who I am is because I need your help to save Elizabeth. I need you to teach me how to deal with the slayers and to keep Danny safe here." I was now a foot away from my grandfather, waiting for him to react and to say something.

He put his fangs away and gave me a friendly smile. I took a step away from him in shock. I was ready for him to shout, to strangle me again, not smile at me. "Come into the back garden in 5 minutes and I shall teach you how to deal with the slayers." He walked pasted me and out of the room, my eyes following him as he left. I turned to look at my grandmother, trying to see if she could help me understand what had just happened.

She smiled at me as she stood up and put Danny on the chair.

"You don't need to worry about your grandfather. He just wanted to see the vampire side of you, not the scared girl that turned up at our house. You need to remember that it was his daughter that the slayers took, he is going to be cation when people turn up and say that they are their missing granddaughter." She gave me a hug, "But like I said, your grandfather accept you and you are finally home with your family." She sped at out of the room using her vampire speed without looking back at me.

I turned to look at Danny and smiled at me. I was finally home with my family.

Chapter 22

I left Danny inside the house with my grandmother and went into the back garden to find my grandfather. The only light in the garden came from the moon which lit up the garden in a white glow. The edge of the garden was covered on all sides with tall trees that made it impossible to see through from next door garden or the house. The grass in the garden was overgrown like the front and was starting to knot in a few places. The only bit that was clear was a circle at the bottom of the garden where my grandfather stood waiting for me.

I took a couple of steps forward when I heard my grandfather shout.

"STOP." His voice echoed in the garden, my foot froze mid-air, what have I done wrong? I saw him smile at me and I lowered my foot to the floor and smiled back at him. "You here to learn how to use your powers remember. So use your powers to come here." He crocked his finger in a come here movement. In a blink of an eye I was standing in front of him. Since accepting my true nature, it feels like I now have complete control of my powers. "Well done." He started to circle me, keeping in the grass circle with ease. "One of the first things you will need to be able to do is to hunt. If you can't hunt, you won't be able to survive if you get hurt. Blood won't be served to you on a plate, you need to get it yourself."

I nodded understanding that I might need to hurt someone to keep Elizabeth and myself safe.

"You first need to circle them if they are an enemy, make them feel fear and dread. It makes their heartbeat faster, pumping the blood round their body even more." He carried on circling me as I stayed in the middle of the circle, turning my head to make sure I kept my eyes on him. "You need to keep looking into their eyes, make them freeze to the spot. Make it easier to attack them and kill them. If they can't move, they can't fight back, which for someone who an enemy is a good thing." He smiled showing his fangs. "Then again, some vampires like it when they fight back, pumps the blood round the body faster. Let see what you can do."

I nodded and went to the edge of the circle and walked round it like he was doing, keeping an eye on my feet as I kept catching the edge of the grass. "Keep your eyes up, don't take your eyes off me, they can attack you if your eyes are down."

"OK." I moved around the circle again, still catching the overgrown bits but not looking down. My grandfather smiled at me and I smiled back as it became easier and easier to move around the circle.

"Good, well done, you are a fast learner." He suddenly stopped moving and I stumbled a bit trying to stop so quickly. "Now you need to be able to defend yourself against vampires and humans. The circling can be used when you are hunting and fighting. People won't be standing still when you are feeding from them and attacking them. They will fight back."

"I manage to defend myself when I was attacked at a party, I stopped the knife as it came towards me. I know how to fight back."

My grandfather shook his head. "Doesn't count when you are high on power, have you fought since then?" He asked.

I shook my head. "No I haven't."

"Thought so. Now if you can defend yourself against vampires, then you can easily defend yourself against humans." He moved towards me fast, I didn't even have time to move out of the way before he knocked me to the ground. I landed on my back, but he made sure I didn't hit the floor hard. "If you were human, then you be dead by now. I would have drunk all your blood from your body."

I shook my head with a smirk as he helped me up. "Now..." I didn't finish let him.

The second he helped me up, used my leg and tripped him up, knocking him to the ground himself. He looked shock when he landed on his back. He smiled when he saw me laughing.

"If you were human, then you be dead by now. I would have drunk all your blood form your body." I repeated the same words to him as I helped him off the floor.

He laughed. "Good job with knocking me down, you need to get them down when they least expect it. It may be a dirty to kick someone down when their back is turned, but it will save your life and others. They will do the same to you if they have the chances."

"It will help save Elizabeth." I sighed and looked down, remembering why I was doing all this training.

He sadly nodded and started to circle me again and I did the same.

"OK. I'm going to try and attack you and you will need to block me. You can't always be able to attack them, that's not how the real-world works. They might be able to attack you and you will need to be able to do something about it. Even a human might be able to get some lucky shots in. I'm doing it with vampire speed, so you can defend yourself against the slayers. They are slower, weaker and be easier to defend yourself against them."

I nodded, but when his arm came towards me, I still ducked out of the way.

"You can't dodge if you been knocked on the floor, if you are pinned down and someone punching you."

I nodded my head and his arm came towards me again. This time I blocked by catching it in my fist.

"Good, good again." This time I missed his arm and he grabbed my shoulder. "I got you. You can't miss any at all, it only takes one lucky shot for you to be dead. Now listen, I am going to grab you 10 times and I will keep doing it to you bloke all 10."

"Ok."

He grabbed me again multiple times with speed and I only manage to block 3 of them.

"Not good enough, not even close. If I was attacking you for real, you be on the floor with a stake in your heart and both you and Elizabeth will be dead. Remember, what happens to one of you happens to the other. So let's keep going then. I need to learn, and I need to learn fast."

He grabbed me again and again and this time I managed to get 5 out of the 10.

"Halfway not good enough Ingrid, you need 10 out of 10."

"I think hallway is good for my second try." I pointed out to him.

"Still not all 10. Let do it again."

The 3rd, 4th, 5th and 6th time I kept getting 8 out of 10, always missing the last few. On the 7th time I manage to get all 10, catching every one of his attacks.

"Well done." He smiled at me as I took some deep breath as I was getting tired, but I knew I needed to keep going.

I heard some clamping coming towards me and I looked up and saw Danny clapping and coming towards us with my grandmother.

"You are doing really well so far Ingrid." My grandmother beamed as she spoke. "It is good to see that you are keeping up with your grandfather. I am just going to get some blood for everyone. Since you told us that you have done the blood test. And because when Elizabeth retuned the cups, there were still traces of blood in them." She gave me a knowing look and I couldn't help but laugh. "I guess you got a type."

"AB positive." I didn't hesitate in answering her, no longer caring about drinking human blood.

"AB positive it is then. Danny you stay here while I am away. But stay out of the way so you don't get hurt."

Danny nodded and stood by the edge of the circle.

"Where are you getting the blood from?" I asked. "I know that there is a limited amount in the village."

"Don't worry, I know where to get the blood from in the next village. Elizabeth made me aware of the blood types in the village." She walked away with a sad smile and I knew it was because she said Elizabeth name. I looked to the ground and I felt the same way.

"How can I do the attacking?" I turned back to my grandfather. "I will need to be able to attack the slayers as well." I needed to know everything if I am to save Elizabeth.

"You need to use your vampire speed to your advantage. You need to keep punching and going forward. Don't stop, don't slow down, don't give them a chance to attack you back." I went to grab his shoulder like he did with me and he blocked me without even trying, I tried again, and he grabbed my hand before I was even close to him. "You need to work harder if you want to make contact with the person."

I took a deep breath and threw as many punches as I could towards my grandfather, and he stopped each one without breaking a sweat. I bent over to catch my breath and I saw him smirking with his arms crossed. I decided to play dirty as I hated not being able to do something. I went to attack him again, this time aiming near his face. This made his hands go up to block me, thinking that was all I was going to do. This means I could use my legs and take his out from under him. He landed back on the floor.

"Hey." He started laughing and even Danny laughed from the side-line. "We are not focusing on the legs, stop cheating. Try using both hands this time, don't get into a patten that they can learn."

I smiled at him, but I was still annoyed that I couldn't do it right. I don't think slayers would fall for a trick like that. If they did somehow and ended up on the floor, they would most likely put a stake in my leg while down on the floor. I helped my grandfather of the floor.

"Let's try again." I said.

He nodded and raised his arms and I took his advice and used both my arms. I threw 15 punches and I was shocked when I manged to grab his shoulder on the last one.

"Good." My grandfather beamed. "Let's try again. Keep punching and don't stop."

I nodded and we tried again. I didn't stop after 15 this time, I just kept going and was getting a fair few past my grandfather. He grabbed both my hands and stopped me; I opened my mouth to asked why we stopped when I heard my grandmother voice coming from the house.

"I got the blood. Come in now, the sun coming up soon."

When did she get back to the house?

I looked up at the sky and notice it was starting to lighten up in the distances. It was the middle of the night when we started training and it was dark when my grandmother left. I picked Danny up and walked back towards the house. Danny was starting to fall asleep in my arms and I stared to yawn myself. It dawned on me that I have been up for nearly 21 hours and I could feel my body starting to slow down. I walked into the house and saw my grandmother by the door with a cup in her hand.

"I set a bedroom up for Danny in the spare room. You have got your own room already." She walked towards the stairs

"What do you mean I have got my own room?" I repeated back to her.

She turned back to me. "Every house that we live in has always had 3 bedroom and a cellar. Your grandfather and I have the cellar as it dark and no sunlight can get in there. 2 of the rooms are separate bedrooms for you and Elizabeth and the third one is a shared bedroom for you and Elizabeth. We used to lie to your grandfather and said your room was a hide out for Elizabeth and a spare room for guests. You might not have been here for with us, but you have never been far from our mind." She smiled and went to the stairs and I followed her up.

I got to the bottom of the stairs and saw my grandfather going through a door that must lead to the cellar with 2 cups in his hand. He looked up and saw me, he smiled with nod before going through the door and down some stairs.

I walked up the stairs and onto the landing where my grandmother was standing by an open door.

"This is the shared room." She walked into the room and I followed her in. "I made the fire up already as we don't have lights in the house so everyone room have a fireplace."

I didn't take in much notice of what she was saying as I was too busy looking around the room. In the middle of the room were 2 coffins that were both purple with a red ribbon painted on them, the light of the fire making the coffin look darker from the fireplace on the far wall. The other light in the room came from 2 tall black candle stands that stood either side of the coffins that matched the black stripped wallpaper that were on the wall. It was the type of room you would see in a haunted house and I loved it. I carefully placed Dany in the coffin closest to the door, making sure that the lid stayed open for him and left the room with my grandmother.

"Come on Ingrid, I show you where you are sleeping." She took me to the door to the other side of the room. She nodded at the door. "Have a look."

I pushed open the door and stepped into my room. The walls were mixture of deep pink and purple that went with the soft black carpet that felt like you would sink into it and never stop. The fireplace matched the one from the spare room which gave the room a warm glow and light. The candles in this room were deep red colour and were in candle holders on the room like old vampire movies. In the middle of the room was my coffin which was red in colour and the word Ingrid written in a deep glitter purple.

"Wow." I gasped.

"I thought you might like it. We kept a cloth over the coffin so that your grandfather didn't notice your name on it. You do know you can stay, here don't you?" That this is your room if you want it?"

"You mean I can live here?" I asked in disbelief. "I would love to stay here." Why would I go back to a house where my parents killers lived?

"Do you think we want to lose you after we just got you back? We left the sides bare so you can put what you want on them. Do you have any stuff, or do you want to buy some things instead? You can nick some of Elizabeth's clothes to keep you going till then."

I thought of the stuff under the floorboards, the vampire stuff I got. I then remembered something else that was also under the floorboard.

The vampire's book.

"The vampire book, it's at the slayer house. Elizabeth gave it to me so I can learn from it and it still there. It's under the floorboard in my old room."

I went to leave the room, but my grandmother blocked the door.

"And where do you think you going young lady. It's morning and the sun is starting to rise. You are tired and the slayer will be there. I will not allow them to hurt you. Go to sleep and we can plan better tomorrow once everyone is rested."

She led me towards the coffin and away from the door and I knew from the look in her eyes that there was no point in auguring.

She handed me the cup of blood.

"Drink this then go to bed Ingrid, I can see that you are tired." She put her hand against my cheek. "I know you are worried, but Elizabeth will be fine till tomorrow, you both are fighters. She will fight back until you arrive and help her. But you won't be able to help her if you fall asleep while fighting."

She gave me a kiss on the head, and she left the room, closing the door behind her. I heard her go downstairs and down into the cellar. I started to yawn again, the tiredness becoming stronger. I knew she was rights and I needed to sleep, I felt more like a zombie than a vampire. I drank the blood in one go, not realizing how thirsty I really was. It tasted better than the first time I drank it, the flavour dancing on my taste buds. I carried on yawning; I really need to go to sleep. She was right I can't fall asleep when I'm helping Elizabeth. All the fighting took more energy out of me then I thought, and I haven't slept for hours. I put the cup on the floor and tried to climb into the coffin but nearly fell onto the floor. I tried again and I slipped of the edge of the coffin. I manage to get in on the 3rd time with a bit of a tumble. I didn't think it would have been hard to get into the coffin as it looks so easy in the movies. I was surprised on how soft and comfy the coffin was, the inside was covered in soft white velvet padding that made it soft to sleep in. I went to close the lid then decided to leave it open. This was the first time sleeping in a coffin and I didn't want to be closed in. Maybe after a few more nights in the coffin, I might be able to put it down. I felt my eyes getting heavy, feeling warm and safe in the coffin and in my home.

I opened my eyes and I saw I was in the cage that Danny was found in the cellar. A place I didn't want to return to again. I went to unlock the cage as I needed to know if Elizabeth was here or not and if she was safe. My hand grabbed the lock and I pulled it to open it. Nothing, it didn't move; it didn't open. I tried again and again but it stayed still. It was stuck, it wasn't going to unlocked from the inside. It needed to be unlocked from the outside. I leant back in the cage sighing, trying to work out what I was going to do next.

"Do you need help?" I heard a mocking voice say.

My eyes went to the voice and I saw Elizabeth leaning against the wall with her arms crossed. A mocking smile on her face that matched her voice.

"Elizabeth, thank god you safe." I could get the words out fast enough, so happy to see Elizabeth. "I'm sorry for everything that I done and said, I'm sorry for..."

"You're sorry." She snared walking towards me with her fangs out.

I heard banging from upstairs and heard people coming down the stairs towards us. Slayers. I could hear Mark and Mr Jones voices coming down the stairs.

"We are going to kill you vampire; we are going to make you suffer for what you have done." I could hear the hate in their voices as they got closer and closer.

"Elizabeth please help me; I know what I did was wrong. I'm sorry for everything I done and said. I know who I am now. Please. I know am a vampire." I was nearly in tears now. Why can't she see how sorry I was, how scared I was. I could hear their footsteps coming closer and closer, the sound echoing in the room.

Elizabeth stood just out of arms reach; arms still folded across her chest.

"You are not a vampire, you told me that yourself. You told me that the same time as you were telling me you are nothing to do with me and my family."

"I know I said that, I was wrong for denying what I was and for denying who you are to me."

"We are coming vampire, are you scared yet? If you are not scared, you will be." I could hear Mark laughing, they were so close now, so near the bottom of the stairs.

"Elizabeth please help me." I was begging now.

"Why? You destroyed my parents shine, not ours but mine. Like you said, you nothing to do with me. So why should I help you? I only help my family."

She turned around disappeared into the darkness.

"No Elizabeth please, I need your help."

I only got laughter back as an answer.

I stretch my arm, trying somehow to open the cage and escape. Someone out of eyesight grabbed my arm stopping it from moving and me pulling it back into the cage. I suddenly felt burning going down my arm, like someone got a hot poker and was moving it down my arm. I screamed as loud as I could, I trying to move my arm away from the pain and the burning. It felt my arm was in an iron grip and it wouldn't move it away.

I heard Elizabeth suddenly scream in the distances. "HELP, HELP STOP IT PLEASE. I'M NOT GOING TO TELL YOU ANYTHING. I WILL NEVER BETRAY MY FAMILY."

"ELIZABETH I'M COMING." I screamed back, knowing that the Elizabeth that won't help me, wasn't the real one but the one asking for help was. "I'M COMING TO HELP." I started to thrust about around, trying to get myself free. I have got to help her; they are hurting her. "ELIZABETH"

I moved my body forward, hitting my head on something hard. I fell back grabbing my head, trying to work out what had happened. I then saw the coffin lid over my head. I hit the coffin lid when I moved forward. It must have fallen while I was having the nightmare. I open the lid and sat up properly, still rubbing my forehead. I hope I've not done any damage to the lid or my head. How can I still be getting nightmare as a vampire? I thought they would stop.

I grabbed hold of the side of the coffin and lifted my legs over. I pushed myself up and got out of the coffin in one go, glad that I didn't fall out or faceplant the floor.

I went to the window in the room and opened the curtains and looked out onto the main street below. The sky was dark, but it was the early morning darkness with only a few hours of darkness left. I must have slept through all day and most of the night.

I heard a banging on the street and looked towards the sound. A For Sales had been placed next door and the wind was making it banged against the fence. Luke's mum must want the house gone fast for the sign to be there already. I looked at the rest of the street and saw there wasn't any other movement from people or animals. Everything was still apart from the wind and the sign. I saw a cupboard in the room and opened it and was glad to see some of Elizabeth clothes in there. I got changed into them, glad that there were dark in colour and more my style. I went to grab a jacket that was in the cupboard when I spotted something on my arm. On my right arm was a faint red mark where I felt the pain in the nightmare. That must be why I felt the pain in my dream because I caught myself on something. I went to the coffin to see if I could find out where I got it from, so it doesn't happen again. I don't know if there was a nail somewhere or if the coffin lid caught me as it fell. I heard the door open and looked up seeing my grandmother standing there.

"Are you OK? I heard you banging your head on your coffin lid." She couldn't hide the smile on her face. "You need to be careful with that."

"Yeah it fell while I was sleeping. I think it might have caught my arm somehow. Look." I showed her the mark on my arm.

Her smile dropped from her face, suddenly standing by my side. She placed her hand on the mark, it felt cold against my skin.

"You didn't do this to yourself. The slayer did it to Elizabeth." She looked in my eyes and I knew what she was saying. Why I could hurt Elizabeth- What happens to one twin happens to the other.

"They are hurting Elizabeth. I had a dream, I could hear her, screaming in pain. She was shouting for help, begging not to be hurt. That she would never betray her family."

She gave me a hug to try convert me, however it wasn't working. I had my mind on one thing.

"I'm going to bring her home tonight." I looked into my grandmother eyes. "And I will stop the slayers, no matter what happens."

Chapter 23

I followed my grandmother downstairs and found my grandfather in the kitchen with Danny. Danny was sat at the table with food in front of him and my grandfather was by the sink cleaning up.

"You do realise the sun sets again in a few hours?" My grandfather turned and smiled at me. "You can't sleep or day and all night you know." He smiled and his eyes fell on my arm and the mark. His smiled dropped and I knew I didn't need to say a ward as he knew what it was and what it meant.

"NO." He screamed, slamming a plate he had in his hand against the side, smashing it to bits. Danny jumped of the chair and ran towards me, I picked him up as my grandmother took a step forward.

"You need to keep your voice down and calmed down right now. Screaming and smashing things up in the kitchen is not going to help Ingrid or Elizabeth. We can't let our temper control what we are going to do next." My grandfather turned to look out of the window and my grandmother walked up to him and placed her hand on his shoulder.

"We got a plan." I spoke up, both my grandparents looked at me. "I know what I am going to do, I am going to save Elizabeth."

"No." My grandfather stormed out of the kitchen. I looked at my grandmother before following him out of the room. I found him pacing in front of the fire. I sat on the chair with Danny on my lap as my grandmother sat in the other chair. "No, no. Don't even think about it, not for one second. You been a vampire for one day, one night. You can't take them on, you be killed and so will Elizabeth. I know that the slayers who have got her, are the one who took my daughter and son-in-law away. The one who took you away for years and tried to make you into a slayer. The one..."

"The one's who have got Elizabeth right now and who needs my help right now." I interrupted him. "I know some stuff so I should be OK. I know how to fight and defend myself. I know can handle them and save Elizabeth." I snapped, why wasn't he listening to me.

"You know the basic stuff, stuff a 7-year-old could learn. They have trained for years and years. You have only trained for one night, there is a big difference there. You don't even know where she is at all, if the slayers know you here or if they are aware that you are a vampire again."

"So the sooner I go, the more time I have to look for her, the more time I have to help her. I can find her; I will find her."

He walked towards my grandmother and sat on the edge of her chair arm, taking some deep breaths.

"You are not going; you will stay here with Danny and your grandmother. I will go, to look for her and the slayers. End off." He said is so calm which made it worse for me to keep calm.

"No, not end off, I am going, not you. If you are worried about me being on my own, I will get Elizabeth friend Matt to help me. He been a vampire longer than me and I know he can help me fight." I tried to match his calmness but failed.

My grandfather just stood up and speed out of the room without even answering me.

My grandmother eyes followed him out before turning to me.

"Will Matt help you?" She asked. "Do you know where he is? What will you do if he doesn't? I've not seen him since Elizabeth left here."

I looked away from her and into the fire, watching the flames dancing in the fireplace and thinking the same thing. Will Matt help me save Elizabeth? He has known Elizabeth for years and he might not like me, but surely, he won't turn his back on her? He must know what I did to Elizabeth when I turned my back on her, if someone did that to one of my friends, I rip them apart before another sound came out of their mouth. So would he even listen to me explain anything before that? I had no idea where to even start looking for him. He could be in a different village by now or right outside the door waiting for me to leave.

I heard a cough from behind me, bringing me out of the fire. I turned around to the doorway where my grandfather was standing,

"Are you sure Matt will help?" My grandfather asked, I was glad his voice was normal again.

"Yes," I lied without hesitation.

He narrowed his eyes, I thought he was going to call me out for lying but he just shook his head.

"Tell Matt from me that if I don't get both granddaughters back by sunrise, he better starts running to a different country and start praying I don't catch him."

I nodded with a small smile of my face.

He then left the room again, I heard him go in a cupboard and started to move stuff around. I took Danny off my knee and walked towards my grandmother.

"Will you look after Danny for me?" I sat on the edge of the chair like my grandfather did before.

"Of course I will look after him Ingrid, you don't even need to ask. But please be careful when you lie to your grandfather, he not daft as you think." She winked at me.

My grandfather walked back into the room with a small backpack. It was black with a white skull in the middle with pink and purples straps.

He smiled when he saw me looking at the bag.

"I might not be happy with you leaving, but I am not going to send you out without any stuff to help you."

He walked to the table and I got off the chair to stand next to my grandfather. He opened the bag and pulled out a knife that had a plain leather cover on it. The handle of the knife was black with a single red ruby at the bottom. My grandfather took the cover off and I saw it was a double-bladed knife and it look like it could do some damage. "I sharpened it so be careful you don't cut yourself, use it when you need to. Promise?"

I shivered and nodded. The thought of killing someone made me feel uneasy, even though I know I might need to do it to save Elizabeth. He then put the cover on it again and put it down on the table. He pulled out a white thick rope and handed it to me. It was wrapped up so that it could be undone quickly, and it had very little weight to it.

He pulled out a small silver flask and he smiled at me. "It A-, I couldn't get any AB* that you like. Trust one of my granddaughters to like the rarest blood type."

I smiled back with a small laugh as he handed it to me. I put in on the table, I know I wasn't going to drink it. I know Elizabeth will need it when I find her, she will be hurt and will need to heal.

"I won't empty everything out but there is a map and compass in here in case you need it. There is a torch with spare battery's, some spare human food and waterproof matches. Be careful with the matches, they burn."

I couldn't help but stick my tongue out at him. "Really? I didn't know that."

He laughed as he put the stuff on the table back in the bag, putting the knife on the very top. He handed the bag to me and I placed it on my back, it wasn't as heavy as thought it would be.

"Do you know where Matt really is?" My grandfather quizzed me as I walked to the front door.

I opened my mouth to lie again when I remembered what my grandmother said about me lying.

"I got one or two ideas on where to find him. Don't worry, we are going to bring Elizabeth back. I promise."

He gave me a tight squeeze, kissing the top of my head. It felt like he didn't want to let me go.

He let go and I gave my grandmother a hug.

"Keep safe." She whispered in my ear.

"I will," I whispered back.

I picked Danny up and gave him a tight hug.

"Be good Danny."

"I am always good." He gave me a cheeky smile and I gave a shaky laugh as I let him go.

I opened the front door and walked out, closing the door behind me without looking back. I looked around the front garden, seeing everything in detail even in the dark. I could see inserts moving in the grass and animals at the very bottom of the street. I could hear people starting to move around in the houses across the street and leaves rustling down the road. I was glad my senses have caught up with my vampire skills. I took a very deep breath, letting the cold cool air enter my lungs. I shifted the bag pack slightly on my shoulder and forced my legs to move as I walked out of the gate. I stood on the edge of the path looking up on down the road. I didn't have the slightest idea on where to find Matt, the only other place I know in the village that was linked to vampire was the den. I walked down the street, keeping an ear out for anything that might cause me harm. I got to the bottom of the street when I stopped. I thought I heard something. I looked towards where I thought the sound came from when I felt something like a truck hitting me, knocking me off my feet and onto my back, the bag being knocked off my shoulder. I felt the air being knocked out of my lungs and I felt the back of my head hitting the floor. I looked up and saw Matt was pinning me to the floor and was the one who had knocked into me. I struggled as I tried to push him off me, but I couldn't shift him in the slightest. I stopped struggling and looked up at Matt face, it was full of anger and I could hear him growling at me with his fangs out.

"Well, well, isn't it the little traitor." He put his hands round my neck and started to strangle me. "Why was you at Elizabeth's house? Trashing it like you did to the den? Trying to kill her grandparents like the slayer that you are? Do you know the slayers have got her? Was it you who told them where she was? Are you going you tell them where the grandparents are? Tell them about me and Danny so that they can finish the job?"

I couldn't answer Matt even if I wanted to as his hands were too tight around my neck. I kneed him in the back to get his hands of my neck. He removed his hands of my neck but kept me pinned down with his knees.

"Look, just listen Matt it..."

He didn't let me finish talking before his fist went towards my face. I blocked it and shoved his hand away.

"Why should I listen to you? You are a traitor to my kind."

He tried to punch me again but I grabbed it and kept hold of it so he couldn't use it again.

"Matt, I know you mad but..." I blocked his other hand going towards my faces and kept hold of it. "For god sake Matt stop it. Look they are hurting Elizabeth; I am trying to save her. I am trying to help."

He pulled his hands back freeing my hands but keeping me to the ground. I rolled up my sleeve and showed him the mark on my arm.

"See, this proves that I am telling the truth. I want to help her; I am going to help her."

"Why do you care?" He demanded.

"Because she family, family look out for each other."

"So you final decided what side you on then?" His eyes narrowed. "Or are you going to change your mind again later on."

"Yes the side of my family and vampires."

He got of me and sat on the floor next to me putting his fangs away. I felt more relax now that he wasn't going to kill me anymore and have gotten off me.

I sat up and grabbed my arm with a hissed.

"Ahh." The burning pain going up my arm again.

Matt carefully lifted my arm up and we saw a deeper and darker red mark underneath the original one.

"We need to find her quick." Matt got up and helped me of the floor. "If the pain is hurting you, then it is going to be much worse for Elizabeth."

I rolled my sleeves down.

"Don't you think I know that. Why do you think I got a bag full of stuff? Or did you think I was going camping in the middle of the roads or something like that?" I picked the bag up and put it back on my shoulder. "So what are we going to do now? We don't know how much longer she can manage on her own."

Matt opened his mouth but stopped when 2 teenagers passed by the bottom of the road speaking loudly to each other.

"I might have got an idea on how to help Elizabeth. It will help her till we can get to her. It will help her heal from what the slayers are doing to her. Let hope you wasn't lying about being on the side of vampires."

He turned to looked at me and I saw he had a small grin on his face and had his fangs showing. I knew straight away what was going through his mind.

"What happens to one twin happens to the other one." I muttered to myself, knowing what he was thinking.

"Can you bite and hunt?" He asked hurrying in the direction of the teenagers.

"I know the basic that my grandfather taught, and I done the blood taste test with Elizabeth. But that all I have done. I've not gone out and hunted someone before." I said chasing after him. I was fine with drinking blood from a cup but biting someone and being aware of it was something completely different.

"Well you need to learn quick and deal with it. You are a vampire and vampires bite. You will heal and because you linked to Elizabeth, she shall heal a bit as well." I saw the two teenagers stopping by a notice board which had the map on the village on it. "We need to be quick and quite when we bite them. We got no time to go hunting somewhere else if they escape. Just keep your mouth shut, I will do the talking. I don't trust you 100% yet, not till I know for sure what side you really on." He didn't even slow down as he walked up towards the teenagers, I was nearly running after him. "Hey." Matt touched the boy shoulder who turned around to look at us at the same time as the girl.

You could see that they were related in some way because their face structure was the same. Same brown eyes, same shape nose, same shape lips and smile. The girl was round about the age of 17 and she looked like she had been on a date or something. Her bleach blond was down her back with curls in places. She had bright red lipstick on with sky blue eyeshadow that matched her strapless dresses, which was finished off with a pair of white high heels with no straps on.

The boy however looked older, only just below Matt age. The boy had short spiky hair, he was wearing skinny jeans, with a plain black top and a black leather jacket on.

"Hi mate." The boy smiled at us both. "We were just looking at the map. Me and my sister are lost and we are trying to work out where we are? I had to pick her up from a party and we broke down the road. Can you help in anyway?"

"Yeah, we notice that you looked a bit lost. This place can be a maze sometime. Yeah, we can help, what do you need?" Matt smiled at the boy.

"Good thanks. Do you have a phone we can borrow? We are not from here at all and mine is broken and she didn't bring hers. I want to ring a breakdown cover to try and help us."

"He threw it against at a wall and wonder why it not working anymore." His sister smirked.

"Yeah mine is broken as well but there is a phone box further down the road. Your sister and Ingrid can start to walk to back to your car. Break down cover fast here, not like some places I know. They be there before you and me and I don't think they wait for us. They a bit funny about that for some reason. Only downside to them am afraid."

The boy looked at his sister with a worry look.

"I don't know about that."

"Don't worry bother, I'm a big girl. I'm sure me and Ingrid can walk back to the car. We will be safe from any murderers. This village looks like a place where nothing happens apart from someone nicking a plastic cone."

"Don't be silly, I am just trying to protect you." He said pointing at he she replied by sticking her tongue out. "Stick together and look after each other."

Matt led the boy down the street and away from us. I knew there was no phone box that worked around here. Lots of the kids break them all the time and no one can be bothered to report them or fix them. They don't normal last longer than a week. I knew that Matt wanted to split them up so that they would be easier to kill. So that it was easy for me to kill the girl on my own.

The girl turned on her heels and walked back the way they came. I followed her, matching my steps to her.

"I'm Sally by the way." She smiled at me.

I nodded and smiled back a little, still trying to relax. "Ingrid." I didn't seem the point of lying to her about my name, not if she wasn't going to survive the night and she already used it before.

We fell back in silence as I kept turning my head to look around the street. I know from all vampire movies I've seen; you can't bite someone in the middle of the street. I know Elizabeth will die if I get caught killing someone as I knew I be trapped and won't be able to save her. I knew I needed to find somewhere hidden from human eye. After a few minutes I finally spotted an alley that was in between some houses, a place hidden from human eye.

"Do you remember what the road was called that you broke down on?" I asked, hiding the fear in voice I was feeling.

"Yes it was called Sweet Lane. My brother and I made a joke about it because of one of our mates. Why?" She sounded worried as she stopped to look at me. She probably thought I was going to say something bad about it. That cars were always been broken into on that street, or someone was killed there, something bad at least.

I pointed to the alley, my hand shacking a bit, lucky she didn't notice or said anything about it.

"That's a short cut, it comes out in the middle of Sweet Lane. Everyone use it, it's safe, we be at your car in no time. Or it going to be longer and we might miss the recover. Your brother and my mate would have made the call already, so we need to be fast." I hope she was gullible enough to fall for it and not ask questions I couldn't answer.

She looked worried for a second, you could tell she was thinking hard. If we went the right way, there would be no place for me to attack her.

"OK then if you think it safe. I trust you." She started to walk down the street and towards the alley.

She got to the alley and started to walk down it without stopping. It wasn't a long alley so knew I needed to act quickly, if I freeze then we could meet someone who show her the real way to Sweet Lane. I felt the pain return in my arm, I clench my teeth, so I didn't scream out in pain and get people running. They were hurting Elizabeth again and I know what I needed to do to help her. Sally was walking quickly and was at the end of the alley while I was still in the middle. I know need her back here in the middle and away from the opening where people could see us.

"Sally," I shouted to her, loud enough so she was the only one who could hear me but no one else. I crotched down on the floor with my back against the wall, making out like I was hurt. I saw Sally walked back down the alley and towards me. I felt my fangs coming out so I kept my head down so she couldn't see them. I knew I needed to be quick and I couldn't hesitate in anyway.

"Ingrid are you OK? Have you hurt yourself?" I saw her crotched in front me. I could see the worried in her eyes and she was looking up and down the alley. She stood up and I knew I needed to kill her now to save Elizabeth. I threw myself forward using my vampire speed and knocked Sally to the floor before she knew what was happening.

"Ingrid what wrong?" Sally sounded scared; her eyes were wide with fear. She didn't scream which was good, but I don't know how long till she does. I knew witnesses were bad, I know that without being told. I put my hand on her throat, turning her head away from me. I didn't want to look into her eyes, I couldn't do it if I could see the pain or the fear.

"Look Ingrid, if that is your real name, if you want money take it, take my jewellery's but let me go please. Ow my god, please tell me my brother is OK? That your mate hasn't done anything to him please?"

"I'm sorry Sally, I'm really am but I need to help me sister. I need your blood to help her as I owe her so much and this will help her."

"What? You need my blood?" She started to move but I kept hold off her, glad that she hasn't thought of screaming yet. I closed my eyes, letting my vampire side come to the surface. "Ingrid please. I..."

I bit down, cutting her off from talking, cutting of her pleading. I felt her blood filling my mouth, this blood was stronger than the ones in the cup. It was a bolder flavour, sweeter and I could taste that it was fresh blood. I could feel it going down my throat and making my body becoming stronger and more powerful. She started to struggle, kicking me in the back and trying to hit me off her. I could feel that she was trying to scream now, but it was too late as she couldn't get any sound out anymore. I kept drinking her blood, the taste and the power taking over my body.

I lifted my head up and looked down at Sally. She was breathing slow and deep, coughing slightly as she tried to breath in air. Her eyes were wide open looking at me, pleading with me to let her live. I bit into her neck again, not taking any notice of her eyes. After a few more minutes of drinking, all the blood in her body was gone. I lifted my head and looked at Sally. There was little blood coming from her neck, with only a small cut where I bit her. My eyes fell on her eyes which were wide open and staring back at me. The eyes of the person I just killed. I shifted my body and was about to stand up when I felt a hand grabbing my shoulder and covering my mouth to stop me from screaming for help. I been caught.

Chapter 24

"Ingrid, shut up and don't scream. If you do, then we are dead." I heard Matt saying from behind me. "If you scream then people will see what wrong. They see the body and then we will be in trouble. They might find out we are vampires and then we won't be able to help Elizabeth, will we?" I felt his hand move away from my mouth and he helped me off the floor. "You got blood on your mouth by the way."
He handed me some tissue he had in his pocket and I rubbed my mouth.
"Why did you put your hand over my mouth, I wasn't going to scream. I might be new, but I am not that stupid. And I was aware I had blood on me." I lied, not hiding that I was annoyed, but I knew by the look he gave me showed he didn't believe a word that I said.
"Where's the boy?" I asked worrying. I looked up and down the alley and noticed that Matt didn't have him with him. Matt didn't answer me and just picked up the girl's body and threw it over his shoulder. "Hey, what the hell are you doing to her?" I demanded. He just

walked down the alley where Sally was heading without saying anything. "Matt." I hissed, chasing after him, not wanting to shout out loud. "What are you doing? Someone going to see you, someone's going to see the body and call the police. Then like you said, we won't be able to help Elizabeth and we be found out."

Matt left the alley and walked across the road and behind a house that looked like building work were happening. I ran across the road after him, waiting to hear shouting from somewhere that we been caught, that someone had seen the body. But the street and the places around us remained empty. I got to the back garden as Matt places the body on the floor of the garden and turning to me.

"We can't leave the body in the alley because it would be seen way too easy for us to get caught. One thing you need to know about hunting, it's don't let the body be found. Hide the evidence."

"What about Mrs Wednesday body?" I challenged. "You didn't hide her did you, you left her in the open for all to see."

"I had my own reason for that, and I've already had an earful from Elizabeth, I don't need another one from you." I walked up to where Matt was standing and I saw what he was standing next to. In the back garden was a deep hole about 6 feet deep and a few feet while. In the hole Matt had already places the boy's body. I notice his eyes was wide as his sister and his neck was nearly ripped opened by Matt. "Here another lesson, when you go to a new place, find as many places as you can where a bodied can be hid. While you were taking your time feeding on your girl, I was digging a hole in an empty house that is going to be knocked down. We hid the bodies in the hole, bury them and when the builders come, they make sure they are hidden even deeper." Matt picked up the girl and places her in the hole next to her brother. I felt a guilty as I looked at them both in the hole. Wondering what they parents will go through when they don't return home, when they find their car on the street and no sign of their children? Never knowing what really happened to them, what Matt and I done to them.

"Earth to Ingrid." I heard Matt behind me. I looked up and saw he had moved away from the hole and was now standing behind me with a plastic sheet in his hands. "You going to help me cover them up, or are you going to stand there like a statue?"

I moved away from the hole and helped him to put the plastic sheet over the bodies. I knew there wasn't time for me to feel guilty. I did what I did to help Elizabeth and that is what was important. Matt placed some bricks over the sheet and started to put the soil back in the hole, within minutes you couldn't tell that there had ever been a hole.

He dusted of his hands and looked at me.

"Where are we going to go first? Have you got any ideas on where to start?" He asked.

"The slayers house where I was brought up. They might be some clues there as I know they were the ones who took her. There is some stuff there that I need to get while we are there."

I left the garden as quickly as I could and walked down the street and headed towards the slayers house. I wanted to get away from the garden and my first kills.

"Where are the slayers now, were they there when you left?" Matt had no trouble with keep up with me.

I shook my head. "No, when I left the house I was on my own. The slayers rang and said they were going to be away for a few days. The house will be empty which means we won't get caught searching it."

We got to the street where the slayer house was in no time. We walked up the street and I stopped when I saw the house.

"What is it?" Matt asked, looking towards the house.

"Someone is in the house. What are we going to do now?" I asked in a panic. Lights were on in the house and I could see movement behind the living room curtains.

"Simple, see who has come home early." Matt smirked at me and we both walked to the gate with caution, my eyes never leaving the house. I got to the gate and opened it, making sure it didn't make a noise and give the people in the house a heads up that we were there. I walked into the garden and looked behind me and saw that Matt was still by the gate.

"What you seen?" I whispered looking at the house to see if he seen something. I couldn't see anything and looked back towards Matt. When I turned my head, I caught of whiff of something in the air. Garlic.

Matt face did not look happy.

"In my defence, I did it when I still hated vampires and Elizabeth. I didn't think to wash it off before I went to my grandparents. I was too focus on Elizabeth being kidnapped."

Matt shook his head and lent on the gate post, armed crossed.

"I keep a look out from here. Shout if you need help and I will help if I can. I can't enter can I without getting bunt by the garlic and I need to be invited into this house. I can feel it."

Why does Matt need to be invited into the house when...? I thought back to the conversation I had with my grandmother about me staying with them. I don't live in the slayers house anymore I realise. I nodded at Matt who moved away from the gate out of sight of the house. I turned away from where Matt was standing and slowly walked to the house, trying to work out what I was going to do if the slayers were home waiting for me.

I got to the door and saw that it was open slightly still due to the damage, making it impossible for the door to close completely. I opened the door with some difficult and walked into the hallway. Whoever was in the house have tidy up most of the damage that had been done. The glass has been brushed into a pile in the corner and I could see black bags packed with broken stuff in the kitchen door. My eyes fell to the side where the family photo had been places with the broken glass had been taken out. Looking at the photo and know the truth made me want to rip the photo up into small pieces and burn it to ash.

I took a step forward and I heard some miss glass that have been missed breaking under my feet. I froze as I heard a voice come from the living.

"Hello?" Ben asked with uncertainty. His head peered slightly around the corner before he walked out of the living, his voice more relax. "Ingrid you back, you home." He sounded glad.

"Ben are the slay... are mum and dad here?" I asked looking round the house, waiting for them to suddenly appear with a stakes aiming at my chest.

"No, they are still helping a mate out as far as I am aware. I only came back here to get some more stuff to take back to Tom's. What happened here Ingrid, do you know anything about it?"

I was about to lie about everything when I heard another noise from the living of someone moving. I raised my hand ready to use them when Tom's head suddenly popped round the coroner.

"Ingrid you back, I thought it was a burglar."

I lowered my hands; human can be so stupid. Why would Ben be talking to a burglar in the hallway? I put my grandfather bag by the door, and I started to walk up the stairs. I didn't have time to hand around here, I needed to get my stuff, have a look for clues and then leave. I couldn't risk the slayers coming home early and finding me and asking questions I can't answer.

"Ingrid, I am trying to talk to you. Wait." Ben chased after me up the stairs and Tom was closed behind him. I got to my room and turned around to face.

"Look what do you want? In case you notice I'm busy." Ben crossed his arms.

"What do you think we want? I came home and saw the house was empty, trashed and smashed up. I know you were was at the house as all you stuff was here and not at a mate's house. I thought you got attacked again or something."

"Have you called anyone about this?" I needed to know if I had a new problem to deal with.

"Not yet. I cleaned up most of the mess and was going to call mum and dad when you came in. Ingrid what is happening?

"Good, don't tell anyone Ben." I walked into my room and grabbed a plain black bag-pack from under my bed. "Just go to Tom's house and stay there. Don't worry about anything here."

I turned to look at Ben when I saw the shoes box behind him, the ones the slayers gave me. They were one thing that weren't going to come home with me. I can't believe I didn't work out that the slayers were trying to bribe me to make out like there wasn't anything wrong when everything was wrong.

"What this?" I turned my head and saw Tom was holding a stake in his hand. It was the stake that Elizabeth kicked out of my hand, the one I was going to use on her. I forgot it was on the floor, I had forgotten it was in my room.

"Give it here Tom and go downstairs. I need to talk to Ben alone." I held out my hand for the stake, not trusting him having it in his hand. Tom looked at Ben and he nodded his head. Tom handed me the stake and left the room, shutting the door behind him. I could hear his footsteps going downstairs and back into the living. I dropped the stake on my bed and lift the floorboard up where all my stuff was hidden.

"Where are you going?" Ben asked when he saw I was packing everything up. I kept the slayers bag in the hole. I didn't want to use anything that the slayers could use in return to hurt me or Elizabeth. I know that the slayers won't find the bag, so I don't need to worry about any of the weapons. I covered the hole back in and stood up to walk to the wardrobe. Ben saw where I was heading and stood in front of the wardrobe. "Ingrid you can't go, what are you playing at?" His voice was getting louder. It's weird how he suddenly seems to be acting older than he is. He has helped keep me and Elizabeth safe from the slayers and doesn't even know it.

"Ben can you please just dropped it?" I put the bag on one shoulder and walked towards the door. I can buy more clothes later and can even nick some of Elizabeth's clothes if needed. I got the book which was the most important thing and the main thing I needed from my room.

I got to the door when my Ben yank the bag off my shoulder and threw it on the bed.

"You are not going anywhere Ingrid; I am not going to allow you to run away. I understand that you are sad about Luke's death and I know you are scared because of everything that has been happening but running away from home won't fix anything."

I pushed past him, going further back into my room, I grabbed some clothes from the wardrobe now that Ben wasn't standing there and shoved them in my bag back as I grabbed it off the bed.

"I am not running away because of Luke's death. I can't explain what is happening, but this is not my home and I can't stay here."

"Ingrid what are you talking about? You are not making any sense." Ben stood in the opened doorway. "I am going to call mum and dad to come home right now."

I opened my mouth to say something to stop him from calling the slayers when I heard a noise of something being knocked over downstairs.

"Tom?" Ben shouted from the room. There was no answer. Ben looked at me and then walked to the top of the stairs. "Tom are you OK?"

There were still no answers from downstairs. I heard my Ben go downstairs and I left my stuff in the room and followed him down. I was starting to worry, something was wrong. I got to the living room at the same time as Ben and saw Tom on the floor tired up.

"TOM." Ben ran to Tom, trying to undo the knots. I looked at the rope and realise that it was my grandfather's rope, someone has been in my bag. I heard noise from the kitchen, and I found myself running towards it, ready to find out who was in the house. I got to the kitchen and found that it was empty and most of the cupboard were now opened and have been stripped of things like food.

"INGRID." I heard Ben screamed from the living room. I ran back to the living room and stopped in the doorway.

"Don't hurt him." I asked the person who had Ben's arms behind his back like he did with Luke. "How have you entered the house without being invited in Matt?"

"I am not hurting him; I am just keeping him in one place. Entering this place wasn't hard, I just got the kid to invite me in by saying I was here to fix the places. I still got caught by the garlic on the door." Matt turned his shoulder slightly and I saw a small red mark where the garlic have caught him. "Finish what you got to do here and then we can get out of here."

He pulled Ben towards Tom and pushed him to the floor, tiring him up next to Tom.

"Ingrid, do you know him? Who is he? You are scaring me, what are you doing?" Ben pleaded, pulling at the ropes behind him.

"Sorry Ben, I don't have time to explain everything."

I left the room and went to the bedroom to get my bag back. I felt more relax now that Matt was in the house, I was glad that I wasn't alone in the slayers house anymore. I got to the room and saw that Matt was now standing by my bed. He lifted his arm up and I saw he had the stake in his hand that I left on the bed. His eyes followed me at I entered the room and I knew what he was thinking.

"The stake belongs to the slayers. Don't start getting ideas into your head that I am planning something when I am not." I opened the floorboard up and pulled out the slayers bag. "Ben found the slayer's bag, I kept it hidden so that slayers can't use it against us." Matt handed me the stake and I put it in the bag and hid it again. "You need to start trusting me more."

I grabbed my bag of the bed and went downstairs, not caring if Matt got there before me or not. I walked into living room where Ben and Tom were still tied up.

"Please Ingrid untie us. You are really scaring me. Please I am your brother." Ben was crying and begging.

"You're not." I muttered to myself so low that I knew Ben wouldn't hear. I saw my grandfather's bag in the corner in the room where Matt must have left it after taking the rope from it. I grabbed it to move it back to the hallway when I notice that now had some weight to it. I put it back on the floor and opened it and saw that the food from the kitchen was in the bag and some loose money.

"You grandfather didn't think to give you any money before sending you out or any food enough for 3 people. But at least we can see with a torch none of us need." Matt spoke as he entered the room.

I had to stop myself smirking as I handed Matt the bag and went to a cupboard where I knew Mrs Jones kept some spare money in case of emergency, money I knew that Mr Jones didn't know about.

"Hey idiot, what your name?" I turned my head and saw Ben was trying to stand up while still attached to Tom.

Matt just put him back on the floor and sat on one of the armchairs and stared at Ben and Tom.

"It's Matt and you should be careful what you say. Trying to act all big and smart when you are just a kid will not end well with you, especially if you call them an idiot."

"You are an idiot if you think my grandfather gave my sister that bag when he been dead for years. Tell me why my sister is suddenly acting weird and tell me why you are here?"

"Matt can you look round the house please." I spoke before Matt could answered Ben. The way Matt was looking at Ben, he could either answer him or kill him and I couldn't let that happen. "See if you can find anything that could tell us where Elizabeth is and where the slayers might have taken her. Don't take anything else from the house, I know what I can take without a trail leading back to us."

Matt stood up and took a few steps towards to leave when he stopped and looked at me.

"You do realise it wasn't us that robbed Luke's uncle's house, it was the slayers to cover up what have happened. We don't take thing of people who we go after, not unless we have to, to keep us safe."

"I know Matt, I know the slayers robbed the house. And I know that Luke needed to be blamed and for his death to be covered up so that we stay hidden and to keep me and Elizabeth safe." I gave Matt a small smile and he returned it before walking out of the door.

"He covered up Luke's death, he killed him." Tom finally spoke, his voice small and frighten.

"Matt didn't killed Luke; Luke's death was an accident." I spoke firmly, I didn't have time to go around in circle to do with Luke's death. I opened the draw and grabbed the money which was hidden, placing it in my bag and put the bag on my back.

"Why are you taking mum's money? Can you please just give me some answers and stop scaring me?" Ben had tears going down his face.

"Hey." Matt head pop round the door before I had a chance to speak. "Come here for 2 seconds."

I followed Matt into the hallway and into the kitchen. "What is it?"

He took a phone number of the notice board and I saw it was the slayers one the Mr Jones left behind. The one that called Luke's uncles house. "It's a slayer phone number, to be exact its Mark's number."

"Yeah, I know, I showed it to Eliz…" I thought struck me, suddenly realising something. "Phone." I sped upstairs and grabbed Elizabeth's phone, putting the battery back in as I went back downstairs to Matt. "Elizabeth gave me this phone so she could keep in contact with me. She might have left a message on it something. We need to wait for it to turn back on, I took the battery out when I was mad." I looked at Matt expertly him to look a bit please, but he had a serious look on his face. "What is it? What wrong Matt?

He nodded towards the living room. "We can't leave them here, they going to tell the slayers we been here, they know too much."

"We are not killing them, they only kids." I half shouted at him. "They have got nothing to do with vampires or slayers. I am not going to let you hurt them, they don't know anything."

"It's the only way to make sure they don't tell the slayers anything about us." Matt took a step towards the door, but I stopped him.

"Wait in the car and take the bags with you. I will deal with Ben and Tom which doesn't involved killing them." I gave him the bag and the phone.

"I'll check it while I wait for you. Don't be long or I will deal with them myself." Matt walked out of the kitchen and threw the front door.

I took a deep breath and walked into the living room. Ben and Tom both had red faces from crying.

"We saw him leave, is he gone? Can you let us go now please?"

I walked over to them and untied Ben first. He jumped up and went straight to the phone and I was untiring Tom.

"We need to call the police now."

"No Ben." I dropped the rope on the floor and grabbed the phone before Ben could. "You need to stop and listen to me."

"Why? You are not giving me a reason to. You just allowed someone to tie us and you are talking about covering up Luke's death." Ben kept trying to grab the phone out of my hand.

"To protect you from dad." I spoke as a matter of fact.

Ben stopped trying to grab the phone.

"What do you mean?"

I took a deep breath.

"Dad and mum were involved in Mrs Wednesday and Luke's death. Dad made me lie about hearing him the night it happened. I need you to stay safe, you need to go to Tom's house and stay there. Don't go with mum or dad if they come for you. They are killers"

I partly lied. He needed to stay away from the slayers without knowing the full truth. He needed to know the slayers were dangouses

Ben shook his head. "Why are you saying that about mum and dad?" He took a step away from me.

"Ben remember what you saw in the bag, what you felt? You know something is wrong here and it not just me. Every time a body turned up, mum and dad has disappeared. They made me lie to you to hide the fact. Matt is not the one to be scared off, he acts before he thinks. He is trying to sort this out, but you can't ring the police, Ben please believe me." I placed a hand on Ben's shoulder, and I could feel him shaking. Tears were freely going down his face.

"Mum and dad are killers." Ben whispered looking at the floor then at me.

"Run to Tom's house Ben and stay hidden. Stay away from the killers."

And please don't let me regret this. I left them in the living and walked out the house, not even taking a second look behind me. I got halfway down the path when Ben and Tom ran past me and ran full speed towards Tom's house. I watch them as they ran, I hope that Ben listens to me and stays away from the slayers and stays safe.

Matt car pulled up in front of the house and stuck his head out of the window. "We need to leave; the sun will be coming up soon and we have to find the slayers now."

Chapter 25

I got into the car, Matt speeding down the road before I even had the door fully closed. Matt handed me the phone as he drove down the road, weaving into the parked cars.

I looked at the phone and saw that Elizabeth had left a 5 seconds voicemail. I put the phone on loudspeaker as I played the message.

"VAMPIRE." I heard Bill voice on the phone and some struggling before the phone went dead.

"She must be at the slayer farmhouse if his voice is on her phone. So how long to the kids end up there and they find out you are a vampire? You shouldn't have kept them alive."

"I know Ben, I know he will listen to me and stay away. He knows nothing about vampires or any of the stuff that is happening, and I am going to make sure it stays like that. Ben and Tom are just kids and I will not let you do anything to harm them in anyway." I threatened Matt who just replied by shaking his head. "What are we going to do when we get to the farm? How are going to get Elizabeth away from the slayers and what are we going to do if for some reason she isn't there?"

He turned up the road towards the house.

"If she is there, we will get her out and kill all the slayer. If she is not there, find out where she is from the slayers and then kill them. I will not stop till I know she safe. She and her family have helped me so much and I will never stop repaying them for that."

"How did my family help you, what did you do Matt?" I asked, turning my head to look at Matt.

I saw Matt hand gripped the steering wheel tightly.

"We are here." He spoke in a low voice, his eyes remaining focus ahead of him. I looked forward and saw Matt headlights lighting up the mental gate that lead to the path. "Stay here while I hide the car. It will be best to go up on foot as it less chance of them spotting the lights or hearing the car driving up."

I nodded and got out of the car and stood next to the gate. I watch as Matt moved the car off the road and made sure it was hidden off the road before walking back towards me.

"Let's climb the fence, I remember the noise this gate made the last time we were here."

I nodded and we both climb the fence with no problem and walked up the path in silence. I don't know if it was because we didn't want the slayers to know that we were coming or because Matt didn't want to answer my questions. We got halfway down the path when we heard the mental gate opening behind us. I looked behind me and saw a pair of headlights coming up the path. I felt Matt grabbing the collar of my coat and pulled me into the ditch the ran along the road.

"Lie down, they see you." He hissed in my ear, keeping his hand on my bag to stop me from moving.

"I know." I hissed back at him as I rubbed my neck where my jacket caught me as he pulled me down. I kept my eyes ahead of me as I saw a Bill drive past in a car. I also saw the body bag that had been placed in a sitting position in the passenger seat like a person. I went to jump up, but Matt grabbed my collar again and pulled me back to the floor. "Stop doing that now." I snapped at Matt, shoving his hands away from my neck.

"Stay down or he will see you and kill you." He growled at me.

"There was a body in that car in case you didn't notice it. They might have killed Elizabeth already; we might be too late to save her." I had to stop myself from shouting at him.

"Use your brain Ingrid if they have killed Elizabeth you would be dead as well. Kill one twin and you kill the other. You drank blood so any injures she had will have healed. The body in the car is not her."

"I am not going to take your word for it, I am going to make sure it is not her." I pushed Matt hand away and crawled along with speed using the ditch as cover as I followed the car.

"Ingrid, what the hell are you doing?" I heard Matt whispered behind me. "Ingrid wait up." I heard Matt starting to follow me, keeping low in the ditch and hidden from the road.

We got to the front of the house where Bill have stopped the car and gotten out. Mr Jones came out of the front door and walked towards him.

"Did you check the house?" He asked.

"The house was trashed and empty, but it looked like someone cleaned up. I checked on Ben at Tom's, but they said that he had left to go to the main house. It felt like they were lying as I could have sworn Ben was in their house. There was no sign of Ingrid but the good news there were no signs of blood either in any of the rooms. There was garlic around the house so someone who know about vampires have been there. Do you think Elizabeth killed her?"

"She has better not have touch Ingrid or Ben. Elizabeth was walking away from the house, not towards it but it didn't mean she didn't go inside first and did something before we got there. The fact that there was garlic around the house is making me worried that Ingrid or Ben knows that something is happening. If Ingrid is starting to realise that she is a vampire, then we will with her once we dealt with her sister. I will not allow any vampire to harm my family. And talking about vampires, stop displaying the one in your car like it's a trophy and burn it. Once you done that, help Mark set up the cage as the sun is going to come up in less than an hour and we need it ready for the burning." Mr Jones left Bill and walked back into the house.

Bill shook his head and dragged the body out of the car and along the floor as he went behind the house.

"Look like your secret is going to be out soon. The slayers know that something is up with you and they going to work out you are a vampire soon. They have no idea what Elizabeth have told you which means they are going to keep her alive till they do. They said that they will deal with you once they dealt with Elizabeth so if anything thing that proves she is alive. However it does seem like Elizabeth isn't the only vampire in trouble." I saw Matt shift a bit and sat up slightly. "Either that or the slayers don't know that the sun doesn't affect Elizabeth. Do you understand what the slayers meant when they were speaking about the cage?"

"I can guess, you don't need to draw me a picture. Vampire in cage, sun come up and the vampire burns."

I started to move again, to the back of the house where Bill had taken the vampires body.

"Ingrid where you going? You're going to get caught and killed." Matt whispered trying not to be too loud. "For god sake, stop acting like a stupid kid and listening to what I am saying."

"I need to make sure it's not Elizabeth. You could have made a mistake and they have killed her. I need to check with my own eyes."

I felt Matt grabbing me leg and pulling me back slightly towards him. When did he catch up to me?

"Ingrid listen to me; the body is not Elizabeth. We need to think and plan what we are doing. We don't know how many slayers are here, there could be 2 or 50 hidden in the house. We can't handle that many slayers, I can't manage that many slayers and I can fight better than you."

"I am going to have a look. You can't understand what is like not knowing if someone you care for is safe or not." I turned to look at Matt who had a grip on my leg still. "You have never put your family in danger before, you won't understand what I am feeling."

Matt let go off my leg and I carried on moving to behind the house, not caring if Matt was following me or not. I got to the back of the house and saw Bill was in the middle of the back garden building a wooden pile. I knew it was to burn the vampire body that was in the body bag next to him. Mark was a few feet behind him, and he looked like he was adding some finishing touches to a cage that I knew was the sun cage. Knowing the slayer it was most likely made of silver to cause the vampire in the cage even more pain.

I felt Matt coming up next to me.

"Ingrid you don't know me. I understand…"

"Shut up they will hear you." I whispered to him, my eyes never leaving Bill or Mark in front of me. I watch as Bill threw one last piece of wood onto the pile than walked over to Mark. He tapped his shoulder and then they both walked into the house. I watched the door for a few minutes to make sure they didn't suddenly walk out of the door again. All clear.

"I am going to have a look."

I moved towards the body bag keeping low to the ground but moving fast. I felt Matt going for my leg again, but this time he missed.

"Ingrid come back you stupid idiot. You are going to get caught and killed if you don't stay hidden." I heard Matt whispered loudly behind me.

I got to the body bag and duck behind the woodpile with Matt only being half a step behind me. We were both now in the open and if any of the slayers came towards the woodpile than they will catch us.

I reach out to open the zip on the body bag when Matt grabbed my arm and yanked it away.

"Matt let go of my arm." I tried to pull my hand free, but Matt had an iron grip on it.

"No. I am not going to allow you to open the body bag. Use your senses, use your smell. There is burnt flesh in the air from the bag. That means that the vampire in the bag have been bunt from the sun, most likely from yesterday sun. Use your brain, Elizabeth can't be burn from the sun, so it isn't her in the bag."

I sniff the air and the smell hit me straight away. The smell of rotten and burnt meat clung around the body bag. How could I miss such a strong and powerful smell coming from the bag? My eyes were still on the body bag when he suddenly pulled my arm and dragged me across the grass. He pushed me into an outhouse that was close by and followed me in.

"Stop pulling me about?" I snapped at him walking towards the outhouse door.

"Slayers are coming." Matt hissed at me.

I looked through the gap in the door and saw Mr Jones and Bill dragging someone out of the house by his arms with Mark helping from behind. Mrs Jones followed the men a few feet behind and not getting involved with moving the male. The male that the slayers were dragging was a vampire in his early 20, he had his fangs out and was hissing and snappy at them all. It looked like the slayer had to use all their strength to keep hold the vampire as he was fighting back hard. Mark moved from behind the vampire and walked to the body bag and dragged it in front of the male vampire. The male vampire went silence and I could see all the fight leave his body. He fell to the floor and I saw the tears flowing down his cheeks.

"NO." He howled in pain, trying to grab hold of the bag and whoever was inside.

I felt myself inching closer and closer to the door. "Ingrid, stay hidden." I heard Matt whispered behind me. I watch as the slayers pulled the vampire towards the cage and away from the body bag. He was no longer fighting back and was almost walking himself to the cage. I moved towards the door, getting ready to leave the outhouse and to try and save him. "Ingrid, get away from the door now." I felt Matt hand grab my collar and yanking me away from the door with such force that I ended up in the middle of the outhouse on my back.

"Matt let me out of this place. They are going to burn him, and I am going to help him. I am not going to let him die." I looked up at Matt stood above me.

"Ingrid you need to listen to me. It's too late." Matt looked up above my head and I turned and followed his eye line. There was a small window above our head, and I could see the early morning sun starting to come through into the outhouse.

"It's not too later, the sun doesn't affect me. I am not going to watch him die." I jumped onto my feet and pushed Matt out the way and ran to the door.

Matt got to me before I got to the door and pulled me onto the floor with him. He kept me close to him and keeping a tight hold so that I couldn't move or fight back no matter how much I struggled.

"Matt please." I begged when I heard a sound coming from outside. It sounded like fire crackling and the sound of hissing stream and I knew by the smell of burning flesh that it was the male vampire burning in the sun. The sound and the smell were getting worst by the second, I looked at Matt and saw his eyes were locked on the door, his hold never letting me go. The sound suddenly stopped, and I looked back at the door, everything and everyone outside was silence.

Matt let go off me, but I knew it was too late to do anything know. I found myself turning around and punching Matt, he didn't even seem to notice it.

"Why did you do that? We could have saved him. Because of you, you are stuck in an outhouse because it daytime. I understand you are heartless vampire, but I aren't, I care about my family."

I sat on the floor with my back to the door, not being able to look at Matt anymore.

"You have no idea what happen when a vampire is burning in the sun." Matt spoke in a low tone, I turned to look at him and saw him staring at me. "I know you don't trust me as far as a human can throw me, but I am not heartless vampire that fell out of the sky at 18. As surprising as it sounds, I had a life in the light before I got my fangs. I have a family and I had an older sister."

"Had?" I questioned.

"Lexi was my older sister; she was 20 and she was traveling the world, not letting being a vampire stop her from having a life. I was 16 when she came home for a week to see me and our parents. At the time I was rebelling against ever rule my parents gave me. Even the one about going out and killing humans, something I have done many times before. I followed a human down an alley, I thought he was alone, but it turned out he was part of a gang that was hanging out at the alley. I was stupid and I thought I could do anything I wanted even without my fangs. When I got to the bottom of the alley the gang joined in and attacked me, there were too many for me to fight back. It wasn't bad enough for me to get my fangs, but it was enough to hurt me and to keep me on the ground. Turns out my sister was out that night, she found the gang attacking me and sorted them out without killing a single one. Neither of us notice the sun as it came down the alley with nowhere to hide. I don't think either of us realise the time or how long we been out. I watch my own sister burn in front of my eyes as I laid on the floor too hurt to even move. When a vampire burns there is nothing that can be done to save them. You can't stop drop and roll or jump in a pool of water to stop the fire from burning."

"You were only 16." I whispered.

"Yes, I was a 16-year-old kid who got his older sister killed. A 16-year old kid who had to explain to his parents about how he got their daughter killed because he didn't care about any of the rules that were there to keep him safe. Because he was showing off and thought nothing could touch him, that no human could touch him. I was a mess after my sister died, I did things I know I shouldn't have because I was still fighting the world. I killed people I shouldn't, and I lost friends because of it. When my fangs came, I left my parent's house, not even saying bye to them as they were away, and I knew they would stop me if they were there. They didn't need a son who messed everything up and get their daughter killed but they wouldn't have seen it that way. You said I don't care about family; well Elizabeth is my family. She and her grandparents helped me when I needed them. Not because they knew my family but because Elizabeth is good person. Because she will do anything to help people even if they don't believe they should be helped, just like Lexi use to do." Matt suddenly moved back into the shadows as sunlight came into part of the outhouse. He went into a dark corner of the outhouse where the sun couldn't reach, he looked at me before laying down on the floor with his back to me.

"Matt I am so sorry." I whispered which I knew Matt could hear but he didn't react in anyway.

I felt guilty about how I treated Matt, I never thought of his background or his family. I just saw him as a heartless vampire and nothing more. I heard Matt sleeping lightly and I knew there wasn't anything else I could do now. I knew I couldn't take on the slayers on my own and now the sun was out, Matt couldn't leave the outhouse till night-time. I saw some old fabric and rags on the floor in another dark park of the outhouse and sat down on them. I looked at the window above Matt thinking about my family, wondering how they were feeling about Elizabeth and I not being back safe yet. I wonder how long my grandmother could keep my grandfather from coming after us and trying to deal with the slayers himself. I thought of Elizabeth, about how close I was to her but not close enough. Does she know Matt and I are here for her, that she will be rescued soon? I snuggled down on the fabric and thought back on what Bill had said to the slayers. Ben and Jake were doing what I asked and are staying away from the slayers and keeping safe. But the slayers are going to work out that I know the truth and then they will no longer need to pretend to be good to me. I started to yawn, and I knew that if we were going to deal with slayers tomorrow, I am going to need to get some sleep. The sun was making me tired and the last few nights I have had little sleep combined. I took one look at Matt before closing my eyes, sending thoughts to Elizabeth that I was here for her and she will be safe soon.

I woke up after a dreamless sleep, taking a few moments to work out where I was. I sat up and looked around the outhouse. The room was covered in darkness and Matt was still sleeping in his corner. I stood up and stretched as my body was full of cramp. My hand caught something above my head, and something hit the floor with a bang.

Matt shot up onto his feet, his fangs out and ready. "What was that noise?"

I opened my mouth to tell him when I heard footsteps and voiced coming from outside the outhouse. My head turned towards the door and the direction on the voices.

"Hey, I think someone is in the outhouse; I just heard a noise from inside." Mark voice came outside.

I felt my body going completely cold as I heard the footsteps coming closer to where we were hiding. The nightmare of being tapped by the slayers returning to my head.

"Didn't anyone check the outhouse?" Mr Jones shouted. "Please tell me someone checked the outhouse; they might have seen us burning the dam vampire."

"We need to get out of here." I felt Matt grabbing my arm and turning me to face him. "We need to get out of here now."

"How are we going to do that? We are trapped." I watched as Matt pulled a shelve in front of the door. The shelve started to rattle straight away with each kick of the door by the slayers.

"Window." Matt walked pasted me and look up at the window. "If the slayers were stupid enough not to check the outhouse, they might be stupid enough not to realise there is a window out back. I will help you up and out."

Matt made it look easy jumping up to the window and pulled himself up. He lowered himself halfway out of the window and lowered his hands down for me.

"Hurry." I ran towards the window and jumped on a shelve nearby, is shifted under my feet and fell to the floor. Matt manage to grab my coat and stop me hitting the floor. "Use your feet, I can't pull you up at this angle."

I put my feet against the wall, and I pushed myself up and partly out of the window. I heard the shelve falling behind me and the door bursting open. I felt someone grabbing my foot and pulling me down and away from the window.

Matt hand tighten on my coat and tried to pull me back out of the window. "Get off me." I kicked the person behind me, feeling my foot hitting them and they let go of my leg. I saw my coat was starting to rip where Matt had hold of me.

"Matt the coat." I tried to push myself back up the wall, but the coat ripped before I could grab anything to stop myself from falling. I saw Matt try and grab me again to stop me from falling, but he missed. I landed on the ground, hitting my head hard and I felt myself starting to fall unconscious.

I heard the person who grabbed walking near me, but I couldn't keep my eyes open to see who it was. I could hear Matt shouting something from outside, but I couldn't work it out before the darkness took over and I felt my body being lifted off the floor.

Chapter 26

"Aah." I groaned, the pain waking me up from my dark sleep. I put my hand on my head where I fell, and I felt a small lump. I opened my eyes and I saw I was in small cage on the floor, which was half my size and I couldn't move my legs away from my chest. I manage to lift myself up slightly and my elbow and looked around the room in front of me. We were back in the cellar where Danny was kept, my eyes fell on the cage next to me and the person in the cage.

"Elizabeth!" I screamed, throwing myself at the bar of the cage.

Elizabeth was curled up on the bottom of the cage facing me with her eyes closed. I check her chest and I was glad to see that she was breathing.

"I am glad to see that you are awake." I heard Matt voice from behind me.

I managed to shift my body around and looked behind me and saw Matt in the similiter cage as me and Elizabeth.

"Matt." I never thought I be so glad to see him. I saw him struggling to move in the cage to face me as the cage was way too small for him. "What happened? How did we end up down here?" I asked trying to sit up more in the cage.

"The slayers were waiting for me by the window when I jumped down. I was focus on Mark when Bill manage to sneak up behind me and got me with a silver chain blanket. They wrapped the blanket around me and dragged me down to the cellar. My skin still burns from where the silver got me. Mr Jones had you in his arms when he brought you down here. I thought you were dead when he placed you in the cage. I noticed that his noise was bleeding, you must have kicked him hard in the face when he grabbed hold of your leg. It was a good thing we hunted before, most of the injuries we had have heal already. You just got a small cut on your head that should heal soon enough."

I smiled at Matt when I heard a movement behind me. I turned to look at the sound and saw Elizabeth opening her eyes and she was starting to wake up.

"Elizabeth." I felt so relief that she was finally waking up.

She smiled weakly at me as she pushed herself up slightly, so she was sitting up a bit more. I saw she was in pain as she moved.

"Are you OK Elizabeth, are you still in pain?" Matt asked and I wanted to know the answer as well.

"I am fine Matt, I'm just a bit stiff from being curled up for the last few days." She looked away from Matt and looked at me. She gave me small smile. "I know what you did Ingrid to help me heal, I understand how hard it must have been for you to do. I'm sorry, I understand…"

"No Elizabeth, let me speak first please." I interrupted her. "You shouldn't be the one to say sorry, I should be. I am sorry for everything I said to you and what I did to our parent's shine. I should have never turned my back on you, I should have stood by you like you were standing by me. I care about you and I know I should show it more." I took a pause to take a breath when Elizabeth used the break to interrupt me.

"I know that you are sorry without you needing to say it. You drank someone's blood to save me, you killed a human. You came here to save me and tried to take on slayers, 2 of them being the ones you lived with for years. Instead of being in a nice warm bed and you in a cage talking to me. I know you care for me." She smiled at me and I returned it, glad that the air is now cleared between us and we can be a family again.

"Great, now that you two have kissed and made up." I turned to Matt who had a sarcastic smirk on his face. "Are we going to work out how we are going to get out of here and try and work out who we are up against? Or are we going to sit in the cages till the slayer come down and kill us all?"

"I can give you information for most of the questions. I don't think the slayers realised how much I heard while I been down here. The only slayers I've seen here while they were torturing me where the Jones's, Bill and Mark. There isn't anyone else here." I looked to the floor when Elizabeth spoke about being tortured, knowing that part of the reason she was in this place was because I told her to leave the house. "They have also been speaking about the human girls from the party."

"Lily, Rose and Emma are still involved?" I asked with concern. I didn't like the idea of Rose knowing about

Vampires and Emma and Lily know a lot about me being a vampire.

"Rose is still not involved with the slayers; she is still being kept in the dark about vampires and the slayers want it to stay like that. They don't tend to like normally humans knowing things about slayers and vampires unless they need too. The slayers know that we have dealt with the police and put the blame on Luke for the party and made out it was nobody fault that Luke died here. Rose doesn't believe any of it, yet it the closest to the truth with only small details missing. Mark want Emma and Lily to stay quiet about what they know, and he banned them from even talking to each other about it in case someone overhear them. Lily have been told that she needs to go back to university and act normally again like she did before she came back here. Emma is staying in Hillstrength and she is going to make sure Rose stay safe by making sure you don't go near her. The only time the slayers want them to get involved if they notice any new vampires coming into the village. I know at least of couple of vampires came through the village a couple of nights ago as they slayers were talking about dealing with them. I guess they did that this morning as I could small the burning when the sun came up."

"We could smell them from where we were hidden, we were so close we could have seen them if we wanted to." I looked at Matt and thought back about I found out about him while we hid.

We all heard the heavy footsteps moving above us. "Look like the slayers are awake. They seem to be doing the same thing most slayer do. Sleep during the day and wake up at night so that they can deal with vampires."

I jumped when I heard the cellar door burst open and Mark mocking laugh drifting down the stairs.

"What are we going to do with our friends?" I shivered; his voice sounded so cold.

Mr Jones voice answered him back, he sounded as cold as Mark did.

"No, leave them down there. We need to sort out the older vampires in the village first. Then we can find out how much Ingrid know before we deal with her and the rest down there."

The closed and the voice became muffled.

"Danny." I whispered. I lifted my head up fast, forgetting I was in a cage and hitting my head hard.

"They are talking about our grandparents, Elizabeth I left Danny there to keep him safe. They are going to go after them, and it doesn't sound like they are going to wait any longer."

"We need to get out of here now." I could see the panic in Elizabeth eyes, and I could see her looking around the room for anything that could help. I tried to kick my cage door, but it didn't do anything to open it.

"I got this." Matt spoke up. I looked at him as he put his back against the side of the wall and kicked the cage door with all his strength. It took 5 goes before the cage burst open and the lock skidding across the floor.

"Yes." I could help but shout.

Matt smirked at me as he climbed out of his cage and quickly came over to mine. He grabbed the lock but let go of it quickly when his hand started to smoke, and I could smell burning in the air.

"Dam it, silver locks. I am getting sick of being burnt by silver because of the slayers. I am going to make them suffer when I see them." He took of his jacket and wrapped it round his hand before grabbing the lock again and pulling it, snapping the lock in his hand. He walked to Elizabeth cage as I pushed open my cage and stood up. I had to grab hold of the cage as my head felt dizzy as I stood up, either due to my head injury or because I stood up too fast.

I heard the lock on Elizabeth cage snapping, and I looked towards them as Matt was helping Elizabeth out. Elizabeth stumbled and Matt had to catch her before she hit the floor. I rushed toward them as Elizabeth was leaning on Matt for support. She looked in pain with every moment she made, and she was breathing fast and heavy. How much damage did the slayer do to her if this was how she like after she healed?

"I am going to check if it cleared upstairs." Matt moved Elizabeth body weight, so she was now leaning on me and walked to the bottom of the stairs. "Keep quiet and don't move until I come back."

I nodded at Matt went up the stairs making very little noise as he went. I looked at Elizabeth who looked even worse now I could see her up close.

"Are you OK Elizabeth? Don't lie to me and say that you are fine when I know you are not."

Elizabeth gave me a weak smile and a small laugh.

"It's nothing, don't worry Ingrid. I am just stiff from being locked in a small cage for so long. I be fine once my body start moving again and I stretched a bit. The only tight space I can stand to be in for a long time is my coffin." She smiled a little wider at me, but I could see it hurt her to do it.

I retuned a small smile back to her, wanting to keep Elizabeth humour up.

"Yeah I slept in my coffin a couple of nights ago. I slept better than I had in a while. Minus the nightmare about me being in this place." I shudder at the memory. "I had to sleep with the lid open as it was my first time in a coffin."

Elizabeth chuckled slightly before it turned into a cough that seem to shake Elizabeth whole body. I tighten my grip on Elizabeth, I don't know if it was because I was scared of her collapsing or scared of losing her again.

The door at the top of the stairs banged open and a pair of footsteps came running down the stairs. I looked round the room to see if there was somewhere, I could hide Elizabeth but the only thing in the room were the 3 broken cages with the locks in different places around the room. I shift Elizabeth so she was standing more behind me and I kept my eyes on the stairs, waiting for whoever were coming down them.

Matt appeared and I felt myself relaxing.

"The slayers aren't up here anymore. I don't know where they gone or how long they are going to be, so we need to move fast and get Elizabeth out of her and somewhere safe." Matt came down and helped hold Elizabeth on the other side and helped me get Elizabeth up the stairs and into the hallway.

"We need to go to our grandparents; we need to tell them about the slayers." Elizabeth spoke, the determination and fight coming back into her voice.

"That's the plan." Matt answered as he left Elizabeth to lean on me and went into the living room.

"Matt what are you doing, we need to get Elizabeth to safety. We need to make sure the slayers haven't gone after Danny or our grandparents." I said with urgently, looking round the empty house for any other sign of life.

"Don't worry, I am just making sure we don't leave any clues that we were here. The slayers have our bags with stuff in it that they can use against us. The vampire book you got from the slayers house is in the bag. I know your grandparents wouldn't be happy if that fell into the hands of the slayers." Matt kept his voice as low as mine, the sound just being above a whispered. "Got them."

Matt came back out of the living room with the 2 backpacks in his hands. I took one bag of Matt and places in on my shoulder, keeping a tight hold on Elizabeth.

"We got the bags and we got the book; can we please go now in case the slayers suddenly come back?"

"Yeah we are going now. I am going to get you and Elizabeth to a safe place and then I am coming back to deal with the slayers on my own. And don't bother to argue with me Elizabeth because you know me well enough to know I won't listen to you." Matt walked pasted us and walked towards the front door, Elizabeth shaking her head with a smirk beside me. Matt just got to the door when a key was placed in the lock from the outside and the handle was being turned. Someone was coming into the house. Matt moved next to me and Elizabeth with speed, none of our eyes leaving the door. Bill enter the house first, stopping in the doorway when his eyes fell on us.

"The vampires have gotten out of the cages." He shouted, the rest of the male slayers suddenly appeared behind him, stakes already in their hands.

Matt had his fangs out but neither party seem to want to make the first move of taking a step forward.

"You got lucky getting out of them cages. But if try anything stupid now, then we will kill each and every one of you. Then we will go for the grandparents and any other vampires we might come across while we there." Mark threatened, his eyes daring us to do so.

"Matt." I hissed, keeping my voice low so the slayers wouldn't hear. "Please." I begged. "Think before you do something that will get us hurt."

Matt put his fangs away, but his body was still tense as the slayers walked towards us with their stakes ready. Mr Jones walked behind, and I could hear him moving things behind us, but my eyes remains focus on Bill and how his stake seem to be aimed at my chest personally.

I felt a point of a stake against the back of my neck and I knew it was Mr Jones.

"Put your hand behind your back or I will stake you without a second thought."

I slowly let go of Elizabeth who managed to support herself standing and I put my hands behind my back like I was told. Trying not to move too much as I could feel the stake digging slightly into my neck. I felt the bag being took of my shoulder and places on the floor next me. I could feel a thick rope being tired around my hand and waist, them not caring that the rope was digging into my skin and hurting me. I was pushed forward, and I could hear Elizabeth being tired up and being pushed forward into me, somehow keeping her balance and not falling to the floor. I looked at Elizabeth hands and I saw we were being tired up using orange climbing rope. Matt was moved forward, but this time Mr Jones was keeping a tight hold of his wrist and was pushing him towards the living room. Mrs Jones following close behind with both backpacks I looked at Bill who took a step closer to me with his stake and I knew he wanted us to go into the living room. I took a deep breath and went into the living room with Elizabeth, Bill and Mark following very close behind us. I saw Mr Jones tripping up Matt who manage to twist his body, so he landed on his back instead of his face. I felt myself falling next to Matt as either Bill or Mark tripped me and Elizabeth onto the ground. I manage to land on my knees hard, the pain shooting through my body. I saw Elizabeth landing on her back like Matt, her eyes locked on something in front of her. I tried to move my head to see what she was looking at when I felt a stake next to my neck again, pressing hard into my skin.

"You are going to tell us everything you know. And then I shall make you suffer for what you did to my family." I heard Bill laugh into my ear.

Chapter 27
I felt Bill's hand on my shoulders, and I was pushed off my knees and onto my side. I twisted my body and manage to sit and looked up. Mrs Jones was sat on a chair at the back at the room with our bags by her feet. Bill took a step back away from us and stood by Mark while Mr Jones took a step forward towards us.

Mr Jones smirked at me and crouched down in front of me, so he was eye level.

"Hello Ingrid, how are you feeling after your sleep?"

"Great, the cages are so soft to sleep in. You should try it." I don't know why I was trying to sound brave as I was scared stiff deep inside.

He smiled with a little chuckle deep in his throat.

"How much do you know Ingrid? We tried to ask your friend here." His eyes flicked towards Elizabeth and back to me. "But she wouldn't say a word, no matter what we did to her."

"If you lay one more finger on Elizabeth, I will show you how much I know." I threaten, no longer caring if I get hurt protecting Elizabeth.

He smiled evil and lean forward closer to my face. "You shouldn't make threats if you can't carry them out. For example if I said your grandparents will be dead like your parents, I make it happen."

Me and Elizabeth both snared with our fangs at the same time, making Mr Jones jump up onto his feet and taking a step back from us. "Well, I think your fangs have confirmed that you know what is really going on. That you know the truth about everything."

"Yes, I know everything. I know that you murdered my real parents in cold blood. I know that you kidnapped me and made me believe I was a human when I am in fact a vampire. And I know that you are all trained slayers." I growled, making sure my eyes burned into his.

"Yeah, you are right. We are trained slayers." Bill spoke from behind Mr Jones. "But I rather be a slayer than a bunch of blood sucking monster. You will kill any human that you meet without a second thought and drink them dry."

"You rather be something that kidnapped a child after you murdered their parents." Matt spoke up behind me. "And I am not from here and I know that there were a couple of kids found in the woods that were killed by slayers. Your hands are as dirty as ours. And we don't drink from every human that die. Luke died right here, and we didn't drink from him. Then again I rather starve then drink his tainted blood."

Bill suddenly came rushing forward but Mr Jones put his hand in front of him to stop him.

"You better keep your mouth shut you leach. I can't wait till you meet the end of my stake as I push it through you cold stone heart. Something I have wanted to do since I first saw you."

"Well at least I am not a walking blood bag begging to be bit by a vampire. I can help you with that if you want."

A stake suddenly appeared in Bill's hand and I flinched away from it as he made another lunge for us. Mr Jones grabbed his arm and yanked him back away from us.

"Bill, you need to stop it. We need to get more information from Ingrid. You fighting with the male vampire is not helping. Stay back and keep your mouth shut till I say so."

Bill eyes were burning with hate, but he still took a step backwards and stood next to Mark. Mr Jones opened his mouth, but Mrs Jones spoke first. Getting up from her chair and standing by Mr Jones.

"Where is Ben, where is my son? If you have killed him, at least tell me where his body is?" Her voice was full of pain and sadness, her face full of emotions.

"He isn't dead, he is safe." I was the one who answered. "I am making sure he won't get drag into this life of hell by making sure you don't have a clue where he is. You will never find him, and he will grow up knowing nothing of this world."

"I am his mother." Tears were now flowing down Mrs Jones cheeks. "And I demand that you answer the question and tell me where my son is."

"She answered your question, it's not our fault you don't like the answer. I think it's fair if we can ask a question if you can." Elizabeth spoke, lifting her head up and looking straight at the slayers. I looked at Elizabeth as she spoke. "How did our parents die? I have always wanted to meet the slayers who killed my parents and took my sister away from me. I want to know why? Why take Ingrid and bring her up as one of your own?" Her voice was shacking but strong. I looked away from Elizabeth and towards the slayers. Why have I been living with them for years?

Everyone turned to Mr Jones who walked towards us and crouch down in front of me and Elizabeth. He took a stake out of his back pocket and put it on the floor next to him and had a smile of his face which made me think he would do anything to us.

"You want to know the story." He looked at both me and Elizabeth, not even bothering with Matt. I swallowed and nodded at the same time as Elizabeth. "OK I will tell you the story. Once upon a time, many years ago there was a family of blood suckers who just moved into a village. We made a mistake when checking out the family and thought there were only 1 devil child, but it turned out there were 2. The second one had been hidden away at another monster house. We only found out about her a few years later, but she was kept hidden from us so we couldn't deal with her. The mummy and daddy vampire went out one night where they killed a human for food. Luckily for humanity, there were some local slayers that saw them and knew they needed to kill them. So they followed them back home and the vampires didn't even have a clue that they were the ones been hunted by the people they would hunt. They got back to their house where they checked on their devil child, their stomach full of blood from someone else's baby. They slayers broke into the house and managed to trap the vampire inside house. The daddy vampire fought back against the slayers, trying to save the wife and child, but the slayers won and killed the daddy. During this time, the mummy was trying to save her baby girl. But you see my children." Mr Jones lent closer to us and was now nearly whispering. "The slayers were faster and stronger than the vampire, the slayer won and like the daddy vampire, the mummy vampire was killed. The slayers find a baby sat in their cot, not having a clue that she was now an orphan. The slayers were going to kill the baby when they had a brilliant idea. They knew that they would have to deal with more vampires soon, so they were going to train the vampire baby to kill her own kind. That's was what we were going to do with your Ingrid. We were going to start you training during the summer, fighting and self-defence. We weren't going to tell you about vampires till your first kill, getting you under are control before your fangs came. Getting her to kill her own family and twin, ending the family bloodline for ever." Mr Jones laughed, showing all his teeth. I couldn't take my eyes on him as he laughed. Feeling sick on how much he enjoyed killing my parents and telling us in detail how he did it.

"Well that failed didn't it." Matt mocked, I turned to look at him. I had forgotten that there were other people in the room with us.

Mr Jones signed before swinging at Matt without warming and hitting him in the mouth. I saw Matt biting into Mr Jones hand. He screamed and pulled his hand back, grabbing the stake of the floor and stood up. He put his hand to his mouth and sucked the wound.

"You better behave yourself vampire right now" Mr Jones threaten, aiming the stake toward Matt. "Or like your female friend here, you see what we do to vampires who are not careful."

I turned my head to look at Elizabeth, but she lowered her eyes to the floor.

"What did you do to her?" I demanded. "TELL ME." I shouted, surprising myself on how angry I sounded.

Bill took a step towards me, a nasty smile on his face. "It's simple. We placed her on a chair and wrapped silver chains around her so she couldn't move. You should have seen her skin burn and blistered." I knew he was trying to get a reaction out of me, but there was no way I would give him the satisfaction of that. "We used a silver and garlic knife and cut into her arms and watching her blood smoke, letting her heal a bit and then doing it all over. If she didn't say anything or said something we didn't like, we made the cut even deeper and longer. You should know she told us everything, we now know everything you know." He smirked and have gotten so close to my face, but I could see though him and knew he was lying.

"You are lying. I know she didn't tell you anything, no matter what you did to her." I feel my blood boiling now I know how they tortured her and how they enjoyed doing it. "You have no idea of the depth of information I know about slayers because you know no idea when I found out the truth. And if you ever lay a finger on Elizabeth again, you will see first-hand how much of a vampire am really am. You wouldn't be doing all this if you still didn't need us to tell you everything."

Mark put his hand on Bill shoulder who moved away and stood by the other slayers leaving Mark standing in front of us.

"You need to think things through vampire. We don't need all 3 of your to be alive to get what we need. So as you seem keen to throw yourself on a stake to save your sister, I will allow you to choose which stake it shall be. Some of us will enjoy it more than others." He grinned at me in a way that made me feel scare again as I knew he would be the one to stake me. I was so glad that Matt was the one to speak because I didn't know if I could trust me voice to speak.

"Well if you are bringing stakes to the party, we get to bring the fangs to it. You have 3 very sharp pairs to pick from. Some of us will enjoy it more than others." I didn't even need to look at Matt to know he had a big smirk on his face as he spoke.

"You are not in a place to make jokes leech." Mark didn't hesitate as he kick Matt full force in the chest.

Matt hissed in pain as he well back into his hands.

"I like it when food fight back, helps me work up an appetite." He laughed but he sounded wined as he sat up again.

It looked like Mark was going to kick Matt about but stopped when Mrs Wednesday spoke, keeping back behind the males.

"We will always fight to protect our own or to make sure you pay for their death. We know that you killed Luke and Mrs Wednesday. I want to know which one of you took their lives away from them."

I felt my mouth go suddenly dry, all the slayers eyes were on me and I felt my heart speeding up. I had no idea what to say as I knew because of me Bill's nephew was dead and the rest of his family have left the village. Elizabeth answered for me, taking control of the situation.

"I killed Mrs Wednesday; I needed her blood to help Ingrid find out who she was. I could tell you all the details however unlike you lot, I don't get pleasure with describing things in detail about how I slit her throat. Luke…"

"Was me." I interrupted Elizabeth; I couldn't let her take the blame for Luke's death. My eyes fell on Bill's, his eyes full of hate and darkness.

"I killed Luke by mistake. No one drank from him which you will know if you checked his body for marks. We were fighting and he died when he his neck hit the chair."

"I don't believe you; I know you killed Luke on purpose." Bill spoke, his eyes burning deep into me. "You killed him and took away my family from me."

"You are the part of the reason why he is dead." I words were out of my mouth before I could stop them. "You try to turn him into a slayer, and it was your fault he was in the house. You made him kill Danny's mum and you allowed him to come back to the house to finish the job. Don't forget you were the ones that invited us into the house knowing that Luke was going to returned. You left us in the house alone so when Luke came over, he thought we killed you and he went after us. You were the one that let the vampires inside, you are part of the reason why Luke is dead."

Bill suddenly lunged towards me, I jumped back, and I was glad when Mark and Mr Jones grabbed hold of him. Bill had his teeth bare and was acting like a cage animal, screaming an inch from my face.

"Your will shut your mouth you little blood sucker. I had nothing to do with my family death, everything that happened in this house was your fault. I will take great pleasure in killing you so slowly you will be begging me to finish the job. And do you know what, I will not listen, I will make you suffer for what you did to my family, to all of them."

Mark and Mr Jones struggle to move Bill away from me, trying to get him to the back of the room.

"You need to calm down right now." Mr Jones stood in front of Bill while Mark kept his hands on him. "If you kill her now then she will die too quick. When we are done with them, you can have your revenge and we will not stand in your way. You just need to wait, but not for very much longer."

Mr Jones turned to look at me and the hate in his eyes matched Bill's, he was done playing games. He walked towards us and yanked up both bags from the floor. "Let see what you two thinks can help you win against us that can fit into 2 backpacks." He dropped my grandfather bag on the floor and opened the home one and took out the money that I took. "I wonder where you got this money from. Looks like you a thief and as well as a killer."

"Like how you stole me and killed my parents." I said quietly, just loud enough for him to hear.

He paused for a split second, his eyes looking up from the bag and towards me. I had no idea what he was thinking till he lifts his hand out of the bag and pulled out the vampire book. He had a smirk on his face as he spoke.

"What do we have here? This seem to have a vampire theme to it doesn't it?" He flicked through the pages and I was glad that he wouldn't be able to understand it. If he knew that there was a whole chapter on how to really hurt me and Elizabeth, to kill us, then there would be nothing that we could do to survive. He finished flicking through the book before putting on the table next to him. Mr Jones shook his head and turned the bag upside and empties the rest of it onto the floor. All my vampire stuff, clothes and food went all over the ground. I was shocked on how much Matt managed to get into the bag. He was smart as it was food that could be eaten without needs to be cooked. Cold meat. Biscuits, crisps, fruit, bread and some basic tin food. I need to give Matt more credit than I do.

"Look like you took most of the food from the house as well as money. You have not really got anything in here that can save you, have you?" He dropped the empty bag onto the pile and picked up the next back.

A terrible thought hit me.

"The knife is at the top." I muttered under my breath so the slayers couldn't hear. "The bag has a knife in it."

"Who gave you this?" Mr Jones started to undo the straps and I was glad he was struggling because of how tight it was.

"Family." I answered back, the panic coming back into my body. He was going to find the knife and I knew he will use it on us.

Matt suddenly came rushing past me, nearly knocking me and Elizabeth over. He put his head down and ran straight into Mr Jones chest. The bag got knocked out of Mr Jones hand and onto the floor. The slayers all went forward and grabbed hold of Matt who was putting up a good fight with his hands still behind his back. He kicked the bag towards me, and it went behind me. I worked out what he wanted me to do and what his plan was. I kept my eyes on the scene in front of me and managed to get the knife out of the bag without the slayers noticing. I just got the knife hidden up my sleeve, the cold steel against my burning skin when Matt got thrown onto the floor next to us. Matt kicked the bag away from me as he went down to the floor. I looked at Matt and I saw he had a cut on his bottom lip. He licked it once and I saw the cut getting smaller and smaller till it healed completely. I turned my head and I saw Mr Jones whipping his bloody noise on his sleeve from Matt sudden attack.

"This is your finally warning vampire. Don't you try and do ANYTHING like that again, I swear." He grabbed a stake and put it against Matt check. "The girl's death will be on your hand. It a shame one of your blood suckers have got my special knife." I felt my stomach suddenly drop. "I always put an X on it after killing each vampire." I remember the knife from the slayer bag and how many X's that were craved on, knowing that 2 of them belonged to my parents.

Mr Jones stood up, grabbing the bag on the way up and walked towards the table.

I twisted my body to the side so that Matt could get the knife from my sleeve without any of the slayers noticing. My skin burning more where the knife used to be. I looked at Matt and met his eyes and I knew deep down that someone will die today. Only one kind will be able to leave this house alive.

Chapter 28

Mr Jones tipped my grandfather bag upside down and emptied everything onto the floor. The flask was the last thing to fall onto the floor and Mr Jones saw it. He picked it up and turned it over in his hand. He crotched down in front of us again and shook the flask in his fist. "What is in this?"

Knowing that Matt had the knife on him I felt braver again.

"It's Tomato Juice, have a taste if you want."

He smirked at me.

"Aren't we brave suddenly. Don't start getting clever just because you friend caught me. I can guarantee that it won't happen again because if it does, then I will kill your sister without a second hesitation." He opened the flack and pulled the blood onto the floor in front of us. "I wonder what the name of this poor person was before you gutted her and drained her of all her blood." I kept my face straight, not giving him anything new to use against me.

He stood up and put the flask next to the book and walked towards the slayers at the back of the room.

"Why do you have blood in a flask?" Elizabeth whispered to me.

"Our grandfather gave it to us. I saved it for you so you could have a drink and heal better. I knew me drinking blood would only do so much." I whispered back.

I felt a hand yanking me onto the floor and Mark standing above me.

"One more word out of you and you won't get to see what we got planned for your grandparents."

"When?" We all spoke at the same time, the panic in both mine and Elizabeth voice.

"Let's just say that they had their last night sleeping in their coffin in one piece." Mark laughed and walked back towards the other slayers. The had a map on the table now and I knew they were planning what to do with the rest of my family.

I took my focus from them when I heard Matt mutter next to me so low that I knew the slayers couldn't hear us.

"We need to move soon and when I say soon, I mean in the next two minutes. You need to head towards the door and make a run for, do not look back and I will deal with the slayers on my own. This is the plan and there is no arguing with it or changing it."

"No," We both hissed. I looked towards the slayers and it seem like they didn't hear us. I turned back to Matt. "I am not running away, and I know Elizabeth won't either."

"Yes." Matt hissed back. "I will throw you towards the door if I need to get you moving."

Matt moved slightly and I saw he got the knife out from his sleeve and cut the rope with a single movement. The rope fell to the floor, but he kept his hand in the same position as they were still tied. I twisted my body so that my hand was towards Matt and I felt my ropes being cut. I moved my fingers to get the blood moving in them again but like Matt kept my hands in the same position as before. I felt him past me the knife and I cut Elizabeth free and passed the knife back to Matt. My eyes never leaving the slayers who seem to busy planning my grandparent's death to notice what we were doing behind them.

"When I say when, you both go." Matt whispered.

"What about all my stuff that the slayers have?" I whispered back as I watched Mark leave the room as the slayers watched him.

"You risk your life for some clothes?" Matt hissed at me. I looked at Matt and I could see he was starting to get annoyed. "You risk Elizabeth life for a bunch of vampire tact."

"She means the vampire book and the things that belong to our family. Not all the human stuff." Elizabeth defended me, knowing what I was talking about.

I looked back towards the slayers and Mark walked back into the room with slayers weapons in his hand. He handed them to the slayers, and I knew we were running out of time. My eyes caught Bill's; he ran his stake across his neck with the biggest smile on his face.

"What are you going to do if you meet someone who haven't got their fangs?" Elizabeth asked, I looked at her and I knew she was getting worried about Danny. She knew that the slayers were getting ready to move and Danny was going to get caught in the middle.

"Do you mean the son of the blood sucker women who we had locked up to be killed downstairs?" Mr Jones asked with a smile.

"Yes." She answered coldly.

"He won't be alive long enough to get his fangs. Every vampire in this village will be dead, and then we will move onto the next village and the next till we wipe every one of your kind of this planet." He laughed and walked out of the room with Mark, leaving Bill and Mrs Wednesday in the room with us.

I heard the front door open and closed. Bill smirked at me and walked towards me.

"Now I can make you suffer for what you did to me and my family."

I found myself frozen to the ground. Even though I was free, I couldn't make any of my muscle move.

"Not going to happen slayer." Matt spoke next to me. He stood up fast and I saw the knife going into Bill's stomach. Bill stumbled back and Matt pushed him away from us.

"NO." Mrs Jones screamed, and I heard footsteps coming back towards the house from outside.

"Go. Get out of here." Matt shouted at me and Elizabeth. He grabbed Mrs Jones as she came running towards us and pushed her onto the floor. "NOW."

I stood up and helped Elizabeth towards the door, Matt still behind us and dealing with the 2 slayers.

We just got to the door when we saw it bust open and Mark and Mr Jones came in.

"What have you done to my friend and wife?"

"Why do you care what we done?" I said pushing Elizabeth to the living room doorway with my fangs out and ready.

I knew she was still too weak to do any real damage and I couldn't allow her to get hurt any more.

They both ran towards us with stake raised high. I manage to dodge Mark and stamped on Mr Jones lower leg and I heard his bones breaking. He fell to the floor as I turned to block Marks stake in his hand and punched him in the face. I felt Mr Jones grabbing my leg and pulled me onto the ground. He got his hands around my body and trapped me on the floor with him.

"Now you die." Mark said laughing, his noise bleeding from my punch.

I tried to fight my way out of Mr Jones grip, but I was pinned in a way that made it impossible for me to fight or run. "Time to see your parents."

I kept my eyes on him as the stake came towards me. Everything that have has happened to me since Rose's party going through my head. I found out I was a vampire; I had a twin sister and my real family have been dead for years. I have killed multiple people and I have been living a lie all my life. I am glad I get to die knowing who I am really am. Yet for some reason the stake stopped before it got to me. I looked at Mark and I saw his eyes getting wider. Blood started to come out from his mouth, and he started to cough blood up. I looked behind him and I saw that Elizabeth had gotten the knife and had stabbed Mark in the back of his neck. He took a step forward before collapsing onto the floor dead.

"NO." Mr Jones screamed.

Matt came in front of me and yanked Mr Jones off me and pulled me onto my feet. I stumbled a bit as I felt the pain in my leg and needed the wall to stop myself from falling. I looked into the living room and saw the room had been trashed. Tables and chairs had been smashed and everything were in pieces. Bill was dead on the floor and Mrs Jones was sat next to him, all the fight and power seem to have left her body.

"She not the main threat at the moment, we can deal with her later." Matt spoke next to me.

"Where's my wife?" Mr Jones asked, I looked towards him and saw him lifting himself up. When did he seem so old and so weak?

"She alive." I picked up the knife out of Mark neck and put it next to Mr Jones neck like he did to us. Not caring that blood was still dripping from it and onto the floor. "But you won't be soon. You killed my parents and stole me, making me think I was something else. You tried to destroy my life and that of my own family. You don't deserve to live for what you did to me." I tried to move the knife down into his neck, but I couldn't make it move. I tried again but I couldn't make myself kill him.

I felt Matt hand on my shoulder.

"Let me do it. I know you are struggling, and I understand." I tried again but I knew I couldn't. Matt put his hand on the knife, and I let go and walked into the living room and away from them, hearing the knife going into Mr Jones skin and him dying.

Mrs Jones aw us walking in and moved into the far corner, tears still flowing down her face. I crotched down in front of her like Mr Jones did to me and Elizabeth. Elizabeth standing next to me and Matt coming into me and standing on my other side.

"We're not going to kill you." I said in an even tone. I saw Matt open his mouth. "No Matt." I stopped him before he could say anything. "There has been enough death here and if we kill her, then more slayers will come, and we got to do this all over again." I saw Mrs Jones let out the breath she had been holding.

"However there a catch and if you break them, then I will allow Matt to kill you. You need to leave this village and not get in contact with me or Ben in anyway. I will not allow him to be dragged into this mess of a life, at least one of us should have a normal life. I will find out if you don't do any of these things and you will suffer."

I stood up and left Mrs Jones crying in the corner. I took no notice as I put my stuff into my bag and walked out the room. I didn't look back at any of the bodies as walked outside the builder. I took a deep breath and allowed the cold air into my lung. I felt a hand on my shoulder and turned and saw Elizabeth standing there. I turned to my other side and saw Matt standing there.

"Can we go home now." I said tired of everything.

"For once I'm agreeing with you." Matt said smiling. "Come on, I'm a day late getting you back. I know your grandfather timeline, I bet he wanted you back yesterday. Your grandfather going to kill me. Stay here and I bring the car up."

I sat on the step and Elizabeth sat next to me. I didn't say anything to Elizabeth, I just kept my eye on the road and waited for the car. Matt came up the drive within minutes and I got into the back seat while Elizabeth got into the front. I was glad that neither Matt nor Elizabeth was trying to talk to me, they knew I needed to be on my own.

Matt pulled up in front of the house.

"You're home." He smiled at me and I smiled back. We got out of the car and we enter the house. I could hear talking coming from our living room and walked towards it, Elizabeth keeping very close to my side. We got to the doorway and we were nearly knocked over as our grandparents came to us and grabbed us into a big hug.

"Thank god you are all safe." My grandfather said as he squeezed me tight.

"I am sorry for not getting them back sooner, but there nothing to worry about anymore." Matt spoke, keeping a safe distance behind us.

"I shall let it slide this time. I will never forget you bringing my family home safe." My grandfather held out his hand and Matt shook it.

My grandfather took Elizabeth into the dining room so he could clear up the injuries that the slayers did to her.

Danny ran up to me and jumped into my arms. I took a step back onto my bad leg and I winced a bit, but I didn't care about the pain anymore. I looked at my grandmother I knew she notice I was hurting.

"Come on, you all need to rest." She took Danny out of my own and took him upstairs ad I made my own way up. By the time I got to the top of the stairs, Danny was in his coffin and my grandmother was standing the door that led to my and Elizabeth shared room. "You did well Ingrid, your parents would be so proud of you and Elizabeth. You will do anything to look after one of another." She smiled and I returned the smile. I walked into the room and she helped me into the coffin, my leg hurting the more I move it. I sat up in it as Elizabeth came into the room and I saw she had bandages on her arms.

"I have never been so happy to see my coffin." She laughed as she got into her coffin next to me with helped and sat up like me.

"I leave you 2 to get some rest." My grandmother gave us both a kiss and left the room, passing Matt on the way out.

"I have got an update from a mate of mine who works at an airport." Matt leant on the doorframe with that smirk on his face. "The female slayer has gone to the America on her own, she only bought one ticker. So it seems like the kid listened and kept away from all this and the female have left without him. Not bad for a new vampire. Your plan worked."

I stuck my tongue out of him and he left, shaking his head as he went. I heard him going down the stairs and into the basement which is where he must be crashing tonight. I was glad that my plan worked, and everyone was now safe. All the slayers were gone, and my family were safe, we can now build our relationship and make up for all the years we missed.

I laid down in my coffin but kept the lid open like Elizabeth.

"So what are we going to do tomorrow?" Elizabeth asked, she sounded sleepy. My grandfather must have given her something for her injury, you could still hear someone pain in her voice.

"Are you still hurt?" I asked with a smile on my face.

"I told you I'm fine." Elizabeth sounded fed up being asked that again.

"OK, I thought if you were hurt, we could go out hunting tomorrow night. You could see some of the new skills that I learnt." I laughed and I was glad when Elizabeth joined in.

"I don't need to be hurt to go hunting. But knowing our grandfather, he won't let us walk out the door. Lucky for you, I know how to sneak out of the house without him knowing."

We both carried on laughing as I drifted of the sleep. Feeling relax knowing my family was safe and finally knowing the truth about my own life.

Printed in Great Britain
by Amazon